C000080303

THE ALCHEMIST'S APPRENTICE

Also by Jeremy Dronfield

Resurrecting Salvador
The Locust Farm
Burning Blue

The Alchemist's Apprentice

Jeremy Dronfield

review

Copyright © 2001 Jeremy Dronfield

The right of Jeremy Dronfield to be identified as the Author of
the Work has been asserted by him in accordance with the
Copyright, Designs and Patents Act 1988.

First published in 2001
by REVIEW

An imprint of Headline Book Publishing

10 9 8 7 6 5 4 3 2 1

All rights reserved. No part of this publication may be
reproduced, stored in a retrieval system, or transmitted
in any form or by any means without the prior written
permission of the publisher, nor be otherwise circulated
in any form of binding or cover other than that in which
it is published and without a similar condition being
imposed on the subsequent purchaser.

All characters in this publication are fictitious
and any resemblance to real persons, living or dead,
is purely coincidental.

British Library Cataloguing in Publication Data

Dronfield, Jeremy
The alchemist's apprentice
I.Title
823.9'14[F]

ISBN 0 7472 2143 X

Typeset by
Letterpart Limited, Reigate, Surrey

Printed and bound in Great Britain by
Clays Ltd, St Ives plc.

HEADLINE BOOK PUBLISHING
A division of Hodder Headline
338 Euston Road
London NW1 3BH

www.headline.co.uk
www.hodderheadline.com

For K.

Part One

THE GARDEN

I

Let me tell you about Madagascar Rhodes; I can't describe how he has been on my mind recently. Old Madagascar; Maddy to his post-colonial cronies and his readers. The former were entirely fictitious, of course, but the latter were very real and positively legion, and they all knew him as Maddy.

I hadn't thought about him – much – for quite a while, but this past week I have thought of little else. It had seemed to me, for all my searching, that all trace of him had gone from the world, but last Saturday I stumbled on an artefact. Aside from the box of valuables which he . . . well, bequeathed, I suppose, it was the first tangible evidence of him I had come across since he disappeared three years ago.

I made this momentous find in Hay-on-Wye; perhaps the ideal place for serendipitous discovery, though not one I visit often. (I have no liking for second-hand books, ironic though that may seem when you hear my story – novels ninety-nine per cent pulp, academic works by definition outdated.) I can't really explain the whim that took me there that day. Some vague notion of old copies of the *Proceedings of the Royal Irish Academy* and Macalister's report on Carrowkeel (God knows why – I've been out of archaeology for years now), combined with slightly less vague guilt pangs about repeatedly overshot invitations to visit my parents which had finally drawn me over from Cambridge.

I spent Friday night with the ageds and drove up to Hay on Saturday morning, unbreakfasted and rife with good bookhunting intentions. After half an hour of grazing the tables and browsing the shelves in the antiquarian sections, though, I was overcome by

3

a welter of apathy, and withdrew down the hill to the Granary for coffee and toast. It being the middle of January, the place was pretty much empty; aside from myself there were two old ladies sipping tea and a ruddy-faced family in hill-tramping gear tucking in to thick-knotted pasties (which were stuffed with dry sticks and blancmange, to judge from the noise they were making).

Fortified by two rounds of buttered white, some strong Nicaraguan and a Gitane, and reluctant to retreat bookless home after so feeble a foray, I trudged back up the hill. Ten minutes later, my boredom was as utterly forgotten as Ewan Brereton (who he? – well, exactly); for that was when I made my discovery.

I was looking listlessly at the cheap paperback bins outside the Cinema Bookshop – picking out a few of the more awful-sounding titles and slotting them back – when my eye lit on a familiar jacket. It was difficult to miss – for one thing, it was the only hardback on the shelf, and for another, it was turned face-out, wedged awkwardly between its pliable but protesting co-shelvees. I stared dumbly at it for several moments, then I levered it out eagerly, sending an avalanche of dog-eared Wilbur Smith cascading to the ground. I couldn't believe my eyes; I had thought I owned the single, solitary, absolutely one-and-only surviving copy of *The Alchemist's Apprentice* by Maddy Rhodes, but here – spine a little buckled but otherwise pristine – was its twin. For a good minute or two, I just goggled at the mere coincidence of it, but then the implications began to sink in.

Got you, I muttered to myself excitedly. *Got you by the tail at last, you slippery sod!* Mopped up every last trace, did you? Well, here's one you missed.

. . . Pause. I've just read these few pages back to myself, and it strikes me as a little bit . . . well, I can almost hear you thinking to yourself (or is it my own interior voice?) – Not the most beguiling, seductive way to begin telling a story, is it? Tea and toast in Hay-on-Wye? Dusty old bookshops and some obscure discarded novel? Don't think much of this guy's style. And where does he get off on *reluctant to retreat bookless after so feeble a foray*? Jesus wept. In reply, let me just say that, contrary to appearances, I had no idea I *had* a style until now (not beyond the drily academic, anyway). To elaborate, I might add that such style as I seem to possess has been

– like this excuse for it – forced upon me. Or I have been forced upon it – whatever; I just want to register my plea of innocence and protest at being treated in such a cavalier fashion. As to how and by whom, we'll come to that presently. And if you would be so good as to leave off criticising, we'll come to it all the faster. First, we have to go back to the point where you interrupted and sent me off on this digression: to whit, myself, standing outside the Cinema Bookshop in Hay, clutching the second-to-last copy of Maddy Rhodes' great work in my trembling fingers.

You won't know it, but in its day it was one of the most well-known books in print. That makes it sound like a hundred years ago, but it wasn't. *The Alchemist's Apprentice* by Maddy Rhodes was first published at the back end of 1994, and was promptly swallowed in the logjam of pre-Christmas books. After the slowest of slow starts, however, it exploded; within a year, it became one of the biggest – if not *the* biggest – publishing bonanzas of the '90s. It's easy to see why it was so successful: its mixture of emotional drama and brooding threat, nostalgia and sentimentality, all tied together with bright threads of magical realism and set down in a sun-drenched yet war-torn Mediterranean location; all these things made it one of those novels which are simply impossible to avoid reading. It told the story of a Jewish family who flee Germany just before the War and fetch up on Malta. It had all the dramatic elements you might expect in a beautifully written family-at-war saga, but focused on the friendship between the twelve-year-old daughter and an elderly Algerian fakir and alchemist; a friendship full of mystical adventure and nuggets of ancient wisdom. I have to say I never cared for it all that much; I enjoyed it well enough, but didn't perform cartwheels of delight. Not exactly to my taste, I suppose, which put me in a middling small minority. (As it turned out, I was right, though.) This was, you might say, a little unfortunate, because Maddy Rhodes was my friend. Indeed, I could go further and say that I knew him about as well as one human being can know another; I could go further still and say that we were as close as brothers, but it wouldn't be true – brothers sometimes fall out, while we never exchanged so much as a cross word all our lives. Whatever, I certainly knew him better than his readers, or the few journalists who were allowed to interview him (rarely, and never face to face). 'Maddy (short for Madagascar) Rhodes,' ran the book's biographical blurb, 'was born in 1948 on the island from which he took his name. After studying history at the University of the Witwatersrand, he served in the South African navy and later as a merchant seaman. After two decades in which he worked variously as a French teacher in Montevideo, a safari guide in his native Madagascar and a diver in the Persian Gulf, he settled in Malta and began writing. This is his first novel.'

Apart from that last sentence, this brief summary was, like his rare interviews, a tissue of the most solidly palpable lies you ever heard in your life. Complete hog-spittle, but it sounded well. Old Madagascar Rhodes, larger than life and every bit as bizarre. His real name was Roderick Bent (Drick to his friends), and he was born (like me) in South Wales in the mid-60s. The photograph used on the jacket was of his father, Lionel, a works manager with British Steel. (Although I have to admit he did look as though he *could* have lived Madagascar Rhodes' extraordinary weatherbeaten life. The Valleys do that to you, I suppose.)

As I've said, we were very close, Drick and I: we met at playgroup (I knocked over his orange squash and made him cry); we grew up together, went to school together, flunked out together, even went off to university together in the end. Influence each other we certainly did, and our mothers could never decide whether the influence was good or bad. We read for the same degree (BA Archaeology, Southampton – my choice) and went off together to do PhDs at Cambridge (definitely his choice). There, after twenty-three years, our ways finally parted. I stuck with my research, got my doctorate, had my work published in prestigious journals, and signed on the dole; he freaked badly in his second-year interview, bummed out and went to live with his girlfriend, Elsa, who was eight years older than him and ran a gift shop near Ely Cathedral. He started writing fiction, had a few short stories published (under his own name), taught creative writing at the local college, and let it be quietly known that he was working on a novel (several novels, if you believed him). In the meantime, he fell madly in love with another girl and dumped

Elsa. The recriminations of that period (to which I bore reluctant eye-witness) were so bitter my toes still curl and innards cringe to remember it; after all, Elsa had been supporting his wastrel ways for a year and a half, and felt she had a right to expect a little loyalty. Not that you would expect Drick to remember it that way – he had a remarkable capacity for blanking out uncomfortable memories. We talked about it once (Elsa, not his blanking habit), and where I remembered tears and hysterical rows (some of which I witnessed first-hand), he remembered a few arguments and a relatively uneventful parting. Maybe it never really registered in the first place, because none of the upheaval seemed to affect his writing in any way, if the speed with which he planked out his novel (the *first* novel, if you believed him) was anything to go by. He then had several frustrating months of flogging *The Alchemist's Apprentice* around the big publishers, with not a flicker of interest shown. He eventually sold it to a short-run cottage press called Obelisk; his advance consisted of a modest lunch at the company's expense, and the print-run was set at five hundred hardback copies. Well, it seemed you couldn't have got it off the shelves with a crowbar during those late months of 1994, but then word of mouth began to play its part. As I've remarked, everyone who read it loved it: they told everybody they knew *You MUST read this*, and bought it for presents. Soon, the cottage press was out of its depth, and the next thing Roderick knew, he had an agent, and was being courted by all the big publishers who had turned him down only a year before. Eventually, Headline bought out the UK rights (Drick, for all his desperation, had been canny enough to reserve foreign rights from the start). He never discussed figures with me, but it was obvious he was now rich; if the sums bruited about in the papers were anywhere near the truth, he notched up over three quarters of a million in overseas advances, and by late 1996 had cleared more than one point two million in UK royalties alone. He stood head, shoulders and torso above everything else in any bestseller list you cared to look at. Madagascar Rhodes, the mysterious colonial adventurer, with his magical, hypnotic, life-affirming prose, was absolutely the biggest thing in contemporary literature.

Now, I know what you're thinking. I can feel you busting a gut to interrupt me again. Having criticised my style already, you are now demanding to know why, if *The Alchemist's Apprentice* was the smash hit of the '90s, bigger than *Captain Corelli*, *Cold Mountain* and *The Beach* combined, why have you, as literate as the next person, never heard of either it or its eccentrically pseudonamed author? The answer is quite simple: Roderick destroyed it. Obliterated it, annihilated it, expunged it from history and memory. You may find it hard to credit, but you can take it from one who knows (the *only* one who knows): you *had* heard of *The Alchemist's Apprentice*; statistically, the likelihood is that you read it, even enjoyed it and passed it on to a friend. You just don't remember it. Because, paradoxically, although you can take every word of what I have told you as gospel, *The Alchemist's Apprentice* and its author do not – never did, in a sense – exist.

Supplied with that admittedly baffling piece of information, you may begin to have some inkling of why my find excited me so much. Own twin to the only – *my* only – copy, sitting innocently amongst the discarded westerns as though nothing was odd with the world. It was almost as though – no it wasn't, it was as stone-cold certain as a certainty can be that it had been *put* there for me to find. And the moment I held it in my hand and gazed at that familiar yellow cover, I was pretty sure I could guess who had put it there, and how. It was a while longer before I discovered why. (That's right, brain-blasting surprise hadn't finished with me yet, not by a long sight.)

I took it up to the shop, paid my 20p, and hurried back through the town. I wanted to study my prize in peace and comfort, so I retraced my steps to the Granary. (It was still quiet, the previous customers having been replaced by a middle-aged man with a stick and a sheaf of maps, and a young couple arguing viciously under their breath at a corner table.) I sat at my same table with another pot of coffee, an ostensible slice of flapjack and *The Alchemist's Apprentice* laid out before me.

It had occurred to me as soon as I saw the book and realised how it must have come there that somewhere in these pages Drick would have left me some clue at last; some kind of hint or pointer to explain what had *really* happened to him; where he had *really* gone. Why else would he have left me my sole copy in the first place? Of course, I had had this hunch before, and my copy of the book was dog-eared from my searching, ragged and held together with sellotape from long evenings spent fruitlessly re-reading the story of that blasted family, their sodding daughter and her infuriating Algerian hanger-on. There *had* to be something there, and finding this copy here brought back the conviction with renewed force.

I poured my coffee, took a sip, had a bite of flapjack, lit a cigarette, and slipped a finger under the cover.

II

He left on New Year's Eve, 1996. I always make a point of staying
in for New Year (and have made the point all the more firmly
since 1996, I can tell you). I'm not much of a hand at celebrations;
they depress me at best, and the enforced good-willing of New
Year makes me want to start lobbing hand grenades. People are
the problem. I don't like them much, if you want the truth. One is
good; any number up to four or five can be fine, but more than
that and I find that the chimpanzee in them starts to take over.
Some sort of pack instinct kicks in, I suppose (or do I mean
flange instinct?), and civilised sociability goes out the window
(rapidly followed by your correspondent).

This party, though, Drick promised would be right up my alley.
He phoned me around lunchtime on the day itself (knowing I
wouldn't be booked up for the evening even at the eleventh hour,
damn his cheek) and turned on the charm I'd never been able to
resist. He had an important announcement to make, he said, and
could I be sure to get there by nine. He had booked the Maltings
for the event; I knew where that was, didn't I? I didn't, so he gave
me directions. It wouldn't be a big party: just a few friends, people
from the trade and a couple of journalists. Nothing to furrow my
brow or take fright at, he assured me. He was evasive when I tried
to get some hint out of him as to what his announcement might
be, and I asked him if all was well. Absolutely well, he said.
Couldn't be better if it tried. Be there for nine, won't you. And
with that, he hung up.

I supposed his announcement must be one of two things. It
might be a book launch of some kind: we had been more or less

10

in and out of touch for some time (since he split up with Elsa, in fact, and became a literary lion), but I had heard whispers that a follow-up to *The Alchemist's Apprentice* was imminent. The presence of journalists, though, in person, in the same room as him, suggested the alternative possibility: that he was planning to reveal himself as the pen behind Maddy Rhodes. A move which, I imagined, would probably be career suicide. It never occurred to me that it was quite another kind of suicide he had in mind, nor that he was lying and that I was to be the only witness.

He had told me not to bother bringing a bottle, but I nipped out to Sainsbury's and got a couple anyway. (Unemployed and taking liquor to a millionaire's party – yeah, right.) Thinking I would be mixing with smart literary types (that was all I knew – I'd never met anyone in publishing), I took care to dress appropriately: black moleskin jacket (half-price in the Next sale earlier that week, and bloody expensive at that on the money I got from Income Support and supervising Part I undergrads), matching trousers and my onlie begotten linen shirt. I decided a tie would be farting higher than my arsehole, and it wasn't that kind of shirt (nor doubtless that kind of party) anyway. Suitably rigged, I climbed behind the wheel of my rusty-trusty Morris Minor and headed for Ely.

As I drove out of Cambridge, I went over what Drick had said on the phone. Thinking back, I wasn't quite so sure about the nature of this announcement he was planning to make. If it was to reveal the identity of Maddy Rhodes, surely he would have worded it differently. He had said, *I've got an important announcement to make.* Somehow, that seemed to imply that it would be news to me. If it were a secret I was already party to, he would have said, *I'm going to be making an announcement* – with a knowing, conspiratorial tone. In other words, there's going to be a scene, and you might want to witness it. No, I was to be a recipient of the news, not an observer of its reception. Over-analysis, you may think, but remember, I knew Drick as well as I knew myself, and that's how I would have spoken. What is more, I was absolutely right, though not in quite the way I imagined.

When I got to Ely, there wasn't a space to be had along the

river, so I had to park round the corner and up the hill, near the Cathedral. Even so, I arrived at the Maltings twenty minutes early, and wasn't entirely surprised to find the building shut up and in darkness. Smoking a cigarette, with the bottles clinking in their carrier bag, I kicked my heels until ten to nine. When there were still no signs of life, I started growing puzzled (I could've started growing geraniums for all the good it did me), and stepped under a street light to check my watch. Eight minutes to, and ticking healthily. I peered in through the glass door, but couldn't make anything out, then pressed an ear against it and heard not the faintest whisper. The place was dead and empty as a crypt.

Not so the riverside bar next door to the Maltings, which was bursting with light and life. The obvious conclusion, of course, was that I'd misunderstood Drick's directions: the party was in the *bar adjoining* the Maltings. Still unsure, though, I paced along by the windows, looking in. I couldn't see anyone I recognised, but then supposed I wouldn't; Drick himself would be the only familiar face – but there was no sign of him, either.

Taking a firm grip on my courage and my bottles, I pushed through the door and waded into the press. One thing was certain: if this was the right place, there were far more guests than he had claimed. About twenty or thirty times as many, at a conservative estimate. I struggled a few yards, and paused for breath in a small pool of calm near the centre of the room, looking about me, searching for a face I recognised. As I scanned the knots of people, a blonde woman in a blue dress with a paper streamer coiled around her throat and an empty glass in her hand detached herself from a group, teetered across my little oasis and poised a shoulder to slither out the other side.

'Excuse me,' I said, and touched her bare elbow. She didn't notice me, and in desperation I found myself pinching at her skin – quite hard, I think, because she whirled on her heels and glared at me, half angry, half alarmed, and not less than three parts stewed.

'Excuse me,' I repeated. 'Sorry. I wonder if you could help me. You see, I'm just wondering if I'm at the right party.'

She frowned. 'You too?'

'Sorry?'

She looked me up and down, eyes resting momentarily on the carrier bag pressed to my chest. 'Get yourself a drink, sweetie. Who cares? Get me one while you're at it,' she added, and held out her glass to me. Like an idiot, I took it. 'Tell little Jarvis the same again for the daughter of sin – he'll understand. And the same for you – you look like you need it.'

And with that, she turned and shouldered through a gap between two suits. I tried to stop her, but with a shimmer of blue fabric she was gone, and the suits closed ranks behind her.

Peering over heads, I managed to weave my way through to the bar. I set the woman's glass (a brandy balloon, of all things) on the bar and stood patiently, waiting to catch the eye of one of the three harassed barmen.

'Brandy, hey?' barked a bleary voice beside me. 'And I thought you'd the look of a whisky man. Never can tell, you know, with spirits.'

I turned and found myself looking into the most monstrously booze-pickled old face I've ever seen. I had a vision of white hair yellowing at the temples, watery bloodshot eyes and ruptured purple veins on a pocked nose the shape of a fist. I couldn't swear I didn't actually gasp, but managed not to step back a pace.

'Velvet clad, old boy,' he wheezed, poking me hard in the chest with a claw-like finger. 'Marks you out as a spirit-guzzler.'

'It's moleskin,' I mumbled. 'I don't actually—'

'Get 'em to put another in there, young stripling,' and he planked a tumbler on the bar beside the brandy balloon. 'It's gratis, don't you know? Hey, you down there! Does a fella have to die of thirst, or what?' He gave me an unsteady, appraising stare, and blinked slowly. 'One of Roderick's chaps, are you?'

At last. 'Yes. Have you seen—'

'Work or weekender? Look like a damned muff to me, so you must be work.'

I forced a smile, God knows why. 'I'm a friend,' I said. 'Are you in publishing? Or a journalist?' I can't say he looked remotely like either – that was a Guards tie, I was sure.

He spluttered. 'Journalist? What the devil makes you say that?'

'Oh, nothing.'

At that moment, our drinks (or rather, his and the blonde woman's drinks) arrived, and he cheered up. 'Bottoms up, old son,' he rumbled, and downed half his quadruple whisky in one. 'Now, tell me how you know young Roddy.'

'I'm a friend.'

'Friend, are you? Had a feeling you might be. Can't see any of those chaps he works with dressing in velvet, what? Friends a different pan of mullet, of course.'

'It's moleskin.' I frowned. 'Works with? Excuse me, but we are talking about Roderick Bent, aren't we?'

His bloodshot eyes crinkled up, and he let out a wheezing gurgle. Contrary to appearances, he was laughing, not having a stroke. 'I say, we jolly well might be, but don't let Roddy hear you say so, what?'

I stared at him, and was about to ask what on earth he was talking about, when the blonde woman in blue appeared at my elbow, with a tall, military-looking young man on her arm. 'Ah, is that mine?' she said, indicating the glass in my hand. 'Thanks, sweetie,' and she took it from me.

The old booze-hound tapped her on the wrist. 'I say, Lolly, seen Roddy, have you?'

'No, Uncle,' she said and looked at her escort, who shook his handsome head.

'Do I hear my name being taken in vain?'

'Roddy! You know Douglas, don't you, and er . . .' She looked at me.

I looked at the new arrival. He was a good four inches shorter than Roderick, about fifty per cent wider, and had a moustache Drick wouldn't have kept in a cage. 'You're Roderick?'

'I am. Pleased to meet you, er . . . ?'

'Not Roderick Bent, though.'

'I say, there he goes again. I warned you, old chap, ha-ha!'

'Bent?'

'Shit – look, I'm sorry, I've got the wrong person. Excuse me.'

Excreting bricks of embarrassment, I retreated into the crowd, thankful now for the thick press of bodies. Behind me, I caught a

14

raucous, whisky-sodden voice: 'Well, bugger me down dead, I *thought* he wasn't quite right in the head – dressed in velvet, for God's sake!'

I made it to the door, and was squeezed out of the crush like a pip from a lemon, sticky with sweat and taking great gulps of freezing river air. I walked a little way along the riverside and leaned on the railing, looking at the reflected stars in the black water below. It was only then I realised that I had left my bottles behind – on the bar, probably. Well, I wasn't about to go back in there, not for a year's Giros, so I'd have to consider them dead and gone. (Anyway, Uncle had probably drunk them both by now.) When I'd cooled off and got my breath back, I lit a cigarette and wandered round the corner to the door of the Maltings. Still dead, and as it was now nearly half-past nine, Drick's party was clearly a wild goose; some sort of pointlessly unfunny practical joke.

He had a house further along the river at Waterside (a three-storey Georgian affair bought and renovated with his literary winnings), so I decided to call for him there and let him have his laugh. I can't think why I reached the practical joke conclusion so readily, unless it was sheer disorientation; he'd never done such a thing to me – nor anyone else, so far as I knew – in his life. Nor, as I went storming along Waterside in a horrible temper, did it seem very likely that he would be there. As well as the house in Ely, you see, he had a flat in Wapping, and he'd surely more likely be in London for New Year.

When I arrived at the house, though, it was lit up like . . . well, like New Year's Eve. Oh, I thought, maybe there was some innocent explanation after all. Through the open curtains I could see a party going full steam in the big living room – altogether more stylishly populated than the one I'd just crashed, I noticed, and much less crowded; I could see maybe a dozen people standing about with civilised gaps between them and, while they were talking and laughing in full animated party style, they weren't bawling in each other's ears over the din, nor leaning drunkenly on their neighbours' shoulders or spilling their drinks on the carpet.

15

I went to the front door and knocked. I had to batter the knocker three times before it was answered. A female voice separated itself from the muted throng, calling *I'll get it!* and the door opened. I looked, and got such a shock I actually stepped back: the woman standing there with the doorknob in one hand and a glass in the other was the same one I had accosted in the bar. The same blue dress, the same bobbed blonde hair, and ... to my relief, I saw that the glass was a champagne flute rather than a brandy balloon, and that the face was definitely different. Decidedly older, but nevertheless disturbingly attractive.

'Hello?' she said, smiling. She had been in the act of standing aside to let me pass in, but seeing my backwards step, she peered curiously at me. 'Can I help you?'

I recovered my poise. 'Sorry. Yes, I'm a friend of Drick's. I tried the Maltings, but I presume the party must have moved here.' I smiled in a way which I hoped indicated intelligence momentarily confounded but now back on track.

'Drick?'

'I mean Roderick.' She looked blank, so I elaborated. 'Roderick Bent. Maddy Rhodes.'

Since I assumed these would be close professional associates of his, I didn't think I'd be letting any unexpected cats out of bags by referring to his pseudonymity. As it turned out, breaching his cover was the least of my concerns. Her smile had completely disappeared now, and I experienced a terrible sinking feeling. I had got the right house, hadn't I? It was awfully dark on Waterside, and I'd only been here once before. She had stepped back further inside, and was pushing the door slowly closed. 'Hang on there,' she said. 'I'll ask. Oh, Gabby, there you are.' A man had appeared through a door at the far end of the hall, carrying a bottle in each hand. 'Gabby, do you know anyone called Roderick?'

He glanced at me, his face as blank as hers, and leaned towards her as she spoke *sotto voce* in his ear. I caught some of what she said: '... drunk, I think ... let him in? ... said something about muddy roads ... no, neither do I ...' While they conferred, I looked at the number on the door, which was now half-closed.

Yes, this was definitely the right house, so what on earth was this all about?

They both turned to look at me, he wearing a puzzled frown, she a ghastly caricature of a smile. 'Sorry,' she said, 'there's no Roderick here. You must have the wrong—'

'No,' I said, 'this is his house . . . Look, Roderick Bent? Maddy Rhodes? You must have heard of Maddy Rhodes – the author?'

In unison, they pursed their lips and shook their heads – it would have been funny if I hadn't been so bewildered. The only people in Britain who had never heard of my best friend, and here they were barring the way into his house.

Suddenly, daylight broke on the man's face, and he snapped his fingers. 'Rhodes!' he exclaimed. 'I *knew* I'd heard it recently. What did you say your name was?'

'I didn't,' I said impatiently; I'd had nearly as much of this as I could take. But not quite; true to form, I resigned myself to going along with it a few more yards. 'Jeremy,' I admitted. 'Jeremy Dronfield.'

To my astonishment, he snapped his fingers again, and slapped his fist. 'Why didn't you say so? We've got something for you – come in.'

The woman shrugged and stood aside, and I followed him down the long hall to the dining room at the back of the house. This, I remembered from my only visit, was where Drick had his office, with big bookcases either side of the fireplace, a hefty Denon stereo system and half an acre of desk in the middle of the room, looking towards the French window and the garden beyond. Now, the desk, stereo and filing cabinets were gone, the bookcases were empty, and the room was piled high with cardboard boxes and stuffed bin-liners.

'We only moved in today,' he was saying as he began moving boxes and slinging black bags. 'Bloody inconvenient time of year to move, but she wouldn't listen. Front room's the only one we've got even half-organised . . . Where the hell is it? I could've sworn it was under the videos.' He paused and rubbed his chin, then gave his fingers another click. 'It was waiting on the pavement when we arrived,' he said over his shoulder, setting

17

about disarranging another neat stack on the other side of the room. 'Damned puzzling, I can tell you.'

The vague, growing unease I had been feeling as I stood on the doorstep had gone now, to be replaced by a deepening resentment: how could Drick have sold up and moved without mentioning it to me, his oldest, best friend? I mean, we had only spoken a few hours ago. Was this the great announcement he was meant to be making? And that was another thing: what the hell had happened to his bloody party?

'Got it!' He had delved an alleyway through the boxes, which were now towering, dangerously unstable, on either side of him. With a great deal of grunting and huffing, he dragged out a heavily taped box and shoved it into the middle of the room. 'Here we are. Yours, I believe.'

I looked at it. It was a big box, about the size you'd get a widescreen television delivered in, probably (as though I'd know), but unmarked except for the logo RHODES in bold capitals on the side and a large printed label covered with layers of sellotape. Sure enough, it was addressed to me, c/o 70 Waterside, Ely. I frowned at it. There was no sender's name other than 'Rhodes', which should have been a pretty clear hint, I suppose, but looked for all the world like a company logo.

'You don't know who delivered it?'

He shook his head. 'Like I said, it was waiting when we got here this morning. Couldn't get in the front door for it.' He looked at me. 'D'you mean you weren't expecting it? I rather assumed this was what you'd called for.'

'What? Oh, er, yes, of course. I, er ... thought it was going to be a bit smaller, you see.' I'm not much of a hand at dissimulation, but he smiled obligingly. 'You don't mind, do you? I mean, I'm really sorry about this. I, er, I wasn't expecting you to have moved in just yet. I thought Mr Bent would still be living here.'

'Not at all. Don't worry about it. Lodger, was he?'

'Who?'

'Your Mr Bent.'

I hesitated. 'Er ... sort of.'

He gave me a knowing look. 'Sort of, eh? Hmm . . . Did you know old Mr Thornley well?'

'Mr Thornley? No . . . er, I never met him.'

'No? Splendid old chap – old colonial sort, ex-Navy, I believe, lived here donkey's years. Odd, though. Had quite a succession of young *sort-of* lodgers, you know.'

'I see. Right.'

The way we both stared at my newly acquired box while we talked, you would have thought we expected Roderick and old Mr Thornley (*who?*) to come springing out of it in a fountain of party streamers. At last, I made *oh well* noises and stooped to pick it up. I managed to get it about eight inches off the ground, my eyes bulging, before it lurched from my fingers and hit the bare boards with a boom like a cannon.

'Need a hand?'

I nodded. 'If you wouldn't mind.'

Between us, we dragged and shoved it out of the room, along the hall and through the front door onto the pavement. There I left it while I walked up the hill and collected the car. To my surprise, he was still waiting when I pulled up, and helped me squeeze it over the front seats and into the back of the car. It would only fit by resting it against the back of the tipped-forward passenger seat, and even then it blotted out the rear window and one of its corners began furrowing a tear in the headlining. My friend remained on the pavement and watched benevolently as I drove off, giving me a cheery wave as I rounded the corner. Acting as dead-letter postmaster had clearly made his New Year; going back to his party must have been rather an anticlimax.

III

My coffee was almost cold, my flapjack half-eaten, and the ashtray contained the corpses of no fewer than four cigarettes. The couple in the corner had left off arguing; she was staring at her plate of salad, and he was contemplating the wall. On the table by my half-empty coffee cup, *The Alchemist's Apprentice* still lay unopened, its cover resting on my index finger. Dragging my mind back to the present, I turned the cover over and looked at the title page. It was inscribed, *To D. – Hope you enjoy this as much as we enjoyed Cyprus. Love E.* I wondered how many thousand copies must have been given bearing some similar inscription, or at least with some verbal recommendation. Judging by the condition of the spine, D. hadn't read it, let alone enjoyed it as much as Cyprus. Ironic, really, that this unlikely survivor must be about the only copy ever to have been so neglected. It occurred to me that Drick would have enjoyed the irony, and the less distracted part of my mind replied that of course he had enjoyed it, and that it was all part of the joke he was playing on me; a joke begun over three years ago and only now on the verge of delivering its punchline.

It hadn't seemed much like a joke at the time; for the first few days, in fact, I wondered seriously if I was going mad. I woke on the first day of 1997 feeling shabby and bleary, a condition which had nothing to do with drink or festivity, and everything to do with an evening spent not going to a party and a sleepless night spent puzzling over it thus: Drick had invited me to a New Year party. Oh-kay... He'd then cancelled it without telling me. Right... He'd also neglected to tell me that he'd sold his house in Ely and moved on... Though he must still live in the area, or the

20

Maltings wouldn't have been booked for his party. If it ever had been. Hmm . . . Finally, there had been that big box left for me. It could only have come from Drick, with or without a sender's name; even overlooking the 'Rhodes' logo (a peculiar touch, that), who else would leave me something there? But the thing that kept coming back and nagging at me was that stuff about Mr Thornley and his lodgers. Some misunderstanding, surely, but how? Was it really possible to buy a house without knowing who you were buying it from? Not only that, but to have so much gossipy knowledge of a completely spurious former owner? Maybe they bought it absent-mindedly (eh?) from a third party and never met Roderick; Mr Thornley must have been the person Roderick bought it from, and the local gossip had skipped a generation, as it were. That, convoluted as it seemed, must be it.

I was nodding with satisfaction when . . . of course! I jumped out of bed and went to the phone. I tapped in 1471, but Drick's number had gone, replaced at nine-thirty p.m. by my parents' number. I dithered by the phone for a couple of minutes, swearing under my breath and wondering whether to call my mother back, then went and got dressed.

Ten minutes later, I was down in the car park at the back of the building, sweating and cursing as I pushed and pulled at the cardboard box, jiggling it this way and that to dislodge it from the back seat. I hauled it up onto the back of the tipped-up passenger seat, where it sat with one corner wedged against the door-post; one last great heave, and it came slithering out like an overweight cardboard baby, dragging an umbilicus of tangled seatbelt, and crunched onto the tarmac. I tipped it upright and sat on it, breathing heavily, wondering how I was going to get it up the long flight of stairs to my flat. Sheer hard labour was the only answer, so I paused to smoke a roll-up and get my breath back.

It took me nearly half an hour to inch that damned box across thirty feet of tarmac to the steps which led up to the main entrance, then up the steps one at a time, through the security door and up the stairs, stopping for breath on each step with my arms flung round the box to steady it, my face red and dripping sweat. (It hadn't occurred to me to open the box in the car park;

21

since I had assumed it must contain some almost equally large and unwieldy object, I didn't see it would help much.) Finally, feeling like the last survivor of Fort Nohope staggering back to camp, I struggled across the threshold, skidded the box across the kitchen lino and desposited it on the carpet in the middle of the living room, collapsing beside it wheezing like a consumptive, hauling up great wracking, barking gusts of breath and phlegm. This time next year, I would definitely, *positively* be a non-smoker (I make the same prediction every year; I'm still waiting for it to come true.)

After restoring myself with another skin-up of Old Holborn, I got a knife from the kitchen and slit through the thick layers of parcel tape sealing the top of the box. Inside, to my intense disappointment, it appeared at first to be filled entirely with empty, unused Jiffy bags. I must have pulled out and discarded nearly a dozen of them (peering inside some to check that they were definitely empty) before uncovering the box's proper contents. These are simply itemised: about forty or fifty separate brown packets (I was too intrigued by now to curse myself for not breaking it open in the car park and saving myself a pair of near-burst lungs), ranging in size from thin manilla envelopes to hefty packages wrapped in brown paper and bound with parcel tape, like the proceeds of a post-room robbery. Each bore a white label with writing on, in Drick's unmistakeably orotund hand. The labels didn't give much away; they were simply marked *Packet 1, Packet 2, Packet 3,* and so on. Taped to Packet 1 (a thinnish A4 manilla envelope) were a couple of sheets of paper, also written in Drick's hand. The top sheet was a note:

Jeremy,

How strange to be addressing you this way – and how strange it must seem for you to be so addressed. First, I should apologise for the party last night (I know you won't get around to reading this until the morning after). It was a pretty shabby trick, but I couldn't think of any other way.

I've gone away. Where is no concern of yours, or indeed anybody's. You're the only person I shall be telling about this. You are, after all, the only person who will remember me. I shan't be coming back, ever.

Since we haven't seen each other as much as we should these last few years, I'm leaving you some papers. Some will go some way towards explaining what I've done, and my motives for it. The remainder are a gift: do with them what you will, so long as my name isn't associated with them. I simply want to be forgotten, and have taken steps to ensure that I am. Wherever I go, I shall remain

Ever your friend,

Drick

P.S. I don't feel I can take Manni with me. It wouldn't be fair: whatever I'm going to, it won't be for him. You'll find him at the address enclosed. He'll be no trouble, I promise.

P.P.S. Open the packets in order: they won't make sense otherwise. The unlabelled ones you can open whenever you like: they are the above-mentioned gift, and have nothing to do with this business.

I just didn't know what to make of it. Gone Away? I pictured him boarding a plane for Brazil, or setting up home in a shack in the Outer Hebrides. I tried not to think of the possibility hovering between the lines: that he intended to kill himself. But no, not Drick; even if he had reason to (which, ignorant as I was, I couldn't imagine), he just wasn't the type. (There is a type, you know; if it were just down to provocation, the world would be a pretty thinly populated place by now.) Where, then, could he have gone, and why?

After my sleepless night and box-moving, I was too tired to puzzle over it any more. I went through to the bedroom, collapsed on the bed and fell straight into a deep sleep.

I woke in the early evening with dribble running down my cheek and a thundering headache. I sorted myself out with a wash, a coffee and a bowl of cornflakes, then, deciding to leave Drick's packages for the moment, got my organiser out and started dialling numbers. There were four listed for Drick: his Ely number, his London flat, his mobile, and his parents in Wales. The first would obviously be defunct now, so I tried the other three with a growing sense of bewilderment as, one by one, they elicited no response. Not only were they not answered; they didn't even ring. *Dee-dah-dit* ... *The number you have dialled has not been recognised. Please check and try again.*

I sat on the hall floor with my back against the front door and the phone purring softly in my lap, staring sightlessly at the bookcase, my mind a clouded blank. I cradled the receiver, and it immediately started ringing. I snatched it up.

'Drick?'

'It's me,' said my mother.

I sighed. She wasn't disturbing me, was she? No, of course not. She had tried phoning me last night. Oh, I was out. Anywhere nice?

'Just a party ... Drick had a party in Ely.'

'Is he another archaeologist?'

'Who?'

'Rick.'

I paused. '*Drick*,' I said. 'You know Drick. Roderick. Roderick Bent.'

I could hear her breathing. '... No, I don't think I've heard of him. Is he new?'

My brain reeled. 'Roderick! He's practically your nephew! Lionel and Audrey Bent?'

There was a long, uncomfortable silence in which I imagined she was doing the same as me: frowning like a gargoyle and wondering if she had dialled the right number and wasn't speaking to a complete stranger.

'No,' she said at last, speaking in that tentative tone of voice we reserve for the senile and the dangerously insane. 'No, I don't know them.'

They had only been near neighbours for twenty-odd years, their son practically a fixture in our house from the age of eight to eighteen. What the leaping Christ was going on?

'Forget it,' I said, feeling that this conversation could only end in madness for one or both of us. 'It's not important.'

I half-listened while she gamely went on to tell me about their Christmas, none of which I can recall, occasionally pausing to ponder fruitlessly over the name Bent.

'Sorry,' she concluded. 'I must've forgotten them. Was it a long time ago? The name rings a bell. I had a teacher at school called Mrs Bent.'

'I know, she was still there in my day. No relation. Look, just forget it.'

I'd decided her brain was going. It had to be; a person – a whole family – couldn't just vanish! Maybe I should speak to Dad. Not now, though. I excused myself, said goodbye and rang off.

I wandered back into the living room, slumped on the sofa and contemplated the cardboard box and its attendant litter of empty Jiffy bags. I gazed at it for several minutes, then reached over, took Packet 1 from the top of the box and tore it open.

Packet 1

Hello my lovely darling. (Lostmacarkeys, as we used to say in Wales.) If you are reading this (which of course you're not, since I'm still writing it – there you are, only a couple of lines in and already we have a neat little aoristic conundrum; I must be on form), then the first question you will want answered may be expressed thusly: *Where in the kingdom of cunt have you got to, Bent?* Well, my friend, everywhere and nowhere is the simple answer; though not a very satisfactory one, I imagine.

Sorry, I'm getting a bit hysterical. But with reason – you see, I've hit upon the solution to all my problems; I've set in train a series of events which, at the merest additional stroke, will concatenate and wipe away forever that smirch the world calls Roderick Bent. The closure created will be absolute, and only you and I will know what has happened. But first of all I owe you an explanation.

Yes indeed. But how much easier said than done that is. Stuffed as I am with good intentions, I find myself gazing now hopelessly at the plank of words hanging unsupported above the blank space of the screen, drawing me, tempting me to run to the end of the sentence and dive into the deep. I'm a novelist, Jeremy, a paid (some would say overpaid) professional liar; writing a true account – or writing an account which cleaves as close as I can force it to that part of my memory we consider to be true – is not at all like writing fiction.

Now, I don't want to bore you with a lot of writerly navel-gazing, but it does happen to be relevant; and in a way which you could never begin to imagine. For a start, forget all that basic,

26

obvious stuff about checking of facts (which we do when we write fiction anyway) and forget all about the relationship between data and theory, theory and interpretation, writer, reader and text and all that other Crit Theory bollocks they taught us at university. *Il n'y a pas d'hors-texte.* True enough, from a certain point of view, but what I mean is that writing reality is a different *psychological experience* from writing fiction; a paradoxically different experience, if you like. Am I making myself clear? Probably not. I'll explain further.

The paradox lies in life; real characters, for instance, when written into a real–life drama which actually happened, have so much less *life* in them than invented characters in an invented story. Real people's real actions are teleological and tendentious; when I write them, I already know their life histories, their personalities and their motivations and, at the beginning of that slot of time we call a story, I know what they will do in the story and how it will end. These allegedly real people are automata hermetically sealed inside a membrane circumscribed by what actually happened, which is in turn surrounded by a teemingly vacuous infinity of what did not actually happen, if you'll excuse the oxymoron (I know how your academic mind disdains such tricksy devices). When, on the other hand, I write fiction, the invented characters with their invented personalities and their never–really–happened histories really *live* in the text. Let me illustrate: When I was a child, I had a toy which consisted of a pile of iron filings (I should say about a spoonful) trapped under a transparent plastic sheet. The object was to use a sort of magnetic stylus to pull the filings around and make pictures. The trouble was that I could never accurately determine how much of the black powder the stylus dragged; bits of it clung to other bits as I tried to pull them around, and if I let the stylus wander too close to some previously deposited filings, bits of those might be drawn away from their designated place. That is rather like writing fiction: although I have central control, the characters and their actions live by themselves. I may move them around, but their relations to each other – character to character, action to action, action to character and back again – shift exponentially, and the

27

end result, like life, can be unpredictable. Therefore, it has always been my guiding principle that my lies are truer than the truth. Or they should be. If they're not . . .

Still, we can but make the effort. More comfortably than this, though. A comfy chair is called for; I'll swap the clinical Apple for a good old-fashioned pad and pen, and type up later.

Okay, all set: pot of coffee, ashtray, fags, lighter – all neatly arranged at my left elbow; cheap biro in right fist; crisp, blank pad in front of me.

(Actually, not blank – now the top sheet has an optimistic (1) in the top right corner, one short paragraph and now the beginnings of an irrelevant parenthesis – but you know what I mean. Let's consider it blank for the sake of figurative simplicity.)

Okay again: I shall speak upon the ever-compelling subject of myself. Unlike Holden Caulfield, I'll set down the *David Copperfield* crap first and come to the madman stuff by and by. I suppose the first thing you'll want to know is that I splatted into the world on 15 September 1965 in Tredegar, South Wales. (I know you know this, Jeremy, but I can't help playing to the gallery, even when there's nobody up there.) Tredegar is the sort of town which manages to be both too small and too large – too small to offer much in the way of diversion (unless your tastes run to sheep), too large and grim to charm. Not that I ever cared; I never lived there. My parents fled the Valley wastes for fresh woods before I was more than half-sentient, and I found myself coming-to in . . .

Look, it's no use; I can't do it. It's like turning out your pockets on the custody sergeant's desk. (I've been there – forensic frown as a particularly unpleasant collection of boyish treasures is nudged with the point of a pen into a plastic bag.) How anyone can write autobiography without developing a permanent crouch due to prolonged rectal clenching is beyond me. But I've set myself this task now, and there's no backing down. I'll retreat a moment and think about it.

Later. I have it. Unbearably precious as it may seem at first glance, it's the only way; instead of levering out the turds of personal experience at close range with my own fingers, I shall, like Caesar, take the third person. Trust me on this; it'll work.

Very well, let's begin again . . .

Roderick Bent was twenty-three years old. (There – it feels more comfortable already; and you can take that disapproving look off your face this minute, Dr Dronfield – if you want the madman stuff, this is the only way you're going to get it. Run with me, okay?) Roderick Bent was twenty-three years old. It was an age he liked – the very peak at which the recently acquired word 'man' only applied with the qualification 'young' – and he stayed that age for some time (exactly a year, in fact) before becoming twenty-four; an age which was also quite good, though not as good as twenty-three. He tried out twenty-five thru' twenty-seven in quick succession – and didn't care much for any of them – before sliding full-tilt into twenty-eight and teetering on the edge of twenty-nine. He expected the next – and last – click of his twenties to be the worst of the lot – worse than thirty itself (on the premise that waiting on Death Row must be worse than going to the gas chamber), and so he set up camp eighteen months before thirty and never moved on.

Impossible, you say? Certainly; he was an impossible man (that's what Elsa said, anyway). A liar? Given to premature vanity? Certainly not; Roderick was many things, but easy liar and anxious narcissus were not among them. If the reasons why he liked himself at twenty-eight were so hard to explain (and they were not the fame, the money or the esteem, as his friends might have guessed), the means by which he stayed there were in an alto-gether higher league of inexplicability. A clumsily doctored birth certificate and lots of moisturiser weren't in it. He didn't become immortal or anything hyper-impossible like that, nor did he set the brake on the oncoming slow train of death – he just stopped getting older, and nobody noticed.

Packet 2

It began with a perfectly normal walk by the river, on a perfectly normal, though beautifully, crisply bright, June day. But isn't that always the way; this kind of story always begins with 'It started out as a perfectly ordinary day/journey/shopping trip/criminal trial/piano lesson', followed by extraordinariness and weird stuff. A storyteller's device, of course; counterpointing the everyday against the abnormal. If it had *begun* as a totally bizarre day/ journey/shopping trip/criminal trial/piano lesson, then the telling of it would have to pull focus, drawing attention to the completely ordinary week/month/year preceding it. You *can't* slam people over the head with the weird shit straight away; they won't stand for it.

So, it was a perfectly normal walk. It wasn't destined to turn weird, exactly, but it certainly became extraordinary. Roderick's life was never the same again.

He got out of bed late (which was perfectly normal) and had breakfast in the little kitchen above the shop, sitting in his socks and boxers at the small pine table and gazing through the tiny, crooked window with its view over the eaves of Steeplegate to the Cathedral beyond. From time to time, he tore pieces from his buttered toast and dropped them for Manni, smiling as the big, sleek dog ducked his head and hoovered up the greasy wedges. It was as well Elsa was hard at work in the shop, because she strongly disapproved of him feeding the dog from the table. It offended her sense of discipline as well as her sense of hygiene; encouraging begging at mealtimes might be tolerable in a little dog, but not in one tall enough to rest his chin flat on the

30

table-top. Drick encouraged it in spite of her, since he believed (rightly) that Elsa had never liked Manni much anyway. She liked small dogs; she had wanted (if they really *must* have a dog, which she had never been convinced of) a dachshund, or perhaps a little cocker spaniel; certainly not a Weimaraner, much less the biggest pup of the litter. But Drick was wilful and could be persuasive, and those nine wrinkly, blue-eyed, silver-grey puppies had been monstrously gorgeous; what was more, it was Drick's money to spend, saved from the sale of some of his short stories. Forever after, she couldn't shake off the feeling that she had been well and truly railroaded; she was resentful, and Elsa resentful was an uneasy partner. Her ill will was mostly aimed at Drick (and was rooted in much more than just his choice of dog), but was frequently expressed at Manni. The more he grew and the less puppyish he became (he was nine months old now, and almost fully grown), the more she disliked him. Manni, of course, sensed both the dislike of himself and of his master. As dogs will, he responded by making things worse, laying back his ears and growling if she went to touch him; when Drick rebuked him for it, he would skulk round his master's legs and gaze at Elsa with his baleful grey eyes. Even Drick, who was fiercely loyal to Manni, would have taken Elsa's side over this behaviour if it had been a typical expression of the dog's character, but it wasn't; Manni was the softest, silliest man's-best-friend on earth, and would rather fool and frolic with humans than eat his dinner. If he took a dislike to somebody, there was invariably a good reason for it.

'Walkies, Manni?'

The dog's ears went out like sails. He pushed his nose into Drick's bare chest and tried to climb into his lap, coiling himself round in a tangle of long limbs and licking at Drick's bristly chin. Drick grasped his forelegs and pushed him off.

'Where's your lead?'

With the dog following at his heels, he went to the bathroom and, having completed his ablutions with excited paws clawing at the backs of his legs – shouting 'Down, Manni!' through a froth of toothpaste – they had their ritual tug-of-war with T-shirt, clean socks, boxers and jeans. Gradually, Drick won the games and dressed himself in his prizes. Down the stairs to the little vestibule at the back of the shop – boots on, collar, lead – and a final check on the contents of the walkie-bag: biscuits, water bottle, flexi-lead, poop-scoop (like a soldier's gas mask – essential to carry, but God forbid he should ever have to use it); cigarettes, lighter. With everything sorted out, he opened the back door and they reeled out into the alleyway.

'Heel! Heel, Manni!'

The dog stopped hauling like a husky and settled into an eager trot at Drick's side. They crossed the High Street to Steeplegate and walked through to the sun-soaked Cathedral green just as the bells of St Mary's were chiming ten o'clock. They strolled down Back Hill in the direction of the river, and half an hour later were making their way along the worn path through the long grass by Middle Fen Bank, following the line of the railway track.

As they walked – or rather, as Drick walked and Manni bounded through the grass like a porpoise – he reflected on his relationship with Elsa (Drick's, not Manni's, which was foregone). She had her attractions, certainly, and she had given him refuge when his studies went down the pan, but although he had once been fond of her, he had never really loved her. They had met two years ago, when he was still a student attempting (unsuccessfully, it turned out) to get permission to excavate in the Cathedral precincts and she was a power in the local historical society. She was keen – on him as much as his researches, and given the state of mind he was in then, she fitted his prescription to a T: eight years his senior, self-sufficient, stern and stable, pretty in a country-lass sort of way, with marvellous breasts, rolling hips, and buttocks you could buffer trains with. And oh so willing to indulge him.

Well, that had worn off before long, and now they lived in a permanent state of détente. He anticipated the day when she would finally ask him to take his belongings, his cronky little Mac, his boxes of manuscripts, and his damned dog, and remove himself from the flat. Each day it didn't happen was a perpetual surprise to him. If he'd had enough money, he would have left by now of his own accord. What he earned from teaching wasn't enough to keep Manni in dog-chews. If only he could get someone to take his novel. Any one of them – he wasn't fussy, and he didn't expect a king's ransom for it.

'*Manni! Leave it!*' he roared, and the dog, who had been sniffing at the decaying carcass of a squashed hedgehog, came bounding back to him. 'Here, have a biscuit and behave. Sit. Good boy.'

No fewer than fourteen publishers had turned down *The Island* now. Maybe he should get an agent. Or a silenced revolver and a ticket to London. He had exhausted all the big imprints, and his copy of *The Writer's Handbook* looked like it had been gone over by a demented and extremely angry proofreader. The last batch of samples had gone out to little back-street presses; if they proved as obdurate and purblind as the big houses, all that would be left would be the vanity publishers. The problem was, he *knew* he was a good writer. And not in the vain, deluded, self-pitying way of the born failure; if Roderick Bent had one virtue, it was honest self-appraisal. He knew when he had written good work, just as he knew when his outpourings were shit. (After all, he was a published writer, wasn't he? He had some considerable skill with words, hadn't he? People – professional publishing people – had told him so. Fuck it, he *taught* creative writing, didn't he?) Had it been his first or second novel, he wouldn't have been surprised if they turned it down; he never bothered submitting them because he knew they were poor efforts. The third and fourth he was delighted with, but *The Island* had been tailored for maximum publishability, even to the extent of betraying his principles by allowing its writing to be guided by his perception of the market. He had chosen its setting to capture the heart of the holiday-bound or holiday-nostalgic reader, its characters had been designed to charm and delight, its narrative to wring the emotions, its ending to leave a lingering sweet aftertaste in the mind. And it worked; he *knew* it worked, even though he had exercised (for him) too dictatorial a degree of control over its form and had, ultimately, forced it.

Ah, bollocks, he thought. *Dans la derrière* with it, as Zola would have said. He'd wait and see.

'STOP! Manni, STAY!'

The dog had paused in his exploration of the reeds bordering the marshes, and was poised, pointing ahead up the track; coming towards them was an elderly lady with a wiry little Jack Russell trotting at her heels. This was Midge, and Manni had met him once before. On that occasion, he had bounded forward with his usual exuberant exhortations to play; the little terrier – remarkably for a member of his breed – had taken fright and run. Although Manni had given up the pursuit within ten yards (more interested in meeting the owner than her dog), Midge, in blind panic, had burned paw the whole length of the riverbank, not stopping until he reached his home in Queen Adelaide, where his owner found him an hour later, panting and trembling on the doorstep.

Luckily, this time Drick spotted him coming at a good distance. 'Here, Manni, this way!' he called, and veered off the track onto one of the little rush-lined pathways leading down to the river's edge. Manni followed with reluctant obedience, pausing now and then to gaze wistfully back over his shoulder until the old lady was lost to sight beyond the reeds.

It was pleasant down by the river; usually they gave this stretch a wide berth to avoid the dog-hostile horses which sometimes grazed on the bank. Today there was no sign of them, and Drick slowed his pace to a gentle amble, taking advantage of their absence to enjoy the peace of the river. It was midsummer, and the hawthorn hedgerows were thick with dog-rose and spattered with cow-parsley, and the surface of the river – still and slow as a canal – was a regatta of water-lilies. Here and there, pads were tilted up like the hulls of sinking boats (perhaps, it occurred to him, where animals had tried to walk on the solid-looking surface, as Manni was doing now, dipping a paw and frowning as the pads sank and bobbed); amongst them, the thick, orange-capped stems curved up like the arms of drowning sailors.

They had reached the half-way mark of their morning walk (from here, they would re-cross the river near the pumping station and make their way over Cuckoo Bridge to Roswell Pits and Springhead Lane woods, then cut up through the town), and Drick decided to spin it out; the weather was gorgeous, and he had no desire to hurry back for the usual moody lunch with Elsa.

34

He sat down on a tussock near the water's edge and opened his bag. He poured out a bowl of water for Manni and scattered some biscuits on the turf, then lit a cigarette and enveloped himself in luxuriant smoke.

While he sat, he reached up to the cluster of dog-rose drooping above his head, idly plucking off the pink blooms and laying them on the grass at his side. Then, smiling to himself, he beckoned Manni to him, told him to sit, and began weaving the stems into the links and buckle of his chain collar. Drick half-expected him to claw and scatter them, but he just sat panting patiently; when his garland was complete, he sniffed around in the grass for a few moments and, with a deep, growling sigh, lay down and closed his eyes. Lulled by the thick, clotted river warmth, Drick did likewise, and within minutes both were snoring gently on the deep carpet of turf.

The dream he had then haunted his memory forever afterwards, but he slipped into it so seamlessly that it didn't seem like a dream at all; not even when he woke.

In the dream, he was still lying there on the grass by the river, his eyes filled with the glare of the blue sky and sun. He sat up, shading his eyes and looked about him. Manni was gone; there was a crushed area of grass where he had lain, and a single pink petal torn almost in two. Frowning in bewilderment, but still not rising to his feet, he picked up the petal and rolled it between his fingers. He was struck by how quiet it had become; the sounds of geese croaking in the reeds had disappeared, as had the distant sound of traffic on the Stuntney Causeway, the rattle of trains on the park bridge and the gentle putter of boat engines passing up- and downriver. In their place was a dense, oppressive silence; he couldn't even hear his own breathing. Then he heard a thin, distant sound; a gentle keening like a dog crying softly in its sleep, but far away. Manni. He stood up – or rather, he tried to; his legs wouldn't answer, and the best he could do was rise heavily to his knees, supporting himself with his hands. He looked about, trying to tell the direction of the sound. It seemed to be coming from the water. He crawled forward to the edge, afraid he would find pawprints in the mud and no sign of Manni. To his relief, there were no prints; the mud was smooth and unbroken. Yet the keening – slightly more distinct now – was definitely coming from the water. He stared at the twinkling, blinking reflection of the sun among the lily pads. Suddenly, the green pads parted, there was a rush of water, the keening wail burst out abruptly, turning into a howl of anguish, and a human form rose up out of the water, brown with mud and trailing a drapery of slimy green weeds. He started back in alarm and sprawled on the grass, lying helpless as the figure made its way to the water's edge and up the bank towards him. He tried to call for Manni, but couldn't make any sound come out of his gibbering mouth. As it came closer, he realised that the figure wasn't the enormous, diabolical monster it had looked like, but a young child. Under the weeds, the streaks of mud and runnels of water coursing down her face, she was pale and drawn, and in her eyes was such an expression of anguish that he felt his insides wither and perish just at the sight of it. As he lay, unable to move, she came closer and closer. She knelt beside him and peered intently into his face; as she bent over him, her hair, bedraggled with weed-slime, licked across his face, and he cried out at last.

Daddy? she murmured desolately. *Daddy, I can't see. Is it you?*

And he woke, sweating and clawing at Manni's velvet face as the dog stooped over him and nuzzled his face with his wet nose. The King's Lynn train clattered noisily across the park bridge, and as it faded away, there was the gurgle of geese strutting through the reeds. He took Manni by the ears and nuzzled him back, reassured by the satin-soft fur.

After a cigarette, he felt fine; he didn't have the foul, clogged throat and heavy head he usually got after sleeping during the day, and the horrible dream retreated quickly to the back of his mind (though it never receded any further than that). By the time he and Manni had walked on a little way along the river, it was as though the episode had never occurred.

It was then – about ten minutes or so after continuing the walk – that he happened to glance across the water and saw the garden.

He had never noticed it before, and he had walked this way more times than he could count. However, he reflected, it wasn't that surprising that he had failed to notice it; unless you looked directly at it from a certain angle, you would almost certainly take it for a continuation – albeit a rather picturesque continuation – of the riverbank flora. It ran down to the water and was enclosed on one side by the high hawthorn hedge which bordered the marshland up to Kiln Lane, and on the other by the thick woodland beyond which lay the water company depot. You wouldn't immediately take it for a garden because, from this side of the river, the house to which it must attach was out of sight, screened by a tall hedge of privet. Within these bounds was a long, narrow sward ending in a strand of bulrushes, where a half-sunk punt was moored at a landing-place built of rotting piles whose few remaining boards hung crazily into the water. Drick probably wouldn't have noticed the garden now if it hadn't been for the person sitting in it.

She was perched on a hummock above the water's edge just where the remains of the landing-stage disappeared into the dense reed-bed. She wore a white dress and broad-brimmed white hat, and had a sketch-book the size of a table-top propped against her knees. She was bent over her drawing, working away at it with intense concentration. From time to time she glanced up and peered across the water, without ever seeming to notice one man and his dog staring at her from the far side of the river (the man at least was staring; his dog was preoccupied with scratching at the turf some distance away). Drick couldn't take his eyes off her; she was undoubtedly the most beautiful girl he had ever seen. (Thinking back on this later and reckoning the width of the river, this certainty seemed strange; with his imperfect eyesight, her face couldn't have been more than a tiny smudge at that distance.)

He thought of trying to attract her attention, but she was too absorbed in her drawing; and anyway, what could he do from this side of the river even if he succeeded? Give her a cheery wave? Still, he was loath to pass on by and leave her unflirted with. He glanced at Manni; interestingly, the dog was now also gazing across the river, his ears raised intelligently. *Oi loike meetin' people*, Drick murmured to himself. 'Don't you, doggie?' he added out loud, and Manni looked up at him and wagged his tail.

Drick rummaged in his walkie bag and unearthed the pad and pen he always kept there (just in case inspiration irresistible came to him out of doors), and wrote a short note. He tore out the page, folded it over and over, and tucked it into Manni's flower-garlanded collar, securing it under the hasp of the buckle. Then he crouched down at the dog's shoulder and directed his attention back at the girl.

'Go meet the lady, Manni. Go fetch her!'

He had taught the dog to do this with Elsa on the infrequent occasions when she came out for a walk with them; inevitably she would lag behind, her interest caught by some wagtailed bluefinch or piebald greenhopper or whatever they were called, and he would send the dog back to fetch her. Of course, with a stranger (Manni adored all strangers), he surely wouldn't do what he did to Elsa, which was to round her up like a stray sheep, driving her along with little nips at her calves and ankles. Of course not.

'Off you go – fetch her!'

Manni reached the river's edge in two great bounds and launched himself into the water like a four-legged depth-charge, landing with a splash that sprayed Drick at a range of ten feet. (The girl still didn't look up from her sketch-book – she must have powers of concentration bordering on self-hypnosis.) He disappeared below the surface momentarily, then came up in a froth of churned water and dog-rose petals and began driving like an otter for the far bank. He drifted downstream a little and came ashore under the eaves of the woodland to the right of the garden. By the time he had scrambled up the muddy bank and shaken himself, only a few blooms still clung to his collar – along with the note, Drick was glad to see. He looked about, getting his bearings, then spotted the girl through the trees and went bounding towards her, crashing through the undergrowth.

At that moment, Drick had what could only be described as a premonition; the girl still hadn't noticed the dog loping out of the woods, and Drick could see with startling clarity what was about to happen. Manni hit the turf at a gallop; at that moment the girl looked up from her drawing and twisted round to see the huge dog bearing down on her. He slammed on the brakes a few feet short of her and met her eye, and for a few pregnant seconds they gazed at each other. His entire backside wagged like a flag, he laid back his ears in greeting and leapt. His front paws, slathered in river mud, planted themselves firmly on the front of her white dress, she staggered back, and her sketch-book flew out of her hand like a huge frisbee as she fell backwards onto the grass.

Drick didn't see any of this; he had flung himself flat on the turf behind a cluster of tall rushes as soon as Manni made his leap. He lay there for several moments, listening, and when he failed to hear any screams or shouts, he got to his knees and peered cautiously through the tops of the rushes.

All he could see over the hummock above the landing stage was Manni standing over something – presumably the supine and struggling girl – wagging and licking. Raising himself a little higher, he noticed that the girl's sketch-book was drifting like a raft on the slow, gentle current. Well, he had only two choices: abandon Manni and hope he would find his own way home, or . . .

Seized by a sudden resolve, and acting quickly before he thought better of it, he followed the dog's footsteps down the bank and waded into the river. By the time he was ten feet out the water was up past his knees, and he thought he might have to swim for it. Luckily, though, it didn't get any deeper; he managed to overtake the sketch-book and, holding it out in front of him like a swimming float, made it through the rushes to the landing stage. With an effort (sodden, it was the weight as well as the size of a table-top), he pushed the book up over the rotting timbers onto the bank, then hauled himself up, squelching and out of breath, after it. He paused for a second with his palms and face on the ground, bracing himself for recrimination, then rose to his feet.

The scene before him was so unexpected that he wondered if he had come ashore in some other garden: but no, there was the hawthorn and the privet hedge and the woodland, and there was Manni, head still bowed, guzzling biscuits off the ground; but there was no sign of the girl. He went to the dog, who looked up with a politely inquiring expression, wagged his tail a little, then went back to snorting over his biscuits – chocolate chip cookies, by the look of the remains he was now vacuuming up.

'Would he like some more, do you think?'

Drick turned to find the girl standing by the hedge, as though she had stepped through the solid wall of privet like a ghost. As he looked, he realised that the hedge was cut in such a way as to enclose a small alcove – not noticeable from a distance – which contained a white wrought-iron table. On the table was a tall glass pitcher and some tumblers, as well as a plate of biscuits. The girl picked up the plate.

'He seems awfully hungry,' she said with a smile.

'He always is,' said Drick absently, still palpitating from his struggle across the river and the shock of the girl's disappearance and sudden reapparition. 'I'm sorry about his behaviour – he's never done that before. Did he hurt you?'

The girl didn't seem to hear him. 'I love dogs,' she said. 'I was never allowed one.' She put down the plate and took a cookie from it. 'Here,' she said, holding it out. Manni loped over to her and took it with the utmost delicacy, not grabbing the way he usually did. (Drick's fingers had once been covered with little nip-marks acquired before he learned to toss Manni his treat as he lunged for it.)

'Good boy,' she murmured. 'And to bring me such a nice note.' She took the piece of paper – thoroughly crumpled, but not at all soggy from its immersion in the river – from the sleeve of her dress, and read it aloud: '*Der prety lady, mi mastr say howdedoo. P.S. got eny snaks?*'

Drick coughed and felt himself beginning to colour. 'Er, well,' he smiled, 'I apologise again for his behaviour and his presumption, but I can't be held responsible for his spelling. I don't know how many times I've told him there are two t's in pretty.'

She laughed – a light laugh which was soft and warm, and for some reason made him think of a chenille scarf he had worn and cherished as a child – and looked directly at Drick for the first time. He noticed then that there was no trace of dirt on the snow-whiteness of her dress. Surely she couldn't have got changed in the half-minute or so it had taken him to cross the river? Certainly not; yet where he would have expected great

40

splats and skid-marks of brown mud (not to mention grass stains), there was only pure white – and such a white; bright and absolute, like light. Her plimsolls were also white, as were the strap of her watch and the ruffle she wore on her right wrist, and the broad-brimmed hat. Her skin seemed to reflect the brilliance of her clothes: pale almost to the point of translucency. There were only three touches of colour in her: a ribbon loosely bound about the crown of her hat which was printed with a pattern of strawberries, her eyes which were deep serpentine green and her hair, which was a rich, dark chestnut. She was older than he had thought; something juvenile in her figure and manner of dress had led him to expect her to be in her late teens, but she clearly wasn't: her figure – narrow-hipped and with small, bud-like breasts – could have belonged to an adolescent, but her eyes were clearly much older. They were bright with youth, but there were tiny care lines about their corners which could only belong to a mature adult. He was hypnotised by her, and found himself describing these details to himself as if to inscribe them in his memory – somehow feeling he would never get a chance to memorise her at leisure. There was something ethereal about this girl, and he wouldn't have been surprised to see her dissipate like mist and vanish before his eyes.

Dully, he became aware that she was speaking to him. 'Hnh?' he said thickly, and was conscious of an amused smile on her lips – lips, he thought to himself in a flurry of inspiration, like two pale satin pillows which . . . – he banished the simile, noting it for later consideration, and fought his way back to full consciousness. 'I beg your pardon,' he said with massive gallantry, 'I was distracted for a moment there. I can only say I can't be blamed for it.' And he gave her what he hoped was a suitably Galahad-like smile.

'I said, you rescued my book.'

'Oh, that. Yes, well, it was the least I could do.'

He picked it up off the grass and, shaking off the drips and removing some pieces of weed, held it out to her. 'I hope it's not too spoiled.'

She grimaced and folded back the cover. 'No, it's fine,' she said. 'It'll dry out.'

He looked at her drawing, and found it wasn't a drawing at all. The huge sheet had been divided into rectangles – like the panels of a cartoon strip but much more irregularly set out – and each panel was filled with pencilled writing, ranging in size from book-print to signboard, and all beautifully calligraphed and justified, with little blocks of illumination in each panel.

'Concrete poetry,' he said. 'How interesting.'

'Is it? It's just an experiment; something I've been playing around with.'

'You're an artist?'

She laughed. 'Goodness, no. I can't draw.'

He raised his eyebrows sceptically at her, then went back to studying some of the panels. 'You can write, though ... I'm a writer myself,' he added, and felt ten buttocks-worth of an arse saying it; but then, why should he? He was published, wasn't he?

'Really? Oh, you won't want to look at this, then.' And with a little self-deprecating laugh, she closed the book and set it aside on the iron table. 'What's your name? Have I heard of you?'

'Roderick Bent, and I doubt it.'

She stared at him – quite alarmingly, actually. 'I have! The boy – in Wales – the boy who fell off the bridge. It's you!'

The moment she said it, she looked as though she could have bitten her tongue off. All he could say was, 'Eh?'

She was far too pretty to be described as 'gibbering' at this point, but she came close. 'Er, it's a story. One of yours. Isn't it?'

He frowned at her. 'I think you've mixed me up with someone else,' he said. 'A bridge? No, that's not me.' He laughed. 'I haven't published enough that I'd forget anything.' He would have taken more notice of her reaction if he hadn't been wondering why her words rang a very, very faint bell. He *hadn't* written a story like that, had he? 'No, that's definitely not me,' he said.

She looked doubtful. 'Oh, I could have sworn ... Never mind. It was a good story, though.' She gazed into the middle-distance, frowning slightly, as though trying to recall a distant memory. 'I've got muddled,' she conceded.

'I am Welsh, though,' he said. 'You got that right.'

'Are you? You don't sound Welsh.' Having been so sure of her facts a moment ago, she now seemed quite sceptical, and Drick couldn't help feeling that, having failed to be the person she thought he was, he was now being viewed like an unknown interloper at a party. She didn't turn frosty; just dubious.

'Born and bred,' he assured her. 'In Wales we don't need an accent; we have a language.'

'You speak Welsh? Say something for me.'

He took a deep breath. 'Llanfairpwllgwyngyllgogeryd-dwyrndrobwllllantisiliogogogoch,' he said confidently, and added: 'Mai hen wlad fyn hadae.'

'What does it mean?'

'It means, "The beautiful church where Gwyn the Mighty slid down the mountain on one knee and played the flute to his girlfriend while she go-go danced in the lych of St Tisilio's chapel and a May hen laid a haddock." '

She pursed her pretty pale lips, then laughed. 'I think you'd be better off with the accent.'

He shrugged. 'Can't oblige you there, I'm afraid. Like Oscar Wilde, it was one of the many things I forgot at university.'

She looked blank. 'You forgot Oscar Wilde? Why?'

'No, he forgot his Ir—' Drick looked at her and stopped. 'You're teasing me,' he said. 'One-all.'

She went over to the table and poured out a cloudy tumbler from the pitcher. 'Lemonade?' she asked.

'Yes please.'

'Aren't you going to ask me my name?' she said as she poured and handed him a glass.

'Of course. What, dear lady, is your name? I'm sure it must be something simple yet pretty, diminutive yet elegant.'

'Kismet,' she said.

'Sorry?'

'So am I. Kismet Lillystone.' She spoke deliberately, looking steadily at him.

He got the impression she expected the name to mean something to him, but he couldn't imagine why. He settled for a different interpretation of her look. 'I'm being willed to ask: why Kismet?'

Was it his imagination, or did she seem disappointed? 'My father named me,' she said. 'You know how Lord Nelson is supposed to have said *Kiss me, Hardy* as he was dying? Well, he didn't, apparently. According to my father – who worshipped Nelson – the Admiral and his Flag Captain had this perennial debate about kismet – fate – in which Nelson believed; the idea that everything in our lives is preordained. Being the man he was, he couldn't resist having the last word in the debate, even as he lay dying. His verdict on his death: *Kismet, Hardy*. You can imagine his slurred speech and the noise of battle causing the witnesses to mishear him; hence the *Kiss me* tradition.' She smiled thinly and peered into her lemonade. 'Given the circumstances, my father thought it was an appropriate name for me.'

Drick was about to ask what circumstances when he felt a wet snout nuzzling at his hand. 'What d'you want, pest? You've guzzled all this lady's cookies, you greedy beast.'

'Poor thing's hungry,' she said. Squatting down, she took one of his paws in her hand. 'I wish I had something for you, you handsome boy.'

'I think he's had quite enough.'

She made a sympathetic moue at the dog and let go of his paw. It slapped against the skirt of her dress, and Drick was intrigued to see that, slippery with mud though the paw was, it left no mark – either on the fabric or her hand. (He didn't notice until much later – when they were walking home, in fact – that, even stranger, his jeans were dry, and – he simply *knew* by examining his memory – had been dry within minutes of getting out of the water. It was a hot day, but not that hot.)

'So,' she said, rising to her feet and taking a sip of her lemonade, 'tell me about being a writer.'

He sat in the kitchen as he had done that morning, staring out of the window at the Cathedral. Manni lay on a blanket at his feet, dreaming, no doubt, of chocolate chip cookies and lemonade while his master stroked absently at the legs of his mysteriously dry jeans and wondered.

For the second time that day, they had failed to encounter

expected recrimination: 'Your lunch went in the bin,' said Elsa indifferently, hardly sparing him a glance as she stuffed carrier-bags into her hold-all and headed off to catch the supermarket before it closed. (Shopping was normally his job, and this indicated the extent of her concealed anger: when she had a strop, she always took over his tasks as a means of stoking up the resentment she felt, so that it would be all the more awful when it finally boiled over.)

Deducting the time he had left that morning from the time he arrived home, with allowance made for the first half of the walk, he calculated that he had spent more than six hours in that garden while the strange pale girl plied him with lemonade (the real article – home-made and tasting of fresh lemons, with the soft fizz of sugar on the tongue – not the carbonated battery acid that usually masquerades under the name) and drew talk from him like water from a well. He tried to recall their conversation, but from the hours of it that there must have been, he could only bring back to mind the barest fragments, along with an inchoate sense of ease and well-being. He remembered telling her about his unpublished novels and his little triumvirate of published stories. (Again he had to deny having written the story of the Welsh boy and the bridge, which was the one aspect of the afternoon that made him uneasy; many things puzzled and bewildered him, but only that was vaguely disturbing, and he wasn't sure why.) Her interest in his work seemed genuine; not merely the polite – however sincere – interest he was used to, but the thirst of a fellow-traveller. She admitted having attempted to write herself (orthodox prose and poetry as well as the more experimental kind he had seen) but insisted that her efforts were of the sorriest quality; which he didn't believe for a moment. He invited her to come and join his next creative writing course, which was due to start in a few weeks' time. She said it would be impossible, but eventually agreed to see what she could do.

And that was all he remembered with any clarity. The rest was just a memory of how happy he had felt with her there in her garden by the river. And how drear by comparison the little flat above the shop seemed – the little flat and the drab hostility of the life he lived in it with Elsa.

He was spared the inevitably drawn-out continuation of this last line of thought by the phone ringing. He let it go for several rings, then hauled himself irritably off his chair and went out to the alcove off the landing. He yanked the receiver off the cradle with such force that the rickety table wobbled and nearly fell over.

'Yes?' he said with unconcealed annoyance.

'Hello, is that Mr Bent?' said a man's voice against a background of audible office bustle.

'It is.'

'Hello. My name is Nicholas Lovell. I represent Obeli—'

'Then you have my commiserations,' Drick interrupted. 'We're not buying anything, so fuck off.'

He slammed down the receiver, feeling noticeably better than he had before picking it up. Perhaps there was something to be said for telesales after all, even if it was only the opportunity to be rude to unsolicited callers. He picked up the receiver again and dialled.

'Jezza? Hi, Drick here. How are you fixed for tonight? Fancy a wet? . . . No, it's okay, I'll come to you. About an hour? . . . Okay, see you then. Cheery-pip.'

He went back to the kitchen, took the car keys off their hook and picked up Manni's collar and lead. 'Come on,' he said. 'Walkies time again.'

If anything was guaranteed to push Elsa's blood pressure into the red, it would be coming back laden with shopping to find her car gone and him with it. Well, she was spoiling for a fit of the tempers, so the least he could do was help her to the crisis point.

Perhaps she had more patience than he had bargained for, or he had behaved less badly than he reckoned; it took another two days for the crisis to come. Manni was the spark to the gas: coming into the living room and finding him curled up in her armchair, she seized him by the scruff and hauled him out. As he rolled onto the floor, he gave a low growl of indignation – just that, no threat, only a huffy, Muttley-like grumble prior to skulking off.

Elsa flushed at the affront, grabbed the nearest object – the television remote – and swiped him across the muzzle with it. He yelped and scurried across to Drick, who, with a furious glare at Elsa, took the dog's head between his hands and examined his snout. There was a small cut on the lip, leaking a dribble of blood onto the fuzzy grey chin.

The blow-up that followed needs no repeating; it was all too predictable and banal, bouncing erratically between his outrage and her semblance of calm: he knew she was a vicious bitch, but he couldn't *believe* she had done that; if he couldn't control his dog, then he knew what he could do with it and himself. She was sick of it. Had he seen the state of the car after the other evening? Dog hair everywhere. And so on. If it hadn't been for stark necessity, he would have upped sticks and decamped there and then in the middle of the night. But, as she never tired of reminding him (and she did so now, of course), it was *her* flat; *her* car; *her* earnings that kept them while he wasted his time writing garbage that nobody in their right mind would want to read, let alone pay for. She had a way of putting it that implied that her own work – selling lacy doilies and clerically gowned teddy bears to pensioners on coach trips – was of more eternal worth than his, simply because it earned money. And he had to admit, on empirical grounds at least, that he didn't have a leg to stand on in the face of her logic. That fact naturally did nothing to assuage his frustration, and he could only seethe impotently while she belittled him and bullied his dog.

In the weeks that followed, he took out his feelings against Elsa by deliberately neglecting his work. How this was meant to spite her was unclear, but the rationale (if it could be called that) went something like this: if she thought so little of his writing, then he just wouldn't do it any more, so stick that in one of her incense burners and smoke it! There may have been more to it than that: perhaps he was saying that her contempt for what he held precious hurt him so much that he was prepared to discard it, however much that might also cost him pain. He took to spending as little time as possible at the flat; Manni's walks began as soon as Drick was up in the morning and, with the aid of a packet of sandwiches and a bag of dry dogfood, lasted until the evening. They walked an ever-expanding bound around Ely: to the villages of Prickwillow, Little Downham and Waterbeach, and across mile after mile of open fen. Most days, though, they would walk the river path between Stuntney Causeway and Cuckoo Bridge, looking out as they passed for Kismet in her garden, but she was never there. Perhaps it was her absence, or maybe the light was different, but the garden seemed somehow less attractive now; it had a look about it that made him think of twilight and abandonment, even though he couldn't discern any recognisable change in it. Each time they came this way, Drick would stop and sit on the bank for an hour or so, waiting to see if she would appear, but she never did. He also tried finding a way into the garden from the landward side, but never succeeded. The woods on one side were blocked off by the water depot, and the hawthorn hedge on the other side was thick and continuous, with no breaches. And as for the entrance to the house to which the garden must belong, there just didn't seem to be one. Repeatedly he traced the meanders of the road between Cuckoo Bridge and the water works, and the tracks and fields that led off it, but there seemed to be no way in: just impenetrable hedgerows and woodland tracks which wandered and turned and finally disgorged him back onto the road. As a last resort, he considered wading across the river (oddly, it never occurred to him to borrow a boat), but something held him back. When he analysed this something, it was to do with a fear of arriving on the other side of the river and finding that his trouser legs were in fact wet. That would prove unbearably that his dreamlike afternoon in the garden really had been nothing more than a dream. (Another part of his reluctance to enter the water – a part which he didn't admit to at the time because its associations were too uncomfortable – was the memory of the dream he had had earlier that same day.)

Slowly, July passed into August, and the extended walks came to an end with the beginning of his summer duties at the Community College. It wasn't the teaching itself (a two-hour session on Wednesday evenings and an additional one on Friday

48

afternoons for the college's summer school) that cut into his walks so much as the time he had to devote to reading his students' effusions. Anyway, since during these tri-annual periods of paid employment Elsa was less able to condescend, he felt less uncomfortable spending time in the flat.

On the second Wednesday morning in August – the first morning he had spent at home in weeks – he was going over his teaching notes (all three pages of them) in preparation for his first class of the term, when the phone rang. With a muttered curse, he squeezed out of the stuffy little cubicle under the stairs which he called his office and went to answer it. The voice on the other end seemed vaguely familiar.

'Hello,' it said. 'Is that Roderick Bent?'

'Probably,' he replied. 'What can I do for you?'

There was a polite little chuckle. 'I've caught you at last. I've tried to call you several times in the past couple of weeks.'

'Well, I've been out a lot. Who are you?'

'We spoke briefly a while ago, but there seemed to be some misunderstanding. Not to put too fine a point on it, you hung up on me.'

'Did I? Well, I must have had good reason.'

Another little chuckle. 'I daresay you did. Please don't do it again, though, not before I've had a chance to explain myself. My name is Nicholas Lovell; I'm publishing director at Obelisk. I'm calling – as I was last time – to say that I've finished reading *The Island* and, well, in short, I loved it and I want to publish it.'

Drick stared at the wall, conscious of a slight sweat breaking out on his forehead and a sudden thumping in his chest. And all he could think about was how dangerously rude he had been. (But if a person had something that important to say, why couldn't they come straight to the point? As in, *Is that Mr Bent? I want to publish your book.*) All he could think of to say was, 'Oh, right. Shucks,' while his stomach did cartwheels.

Lovell described some of the passages in the book which had most moved and impressed him. 'It really is extraordinarily good,' he concluded. 'I have to tell you that we don't normally publish novels, but I'm determined to make an exception in this case. Can I ask whether you've approached any of the larger publishing houses with it?'

'No, I didn't think it was appropriate,' Drick improvised hastily. 'I thought a smaller publisher like, er—' (What the hell was it called? Ottoman?) '—er, Obelisk . . . that it would give it, you know, a more personal touch to it.' He was struggling now, syntax falling to pieces. 'Don't you think?'

'Well, of course. Listen, are you busy next week? I'd like to have you up here to talk terms. Contracts and such, you know. There are also one or two editorial matters I'd like to discuss. Nothing drastic, of course, but I usually prefer to deal with things face to face. Which day would suit you best?'

'Well, whenever, really. You pick.'

There was a pause for diary consultation. 'How about Friday afternoon?'

'Oh, I'm busy then. Sorry. Any other day.'

'Tuesday morning?'

'Fine and dandy.'

When he had put the phone down, he stood on the landing for a long time, winding down. He had imagined getting such a call so many times, and with each imagination of it, it had seemed more remote and unreal – more and more titanically important, until he could no longer picture it as a survivable event; surely some sort of terminal coronary or cerebral trauma was inevitable? Yet here he was, shaken but still alive. He walked slowly into the living room, with Manni trotting curiously at his heels, and stood in the middle of the carpet in a semi-catatonic state. Then, infinitely slowly, a smile began to creep across his face. It grew and grew, turning into a grin of idiot delight. He punched the air and whooped like a Comanche. He was a novelist! A *published novelist*! He had arrived!

At about seven o'clock, he set out for the college, walking on a cushion of air and swollen with a new sense of his value and prestige as a teacher. Manni was with him, as usual; since Drick was an Author (and therefore considered slightly insane), the college administration tolerated the normally forbidden intrusion of a dog into one of its classes as an authorish eccentricity. Which was just as well, because no inducement or prohibition would persuade him to leave the dog in Elsa's care, even if she had been willing to have him (which she wasn't).

It was while they were walking up Downham Road, Drick's thoughts engaged far away, that something in a side road leading to one of the district's housing estates caught his eye. Or rather, it passed through his eye and lodged itself in an unconscious part of his brain. All he experienced consciously was a sudden slight jolt against his distracted thoughts, and he paused. He had a slight feeling of unease which he couldn't identify; that something which he couldn't call to mind was wrong. Had somebody spoken to him? Or had he perhaps seen something? He looked about him, but there was nothing; nobody there apart from two boys riding bikes down the opposite side of the road and a man washing his car in a nearby driveway. Probably just something interior, he concluded. Having a tendency to absent-mindedness, he had had this feeling plenty of times: the ghost of a memory of something important brushing past the back of his crowded thoughts, looking for a way in, and he knew it was useless to venture in search of it. It would come back in its own good time, when his consciousness was less occupied. He couldn't have left the gas on, since the flat only had electricity. On that comforting conclusion, he walked on.

There were a dozen or so students waiting in the classroom for him when he arrived: a handful of new faces, but mostly the usual suspects; the same sad wrecks who came back term after term. Drick wondered about these people's lives, and what benefit they imagined they were getting from repeated immersions in his doubtful pond of writerly wisdom. Certainly there seemed to be no discernible improvement in their writing, and he was never sure whether this was something innate or stemmed from his shortcomings as a teacher. Which interpretation he favoured tended to depend on his mood, but most often he inclined towards the former; especially in one or two cases which seemed beyond redemption. He sometimes daydreamed

...ation of a library dedicated solely to the repose ...npublishable outpourings of incompetent writers. On evidence as he had seen, it would have to be the biggest library in the world; a monument to inability, vanity and immovable self-delusion. Until today, the uncomfortable adjunct to this daydream had been the fact that his great Library of Rejection would catalogue more works of his own than would the British Library. This would have depressed him if he hadn't known that he didn't deserve such a fate, and that the world would give him due recognition sooner or later (and now it had!). Most failed writers (and he had never considered himself *really* failed, not with three stories in respectable print) were so unspeakably bad they couldn't fail to know how awful they were, so just as the talented yearn to excel, they must be motivated by a perverse urge to be execrated. That was his theory, anyway.

There was a small pile of papers waiting for him on the table when he came in, some typed, some word-processed, some obstinately handwritten. These were the samplers requested from each student on enrolment, and he leafed through them briefly, comparing the names with the register he had collected from the college office, looking up from time to time to see if he could match the few unfamiliar names with the new faces.

'Be with you in a moment,' he said. 'Who does this belong to?' He held up a thin sheaf of neatly handwritten sheets which he found lurking at the bottom of the pile. The writing looked remarkably familiar, but he couldn't place it. 'There's no name on it ... No takers? Come on, it can't be that bad.'

There was a ripple of polite laughter. 'Couldn't tell you, old chap,' said a gruff voice from the back of the class. 'Saw it there when I came in.'

Drick looked at old Allenby, who was beaming at him through a haze of whisky fumes and mopping at his brandy-blossomed nose with a large handkerchief. He was a retired Major from some Guards regiment who specialised in rollicking tales of life in the mess and on the hunting field, all lined out, with a doggedness which bordered on perversity, in his own excruciating version of *ottava rima*. He turned up every term, attended astutely to Drick's advice, and never let what he learned detract one iota from his technique or his subject matter. They ought to charge the old bastard corkage.

'Perhaps it's the ghost of a student past,' said Dolores, with a smile at the Major. The two of them had been coming to his classes longer than anyone (in fact, Drick's predecessor had inherited them from *his* predecessor), and had long ago formed their own little cabal. Allenby called her Lolly and she pretended he was her uncle (great uncle would have been nearer the mark). Like him, she had her own resolutely cultivated literary speciality. She wrote murder mysteries. Her highly original take on the genre was to reveal on page one how, why and by whom the murder had been committed, and then have her detective (usually a recurring piece of soggy cardboard called Inspector Wexmorse, if you can credit it) explain, in tortuous, wildly implausible and self-contradictory detail how he had reached his solution. She churned out these stories at such a rate that she must scarcely stop to eat, and claimed, incidentally, to have the largest collection of rejection letters in England. This she attributed to her ground-breaking approach. Drick had once gone to his class with more drink on board than was usual, and made the mistake of explaining to her that there was a difference between being original and simply being fucked in the head. (He didn't use quite those terms.) She just smiled blandly and handed in a story called 'The Case Of The Aunt Murdered For Her Inheritance.' *She* knew which side of the originality coin she was on.

Drick laid the anonymous piece to one side with the others, and got on with the business of getting to know his new class, having each student give a potted autobiography and state his or her literary preferences and reasons for wanting to write. He went through this ritual every term in spite of the regulars, on the principle that the newcomers should not be made to feel like interlopers.

As they declaimed or blushed (according to personality) over their pieces, he began to categorise the new faces. In his experience (which was admittedly limited), creative writing students tended to fall into one of two groups. Firstly there were the

53

hopeless cases (thankfully a minority), like Lolly and the Major, who were here because it was the only way to showcase their genius so long as publishers, consumed with envious spite, refused to give them a more public platform. Then there were those who were here to learn. Or perhaps find things out would be a better way to put it: they appreciated the practical hints and tips which were on offer, but what they really wanted to know was the Secret – the hidden key to getting published. They quite clearly expected there to be such a secret: an instruction expressible in a few concise sentences which would tell them *how to be a published writer*. Students he had encountered who actually wanted advice on how to be better writers than they were could be counted on a goat's fingers. Nevertheless, it was towards these that his course had to be geared.

This was harder than it seemed. In his first term, he had begun with not a clue how to proceed, so he had merely set his students assignments and then discussed them *ad hoc*. By his second term, he had decided that there should be some form of instruction involved, and had produced a handout itemising some Golden Rules. Most of these rules (in fact, almost all of them) were simple Don'ts based on his reading of the first class's efforts: Don't begin a piece of fiction with the assertion *What follows is a true story* or any variation thereof; Don't attempt to deal with any technical matter unless you know a lot about it; Don't begin a story with a snatch of dialogue or a declamatory statement such as *He knew he had been deceived, and here was proof*; Don't begin with your protagonist waking from a dream (with or without a hangover); Don't, under any circumstances, philosophise if your intent is to write fiction; Don't use imagery involving the pathetic fallacy (e.g. *the wind howled in anguish* or *the sky wept with rain*); Don't have a character called Jim Steele; Don't over-describe mundane actions (e.g. drinking a glass of water, picking up an item and looking at it, crossing the street, having sex etc. etc.). The list went on, and grew as each term passed and he was offered new affronts to his sensibilities. Since it seemed unduly negative and discouraging, he tried to compile a list of positive pointers, but found himself rather at a loss to know what to put in it; as a consequence, the list of Do's consisted simply of a series of bland, platitudinous tips (Make your characters three-dimensional by taking traits from people you know; Try to plot in an ordered, consistent pattern; Listen to how people actually talk and try to reproduce it in your dialogue; and so on), and he always felt an interior rush of shame when propounding them. Moreover, the whole set of tips and rules seemed pathetically inadequate in the face of some of these people's problems – like pissing on a forest fire. In an ideal world, he would have liked to add a final Golden Rule, written in fiery letters at the bottom of the page and advising: *Unless you can break the above-stated rules and get away with it, you are wasting your time (AND MINE) trying to write; take up knitting bobble-hats instead.*

'Okay,' he said when they had finished introducing themselves, 'I'm going to give you your assignment for next week. What I want you to do is this: Write a story about an interesting thing you've done in your life; something that contains drama, pathos, excitement, or whatever qualities you feel are required in good fiction. It can be a true story or a complete fabrication; the thing to aim for is that the reader will be unable to guess which it is – truth or fiction.'

It was an assignment he had concocted in desperation near the beginning of his first term, and it had become a regular staple. Not that it was any more valuable as an exercise than any other, but it was inifinitely more enjoyable from his point of view. What he had learned was that hardly any of his students had the imagination to make anything up, and there seemed to be an unstated belief that some kind of sanctity attached itself to a literary group (like the impossibility of slander in a court of law); this, combined with their determination to produce the most exciting, dramatic story possible, resulted in a collection of the most steamingly indiscreet personal gossip you could imagine. He would never have guessed that such an apparently respectable place as Ely could harbour such a rich seam of adultery, theft, secret pasts and general illicit behaviour. An anthology of it would be a professional blackmailer's delight.

As they finished writing down their brief, he gave them their handouts and began explaining his Golden Rules.

He was much too excited about *The Island* to read his students' enrolment pieces the next day, or the day after that. He just went about in a daze occasionally broken by the appearance of a triumphant grin. (Elsa made a show of congratulating him but managed to convey that she'd wait and see whether anybody bought it before thinking it worth celebrating. Sour old trot.) By the end of Friday, he had another pile of fifteen to read, all of them by brand new students. Finally, on Saturday afternoon, he felt calm enough to tackle them, and retreated to his cubby-hole with a pot of coffee, a plate of sandwiches and a stack of amateur fiction.

He didn't need to comment on them, much less annotate or mark them; the only purpose of these introductory essays was to reveal whether there was anybody in the current intake who showed any sign of actually being able to write. (For this reason he didn't bother to read the half-dozen or so contributions by students he had taught before, none of whom seemed capable of writing even so much as a readable sentence.) Three or four of the pieces were passable in a bread-and-butter sort of way; that is, they were coherent, lucid and comprehensible, and their authors might have rubbed by in routine journalism, but none had any kind of spark or any shred of talent in them. The rest, as usual, were execrable. He only needed to read the first paragraph of most of them (the first sentence of some) to form a judgement. A neatly typed piece intended as a story of profound romantic tragedy marked *W. Tattersall* (a member of the Wednesday evening-class whom Drick had recognised as the bespectacled atavist who ran the family chemist's on Fore Hill) was fairly typical (in quality if not style):

> *Her hair was like corn-gold tresses* [it began] *when she came to him in the morning with her hair up in the way she always did to say how much he loved her. "Do not have pity for me", said he looking down at his one-legged state, "For, I am only a man in love with the morning light, which is you my fair maiden".*

That was unforgivable in itself; when, two pages in, it became clear that this was meant to be a contemporary story (the hero saw his beloved on television), Drick nearly chewed the rim off his coffee cup. Things didn't improve: the next piece in the pile was by a summer school student who had once been a sergeant in the United States Air Force at Lakenheath and now delivered washing machines for a living:

'We got to have somebody we can trust one hundred per cent on this job' said the Colonel, as he stared with hard gray eyes across the city taking in it's rifeness of crime lurking in dark alleys. 'Whom do you suggest?'

'There is only one man for a job like this' said his Number 2. 'And that has got to be Jim Steele.' [Drick ground his teeth.]

The Colonel lifted a skeptical eyebrow at these words. 'But he has been off the payroll since that time in sixty-three' he said, objecting.

Where the hell did these people get the bare-faced, brass-bollocked nerve to commit their abominations to paper? Did they even *read* this stuff before handing it in? The problem was literacy. Would any of these people (who, he had ascertained from their introductions, had all submitted manuscripts to publishers at one time or another) bother to apply for a place in, say, the London Symphony Orchestra without first learning to play an instrument? Or think themselves fit to be cardiac surgeons on the basis of a good grade in O-Level Biology? But because they had all learned to write from the earliest age, abetted by the easy availability of paper and ink, they all thought they could be professional writers. He felt downright insulted.

He shuffled miserably through the papers. Christ on a bike, here was more!

Upside down on the floor, the Master watched as the lines of the floorboards disappeared in a perspective of radiations out of sight through the door, echoing with the footsteps of those leaving. STOP, FOOLS! His unruly pupils did not hear him and went on leaving the room. How they would regret their disobedience! He would show them! DEVILS YOU WILL ROT IN HELL!!

Which pretty well summed up his own feelings. What was he

doing teaching these people? He felt like a prostitute, and a pretty shabby one at that – not a high-class hooker or even a common-or-garden streetwalker, but the most debased, poxy whore, dishing out hand-jobs for a fiver up some stinking alley. A friend of his who had once worked as an editorial assistant for Penguin had told him that, of the tens of thousands of manuscripts publishers received each year, about two per cent or less were publishable or showed promise of good work yet to come; the remaining ninety-eight per cent did not, as you would expect, run the gamut from almost good to downright awful – it just dropped straight off the bottom of the scale; it was *all* indescribable bilge. Drick had been doubtful about this (since it conflicted with his notions of human variability) until he started teaching creative writing.

As he finished reading the last page of the last submission, there were beads of sweat on his brow and the beginnings of indigestion in his stomach; he also seemed to be losing control of the muscles in his left leg. He flung the paper (plastic folder, green ink and all) onto the pile and sat back with his palms pressed into his eyes. How could he even begin to chair discussions on this sort of stuff? It was worse than ever.

He finally opened his eyes and let out a deep, guttural sigh. As he looked about him, trying to regain some grip on reality, he noticed that one essay was still waiting to be read; it had been pushed to one side and got itself half under the computer keyboard. He pulled it out and found it was the anonymous contribution; feeling he might as well suffer the *coup de grâce* now rather than later, he began to read.

Half an hour later, he set it down again having read it three times. (Once in a daze, twice to make sure his eyes weren't deceiving him, and a third time to count just how many of his rules it managed to break.) He sat very still for several minutes, gazing into space, then picked it up and read it a fourth time.

I shall address you directly if I may; simply because what is contained here is unvarnished truth. (Unvarnished or unvanished, it's all the same.) It's a simple enough story, but set within a context so strange that even I can scarcely believe it happened; so how can I expect you to take it as truth? Very well, think of it as a fiction; a childish fancy; no more than a diversion to be followed briefly before finding your way back to the straight path which you know to be real. But what you will find there when you return, if you have followed me the whole way, may be more and stranger than what you left behind.

Right away Drick knew the identity of the missing, anonymous student as surely as he knew his own name. He also knew what it was that had made him pause on the way to college the other day.

It was nearly midnight when he walked up Downham Road. He half-expected to see her there, waiting under the yellow glow of the street light on the corner, but there was nobody about aside from a white cat poised on a garden wall, and the only sound was a distant, high-pitched barking echoing from somewhere beyond the school grounds.

He stopped on the pavement near the spot where he had paused two days ago and looked at the entrance to the housing estate; and there was the thing which had clicked silently in his brain. The street sign crouched under a hedge, and in the darkness he had to squat down close to read it: LILLYSTONE ROAD.

He stood up and followed the road onto the estate, reading off the signs of the little branch roads as he went. There were three of them (it was only a small development): Nile Close; Trafalgar Way; and, an orderly queue of small detached houses forming a loop at the end of Lillystone Road: Kismet Crescent.

As he walked back towards the main road, he turned the possibilities over in his mind. She had give him a false name, made up from the street-names of this estate (and had taken the Nelson connection from here also). Why on earth would she do that? The more alarming alternative was that he had dreamed the whole thing, and had supplied the names himself from some uncon-scious memory. The fact that he had no recollection of ever having ventured onto the estate made no difference. This might be just another Stoakley Bookbinder mystery (now *there* was a good name for a detective).

During his first year at Cambridge, he had become puzzled by a strange phenomenon: whenever he walked along Sidney Street, he found himself, for no apparent reason, thinking of the name 'Stoakley Bookbinders'. This seemingly spontaneous and utterly bewildering occurrence went on month after month until, one day, he happened to glance into an alley near Whewell's Court and saw a tiny sign on the wall bearing that very name. So far as he could recall, he had never looked into that alley before, much less noticed the sign; somehow, it had entered his conscious mind through a perceptual back door, and bubbled up like marsh gas each time he passed that place; like those flash-frames on television that are supposed to make subliminal suggestions to the unwary.

Bearing this in mind, he was perfectly prepared to accept that the names of the Lillystone Road estate had lain buried in his memory without him knowing it. On the other hand – and this was an even more startling thought – perhaps Kismet and her riverside garden had been real and *this* was the dream. And why not? If he could accept the former as a dream, then why should this present set of perceptions – no less vivid – necessarily be real? The realisation excited him; he had heard of people who were conscious of their dreams while they were in them, but it had never happened to him before. If this wasn't the real world, then he could do whatever he desired, with complete impunity; make anything happen, however unlikely. And so he wasn't the least bit surprised when, coming back onto Downham Road, he met Kismet, standing beneath the street light just as he had imagined her.

The dream cracked open with the first words she spoke; the chill midnight air rushed in on him, the distant dog barked again, the white cat leapt off the wall and ran across the road, and he knew beyond doubt that this was no dream.

'You read the story,' she said, and it wasn't a question.

'Yes,' he said. 'It was incredible.'

She smiled. 'Since you seemed so determined to deny it, I thought I'd write it for you. Did I get the details right?'

He looked down at her; despite the dim light, he could see

every finest feature of her face as though it were lit from within. She was looking at him knowingly, expectantly, with a curious little twist at the corner of her mouth.

'Details? What details?'

'You still don't remember, then?'

He shook his head. 'I don't know what you're talking about. The *names* I recognised – and the places. How did you know about those? You know . . .' He paused. 'I've got the weirdest feeling – as though we've met before. Even though I know we haven't.'

'We have. In my garden.'

'I mean before that. Long before.'

She shrugged and turned away, stepping lightly along the pavement. He noticed that she was dressed as she had been in the garden, with the addition of woollen stockings and a light coat against the cold night; like everything else she wore, these were also brilliant white, and she seemed to gleam in the darkness, radiating a glow like a ghost. *Had* he seen her somewhere before? If he had, he couldn't imagine where.

He followed her as she walked. 'How did you know?' he repeated. 'I mean, am I *supposed* to remember it? Is that meant to be me, in the story?'

'Not necessarily, not if you don't want it to be. As it says, just regard it as a childish fancy. Just say I felt it. In you. You *could* have written it – in fact, I'd swear you did.' Suddenly, she stopped and turned to him. 'Where's your dog?'

'Manni? I left him at home. He's with . . . with the person I live with.'

She nodded. 'Elsa,' she murmured, and started walking again. 'You don't like her very much, do you?' Without giving him a chance to answer, she went on: 'You don't feel she's right for you. And she doesn't like your dog.'

'Well, she isn't,' he said, making a deliberate decision to set his astonishment aside. 'And she doesn't.'

'Of course not. You chose each other at random; she because she liked your manner, you because you liked her big, comforting body. There's a pattern to the universe, and your life has run contrary to it for as long as you can remember. So has mine. It isn't our fault; we didn't plan it that way. I saw it in you from the first moment I set eyes on you.' She stopped suddenly again and looked up at him. 'Would you like to go to the garden now? It's beautiful in the moonlight.'

He nodded silently, and she took his hand (her grip was soft and cool, and so delicate that he could almost believe it was made of nothing more substantial than light) and led him away through the streets.

Once again he found himself on the bank of the Great Ouse, gazing across at the garden he had never been able to find his own way into. Again, his memory of the hours he had spent there – under a bright midnight moon this time, and without Manni's distracting presence – was diffuse and unclear. He had an image of moonlight glancing off the water and illuminating the garden with an after-twilight glow, and he could see her silhouetted above him as he lay on the cool grass. But he couldn't call to mind the words she had spoken or his own replies; nor what they had done together. When he thought of those hours that seemed like long, slow minutes, all he could remember – just like last time – was a sensation of infinite contentment, an understanding of the universe and his place in it. But over it all lay an unspoken mood of foreboding. In the only clear memory of that night, he saw her gazing at him with an unspoken pleading in her eyes, while he told her it couldn't be done. What couldn't be done he was unable to recall, but he remembered the disappointment in her face.

She had led him down dark lanes and through a gap in the hedgerow where it had looked as though there was no gap, and he had tried to memorise its location, so that he could return. That had been two weeks ago. With a sick inevitability, when he came back by daylight he couldn't find the gap, and day after day he spent an agony of hours fruitlessly searching the hedges and woods. On a couple of occasions, he had thought he heard her voice, but could never be certain of the direction it came from. He had a feeling it probably came from inside his own head. Now, just when he had come to accept that she was real and not a figment of his dreams, she seemed to be slipping through his fingers.

As he tore his eyes away from the far bank of the river, calling Manni to him and continuing on towards the pumping station and Cuckoo Bridge, he realised that he had never asked her about her name. He made a mental note to mention it next time they met.

He never got the chance, because, to his utter dismay, he lost her altogether. He had an awful feeling that it was his fault – that it had something to do with the thing she had asked of him and that he had denied.

He saw her twice before she went. On the first occasion, he and Manni were coming up Fore Hill on the way home from their walk when he saw her – all in white as always – standing in the middle of the market square. He stopped short, their eyes met for a moment, and then she was gone, walking away into Market Street, lost in a moment among the crowds of shoppers. A few days later, he looked out of the living-room window after switching out the light. It was just after midnight, and he saw her standing in the shadow of a shop doorway across the street, looking up at him. Like the first time he had seen her, back in hot midsummer, he could see her face clearly despite distance and shadow, and there was a look in it of profoundest loss. Again, before he could react she turned and walked away, and he was left with the desolate view of the empty street and the sound of Elsa snoring in the next room.

And that was the last he saw of her.

Packet 2(b)

I shall address you directly if I may; simply because what is contained here is unvarnished truth. (Unvarnished or unvanished, it's all the same.) It's a simple enough story, but set within a context so strange that even I can scarcely believe it happened; so how can I expect you to take it as truth? Very well, think of it as a fiction; a childish fancy; no more than a diversion to be followed briefly before finding your way back to the straight path which you know to be real. But what you will find there when you return, if you have followed me the whole way, may be more and stranger than what you left behind.

Duxy was the leader. It wasn't up for discussion: he led, and that was all there was to it. If there had been a vote, Duxy would still have been leader, so where was the point of democracy? Nowhere, that's where; a waste of time that would be better spent on other things.

Although Duxy led, it was Rod who chose the place wherein he should lead them. Three Bridges Corner was a ready-made adventure playground, and was a favourite with all of them, but Rod was especially – perhaps a little abnormally – fascinated by it. There were three bridges at Three Bridges Corner. (But no corner, so the name wasn't perhaps as obvious as it seems: there was a touch of childish adventurism – a desperado flavour – in the 'Corner' addendum.) The main bridge was a hefty steel-girder affair which carried the Newport road over the Afon Llwyd and sent it off towards Llantarnam. It had that criss-cross parapet look, like something built by soldiers. From a point adjacent to the south end of the main bridge, a footbridge crossed the river at a forty-five-degree angle, so that, in plan, the two bridges formed a broad V. The third bridge crossed the river parallel to the road, passing over the far end of the footbridge, making the V into a slightly crocked N. This bridge was the most interesting, because it didn't carry a road or a footpath, but a pipe.

It was a gas pipe, Jeremy said. It was two feet broad and coated with some black tarry substance, with great bolted iron collars at regular intervals. It rose up out of the ground at a steep angle, and climbed up a stone-built slope enclosed on either side by high stone walls and at the landward end by iron gates. About twenty feet up, the stone stopped and gave way to the horizontal span of the bridge, which was made of black-painted steel. There were steps in the slope on either side of the pipe; at the top, they gave way to terrifyingly precarious-looking metal walkways made of slats, with wide gaps between them and the bridge's sidewalls.

As the whole area was hemmed in by dense woodland, it was obvious to any boy with half a brain that Three Bridges Corner made the best, most challenging follow-my-leader course in the world.

And, as always, Duxy went first. That gave him the prerogative of dictating the order of followers. Jimmy Hughes, who was actually the best climber and should on those grounds alone have been leader, went second. After him came little Christopher Evans (Cribbo), who was more than a year younger than the rest of them and a weakling with it. Technically, he should have gone last, but Duxy regarded himself as Cribbo's surrogate big brother, and wouldn't let the snivelling little bugger out of his sight. Then there was Spam Williams (who stank like a dead fishmonger's socks), then Jeremy, then, in last place, came Rod. He didn't mind being last (not as much as he minded being called Rod, anyway), since it meant long pauses while the boys ahead of him negotiated the obstacles, leaving him free to study the structure of the bridges, which was what interested him about the place.

'Oi, pay fuckin' attention, Roddyprick.'

Rod looked at Duxy. 'Eh?'

'Orders, spaz.'

Duxy had a way of being abusive without rancour: he did it with a sudden grin (scaled up to a giggle if he called you something really foul) which managed to convey that, even if he meant it, it didn't matter that he meant it, because he was such an irresistibly great mate. It fooled Rod every time, even when Duxy called him Roddyprick, or Bender.

'Listening, Dux.'

Duxy surveyed his troops, a charismatic half-smile on his thin lips. He always adopted this expression, implying that he was about to deliver a long talk, when he was going to do something unexpe—

'*Rampike!*' he yelled, turning and crashing off through the woods, whooping like a Red Indian.

They took up the cry as they followed, dodging between the trees, ducking under branches, leaping clumps of undergrowth like so many Chingachgooks, oblivious to the brambles that scraped at their shins. All order vanished in the race to be first to the Rampike.

The Rampike (Rod had discovered the word and been first to apply it to one of the obstacle course's principal landmarks) was a dead tree which stood in the middle of the cow pasture on the other side of the woods. It was barkless and white, with two crooked, withered branches, and was blackened down one side where, according to a local legend invented by Jeremy, it had been struck by lightning. The bolt had simultaneously killed the tree and a shepherd who was sheltering under it, and you could see the man's tortured silhouette in the scorch-marks on the trunk (if you squinted from the right angle). What a shepherd was doing in a cow pasture Jeremy had no idea, and (to his relief) was never asked to explain. It was a good story, and everyone, including Jeremy, believed it unquestioningly.

Duxy was first out of the wood, hitting the tussocky grass of the pasture at a headlong run, with Jimmy and Spam close behind. Then came Rod and Jeremy, with Cribbo trailing behind, flapping his arms like a gull. (Cribbo could never be shaken in his belief that this eccentric habit helped him run faster.)

Jimmy, who was by far the most athletic, slapped the Rampike first. He braked sharply and was flung to the ground by Duxy and Spam, who had both built up an unstoppable momentum and crashed into him with an *oof!* that even Rod and Jeremy, far behind by now, could hear.

When they had all come up and got their breath back, they fell into line and began the course. First they took turns to climb the Rampike, shinning up the unscorched side, hand-over-handing out along its horizontal branch and dropping to the turf. That was easy enough, except for Spam, who landed feet-first slap in the middle of a fresh cowpat. Some of it went up his legs and lapped over the tops of his shoes (he didn't care; it added to the festering bouquet he always carried with him), but most shot in a great green spout up Cribbo's side. Jeremy was hanging from the Rampike, and Rod was half-way up the trunk, so they escaped altogether.

'*Yes!*' Spam cried. Amidst the laughter, he tried to persuade Rod to drop on the remains of the cowpat. If Duxy had joined in, he might have done it, but Duxy was torn between laughing and making sure (with a stern glance) that the tears welling up in Cribbo's eyes didn't spill over. When Rod and Jeremy had made the drop, Duxy set off back across the pasture at a trot. The incident under the Rampike had given him an idea.

'Follow on!' he called, and stamped a foot on the fringe of another fresh green dollop, taking care to hit it at an angle, so that the spray shot away from him. Jimmy did the same, Cribbo pretended to stamp on it, and Spam ran right through the middle of it. That amused him so much he doubled back for another go, kicking up a big slobbery clod that splattered up Cribbo's back. (Duxy wasn't looking, fortunately.) By the time Jeremy reached the pat, all that was left was a patch of slippery grass, which he could stamp on with complete impunity.

Duxy led them a tortuous route through the woods, then down to the riverbank, where they had to leap like mountain goats from rock to rock (the most convincing impression being by Spam, who smelt like one) as far as the foot of the road bridge, where they climbed up onto the concrete pier and ran through to the far side. While he waited his turn to get up from the last rock, Rod looked up at the underside of the bridge. There were birds nesting up there, he noticed. Then his turn came, and he levered himself up and ran on.

On the other side, the bridge was revetted by a steep grass bank. Scrambling up it got harder and harder as the leaders destroyed the few handhold tufts in their haste to pull themselves up. By the time Rod made it up to the roadside, the front-runners had crossed over and were disappearing down the entrance to the footbridge. When he got there, Duxy was climbing over the wire fence at the far end and heading off back into the woods, with Jimmy vaulting like a gymnast after him. Rod pumped his legs faster, shoving Jeremy in the back to urge him on. But Jeremy was being held up by Spam, who was sweating like a pig (his fund of near-perfect animal impressions seemed limitless – sweated like a pig, smelled like a goat, scratched like a dog, belched like a cow – he was a one-boy menagerie) and beginning to tire badly. He studied the back of Spam's jumper, looking for a clean place to shove. (Clean being a relative term with Spam, who owned a selection of filthy jumpers which he wore in all weathers, even today's sweltering heat, temperature being more or less regulated by the number of vests underneath. The jumpers came in a variety of jazzy patterns, but all had the same grey, greasy pall and spotty collection of stains.) He found an area near the left shoulder where the cowshit splatter hadn't touched, and pushed. Spam grunted and almost fell, but pressed on harder.

Luckily, Duxy was tiring too, and he paused a little way into the woods, on the pretext of letting the poufs and ponces catch up. When they were all gathered, Rod noticed that he had that expression on his face again, and he braced himself for an extra special challenge, thinking he could guess what it might be. There were a few obstacles they hadn't tackled yet, but only one which engendered that degree of sly anticipation. The pipe bridge.

He was right. When he judged that even the weakest of them were recovered (i.e. when he had got his own breath back), Duxy led them to the tall iron gates. The padlock had been broken off years ago, and the thick steel chain which had once secured the gates against intruders lay caked in rust amongst the litter. The gate squealed on its hinges, and Duxy started to climb the narrow steps to the left of the pipe. They were as steep as a ladder, and Rod used his hands to help himself up. When he reached the top, he had to make a deliberate effort to stand upright and step out onto the metal walkway. On either side, and between the slats of the walkway itself, he could see the river thirty feet below, swirling with yellow froth as it licked the edges of the jagged rocks. Concentrating on the slats and letting the view between and around them go out of focus, he took two steps forward and joined the queue. At the head, Duxy was crouching and peering down through the gap between walkway and sidewall.

'Here,' he said.

Jeremy looked back over his shoulder, and Rod saw apprehension in every line of his face. He had seen what Duxy was planning to do, and Rod could guess. Merely crossing the precarious walkway wasn't daring enough, apparently. About a third of the way along its span, the pipe bridge passed over the footbridge, and Duxy was going to try dropping from one to the other. Rod put a hand on the sidewall to brace himself, and looked down through the gap. From ground level, the two bridges appeared to pass very close, but from up here the concrete footway and its steel girder rails looked almost as distant as the river beneath.

Leaning out like this, he could watch Duxy make his attempt. He sat down on the walkway and grasped the lip at the bottom of the sidewall. His face tense, he rocked his hips back and forth, and Rod could see his lips moving silently: *one, two, three* . . . Then, with an audible grunt, he took his weight on his hands and swung forward, dropping down through the gap. He probably intended to swing by his hands before dropping, but the momentum of his fall whipped his fingers off the slippery steel, and he went straight down. After what seemed like a horribly long fall, his baseball boots hit the concrete with a loud thump, he rolled over and over, and came up yelling in triumph, shaking his fists in the air.

'C'mon!' he shouted. ''Seasy!'

Jimmy went next. Inspired by Duxy, he deliberately took the drop in one go, and landed like a paratrooper. Cribbo took a lot longer, lying out flat on the walkway before swinging his legs out

69

over the drop and twisting his body in search of a handhold. While Duxy called encouragement and Cribbo tried to get a firm grip on the lip of the sidewall, Rod dragged his eyes away and concentrated on the bridge, looking for some feature to study. At the centre, a stub stuck out from the pipe, and he fixed on that; it led into a big metal box with a ladder up the side and a large black handwheel on top. He tried to work out what it was for, shutting out the grunts, gasps and cries from the boys ahead of him.

He didn't see Jeremy go. When he brought his mind back to the game, he found himself alone on the bridge, and they were all yelling at him to hurry up. He edged along the walkway until he judged he was exactly above the footbridge. Not having watched the last few jumpers, he found it difficult to tell which precise spot they had dropped from. They saw what he was doing, and started calling out directions: *Left a bit – nuh, right – back the other way, spastic!*

He gazed down, and suddenly his attention was caught by something in the river below the edge of the footbridge. For a moment, he thought he saw his own face reflected in the water, peering back up at him, but it didn't seem like a reflection; it seemed as though the face – surely his own – was *under* the water. It only lasted a split second; he blinked, and it was gone.

The other boys were beginning to lose patience now. Duxy was leading them off up the footbridge towards the road. Only Jeremy and Spam were waiting, and they were looking edgily after the others. He laid his hands on the lip, rested his weight on them, and with a single heave of his hips, launched himself down through the gap.

The drop made no visual impression on him whatsoever, not even a blur. He felt a brief sensation of falling, then a sharp clout on the chin, and thought for an instant he had hit the lip of the pipe bridge. Something scraped violently up his side from knee to armpit, and when his vision returned, he found himself clinging like a monkey to the outside of the footbridge rail. His left arm was hooked over the top girder, and the rest of him hung in space. He glanced down, and saw the river swirling by far below his swinging feet. And again he thought he saw the face looking

70

up at him, and it definitely wasn't his reflection; he was conscious that his own face was surprisingly calm (if a little startled), not horror-stricken and screaming like that.

He had no memory of getting back over the rail. The next thing he knew, he was lying on his back on the concrete, with Jeremy and Spam looking down at him. Whether he'd hauled himself over, or they'd helped, he had no recollection. Other faces joined theirs: Jimmy, Cribbo, Duxy, and another he didn't recognise; a girl. He had no idea where she had come from, but he knew where he had seen her face before: just a moment ago, under the water. Oddly, she had a purple bruise on her jaw, just like the one he could feel forming on his.

The other weird thing, which he noticed just as he slipped into unconsciousness, was that Jeremy's hair was soaking wet, and so were his clothes.

He learned a few things that day. For one, he learned a deep respect for high bridges. Second, he learned not to look too carefully before leaping. (Close examination led to indecision, which led to error, he decided.)

Finally, he learned not to place too much trust in the evidence of his eyes. He had so obviously imagined the face in the water and the girl looking down at him. And Jeremy's wet clothes.

He didn't play at Three Bridges Corner from that day onwards, although he did go back occasionally to look at the great stone-and-steel N. What puzzled him was that the others stayed away from it too. Even more surprisingly, they didn't take the piss as he'd expected; they never even mentioned his fall. As he got older, it seemed to make sense. Remembering the looks on their faces as they gathered round him, it seemed clear that they had been more frightened by the incident than he had. Jeremy especially; he seemed reluctant even to talk about it. Rod discovered he had a strange, unexpected power: whenever he talked about it, his friends clammed up and looked nervous. They became easier to persuade, and would often do his bidding. He grew in confidence, and the diffident little boy he had been went away, replaced by a new, more robust model.

71

A few months after, Drick (he acquired the name about this time, ditching the hated 'Rod' at last) did a drawing of his fall. He hadn't intended to; he had meant to make a purely technical representation of the bridges, but he couldn't resist adding the figures: stick-boys with round heads watching him plummeting towards the footbridge. As an afterthought, he put in the girl's face under the water.

He never showed it to anybody. He folded it up and put it in an envelope, which he put inside a jigsaw box, which he put at the back of his bedroom cupboard under a tall stack of old annuals.

Many years later, shortly before he left home, he cleared out the cupboard. He filled a bin bag with junk, and put the annuals in a box for his mother to take to the WI jumble sale (setting aside the *Beanos* and *Ruperts*, which he had a notion might be worth a bit of money), along with some dusty old jigsaws. He opened the boxes to check that their contents were intact, and found inside one a brown envelope containing a tightly folded sheet of paper. Puzzlingly, the paper was blank. Why would he have hidden a blank sheet of paper? It obviously had been him, since neither of his parents did jigsaws, and anyway never went in his cupboard.

He puzzled over it for a minute or two, holding the paper up to the light to see if there were any faded marks on it, then, with a shrug, screwed it up and tossed it in the bin bag. He put the lid back on the box and placed it with the others, noticing in passing that the picture on the puzzle was of a tall girder bridge spanning a frothing river. He didn't remember doing that one.

He carried the jumble sale stuff downstairs for his mother to take away, then went back to his room and started sorting out his clothes. He couldn't *believe* he'd ever worn half the stuff he found. Snoods? Christ, no. New Romantic shirts with lacy cuffs? He'd sooner fall off a—

He hesitated. Fall off a what? Again he thought for a moment, and again he shrugged. A cliff, he supposed. What else did he have in here? *Pixie boots?* God's hairpiece, he must have looked like a pimp's houseboy. It couldn't get worse than this. Exasperated, he spread his arms wide, embraced the whole lot – hangers and all – in one big hug and wrestled them into a giant bin-liner. He tied the top, rolled it to the top of the stairs and, with a big, satisfying kick, sent it bounding to the bottom.

IV

I only read the first couple of packets that first evening of 1997. I was still tired, and even coffee and adrenalin couldn't keep me awake. And so I went to bed knowing – if nothing else – a bit more about Kismet. Drick had been extremely vague – not to say downright evasive – on the couple of occasions I'd asked him about her. (Incidentally, you will have seen what I meant about his selective memory where Elsa was concerned – not to mention other things, about which I'll say no more at the moment. Their relationship was far worse than he makes out. Détente my shirt tail – it was trench warfare, with periodic cease-fires for the tending of wounds.)

However, I was still none the wiser regarding his sudden disappearance. Presumably, there was going to be an answer of some sort contained amongst the packets of papers in the box, but I was damned if I could keep my eyes open any longer.

If you want the truth, I hadn't been sleeping all that well lately anyway, and my trip to Ely the night before – and subsequent sleepless night – had been the last straw. The reason for my near-insomnia was worry over my career. To put it shortly, it was not only not going in the direction I'd hoped, it wasn't going in any direction at all other than a downward spiral (if it's possible to go downwards from the basement). I couldn't figure it out: dazzling qualifications, published papers, and a proven ability as a good teacher. The worst thing was that I had caught myself imagining, in the dark, deep reaches of my sleepless nights, that I was the object of some conspiracy; that I was being kept from a suitable university post by a cabal of dullards who were envious of my talents. Sly figures loomed out of the darkness (faces I knew well, and which appeared so friendly in daylight), whispering to each other and rubbing their hands together like so many Obadiah Slopes, patting each other on the back and handing out lectureships, fellowships and sinecures to each other, deals sealed with a secret handshake.

Luckily, I caught myself in time. I had seen other people's minds turn down that path, and knew it led to a bottomless pit of isolation and obsession. Instead, I began to turn my back on my researches. This wasn't difficult to achieve, since without institutional support (I was still affiliated with the Archaeology Department at Cambridge, but that routine status didn't bring any money with it) I couldn't travel, excavate, do lab analyses or perform any of the myriad and expensive tasks needed to put my doctoral research on a more substantive footing. I was . . .

Sorry, I didn't mean to tell you any of this. It's got nothing to do with the story I'm telling. What I meant to tell you was . . . what? Oh yes, the day after New Year. It was a Thursday that year (I hate it when it's a Sunday or, worse, a Saturday), so the working world should have come to at least partial wakefulness.

Fortunately, I'd had one of my rare nights of passable sleep, and I woke ready to tackle the mystery of Roderick Bent and Maddy Rhodes. Instead of going back to the box, I decided to try and track him down, still unable to believe that he had disappeared as irrevocably as he claimed in the covering note that accompanied the packets. I tried his phone numbers again, but they were still dead. I wasn't going to get any sense out of my mother, so I left her out and concentrated instead on other people who had known Drick. I began with the most neutral: his publisher.

Headline was open for business – at least, they had a man answering the phone. I remembered the name of Drick's editor, so asked to be put straight through to him.

'Who?' the man asked.

I repeated the name. There was a brief pause, in which I heard him consulting somebody else.

'Sorry,' he said when he came back on the line. 'He doesn't work here any more.'

'Doesn't work there? Since when?'

'About a year ago, apparently. I'm new here myself,' the man added in a confidential tone.

'A year ago? Do you know where he is now?'

Another muted consultation. 'No. Sorry.'

'Well, is there anybody there who does know?'

A significant pause. 'I doubt it. He left . . . Apparently he was let go. He doesn't work in publishing any more.'

'You mean he was sacked?'

Another pause. 'I didn't say that. He was let go. Early retirement, I imagine.'

He was starting to sound tetchy, so I thanked him and put the phone down. I waited a few minutes, then called again, taking my voice down a tone or two. He had reset his mood to bland indifference, and didn't recognise me.

'I'd like to speak to Maddy Rhodes' editor, please,' I said, trying to sound authoritative, as though I wouldn't suffer delays gladly.

'Who?'

I wondered briefly if Headline was using a loop tape to answer inquiries, then repeated, 'Maddy Rhodes' editor, please.'

'Maddy Rhodes?'

'Yes, Maddy Rhodes.'

'Is she fiction or non-fiction?'

'*He* is fiction.' I began to lose my cool. 'The fact that you've only been there a few weeks *might* excuse you not having heard of him, if he wasn't the biggest-selling author in Britain, possibly the world.'

He treated me to another of his pregnant pauses. 'How do you know I've only been here a few weeks?' he asked suspiciously. 'Did you phone just now?'

'Er . . .'

'Look, mate, I can do without wind-ups. If you'd be good enough to get off the line, I'm sure there's genuine calls I could be taking. Goodbye.'

I sat on the hall floor with the receiver buzzing in my ear and stared blankly at the bookcase opposite me. After a couple of minutes, I found my gaze focusing on a particular spine. I put the receiver back and took the book out.

The Alchemist's Apprentice, it said on the title page. *Maddy Rhodes*. Over the page, it said 'Copyright © 1994 Maddy Rhodes'. Below that was the declaration, 'Published in hardcover 1995 by HEADLINE BOOK PUBLISHING'. Hard evidence, if ever there was such a thing. If anyone was going mad, it wasn't me.

On the page opposite the copyright declaration was the dedication, *For K.*, which I had always assumed stood for Kismet. I tipped the book open at the endpaper and looked at the photograph on the dust-cover flap. It showed Lionel Bent in his familiar pose as Maddy Rhodes. I closed the book again and stared at the maze on the cover. Drick had always hated that maze – *What the fuck's a maze got to do with wartime Malta?* he ranted. He was convinced they'd found the drawing down the back of a filing cabinet and stuck it on the jacket out of sheer laziness. Well, now it had found a symbolic association of sorts. That silhouette was me, and there was only one route left to follow.

The *book* still existed. Lionel Bent still existed. Somewhere. I tried Directory Enquiries and asked for his number.

'Address?' asked a dismal-sounding female voice.

That got me. I decided I'd better aim wide. 'Gwent,' I said. 'Sorry, I can't be more precise.'

I heard computer keys chattering irritably. 'I've got two L. Bents in that area,' the woman said monotonously, plainly oblivious to the pun in the name, which Drick and I had always found stupidly amusing. 'Do you want both?'

I did, and wrote down the numbers. One had a code which I eventually worked out was Chepstow, the other Tredegar. Since Drick's parents had lived in Tredegar before moving out of the Valleys in 1968, that one seemed most promising. Even if it wasn't them, it might be a grandparent. I dialled the number and felt a flood of relief when I heard the familiar voice of Drick's mother.

'Hello,' I said warmly. I was about to introduce myself when I was seized by a rush of doubt. I had butted against so many brick walls by mentioning Drick's name (either of them) that it seemed best to go cautiously and assume nothing. 'Is that Mrs Bent?'

'It is.'

'Audrey Bent?'

'Yeees.'

'My name's Jeremy. I'm a friend of your son.'

'Jeremy? He hasn't mentioned you. Are you a school-friend?'

'Well, yes, I was. That and other places.' I gave a light laugh, and silently willed her to put him on or tell me where he was. I knew what she could be like; she'd embroil me in chit-chat for half an hour before telling me he was out. At least, that was what she had once been like, when she still knew who I was.

'Was?' she repeated. 'Have you left?'

'Well, yes,' I said without thinking. 'Quite a while ago, actually.'

She started to say something, but was interrupted by a male voice in the background. I heard the words *Jeremy . . . friend from school*, followed by a quizzical grunt, then I heard a rustle as the receiver was handed to someone else, and a hauntingly familiar voice came on the line.

'Hello?' it said.

'Dri–' I cut myself short. 'Is that you, Bent?' I said instead.

He spoke cautiously. 'Yeah. What d'you want?' There was more Welsh in the accent than I remembered, even from childhood, but otherwise it was Drick to the life.

'Just wanted to know if you remembered me, that's all.'

There was a long, calculating pause, then he said with deep, slightly amused suspicion: 'Is that you, Baz?'

'Baz? No, no, it's not Baz.'

'It is, isn't it?'

'No, Drick, it's—'

'Look, Baz, you can just fu—' He stopped abruptly, then resumed in a quieter voice (Mrs Bent was presumably still in the room), 'You can just fucking well wait till Monday, okay?'

My heart, which had been pounding with excitement, began to slow and sink. Mrs Bent's remark about school suddenly made sense, and I realised I hadn't reached Drick after all. Drick's voice it might be (notwithstanding the accent), but the tone and manner were unmistakably those of a teenager. What was more, the Drick I knew (at any age after about ten) had never had any qualms about saying 'fuck' in front of his mother.

'Listen,' I said. 'I think there's been some misunderstanding. My name isn't Baz.' I had a flash of inspiration. 'I seem to have got Bent junior – is there a Bent senior by any chance?'

It was a desperate throw: Audrey Bent was majorly unlikely to have given birth more than once. She and her husband were, if such a thing exists, archetypal only-child parents. You could tell just by looking at them that they'd had occasional sex until they had succeeded in reproducing, then cut the unpleasant habit out.

'You mean Dad?'

'No, I mean an older brother.'

'I haven't got an older brother.'

I sighed. 'Listen, this may seem a funny question, but what's your name?'

'Roddy. Look, who are you?'

'Please, humour me. How old are you?'

'I'm seventeen, if it's any of your business. Look, mate, who the fu— who the hell are you?'

'You know, that's a very good question. I *think* I'm an old friend, but having spoken to you, I'm not so sure.'

And, with that, I hung up, feeling a little consoled at having made someone else (a Bent, to boot) feel as confused as I did.

I won't bore you with any more of my fruitless searching. As far as the world was concerned, Roderick Bent no longer existed except in my memory. Nor did Maddy Rhodes. I had yet another ridiculous, nonsensical conversation – with his agent this time – then spent the afternoon trawling the bookshops and libraries of Cambridge, searching for a copy of *The Alchemist's Apprentice*. As you've probably guessed, I found not a single one: no copies, and no record in any catalogue I looked at – printed or online. The book and its author, I finally accepted, had ceased to be. More than that: except in my own mind, they had *never been*.

And that reminds me of what I *really* meant to tell you about. It's all so confusing, I still get lost thinking about it: the dates and events play leap-frog in my head, and before I know it I've got everything back to front. Not a good sign in someone with archaeological pretensions, I admit, but there you are (perhaps a clue to the still-birth of my career). I have to keep a firm grip on the dates.

So, that all happened on the day after New Year, 1997. What I really wanted to talk about was what happened on 15 January 2000 (which was two weeks and one day ago), in Hay, in the Granary, at my table, with an empty coffee pot and a few flapjack crumbs remaining on my plate.

It's hardly surprising that I've digressed into all the stuff I've just been telling you about, since that is precisely what had been clogging my mind as I sat there, with the tables gradually filling about me, and the waitress casting increasingly pointed glances at my empty plate and cup. I'd also been thinking about how my life had changed in the past three years. I had, in a sense, taken Drick's place. From being an incipiently embittered failed academic, I had become a passably successful novelist. Never in Maddy Rhodes' league, of course – nowhere near – but comfortable enough, and with three books to my name.

I looked up and noticed the waitress heading in my direction wearing an expression of resigned determination. I pacified her with an order for more coffee and a slice of that delicious-looking pie. Yes, the leek one. With salad, yes, thank you.

As she headed off, I finally – absolutely and utterly finally – got round to looking properly at the book in my hands. And got the shock of my life. It made Drick's disappearance look like a rather elementary conjuring trick.

I've described my find already – a very slightly buckled but otherwise pristine hardback copy of *The Alchemist's Apprentice*. The only copy in the world beside the one which sat in my hall bookcase at home. It had apparently been given as a gift, looked at by its recipient, but never read. Well, I would be the first to broach its pages. Squashing down the memories that had so far distracted me from it, I turned over the title page and glanced briefly at the dedication. *For K.* Having read the contents of Drick's packets (don't worry – you'll get to read the rest of them soon enough), I now found the dedication really quite poignant. I turned the page and found myself looking at the words, 'Part One – THE GARDEN'. Odd. I didn't remember that bit. I turned over and looked at the opening lines of the first chapter.

When the waitress returned with my lunch, I was still staring dumbly at that first page. I didn't notice her; I just happened to glance up and saw a plate of pie and salad in front of me. I gazed at it blurrily for a moment, then looked back at the page, unable to believe my eyes.

In place of the familiar prologue describing the voyage of the *Mistel* from Danzig in 1938 were the following words:

Let me tell you about Madagascar Rhodes; I can't describe how he has been on my mind recently. Old Madagascar; Maddy to his post-colonial cronies and his readers. The former were entirely fictitious, of course, but the latter were very real and positively legion, and they all knew him as Maddy.

I hadn't thought about him – much – for quite a while, but this past week I have thought of little else. It had seemed to me, for all my searching, that all trace of him had gone from the world, but last Saturday I stumbled on an artefact. Aside from the box of valuables which he . . . well, bequeathed, I suppose, it was the first tangible evidence of him I had come across since he disappeared three years ago.

I made this momentous find in Hay-on-Wye; perhaps the ideal place for serendipitous discovery, though not one I visit often . . .

V

I never got round to eating that pie. Or drinking my third pot of coffee. (Which was probably just as well; another dose of caffeine to my already jangling synapses could have precipitated a critical neural overload and brought on total meltdown.) For several minutes my mind lurched up and down those opening paragraphs like an over-revved car straining against its locked handbrake, then something gave way, and I raced on over the page.

You know that tiny disconcerting feeling you get when you walk past an electrical shop and see yourself (usually ill-tuned, with too much green or red) walking by in the opposite direction? Automatically, you glance around the window, trying to work out which of the camcorders on display is the one watching you. Well, imagine this: As you're passing the shop, you bend down to tie your shoelace. Half an hour later, you're walking past the shop again and glance in to see, not yourself passing in the other direction, but bending down tying that slippery lace. Later again, you pass the shop once more, look in and see yourself staring in bewilderment as you watch yourself tying your lace. You can imagine that? Well, wouldn't it make you feel a bit paranoid? Now imagine that feeling multiplied about a zillion times and you're beginning to get close to how I felt as I read that book.

I read on, and saw myself sitting where I now sat, but with an earlier instalment of coffee, then I was at the Bookshop, finding this very book. I flipped rapidly over several pages and saw myself returning here, losing myself in memories; I turned over a whole chunk of pages, hoping to find some shred of the real *Alchemist's Apprentice*, and there I was, gaping in stupefaction at the words

'Let me tell you about Madagascar Rhodes . . .'

I closed the book and took several deep breaths. When I looked again, I assured myself, it would be normal. This was some weird delusional state which would pass if I calmed down. I deliberately regulated my breathing, and duly calmed down. I reopened the book, turned a couple of pages, and gazed calmly, then stared, then goggled with rapidly snowballing horror, at the sentence, *'This was some weird delusional state which would pass if I calmed down.'*

'You're fucking telling me!'

It was the sudden silence around me that made me realise I had said this aloud. I looked at the startled faces of the people at the other tables, and felt strangely reassured. What I really couldn't stand – what I hadn't been able to stand back in 1997 – was the sensation that totally fucking crazy shit was going on, and that *everyone but me* thought everything was totally normal. It was like a sudden, giddying and comprehensive vision of what it must be like to be insane.

I wasn't insane – I really wasn't. Nor am I now. If I were I'd admit it, believe me. It would be a lot easier to deal with.

I didn't read on any further than that until a lot later. The impossible narrative had reached the present moment, and it was like running at reckless full tilt towards a precipice you know is there, pulling up at the last possible moment, maintaining your balance on the teetering brink by not looking down. I didn't want to know the future, especially if, as it seemed, it had been predetermined.

At least . . . Well, what would you have done? Yes, that's right – I couldn't resist a tiny peek. I did it sidelong, so I could snatch my glance away if it happened to touch something unpleasant. It didn't; I was safe for the moment at least, since my part in the tale was interrupted at that point – right in mid-sentence in fact. There was just a

Part Two

THE BOOK

Packet 3

Get thee behind me, Caesar. I want to step out from the refuge of my third person for a moment and address you directly. (Not you specifically, J.D., but the more generalised yet intimate 'you' whom we writers like to appeal to from time to time.) And what I want to say to you is this:– Some people will believe anything. You probably already realise this, but I would go further and paraphrase Uncle Abe (whom I knew personally, believe it or not):– Some people will believe anything all the time, while all people will believe anything some of the time. I'm tempted to assert (*contra* Abe) that *all* people will believe anything *all* the time, but the case isn't proven. (I believe it, though, which just goes to show.)

At Cambridge, Jeremy and I were founder members of something called the Conspiracy Club (we brought it with us from Southampton, where we cooked it up during a caffeine-fuelled morning in the SU refectory, but Cambridge was where it came to life). Like most Cambridge student societies, it was essentially a drinking club. Being exclusive to postgraduates, however, it was a shade more purposeful than the baked bean appreciation, haddock resuscitation and parrot sketch enacting enclaves which still flourished on the Granta at that time. The premise was simple enough: we collected conspiracy theories. Collected them, not believed them, I hasten to add. If I tell you that the Club's constitution subtitled it as 'The Society for the Celebration of Human Credulity', you will have some idea of the mind-set behind it. Our principal meetings were called 'cullings' and took place at the big round table in the bar of the Mill on the first

Monday, fourth Wednesday and seventh Friday of each term. (The significance of the numbers and days eludes me now, but they came from one of the richest seams known to conspiracists: the Knights Templar.) To the culling, each member (there were never more than seven or eight at any one time) had to bring a newly discovered conspiracy theory and expound it to the group, along with evidence that somebody somewhere believed it to be true. At the end of the culling, points out of ten were awarded to each theory, based on such factors as originality, incredibleness, startlement and (spurious) plausibility. The theory had to come from some identifiable source, and an appropriate difficulty multiplier was applied to the score thus: 1.5 for a website (the 'net wasn't quite as big then – it would probably have been reduced to 0.75 a few years later), 3 for a printed publication, and a maximum of 10 for word of mouth, the instigator and/or believer having to be brought forth in person at the culling. The payoff was that the winner's points translated into the number of drinks he would be bought by the other members in the weeks leading up to the next meeting. It didn't usually work out that expensive, since scores never hit above the thirty mark except on a few memorable occasions, one of which I shall tell you of largely, Prince.

All the theories culled were written down in a big ledger, along with source, member and score, and by the end of Lent Term 1992 we had a big collection. Quite a few concerned the obvious suspects and variations on pretty well-worn theories – Roswell, aliens, the CIA and Aids, the CIA and LSD, Princess Anastasia, the Belgrano – but some were more startling: the Queen Mother was a Soviet android, JFK was Christ reborn and had been assassinated by a cabal of Islamic fundamentalists associated with Malcolm X (I swear it – there were people who believed this stuff). Despite having invented the game, Jeremy and I had won only once each (like football, cricket and tennis, I suppose – the originators of games rarely excel at them), and both of us were determined to buck our ideas up. Especially me, since the third culling of Michaelmas Term (that's autumn to you) was to be my last.

I had decided that the academic life wasn't for me after all, and

I was getting out. Earlier in the term, I'd gone badly off kilter at my second-year interview, in which a gang of lecturers grill you on the progress, value and reliability of your research and methodology. I don't remember much about it, except that (very memorably) I told the professor chairing the do (an unctuous twot with interests in Greek pots and a line in supercilious scepticism and feeling little girls' bicycle saddles, I shouldn't wonder) that he was an ignorant motherfucker with all the vision and imagination of a retarded moose, and that he could stick his interpretation of my data tables under a Minoan jug and fuck off while he was doing it. The rest of the interview is a bit of a blur. One or two of the other nodders and frowners had been on my side to start with, but I think I was on my own from that point on. Roderick Bent MA was on his way out and no bones about it. Not that it mattered much; I'd have been gone soon enough anyway. The scholarly pursuit hadn't lived up to my expectations once I was let off the leading rein of undergraduacy. I had thought it was the great quest for truth, but it was just a search for a more plausible story. And since the measure of plausibility seemed to be whether these witless clods had heard the story before, I was onto a loser from the start.

I've galloped off the track, haven't I? Where were we – oh yes, my last culling. I was determined to go out on a sure-fire winner, a killer theory that would have the other members squirming with envy. But I just couldn't come up with a bloody thing. Not a conspiratorial sausage. I scoured the Web and every magazine I could think of, from the *Fortean Times* to the *National Enquirer*, and drew nothing but dross. I talked to Jeremy in the Copper Kettle; he tried to be helpful, but in such a self-satisfied way that I was convinced he had a real ball-buster in his back pocket, something I couldn't hope to beat.

After he left (*his* interview had gone swimmingly, and he was off now to yet another highly fruitful meeting with his supervisor), I sat over the dregs of my coffee, staring out at the people passing to and fro on King's Parade, wondering if I could get away with simply concocting a conspiracy. (This was allowed under the rules, provided you could persuade at least

89

three independent witnesses to believe in it.)

My reverie came to an abrupt end when my view of King's Chapel was suddenly blotted out by an enormously fat man easing himself into a chair at the window table. He planked down a tray of tea and a huge, apparently homemade ring binder. He was sitting side-on to me, and I gazed incuriously at him while he mashed his tea, poured it, and leafed through his binder. He was right out of the stereotype catalogue (so many people at Cambridge are, you know; it's as though they're determined to live up to the university's exacting standards of uniform oddity). He dressed older than he looked, in dog-eared tweed and blue polyester trousers. Above his little pink eyes was a forehead tall as a pint glass, topped with a froth of unkempt, oily black curls. Definitely a mathematician, I thought, or failing that a medieval historian . . . Or maybe not: as he turned his close-written pages over, I caught a glimpse of some xeroxed photographs inserted between them. As they flicked past, I was sure I recognised the shapes of aeroplanes: a Spitfire, certainly, and a couple of bombers; also some ships. Having nothing better to do, I went and queued for a second coffee. When I came back to my table, my fat friend had closed his binder and was busily scribbling on a loose sheet. As I squeezed past him to my seat, I glanced over his shoulder at the binder's cover. On it was a title printed in dot-matrix and sellotaped to the rumpled card. A slow smile spread across my face. Now, that would be the theory to end all theories. Without a moment's hesitation, I changed course and halted by the long bench beneath the window.

'Mind if I share your table?' I asked.

I mentioned earlier my view that all people will believe anything some of the time. It's just a matter of choosing your moment, I suppose. The culling that Friday took place pretty much as normal. We met at six-thirty in the Mill, and after dealing with Any Other Business (establishing that Nicky Somerton had received the due number of drinks he had won at the last culling – twenty-four receipted and filed, which was an indication of how unfulfilling our quest was becoming), we got down to cases.

There were five of us present: my good self, Jeremy (looking more smug than ever), Nicky Somerton, Colin Bakewell (a relatively new member who had made a distinguished debut the previous term with an almost winning theory culled from the Web which claimed that all Murdoch newspapers were impregnated with a psychoactive substance designed to be absorbed through the skin and heighten the reader's reactionary tendencies), and finally Joe Strebonewski, a tall, basketball-playing American anthropologist who was currently club chairman and three-times prizewinner.

Nicky, Colin and Joe presented their culls first (and a damned uninspiring lot they were) while Jeremy sat there smiling indulgently and I tried to keep a poker face with one eye on my watch and the other on the door. After listening to these three fairly routine contributions – none worth more than fifteen points – Jeremy looked at me and asked if I wanted to go next. I shook my head and offered him back the courtesy.

'No, the floor is yours,' I said. 'My informant isn't due yet.'

That rattled him, I could see. An informant, as I've told you, merited the maximum multiplier; if the theory was a good one (and this was the best ever), the score could shoot up as high as 100. A booze century.

'Oh,' he said. 'Right, okay.' He rallied quickly, I'll give him that, and within seconds he was looking as pleased with himself as ever. He reached under the table and took out a book, leather-bound and very old. With a dramatic flourish, he set it on the table among the glasses, empty crisp packets and ashtrays, and laid a hand on it reverently, as though it contained holy scripture. Which of course, it did.

'The Bible,' he said portentously.

The other guys' eyes lit up. Bible conspiracies were always juicy, and we hadn't heard a good one in months.

'Oh, my word,' said Nicky. 'What now? Templars in the woodpile? Book of Revelations? Right-wing evangelists in league with the Secret Government?'

Jeremy pursed his lips and shook his head firmly. 'The Bible,' he repeated simply.

We all frowned at him, uncomprehending, for several seconds, and then understanding began to dawn. Joe was the first to speak.

'The Bible?' he said. 'You mean the actual Bible?'

'None other. From Genesis to Revelations, the biggest, most comprehensive conspiracy ever foisted on mankind, and the most conclusive proof, if we needed any, of human credulity.'

This sally was greeted by hoots of derision which quickly built into a vigorous argument. Not about treating the Holy Bible in such a fashion (I won't add 'obviously' because, it may surprise you, several people who were members of the Society for the Celebration of Human Credulity at one time or another were actually quite committedly religious – which, if you think about it, is as good a measure of credulity's bounds as you could wish); no, the argument was about whether Jeremy's cull was valid or not. The conclusion eventually reached was, to Jeremy's chagrin, that: 1) The Bible itself (i.e. its content) was not a conspiracy theory, since it was available openly, was not widely believed to be sinister and did not seek to blow out any pre-existing cover story; 2) The Churches might be arguably conspiratorial; but 3) if that were the point on which Jeremy's case rested, that made *him* the theorist, and he had not brought forth the independent witnesses required under the rules. The vote was split between Nicky and myself, who wanted to award him 10 points for scope and scale with a compromise 3.5x multiplier as originator, and everyone else, who wanted to disqualify his cull altogether. Eventually, he was grudgingly awarded an arbitrated score of 30. Since that was the best he could have hoped for from a printed source and it put him well ahead of the field, he should have been well pleased. But having been put through the constitutional mill and been found intellectually wanting, he was more truculent than satisfied. He tried to raise his spirits by looking at me and challenging me to beat that.

I looked at my watch. It was after eight and my informant still hadn't shown. If I didn't have my cull in the bag by nine, I would be disqualified. (Nine was another significant Templar number, apparently, and cullings always ended split on the hour.) Maintaining my impassivity, I offered to buy a round. It was while I was standing at the bar counting out my change that the door opened and in waddled my darling fat bag of tweed, bulging binder cradled in his arms like a new-born babe. He scanned the room nervously, like an adolescent in a brothel, then spotted me and came over.

'Sorry I'm late,' he muttered. 'Are your students here?'

I'd told him I was a historian at Peterhouse (having discovered he was a mathematician – natch – at Caius) and was eager to have him expose his work to a group of my tutees who might benefit from his revolutionary thinking. The lie was probably unnecessary; in my experience folk like him will expound their crackpot theories to a brick wall without any encouragement from the likes of me. Probably for that reason his face had only fallen slightly when I told him our little seminar would take place in the pub rather than in College. I gathered pubs made him uneasy. (I should have asked him why; I might have got two culls for the price of one.)

'Grapefruit juice, please,' he said to my offer of a drink, and added, completely straight-faced: 'Slimline, if you don't mind.'

I thought of the number of Danish pastries he'd engulfed the previous afternoon in the Copper Kettle (at my expense, too – I'd insisted), but let it pass. I led him over to our table and introduced him to my 'tutees'.

'Guys, I want you to meet Dr Arnold Smith. He's—'

'Smythe,' he interrupted, and paraded a pudgy smile around the table. 'Actually it's Pennington-Smythe, but we needn't stand on formalities here, need we? Ha-ha.'

'Dr Arnold *Smythe*,' I continued, 'is going to talk to us on "The Myth of World War Two".' I pulled out a chair. 'Please, Dr Smythe, take a seat and begin when you're ready.'

He sat down, and from the first moment I knew he was going to play me a blinder. First, he gazed earnestly at each member of his audience in turn, and then opened his great tome, which sighed and crackled with its weight of accumulated paper. Just from his manner I guessed he'd been rehearsing assiduously – in fact, I reflected, he'd probably done little else *but* rehearse The Myth of World War II for years without count, and it showed. He began with a little speech on the totemic significance of the War,

touching all the usual bases: the fight against fascism, the extermination of the Jews and so on, and concluding with the central
place of the conflict in world history and mythology. So far so
orthodox, but the sagacity of his presentation, I noticed, had
them nodding like a bunch of courtiers. (The old interrogator's
trick of building up a rhythm of agreement, you see.) Then, when
he had their trust entire, he hit them between the eyes with the
brunt of his thesis. The Second World War, he asserted mightily,
never happened.

For several moments, you could have heard a pin drop; if I
were fanciful, I'd remember every head in the room turning to
look at him, the barman with beer flooding over the rim of the
glass he was in the act of filling, the fruit machine and even the
jukebox falling silent. It wasn't quite as dramatic as that, but in my
memory it has some of that flavour. Dr Smythe looked at his
audience again, and despite his confidence in his thesis, there was
a shade of anxiety in his eyes. But if he was expecting snorts of
disbelief and guffaws, he didn't get them. The moment of shock
slipped smoothly into one of eager anticipation: wide eyes and
knowing smiles – the expressions of connoisseurs of fantasy
anticipating the conspiracy equivalent of Chateau Mouton Roths-
child, had he but known it, but he read the mood as awe awaiting
enlightenment, and his confidence went up several gears. He took
a sheaf of xeroxed photos from his binder and, with the panache
of a Dodge City faro dealer, whisked them across the table at us.

Mine showed a flight of Spitfires against a cloud-strewn sky. It
was a good quality reproduction – none of your blurry high-
contrast copies, but crystal-clear halftone. I glanced at Jeremy's
photo, which appeared to be of a tropical beach.

'These photographs,' Dr Smythe was saying, 'were the spark to
the powder, so to speak; the loose strand which led to the great
unravelling that is my research. All are available in published
works – indeed, one or two of them are among the most
well-known images of the Second World War. Each one, however,
contains at least one anomaly which has enabled me to establish
that it is a fake. Let's see if you can spot the mistakes.'

I studied my Spitfires, but try as I might, I couldn't see anything

94

wrong with them. A glance at the others told me they were no wiser; frowning and shaking heads seemed to be the general consensus. Dr Smythe smiled and said he wasn't surprised; it had taken him years of staring at these and similar pictures to notice their peculiarities.

'This is the one that started it,' he said, and took my picture back. 'It was ostensibly taken by an official War Office photographer shortly before the Battle of Britain, and the original is held in the Public Record Office, freely available. Now, perhaps you are unaware of the technicalities of unpressurised flight. Above ten thousand feet, it is necessary for aircrew to be supplied with oxygen. The two aircraft in the foreground of this picture are close enough to discern that the pilots are not wearing masks. Not significant in itself, perhaps, until one realises that the type of cloud formation above which they are flying does not occur below *fifteen* thousand feet. These men should be unconscious from anoxia. Now look at this image,' and he took Joe's sheet. 'It appears to show a German Heinkel bomber over the coast of England. But compare the shadows on the aircraft with those of buildings on the ground. They are misaligned by more than two and a half degrees.'

Those two photos were obviously his prize pieces. Others were pulled apart by more subtle means. A shot of battleships sailing in convoy towards the camera required an acetate overlay scored with lines and arcs to demonstrate that the rearmost ships were out of scale. Jeremy's Pacific island beach contained the dead bodies of several GIs who were clearly wearing a pattern of gaiter not issued (according to official records) until a year after the battle whose aftermath the photo allegedly depicted. And the French partisan proudly displaying his Bren gun in another photo bore such a close resemblance to an SS soldier seen in yet another that he had indisputably to be the same man. (I squinted at both and I have to admit they did look alike.)

This was better than all my expectations. I had thought him eccentric when I heard his synopsis in the Copper Kettle, but now . . . well, the guy had more loose screws than B&Q. Mad as a toaster, as my old dad used to say; slammed down and browning nicely. But while his thesis was the most breathtakingly outrageous conspiracy theory ever conceived, it had sufficient meat to it that it couldn't fail to attract a substantial (if lunatic) following. Sound all round, and worth an easy 100.

And it only got better. When he had disposed of all his photos, he moved onto documents, which he pulled apart just as skilfully: to this day I could quote you chapter and verse on anomalies in official Air Ministry figures for aircraft production, pilot training and operational strength during the Battle of Britain, or the collated ration and casualty returns which suggested that the German army contained several times more men than existed in Germany at the time (even excluding Hiwis), and enough were killed to repopulate it twice over with corpses.

Like all masters, he saved the best for last. His peroration on the reasons for such colossal shamming took in American economic imperialism, western ambitions for a foothold in the Middle East after the inevitable decline of the British Empire, justification for experiments with nuclear weapons and the covering-up of massive Stalinist extermination programmes in the Soviet Union. I'm sure it ranged wider than that, but those were the salient issues. The world's great powers had colluded in unprecedented ways to pull the wool over the world's collective eyes. When he came to the matter of how come millions of old people thought they had lived (and indeed fought) through a global conflict fifty years ago, and raised the desperately amateurish old chestnut of mass hypnotism (backed by the power of newsreel and other propaganda), though, I half expected the guys to finally laugh in his face.

They didn't. I looked around that table, and you never saw such a set of earnest, attentive expressions in your life, almost as though they were his disciples and he were rehearsing sacred gospel. Hang on, I thought, that's carrying professional commitment a bit far; keeping natural reaction so firmly under control even unto the end. Almost heroic, I thought. Only Jeremy remained detached, sitting back in his chair with a faintly sneering smile on his face, occasionally putting peremptory, sceptical questions. (Probably just narked because I was going to beat his feeble Bible effort. I didn't know why he bothered, really; the little snirp didn't even drink. He had once been as big a gorger and puker as you could wish, but had been a confirmed orange juice and Coke merchant since . . . – ah, but I shouldn't be using these pages to perpetuate tittle-tattle.)

After Dr Smythe had packed up his binder and departed, glowing, I took my inevitable triumph with good grace, buying another round – even though it wasn't my turn – as last orders was called (the official and sacred culling time, you'll note, had been well and truly overrun without comment). Jeremy, to his credit, was gracious enough to come out of his sulk and join me at the bar, raising a glass of orange to my victory.

'Well done,' he said, arranging the pints on a tray while I waited for my change. 'Of course, you realise we'll have to disband the Club now.'

Thinking he was being ironic, I smiled. 'I know. This one's never going to be topped. I've bagged the unprecedented century this night, Horatio.'

'No,' he said, looking aggrieved. 'That's not what I mean. I mean you and your friend have turned the constitution on its head. We can't go on.'

I frowned at him. 'Jeremy, what are you talking about?'

'Credulity. Look at them.' And he nodded at the others, sitting at the table, deep in conversation. I'd looked at them, gloating, while ordering the round, and had assumed that they were debating my score. Now, something told me they weren't; something Jeremy had noticed and I had overlooked in the midst of self-congratulatory stupor, and I started feeling uneasy, like I'd left the gas on at home, the back door unlocked and a cigarette burning in the ashtray.

'You're not suggesting,' I said, and stopped. I grinned uncomfortably and started again: 'You're not telling me they *believe* it?'

He picked up the tray. 'Your friend was very persuasive.'

And he walked back to the table, leaving me goggling. Behind me, the barman gave up trying to get my attention, and deposited my change in a puddle of spilt beer.

Credit it or not (I couldn't), he was absolutely right. The buggers *did* believe it. I won't say they swallowed the line and sinker, but they certainly went swimming away with the hook lodged firmly in their gullets. Firmly enough that we did, in the end, have to disband the Club. They would have carried on, I'm sure (eager, no doubt, for more dribbling, pop-eyed nonsense to take as gospel), but Jeremy and I were sickened, and lost heart. The last we heard, the three of them had formed a new little group dedicated to helping Dr Smythe with his research.

Jeremy had the last word on the subject, just before I left Cambridge (we went for a few drinks to wet my departure, and he unbent sufficiently to sink a couple of lagers).

'Look at my cull,' he said. 'The Bible. I ask you, has there ever been a bigger parcel of bollocks committed to print? And how many people down the ages have believed it, heart and soul? Human beings are lazy creatures at heart, and they'd sooner be gullible than not. The gullible don't have to think. It's not stupidity or ignorance, it's laziness. Like someone said, give a lie a running start, and the truth will never catch it. Funny how the converse doesn't apply. In most people's minds, supercharged bullshit will always overtake truth.'

I've thought a great deal recently about those words, and with good reason. Credulity (belief, faith, call it whatever you want) is a slippery thing. You (again, the generic you), being no doubt intelligent and healthily sceptical, will think I'm telling writerly stretchers; that I can't really have sat there and seen a piggy mathematician with a Tefal head and bottle-bottom glasses persuade three experienced sceptics that World War Two never took place, can I? I must have made the whole thing up. I swear I haven't. It happened exactly as I've told it, and you should bear that in mind as I tell the rest of my tale. (And that goes especially for you, Jeremy Dronfield, faithless dog that you are.)

Okay, now that my little aside's complete, I shall resume the toga of detachment and put that third person 'twixt me and you, and take up my story where I left off.

Packet 4

King's Cross was quieter than Drick had ever seen it; he had no trouble finding a bench on Platform 9 and could wait for the 15:45 to Ely in relative comfort.

There had been no free lunch today; Obelisk's hospitality budget obviously didn't extend to more than one meal. This meeting – second in as many months – had been in Nick Lovell's office, on the top floor of a building off the Charing Cross Road which Obelisk shared with a management consultancy firm and a shop selling mobile phones. The first meeting, in a restaurant in Old Compton Street, had been mostly social and congratulatory; today's was more businesslike. In a grim little office which seemed in perpetual danger of being avalanched by the teetering stacks of books, manuscripts and box-files that lined three of its walls (the fourth was largely given over to an oversize and ancient sash window which leaked loud traffic-noise into the room), Drick listened patiently to his new editor's 'editorial queries'.

He had come to the meeting prepared to field these queries as decisively as possible. He was experienced enough to know that 'editorial queries' meant that some ink-fingered mechanic wanted to chop the vitals out of his precious work, and he wasn't having that at any price. He was mollified to find that Nick put his points in the most disarmingly ingenuous way and seemed to take the view that, since it was Roderick Bent's book, Roderick Bent should have the ultimate veto on any proposed alterations. Civil of him. Drick didn't reciprocate the sentiment; he vetoed every one. His editor maintained his equanimity, even after Drick had signed the contract binding the UK and Territorial publishing rights exclusively to Obelisk. There would be no advance, but a generous flat-rate royalty of twenty per cent was offered in compensation. Furthermore, the company would meet all pro- duction, distribution, marketing and publicity costs (although Drick was scrupulously given to understand that the last two items, given Obelisk's size and budget, would be pretty minimal). The initial print-run was set at five hundred hardback copies, probably priced at £14.99. (Drick did a quick mental calculation which produced a total earning of fifteen hundred pounds if the run sold through, which seemed okay to him.) There was a lot of stuff about remaindering, book clubs, serialisation and subsidiary rights which drifted clean over Drick's head, and he found his mind wandering. What he thought about was how exactly this office matched his expectations, even down to the dusty roller- blind on the window and the rickety, creaky old back-stairs (carpeted in scratchy orange nylon) leading up to the frosted-glass door. Only Lovell himself was out of place: a neatly cut little man in a fashionable four-button suit who looked as though he had lost his way on the dingy stairs and wandered up from the management consultancy where he rightfully belonged.

The meeting was bracketed by two handshakes; two minutes after the second one, he was out in Great Newport Street. He pulled the door to, and as it closed with a snap, as suddenly and surely as switching on a light he felt that someone was staring at him. A sweat broke out on the back of his neck, and he turned quickly and surveyed the street. On the other side of the road, standing in the doorway of a shuttered-down and abandoned shop, was an old derelict, fingering his matted beard and staring at Drick with eyes that shone with extraordinary, unnatural bright- ness in the wrinkled, nut-brown face. He stared for a full minute before shouldering his threadbare haversack, gathering up a number of overstretched carrier bags and shambling off up the street.

It unsettled him at first, but Drick dismissed the feeling quickly enough. As he turned into Charing Cross Road and headed for Leicester Square tube station, though, he found the situation turning itself over and over in his mind, sprouting tendrils of possibility. It had obviously just been a freak occurrence (the tramp had presumably mistaken him for somebody else – a policeman or social worker perhaps), but what if it hadn't been? What depths might lie beneath such an apparently meaningless chance encounter? Layers began to suggest themselves to him, and he saw in what startling, exciting ways the tramp and a notional character standing in his own shoes might be connected.

The idea grew as he descended the escalator to the Piccadilly Line and waited in the windy tunnel for a train. By the time he came up the escalator, through the ascending passages and out onto the concourse at King's Cross, it was more or less fully formed.

As he sat on his bench on platform 9, he decided that it was undoubtedly the fertile seed of a novel. Not a crime story exactly, but something along those lines. Hard on the heels of that thought came the decision that he must get the outline down on paper; he had lost more than one good idea as a result of thinking he'd be able to remember it later. Although he had a bottom drawer at home filled with files containing sketches for novels and stories, he mourned the lost ideas like miscarried children.

He searched through his pockets and bag, but couldn't find any paper. He didn't even have a pen. He cursed himself; what sort of writer goes about without even the most elementary materials of his trade? Virtually every moment of every day he carried about a biro and a shorthand pad – even when he walked the dog – but typically not today. He had seven minutes until his train, so he decided to run back to Smith's on the main station.

He ran out, cutting across the taxi rank and clattering down the echoing tunnel, then turned right and panted along the platform to the concourse where the shops were. Fortunately, there was no queue in Smith's, so he grabbed a cheap reporter's notepad and a Bic biro from the stationery racks, dropped two pound coins on the counter, then ran out without waiting for his change. Back across the concourse, along past the cafés, out through the tunnel and across the taxi rank, where a black cab swerved to avoid knocking him down and jerked to a halt blasting its horn. He made it back to platform 9 with seconds to spare, jumping onto the train just as the doors hissed shut and the engine began whining up to a crescendo.

The train was only half full, and he found a seat in the first carriage, opposite a woman who was busily knitting, with intense concentration and ultra-thin needles, some garment in baby blue with white trimmings. The train jerked into motion just as he was bending his knees to sit, and he was toppled back into his seat with a grunt of surprise. He sensed the woman's glance pass briefly from her knitting, flit across his face, and sink downwards again. He crossed his legs and sat back, watching for a while as the streets and houses jostled by, then took out his notepad and pen. He rested the pad between his raised knee and the edge of the table, flipped back the cover and poised the biro over the first feint line . . .

And nothing came.

The idea, already composed in platoons and companies of words, had been thoroughly ranked and drilled, marched and wheeled in his head as he travelled through London, until he had his first paragraphs by heart. And now they were gone. Not only the words, but the idea itself had vanished like a mist. He couldn't even remember what thought or incident had caused the chain of events which had culminated in his mad dash to Smith's. (Later he would recall the old tramp in Great Newport Street and experience the momentary disquiet of his gaze, but by that time the idea that grew from it had receded out of reach, although he still retained a lingering sense of the exhilaration attached to it, like a body-shape impressed on the surface of a bed. But for now, his mind was blank.) He stared at the little grey-ruled white rectangle for a long time, then gazed out of the window again. The grey-brown brick of the city's core had frayed into the red-block and green-furze of the outer suburbs.

He looked back at the pad, chewing the soft plastic lid of the Bic, frowning angrily and impotently at the blank paper.

Just past Finsbury Park, he was distracted by a metallic rattle further down the carriage. He looked up; a young man wearing an ill-fitting puce waistcoat and matching pimples was wheeling an aluminium trolley along the aisle, piled high with drink cans and packets of crisps. Drick watched him incuriously as he plied his way between the carelessly placed bags and feet in the aisle, leaning randomly into people's private spaces. *Refreshments?* he said softly, making it sound more like a plea than an offer. *Any refreshments?* His smile was like his clip-on bow-tie: artificial, slightly askew and, to Drick's eyes, inexpressibly sad. More from charity than thirst, he stopped the boy and bought a can of lager and a large packet of crisps. As he sat sipping and settling into a kind of resigned gloom, he decided that he might as well use the journey and the notepad constructively. Perhaps if he were to begin writing something – anything – the juices might begin to flow, and he might even recall what he had been intending to write in the first place.

He leaned back in his seat with the pad on his knee and, feeling like a student in one of his own writing classes, began to set down a description of the carriage interior. He started with the carriage itself – the dust-filmed windows filtering fitful sunshine, the creaking, streaked and black-spotted blue-grey seats, the aluminium-edged table in yellowing formica marked with sepia cup-rings – and then moved on to his fellow passengers, beginning with the knitting woman. Sitting diagonally opposite him, on the far side of the carriage, was a young businessman with pallid skin and an incipient peppery moustache. He was wearing a double-breasted suit of shiny, dark grey fabric which revealed a green tint whenever a passing block of sunlight skimmed over it. On the table in front of him was a cheap black attaché case with gold-effect fittings, and propped folded against it was a tabloid newspaper; either the *Mail* or the *Express*. Sitting opposite him was a young woman with dark hair and a sharply pointed nose. She was wearing black leggings and a deep blue, unfaded denim jacket, and was engrossed in a well-thumbed paperback.

(By now, the knitting woman had noticed him furtively examining the other passengers and apparently taking notes, and she kept darting small, suspicious and equally furtive glances at him.)

After about ten minutes, he had filled three pages of the notepad, and he paused to read back what he had written. He was

103

fairly happy with the description of the carriage, but the characters populating it seemed wrong. Starting to enjoy himself, he picked up the biro again and went through the text, altering details here and there, making each character more interesting. Beginning with the man, he changed his description to:

Sitting diagonally opposite me, on the far side of the carriage, was an elderly man with pallid skin and a dark beard peppered with white. He was wearing a dark double-breasted suit in an old-fashioned, pre-war cut, its black fabric revealing a green tint whenever a passing block of sunlight skimmed over it. On the table in front of him was a slim leather briefcase with bent edges and fraying stitching, and resting full open against it was the grey, billowing sail of a copy of Pravda.

He smiled at his revised description, seeing faintly glimmering tendrils of narrative trailing behind his new character, leading away into a dark past. Still grinning, he looked across to compare him with the mundane model around whom he had crafted him. He had seen his ageing Russian so vividly that it took a few moments of staring and blinking before he realised that he was looking at him now across the carriage. The young businessman had gone, and sitting in his place was the Russian gentleman.

To the life. Exactly as he had described him, even down to the copy of *Pravda*. Even the details he had visualised but not written down – like the curved, sharp-tipped nose and hair thinning back from the temples – were there.

Thinking he must have imagined his pallid businessman – that the Russian must in reality have been there all the time – he looked back at the pad, but there, still legible beneath the crossings-out, was the description of the businessman in all his banality.

Minutes passed, in which his brain fluttered haphazardly like a moth, and he became conscious that he was gawping at the Russian district official (somehow he knew the man was a district official – travelling on business connected with agricultural redistribution), and that the man kept glancing curiously back, with an odd, slightly nervous expression in his eyes. Drick tore his gaze away from the man and stared down fixedly at his pad. Then, with a last glance around the carriage, he set about, with intense concentration, changing the descriptions of the other passengers, of the carriage itself, and of the country through which the train was travelling. While he deleted, amended and scribbled, he didn't look up once, but he could sense his surroundings altering as he re-wrote them: the sharp plastic smell of the train became a bitter, dusty stench; the whine of the electric motors and the smooth *sicca-sicca* of the wheels on the tracks was replaced by a dense, grumbling clatter; and the clean, deodorised smell of his fellow-passengers was transformed into a thick odour in which the dominant elements were rancid onions and boiled cabbage. Something else happened also: the snatches of talk he could hear around him took on the sibilant burr of Russian.

After a moment's careful breathing, he finally looked up and inspected the results of his work.

The woman sitting opposite him had shed about thirty years; her hair – no longer a fierce dyed orange – was hidden under a mink hat, and instead of knitting, her fingers toyed restlessly with a pair of fine leather gloves. The most remarkable thing about her, though, was her face. Although he had described her simply as 'a sleek Eurasian beauty', the face he found himself looking at in the flesh was the exact duplicate of the one that had been in his mind when he set down that cursory description. He had seen the face before, in a dozen Bond movies; the beautiful Russian spy who sleeps with Bond and usually ends up dead. And just as he had seen her do in his imagination, she looked at him with a sly, cool, but somehow come-hither smile in her eyes, then looked out at the scenery passing beyond the partly fogged glass. Drick followed her gaze: the soft rolling green and huddled estates of Hertfordshire had gone, and in their place was the snow-covered desolation of northern Russia, blotted out from time to time by the gauze of smoke and steam blowing back from the engine.

He knew where he was, because he had written it; although the only signs of habitation visible in the white landscape were the occasional hamlet or isolated dacha, he knew that in a few minutes the train would be passing into the outskirts of Leningrad. What he didn't know was *when* precisely this was; he hadn't written that down. What was astonishing, though (aside from the fact that any of this was happening at all) was that, as with the woman's face, a general sense of period that had coloured his imaginings as he wrote seemed to have been translated into all the details now before his eyes. The steam train, the air of gloom and the old-fashioned cut of the passengers' clothing suggested a shift backwards of about forty or fifty years.

Leaning forward in his seat and putting his elbows on the table (which was now made of scarred plywood), he tried surreptitiously to steal a glance at the date on the agricultural official's newspaper. It was too far away for his indifferent eyesight, and the cyrillic type was indecipherable, but as the man – sensing the stranger's eyes on him again – lifted the paper high to screen himself, Drick just about managed to read the year below the masthead: 1949.

And here now, flitting by the window, came the first outlying houses and factories of Leningrad – dour grey blocks and smirches under the softening mantle of snow, gathering and rising as the train passed deeper into the city.

The door at the end of the carriage slammed open, and the guard stepped through; a tall figure in a greatcoat of military cut, buttoned up to the shoulder and hanging almost to the ground, a ridiculous peaked cap on his head, with a steep crown like a comedy quiff. Drick stared at him, shocked. He hadn't written this man into the scene at all; hadn't even imagined him. The guard caught his look and stared back, frowning suspiciously. He barked something in Russian, and the other passengers (there seemed to be far more of them than there had been – the train was really quite crowded now) began rummaging in coat pockets, wallets and handbags, producing their tickets ready for inspection. Those nearest the guard held them out towards him, but he waved them aside impatiently, still staring intently at Drick. He repeated his incomprehensible barked order, and Drick felt all eyes in the carriage turn towards him. He took out his wallet and looked inside; his ticket was there, marked King's X–Ely. The guard

106

snatched it from him, and studied it balefully as though it were a dead insect. He issued another demand – still in the same peremptory tone, but with slightly different words – and now Drick sensed the eyes of the passengers turning away and felt waves of fear, suspicion (but also pity) washing over him. He just shrugged helplessly.

'I don't understand,' he said, and the man's suspicious frown deepened.

Suddenly there was a loud metallic squeal and a violent jolt which almost knocked the guard off his feet. He gripped the luggage rack to steady himself and pointed a gloved finger at Drick. He said something which, in any language, was obviously meant to signify *Stay where you are.* The other passengers, with barely subdued haste, gathered together their belongings and began to file out of the carriage. As they passed him, one or two (including the beautiful woman) gave Drick sidelong glances which seemed to convey profound condolence, but most kept their eyes averted. When the carriage was empty, the guard glanced over his shoulder, then fixed Drick with an intense stare intended to pinion him to the seat, then opened the door behind him and went through it. When he reappeared a few seconds later, he had another guard with him, wearing a uniform coat similar to the first man's, but with red beading on the collar. Without speaking, they hauled him to his feet (one of them seizing the notebook and stuffing it into his coat pocket) and marched him up the narrow aisle, through the door and out onto the platform.

He was in no state now to study his surroundings. All he was conscious of was the stench of coal smoke and the intense cold as the guards took an elbow each and force-marched him across the broad platform towards a nondescript office with whited-out windows and a red door. Inside, he was shouted at by a succession of uniformed, mean-faced officials who waved first his British Rail ticket and then his notepad under his nose and then, when he totally failed to understand a word they were saying, he was locked in a freezing, windowless little room which was empty except for a plain wooden table and a bentwood chair. He sank down on the chair, put his head in his hands, and, his brain unassailed at last by bizarre sensations, started to feel his mind drifting free of its moorings.

It was a wonder that, in that moment, he didn't utterly lose his sanity. He kept hold of it by going back in his memory to the words he had written in the notepad. If he had created this nightmare out of his own head, then surely he ought to be able to undo it by the same means. This was clearly some form of self-induced hallucination. That realisation made him feel immediately better; just accepting that none of this was real was a step back towards normality. He no longer had his notepad, but he tried to recreate reality without it, inside his own head. Painstakingly, eyes tight shut, he reconstructed the real carriage with its real, utterly ordinary occupants, the sound of its electric motor, and the Hertfordshire countryside whisking past the window. He saw quite clearly the power lines, the fields and hedges, and even the Bovis housing estate on the edge of Stevenage which he had glanced at on the way to London, finding that he could recall every detail, right down to the imitation victorian gas-lamp in the back garden of one semi and the white plastic conservatory built on the back of its neighbour.

Finally, calm at last, he opened his eyes.

And there, surrounding him as vividly and solidly as ever, was the bare little room behind the office on Leningrad station.

So it was real. He had created it out of his own imaginings, but it was real; more real than King's Cross or the semi in Stevenage or the orange-haired woman and her knitting. He was in Leningrad, under arrest, in 1949. And suddenly it became blindingly obvious why he had been arrested: his inability to understand Russian, his alien rail ticket and his notebook must mark him down as the most blatant, incompetent spy in the whole Cold War. And then there was his clothing: he was still wearing his light cotton jacket, T-shirt and khakis (no wonder he was freezing); in post-war Soviet Russia he couldn't have stood out more dressed in an Arapaho war bonnet and a zoot suit.

The door was flung open, making him start violently, there was a scuffle of boots, and the small room seemed suddenly filled with people. A couple of uniforms (looking even more military

108

than the railway guards) dragged him to his feet, a pair of handcuffs was clapped on his wrists, and he was on the move again. Out of the room, through the office and across the platform. The uniforms (these had submachine-guns slung over their shoulders, he noticed) marched him through a huge archway under a giant clock, across a great pillared concourse which had obviously been very grand once but which now looked grim and shabby, and out onto a broad, snow-slathered street. Before he had time even to glance about him, he was bundled into the back of a black van. The soldiers (or policemen; he couldn't tell) forced him to sit on a rudimentary bench, then sat opposite and gazed indifferently at him while the van grumbled and rattled through unseen city streets. He tried speaking to them, but they obviously didn't understand a word, and showed no sign that they would have cared if they had. One of them grunted and raised the muzzle of his submachine-gun, and Drick shut up.

After numerous stops and starts and several sharp bends, the van came to a halt and the back door opened. He was shoved out onto a wide pavement in front of a tall, utterly forbidding building. It looked like any other government office building in any city in the world, but here it seemed to emanate ill-will and paranoia like an odour. He noticed that the pedestrians who walked by, shoulders hunched and bodies bent against the bite of the cold wind, drew their mufflers a little tighter and stooped a little more as they passed the building. He was met by two more armed guards who escorted him across the pavement and up the steps to the entrance, a panelled double-door beside which a modest brass plaque was fixed to the wall. Engraved on it in cyrillic capitals (which had always looked brutal and alien to him, and now took on an extra layer of menace) were the letters CMEPW. (That, at least, was how they looked to him; later he found that they signified SMERSH, the Soviet security police.)

He was taken along a maze of corridors, down a flight of ill-lit stairs and through another maze lined with blank doors and lit by harsh, bare bulbs. At the end of one particularly long corridor, his guards halted before a closed door and paused. Whether it was deliberate or not, they waited just long enough for him to notice

109

that the door opposite was open – through it he could see a long laboratory workbench with what looked like surgical implements laid out on cloths, and half out of view behind the door, something that looked horribly like an electric chair. One of the guards said something, and they both laughed, while Drick's innards dissolved.

The blank door opened, he was pushed forward, and he found himself in another bare room with another plain table and bentwood chair. The only difference was the portait of Stalin which hung on one wall. Facing him across the table were two men in civilian clothes, one wearing the same expression of glowering suspicion he had seen on all the official faces that had swum in front of him since leaving the train; the other, though, looked almost cheerful, welcoming even.

Hard cop, soft cop, he thought to himself. Mr Soft waved him to a chair and smiled.

'Welcome,' he said in English, 'I will offer no apology for the brusqueness with which you have been treated; I could wish it were otherwise, but there is a certain form here for the handling of spies.'

Now, whatever happened, he must remain calm; he knew that babbling about having got here by accident would only make things worse. Having anticipated something like this, he had been working out his story, and his only hope was to stick to it. With a slight frown which sat convincingly with the quite genuine look of fear on his face, he shook his head.

'I'm not a spy,' he said.

Mr Hard muttered something to his colleague in Russian and leaned forward in his chair. 'You,' he said with a stab of a thick forefinger, which was brown to the knuckle with nicotine, 'spying. Foreigner MI6.'

'I'm not.' It came out in a choked whisper.

Mr Soft chuckled lightly. 'Of course you are not,' he said. 'Will you have a cigarette? Here, and a light? Good. Now please relax. We only wish to ask you some simple questions. First, please, your name?'

'Roderick Bent.'

Mr Soft made a note. 'Your date of birth?'

Drick made a swift mental calculation. 'Fifteenth of September 1921.'

'Good. Nationality British, I presume? Yes. Your occupation?'

'Author.'

'You write? What do you write?'

'Travel books. You won't have read them. You see, that's why I was making notes on the train.' He smiled and avoided Mr Hard's eyes, which were boring into his skull (whether with interrogative suspicion or difficulty in following English Drick wasn't sure). 'I wasn't spying; just taking notes on the journey.'

Mr Soft nodded, and his smile broadened. 'Of course. You weren't spying at all; of this I am sure. You were merely taking notes on your journey in order to describe it in one of your travel books. This, of course, necessitated taking down detailed descriptions of the people on board the train.'

Drick's smile lingered for a few seconds on his lips as the implications of this sank in. Dear God, it hadn't been some sort of official train, had it? Full of Politburo members and KGB agents. He thought of the military-looking guards and almost despaired. 'No,' he said hastily. 'I mean, yes. Describing the local people is all a part of travel writing.'

Mr Soft's smile didn't waver. 'Of course it is. Though I don't imagine travellers on the Moscow-Leningrad Express would be typical local colour. Ha-ha!'

'No, I suppose not.'

Mr Soft produced Drick's notebook and laid it on the table. 'You write well, Mr Bent. But you do not seem to have found much to write about on this journey. I do not blame you; it is not the most interesting journey in the world. Now perhaps you could explain this.'

Drick stared at the ticket as Mr Soft laid it beside the notebook. 'Er, it's an English railway ticket.'

'I can see it is an English railway ticket. You no doubt showed it to the guard by mistake, having accidentally lost your proper ticket and being confused by his abrupt – not to say rude – manner.'

Drick hesitated. Why was this man so generously providing

111

him with excuses? 'Yes,' he said warily. 'That's more or less what happened. You see, I looked in my wallet and couldn't find my ticket. I was confused, and handed over that. It's an old ticket – I can't imagine what it was doing in my wallet still.'

'Yes, that is what I thought. And here, where it says "Date", why does it have "17 Sep 93"? Is England now running to a different calendar from the rest of the world?'

Drick stared at the ticket, and thought quickly. 'No,' he said. 'No. The date is the seventeenth of September, true, but the "93" is a sort of issue number. Tickets in England are only valid for three months, so they don't have the year on them.'

'I see. Yes, that makes sense.' Mr Soft murmured in Russian to his colleague and made to stand up. 'Well, Mr Bent, thank you for answering my questions. Now I bid you goodbye.'

Drick's heart fluttered. 'You mean I can go?'

Mr Soft smiled once more, stood up and left.

Drick looked at Mr Hard. 'I can go now?'

Mr Hard also smiled, but something about the smile told Drick it was neither affirmation or farewell. He nodded to one of the guards, who stepped forward and lifted Drick by his armpits. 'You are liar,' he said quietly, and nodded his head at the door through which Mr Soft had departed. 'He always knows liar. Always.'

Now Drick gave way to utter panic. Reason and rational explanation flew out of the window like birds and scattered to the winds, and he struggled and screamed as they hauled him out of the room. 'You bastards!' he yelled. 'You can't do this to me! I'm a British citizen! I demand to see my ambassador! Stop it, you're hurting me, you Russian cunt! HELP! HELP ME!!' He tried to dig in his heels, but they just skittered and slid on the concrete floor as the policemen dragged him across the corridor and into the room opposite. His screams echoed round the maze of corridors until, with a soft thump, the door slammed shut. Then there was silence. The door to this particular room, understand-ably enough, had been thoroughly soundproofed.

He woke suddenly with sweat running off him and the remains of a scream still gasping in his throat. In the act of waking up, he had levered himself up on one elbow into a half-crouch, ready to leap and make a bolt from the terrors pursuing him, and he remained petrified in that posture, staring through the pre-dawn gloom at his jacket hanging on the back of the door. Slowly he became conscious of a deep, resonant rumbling behind him, and, still palpitating, lowered himself into a sitting position and looked round. Elsa, eyes closed, mouth wide open, lay undisturbed by his violent waking, and was snoring thickly into her pillow.

He swung his legs off the bed and, moving cautiously on limbs that were still weak and trembling from the fright he had had, stood up. Manni scrambled off his bed in the corner and wrapped himself around Drick's legs, wagging his tail and licking the bare, hairy calves.

A dream; the whole thing had been a dream. He left the bedroom and went through into the kitchen with Manni trotting at his heels. He stooped over by the kitchen table and returned the dog's greeting, savouring the comforting velvet fur and the familiar canine smell. When he had filled the dog's food-bowl and made himself a coffee, he sat at the table and replayed the dream. He had always been a vivid dreamer, but that one beat the lot. At least, though, it had brought back to him the story idea that had grown out of his encounter with the old derelict in Great Newport Street; or at least a vague impression of the idea. The story hadn't had anything to do with Russia or spies, he was sure, but the interrogation scene in the dream had jolted his memory;

he had pictured a very similar scene in the proposed novel, and that small detail hinted at the rest of the chain of ideas. Now, as soon as he had finished his breakfast and let the dog out, he would try to work it out on paper . . .

But by God the dream had been vivid! As he sipped his coffee and smoked a tremulous cigarette, he chafed his wrists; he could still *feel* the grip of the handcuffs and the manacles on that hideous chair; the ghosts of those diabolical instruments still pricked and poked at his teeth and nails; and he could still hear the echo of that last desperate, bubbling scream of agony. He grinned at the terror he had felt, and chuckled softly to himself at the memory of Mr Soft and Mr Hard. Now *they* were ridiculous.

He took Manni down the stairs and let him out into the back yard to relieve himself, then, leaving him out there to sniff out the newly-laid scents of the town cats, went up to his office under the stairs.

Under the comforting yellow fug of the forty-watt bulb, he sat down and reached out to switch on the computer, then hesitated. No, he couldn't wait for the machine to start up; he would write in longhand instead. He looked about for some paper, and found the reporter's notepad lying on top of a pile of manuscripts. He vaguely remembered (strange how reality should stick less firmly in the memory than dreams) tossing it aside dejectedly after arriving home the previous evening, full of regret at the lost idea and belching with the beer consumed during a stop-off at The Fountain, which stood conveniently half-way between the railway station and home.

He turned back the cover and flipped past the first three pages with their pointlessly dull description of the Moscow-Leningrad express, and came to the first blank page. At the top, he wrote '*THE DERELICT*' and underneath it began, '*Novel. Thrillerish psychodrama. Possible premise: Concealed relationship between two former members of* – And he paused, pen poised above the next line. But it wasn't a lack of words that caused him to hesitate, but rather a sudden, overwhelming surfeit of them. For a fleeting instant, he saw the novel in its entirety – title, jacket, chapter heads, and words – and the vision dizzied him. He was used to sudden rushes in which an

114

idea presented itself so completely that it seemed less an idea than a finished product, but never quite so suddenly nor so fully nor in such astounding detail. Nor did such visions usually disappear so quickly, effervescing briefly before his startled brain then shimmering and vanishing like vapour. He dropped his pen and sat back, breathing deeply. There was no point trying to write it down now, and no point in mourning its loss, because, in its completeness he had seen all the idea's flaws and the mess that would be made by trying to rectify them; all the problems which he wouldn't normally discover until he was at least twenty thousand words into an abortive project.

Wondering whether this meant he was finished as a writer (a notion that occurred to him at least a couple of times a month and which he had learned to take lightly), he leafed idly through the notepad, thinking maybe his train piece hadn't been so bad after all. He re-read it now, smiling again at his Russian official and the gorgeous woman in the fur cap toying with her gloves. There was some fairly bland description of the winter landscape south of Leningrad and then, at the bottom of the third page, in a frantic, barely coherent hand which he could barely recognise as his own, were the words, '*I woke up in my own bed with Elsa snoring beside me, and found that it had all been a dream.*'

Packet 6

There are moments in life when surprising things happen: for instance, you may be walking along the street, minding your own business, when a six-foot bacon sandwich jumps out of a dark alley and menaces you with a flick-knife; or, as you gaze up at the scudding clouds on a warm summer afternoon, purple seagulls the size of Zeppelins appear out of nowhere and dive-bomb you with macerated copies of *Homes & Gardens*. Things like this happen, and we know instinctively how to cope. Well, no, in fact we don't, because things like that don't happen, do they? Not outside the realm of bad acid trips, anyway. So how does an otherwise normal and well-balanced individual even begin to deal with waking up from a nightmare to find that it is his waking that is a dream and the nightmare is the reality? . . . Or *was* the reality, and is now a dream because he made it so . . . Or something like that.

Roderick Bent coped quite well, considering. Not only did he manage not to go dribbling mad when confronted by the glaring impossible, he actually succeeded in retaining his grip on sanity without recourse to simple flat refusal to believe the evidence of his eyes. As anyone who makes a study of human nature would confirm, this was quite a signal achievement, and should not be underrated.

What he did was this: first, quite naturally, he spent at least a couple of minutes staring at the page with his mouth hanging open. His obligation to convention thus satisfied, he then whipped his synapses into order and forced them to process in a rational manner the utterly irrational information being fed to them. And these were the conclusions he reached:

- *First I wrote what was real, and nothing changed.*
- *Then I wrote what was not real, and I* saw *what I wrote.*
- *On the assumption that I am not mentally ill, nor had I taken any drug, I was not hallucinating.*
- *Therefore, I did not see anything unreal; rather,* reality changed. *What I wrote* became *real.*
- *I have the power to change reality through writing.*
- *The changes I make are permanent (unless I change them back) and follow their own dynamic, since they continued after and beyond the point at which I stopped writing.*

Of course, he didn't reach his conclusions through quite such an orderly logical process (and certainly not as calmly as the above itemisation implies); it is this writer's opinion that he deserves credit for having reached them at all.

Manni was scratching insistently at the back door, and Drick realised that he had been staring at the notepad, hacking through the tangle of reason and logic for a good quarter of an hour. Feeling a bit dazed (shaken but not deranged), he went down to let the dog in, then, switching to autopilot, went to the kitchen to make Elsa's breakfast tea (she was there already, full of pre-work grumps and complaining that her tea wasn't waiting for her) and get ready for morning walkies.

He was so distracted on the walk that day he even forgot to stop near Cuckoo Bridge and contemplate the empty garden. He decided that this incredible new gift needed to be explored and tested.

When he got home, he shut himself in his office and thought long and hard about what to do. Being scientifically inclined, he decided that the first step should be to establish the source of his power. Was it innate, or was it connected specifically with the notepad? He switched on his computer and, while it started up, rummaged through drawers, producing a ruled A4 pad and half a ream of printer paper, which he laid on the desk (having removed the jumble of manuscripts and notes) beside the small notepad. He considered for a moment – for the purposes of experiment, he should do something completely innocuous, brief and self-cancelling. He opened the word-processor and typed, 'A leprechaun, six inches tall, appeared suddenly on my desk, doffed his cap, said "Top of the mornin' to yez" and, just as suddenly, vanished into thin air.' He waited, counting to ten, and when nothing happened, wrote the same words on the A4 pad, then on a sheet of printer paper. Still nothing happened, so he wrote the sentence on a clean page of the reporter's pad. Immediately, with an audible *poof* of smoke (which he had imagined but not described), a little bearded man materialised on the desk before his eyes and swept the feathered green cap off his head.

'Top of the mornin' to yez,' he piped in a laconic, high-pitched voice, then, with a sort of reverse *poof* (a *foop*, I suppose), he vanished.

Drick grinned with a gleeful abandon he hadn't felt since he was about nine years old. It was definitely the notepad. He still wasn't satisfied, though; he still had to prove conclusively that he wasn't the victim of some kind of auto-suggestive hallucination. He left the flat, went across the road to the stationer's and returned five minutes later with four pads identical in size and weight to the 'magic' one. He opened each of the five pads about mid-way, then took off his sweater and wrapped it round his head as a blindfold. He shuffled the pads and laid them out randomly, then took his pen and, still blindfolded, described on each pad in turn the sensation of being tapped hard on the right shoulder. He wrote it twice with no result, then at the third attempt felt a sharp, bony finger jab him firmly on the shoulder-blade. He whipped off the blindfold (checking as he did so that there wasn't actually anyone standing behind him) and examined the pads. The one he had written on last was indeed the Smith's pad.

There remained only one essential test: to find out whether the things he created were subjective. It was nearly time for Elsa's lunch-break, so he would use her as his guinea pig. When he eventually heard her tread on the stairs, he waited until she had gone into the kitchen, then wrote:

Jonathan Peachment wasn't usually a very successful salesman. In the past six weeks, he had only managed to make two sales. Nobody seemed to want double-glazing; at least, nobody seemed to want it from him. Today, though, he felt lucky. There was something in the air. Today he would make a sale, and he would know the house where his success lay in wait the moment he saw it. (The fact that he felt this way every day – and every day was disappointed – didn't seem to deter him.)

He saw his grail within the first few minutes. It didn't look a very likely prospect at first sight – a gift shop in Ely High Street – but where there were shops there were flats above, and the flat above this shop had windows which looked as though they could fall out into the road at the least provocation. He went to the door which he guessed must belong to the flat – a green-painted door down a narrow alley – straightened his tie, brushed back his hair, and knocked; a jaunty, confident knock – Ratta-taTAT!

Ratta-taTAT!

The loud knocking made Drick jump – perhaps all the more for being expected. He waited . . . and waited . . .

'Aren't you going to answer that?' Elsa called impatiently from the kitchen. 'I'm busy. Roderick, are you there? There's someone at the door.'

He kept quiet and still, clamping Manni's muzzle closed to prevent any giveaway barks. Seconds passed, and then he heard Elsa, muttering, go down the stairs. The door opened, there was the muffled sound of conversation, then the door closed.

He came out of his office and stood at the top of the stairs as she came back up. 'Sorry,' he said. 'I was engrossed. Who was it?'

She walked past without looking at him, her face set in a deliberate mask of indifference. 'Double-glazing,' she said as she went into the kitchen.

Drick hurried through to the living room and looked out of the window. He was just in time to see Jonathan Peachment walking disconsolately down the street. At the corner of Market Passage

119

he stopped and looked back for a moment, then passed from view.

Scientifically inclined he might have been, but Drick was not a scientist. Had he been a physicist he might have speculated on quantum mechanics or event horizons or one of those groovy-sounding hypotheticals by which inexplicable things are brought to heel. As an analytical chemist, he could clip bits off the notepad and mix them with chemical reagents, whirling them in centrifuges, burning them in glass tubes, and produce an analysis of the paper's structure which might lead to an hypothesis. He could do none of these things. All he could do, in his own *ad hoc* way, was to study the phenomenon.

Through more experiments he quickly established that it was the notepad rather than the Bic biro he had bought with it that had the power, and that pages became completely inert and ordinary if removed from the pad before writing (although writing on a page *then* removing it had no deleterious effect on what had been written, even when the page was burnt and scattered). In the course of these experiments, he succeeded in creating a plain gold ring bearing his initials on its inner surface (which he later took to wearing on the index finger of his left hand) and a two-foot high goblin with a nasty smile (which he hastily annihilated).

He knew he could never cease to be delighted by these little acts of creation, but felt that he should try to explore the notepad's capabilities in more expansive, demanding ways. Proceeding scientifically and without haste, he set himself a series of questions, discussing them as he went along.

○ *Are the effects of what I create (or change) truly permanent?*
○ *Is it always instantaneous and immediate, or can I manipulate things in the past or the future?*
○ *Are there limits to what I can do? Could I destroy the universe? Or create a new one?*
○ *The above question is immaterial, since in the first instance I too would be destroyed, and in the second I couldn't observe it.*

- *Could I, then, bring about the creation or destruction of, say, a human being?*
- *The case of Jonathan Peachment suggests I can, but I don't know whether he was a permanent or temporary entity.*
- *Could I change my own life? Make myself rich and successful or better-looking and more charming and intelligent? (Do I need to?)*
- *Can I change other people's personalities?*

Questions, questions; he would tackle them all in his own good time. For the moment, one thing was certain: he would have to start conserving the pages of his notebook. He had already used up five sides (three on his Russian adventure and two more with his experiments), which left one hundred and fifty-five. Like everybody, he knew the 'Use your last wish to get three more wishes' rule (or an infinite number of wishes, if you're a clearer thinker), but it didn't seem to apply here, and he wasted another whole page trying to create another notebook, more pages in the existing one, or delete what had already been written. Writing in erasable pencil didn't work either; it was ink or nothing. So in at least one respect – longevity – his powers were finite. The solution was twofold: to write smaller (obviously) and to rehearse carefully each act of creation – writing it out beforehand if necessary – so that no space should be wasted crossing out and correcting.

It was late when he went to bed that night. Before putting the notebook away, he had carried out his first test – an attempt to answer the second question on his list – in which he hoped to displace the event caused from the act of writing. In very small letters, he had written:

The very next day, I made another discovery. I finally found the way into Kismet's garden.

That was all; he added no details, because he wanted what he found there to be completely unaffected by his own imagination. He would only get himself inside by supranatural means; after that, he would find what he would find.

121

He went to bed and had the longest, most frustrating sleepless night since Christmas Eve 1973. He was up at seven, and washed, dressed and out of the door by twenty past, off to see if his spell had worked.

It had.

He and Manni took their usual walk by Stuntney Causeway and along the river towards Cuckoo Bridge. Drick was in a bit of a daze as he walked; almost a stupor, due in part to fearfulness but mainly because of his sleepless night.

As he lay there in the darkness, he had found himself plagued by worries. Not so much about whether the trick would work – he felt fairly confident about that – but about *how* it would work. The *how* of it was suddenly terribly important now that he was wishing for the thing he most desired in the world. He remembered a story he had been told as a child, the story of the Monkey's Paw. It had haunted him all that time, though he hadn't been conscious of it. The Monkey's Paw would give the person who possessed it three wishes; it would grant them anything they desired, but in such a way that they would wish they had never wished for it. The old couple in the story wished for wealth, and it came to them in the form of compensation when their son was killed in an accident at work. When they wished him back to life, he came back as he had died; so hideously mangled and disfigured that they immediately wished him dead again.

Would the notebook turn out like that once he started wishing for things? He thought of the SMERSH torture chamber, and shuddered.

It was a nervous Roderick Bent who crossed Cuckoo Bridge that morning. At first, he thought it hadn't worked after all; he spent several minutes scouring the fringe of the woods and the hedgerows with no more luck than he had had before. Then, as he made his way back along, he realised that at one point where the road turned at a right angle, what he had taken for solid hedgerow in the crook of the bend was only the overhanging boughs of a large, drooping hawthorn which had become laced with a tangle of blackberry vines. Looking closely, he could see that there was

122

no real substance to this apparently solid obstacle. Pushing aside the vines and branches, he managed to make his way through, almost having to crawl on his hands and knees, and found himself standing in what must once have been a narrow lane leading off the road, but was now a thicket of brambles and stinging nettles. He clipped Manni's lead on (making himself rather than the dog feel more secure) and began to work his way through.

After about twenty yards, the brambles thinned out to mud and gravel, and he came to a farm gate. It was slimed with green, rotten and broken, and some of its timbers fell off as Drick dragged it open. Taking a deep breath, he passed through. The lane continued for another ten yards, then opened out into a farmyard or garden (it was so overgrown he couldn't tell which). Off to one side were the remains of some sort of outbuilding, so broken down it was impossible to tell whether it had been a stable or a summerhouse. On the far side of the yard was the house itself.

It is possible, as Drick discovered now, to tell immediately when a house is unoccupied. It wasn't the overgrown lane or yard, nor the state of the house itself (give or take a missing roof-tile or two, it was in good condition); a house unlived-in simply looks so like a corpse. The large sash windows were whole, with no broken panes, and behind them there were curtains, albeit rather dirty and bedraggled ones. But there was no life in them; they were blank – wall-eyed with the accretion of grime which only gathers with extreme slovenliness or long abandonment.

Skirting the house (and keeping a wary, superstitious eye on it), he walked alongside the hedge, treading down the nettles to clear a path as he went. Round the far corner of the house, he found a back garden which was as overgrown as the front. On one side a huge, ragged rosemary bush bellied out from the hedge, and in the centre was a holly the size of a family tent. The garden dog-legged to the right, and Drick followed it, letting himself be carried along its edge by the continuous wall of hawthorn. Until now, he hadn't been at all sure that he had found his way to the right place (he remembered none of this from his midnight visit), but as he turned the corner he found his way barred by an immensely tall, dense and utterly familiar privet hedge. In the centre was a narrow gap which led into the alcove where the white wrought-iron table had stood. It was still there; the first clean, uncorroded thing he had seen since entering this run-down place. And beyond the alcove, the garden was exactly as he remembered it; a fresh-mown green sward stretching down to the strand of bulrushes which lined the riverbank.

Whoever kept the garden neat and weeded clearly wasn't the occupant of the house, since there didn't appear to be one. Perhaps it was Kismet herself (despite having found that it was assumed, he still thought of her by that name – it suited her so well). Well, no wonder her appearances in the garden were so rare, since she didn't live here.

He didn't stay long; just long enough to think those thoughts. Without her presence, the garden, which had seemed the very incarnation of paradise on the two occasions he had been here with her, seemed no different from any other stretch of riverside green; even a little bleak under today's overcast sky. With a heavy sigh, he turned and left.

As he was passing the house, he thought he saw a movement inside; a shadow passing a window. He stopped and stared for a moment, then dismissed it as a trick of the light. He was about to walk on when he saw it again; a shadow passing from left to right, and this time a definite tiny waft of the ragged curtain. Did she live here after all? Having found his way by trickery into her garden, he wasn't at all sure he should meet her. He had been convinced that he had seen the last of her, and even though it had never felt like an act of free will, he remembered it as having been his decision. He wished (wished, there was a word!) he could remember the details of that night; what the proposal had been, and why he had refused it.

In the end, he couldn't help himself. He went round to the front of the house, where there was a small porch which, like the window frames, was peeling its crust of green paint like a shedding lizard, and knocked on the door. It wasn't latched, and it swung open under the force of his two hesitant blows. He looked down at Manni for reassurance, and found that, typically, he was more interested in some pieces of mouldered wood scattered on the ground in front of the porch than he was in spooks. He was pawing at them busily, picking up likely specimens and chewing them to bits. Drick scattered a few biscuits on the ground, tied his lead to the post of the porch, and, bundling up his courage to a usable size, stepped across the threshold.

'Hello?' he called, realised it had come out as a tremulous whisper, and said it again, louder. 'Hello? Anyone home?' Reverting to hoarse *sotto voce*, he added: 'Kismet? Are you here?'

The air of abandonment was even greater inside the house than outside. Dust clung so thickly to everything that it seemed part of the fabric of the house. Open doors had become frozen solid by the accumulation of airborne dirt and rubbish strewn by mice, rats and rabbits, all of whom had left, in addition to bits of rag, paper and dried weeds, a liberal scattering of their shit. The open doorways were curtained with dust-laden cobweb which hung in ropes and shrouds.

He found the room in which the movement had apparently occurred on the right-hand side, off the hallway. It was the kitchen. He would have said that its occupant had just popped out for a moment in the middle of preparing an elaborate meal, if it hadn't been for the ubiquitous dust and cobwebs which coated everything in sight. There was crockery and cutlery on the drainer, a mixing bowl, measuring jug and various utensils laid out on the broad oak table, together with saucepans and a roasting dish containing broken crusts of ancient, congealed food. The door to the larder was open, and Drick could see ranks of jars, tins and mouldering paper packets on the shelves.

But no trace of a living soul. He wiped some of the grime from a window pane and looked out at the spot where he had been standing when he saw the movement. It – *could* have been an illusion. Or a rat running along the drainer and disturbing the curtain.

Back in the hall, he called out again; when no reply came, he decided to explore the house some more. (Now that he was convinced there was no living person in it with him, he had lost his fear.) There were two other doors off the hall, both of which appeared to lead into a single room. He stepped through the nearer one and found himself in a huge living room; about thirty feet long by twenty wide, with a big bay window overlooking the back garden and a sash window at the front. This end – the front – was furnished as a sitting room, with burst sofas and collapsing armchairs, while the far end contained a large oval dining table. On the floor in front of one of the two fireplaces were signs of squatting, and he approached warily. There was a sleeping bag and blankets, along with a small primus stove and some empty tin cans. However, the squatter was long gone. The state of his or her stuff suggested that the little camp had been abandoned years ago; not long after the house itself, probably.

He didn't linger in the room, but he did notice one thing which made him stop for a closer look. On the wide mantelpiece above the squatter's nest was a sort of wooden plinth, about two feet long, flat, and elaborately carved along its bevelled edges. On its top surface were three transverse U-shaped pylons. It was obvious to Drick (who had something of a passion for such things) that it was a cradle, designed to support a model boat or ship; quite a large model, too, to judge from the breadth of curve of the supports. He wiped the dust off the edge of the plinth and uncovered a small brass plaque engraved *HMS 'Victory' – 1765*.

So here was another connection with the story Kismet had told him. Presumably she had explored this house too, and had found inspiration for the invention of her father. Where had the model gone, though? As far as he was able to tell, this was the only evidence of anything having been removed from the house – there was an ancient television and music centre at the far end of the room, and a china cabinet filled to bursting with knick-knacks and crystal. All of this – even the obsolete electrical equipment, once upon a time – must have been worth a fair amount of money. So why only take the ship?

He left the room, listened out for sounds of impatience from Manni, and, hearing nothing, climbed the stairs. He paused on the landing and looked about him. All but one of the doors were standing open, and he could see glimpses of a bathroom and two bedrooms, one of which was completely empty, with bare boards and peeling paper. The fourth door was shut. The fact that it was the only closed door in the house drew him towards it. It had a little ceramic plaque stuck to it; through the dust he could make out a picture of a horse and some writing. He wiped the plaque clean, and almost heaved up his heart on the spot. In Delphian capitals, it said 'KISMET'S ROOM'.

His fearfulness returned in force. He reached out and grasped the doorknob, hesitated, then resolutely turned it and pushed at the door. As it grated on the rug of detritus behind it, from downstairs there came a sudden outburst of furious barking. He caught a glimpse of bright sunlight through the half-opened door, then, swearing to himself, turned and hurried back down the stairs.

He found Manni where he had left him; he was standing four-square in front of the porch, straining at the lead, yelling and frothing like Cerberus, his hackles standing up like *chevaux-de-frise*. The object of his fury was a shortish, rather old-looking man standing a few yards off among the trodden-down nettles. He was wearing baggy twill trousers held up with twine, a threadbare tweed jacket over a collarless shirt, and an expression of unspeak-able, spitting rage. His lean, lined face bore blooms of crimson on the weatherbeaten cheeks, and his wiry fists were clasped round the stock of an old cap-lock shotgun. However, it was less his appearance (give or take the shotgun) than Manni's reaction that alarmed Drick; if Manni feared and disliked a person, it meant there was decidedly something about them to fear and dislike. He had an infallible nose for soul-deep ill will.

'Is that your dog, sir?' the man demanded.

His manner of speech astonished Drick as much as his plainly ridiculous question. Not only was it broad Yorkshire, it was an old-fashioned, curiously abrupt Yorkshire; Drick had last heard an accent like that dressing his maternal great-grandfather's speech. Even that old man, though, hadn't gone in for that antiquated, indignant use of 'sir'.

'Yes, he is.'

'Then quiet him, sir. Ah shan't be girned at by any man's hound.'

127

Drick untied Manni's lead from the porch post and hauled him round. 'Manni!' he hissed, taking the dog's face between his hands. 'Shut up! It's okay. Quiet now.'

The dog's row subsided to a low, indignant growling. But the man wasn't in the least mollified, and he continued to address Drick at full angry pitch as though still competing with the dog's barks.

'Now tell me what business tha 'as on my property.' He glared over Drick's shoulder. 'And in my house, sir, damn tha impidence!'

'I'm sorry. I thought it was empty.'

'Empty! Aye, and if it were, does that mek it public? For any Tom, Dick or Herbert to come gawping? Shame on you, sir, shame!'

It was on the tip of Drick's tongue to say he was looking for Kismet, but thought better of it. If this man was her father (although he found that difficult to believe), then he dreaded to think how the man would react if this was how angry he got about his derelict old house being trespassed upon.

'Sorry,' he repeated. 'I mean, I didn't think it belonged to anybody. If I'd known it was your property, I wouldn't have dreamed of it.'

'Then do not dream of it now, sir!' the man roared. 'Be off, and take that dog wi' thee! If ah catch tha a second time near my house, tha'll be catchin' more buckshot nor harsh words.'

Drick didn't doubt it for a moment; without bothering to offer any more futile apologies, he reined Manni in tight and made his way towards the lane. The man didn't take his eyes off them until they were out of sight under the trees.

Drick was breathing hard and trembling slightly when he pushed his way under the curtain of hawthorn and bramble, picking its claws out of the sleeves of his sweater. He disengaged himself from the last frond and stepped out onto the road.

'Good morning, Roderick!'

Startled, he turned to see a brown-black blur of Dobermann bearing down on him, dragging behind it a round, red-faced

128

bundle of tweed, Barbour green and wild hair. Manni leapt forward to greet the Dobermann, and the two dogs fronted up in the middle of the road, checking each other over from head to tail.

'Morning, Mrs Turnbull. Hi, Frazer.'

'Frazer, calm yourself! You know Mannfred well enough, you foolish creature! I tell you, Roderick, he's had me to the brink of distraction time and again this morning. Dare we let them off, do you think?'

Drick smiled. He liked Marjorie Turnbull; they met from time to time when their walks crossed, and had got to know each other fairly well. She was in her late fifties, and had once, for a brief time in her youth, been an actress. She'd had a number of small parts in films, which Drick had looked up and enjoyed. She had been rather attractive and interesting; a sort of dangerous Sylvia Syms. Now, despite the fact that her career was three decades behind her (or perhaps because of it), she played the full-steam old actress to the hilt, like Miriam Margolyes on speed.

'I don't see why not,' he said.

The dogs' leads were unclipped, and they began chasing up and down the road, bowling each other into the hedge and scrimmaging on the verge.

'Tell me, Roderick, how are your dear children?'

Marjorie liked to refer to his novels as his children. 'Oh, very well. One of them's being published next year.'

Her mouth made a puckered 'o' and she flung her arms around him. 'Oh, Roderick, how wonderful! Haven't I always told you, talent will out? You must send me a copy, the *instant* it comes out. Tell me the title, and who is the publisher? Were you paid a shocking advance? One hears such stories of young authors these days – starving in a garret one moment, rich as Croesus the next. What is the plot? No, don't tell me – a thriller – no, a fashionable tale of erotic tragedy set against a mountainscape of breathtaking beauty bruised by war?'

Drick laughed. 'Close. More a—'

'No, you mustn't tell me, please! I shall read it – and I am sure it will be a work of genius.' She beamed at him, and he wondered if

129

he was right about speed. Miriam Margolyes on PCP, perhaps.

'Miri— I mean Marjorie. Can I ask you something?'

'Your heart's desire, my boy. Ask away.'

'The house back there . . .' He nodded at the hedge. 'Do you know anything about the man who owns it?'

If anyone could give him information it would be Marjorie; she had lived in Ely all her life, and not so much as a hedgehog could live within its bounds for more than a week without her knowing the tiniest ins and outs of its business. Professor Moriarty couldn't hold a candle to her.

She threw back her head dramatically and stared up at him with round, shocked eyes. 'Young Jack Lillystone?' she said. 'What about him?'

Lillystone! 'Young?' he asked.

Marjorie laughed. 'Not so young now, I suppose, though only older than me by the merest handful of years. His father was old Jack Lillystone, so the present Mr Lillystone has always been young Jack to me. Have you met him?'

'Briefly. Just now.'

'I see from your face it wasn't a propitious meeting. Did Manni stray onto his cabbage patch? You've been fortunate if you haven't incurred his wrath before now; you should have learned long ago to give his carriages a wide berth.'

'Sorry? His carriages?'

'Down near the bridge. You must have seen them? I assume that's where you met. You don't often see young Jack straying far from there. Frazer won't go near; he's terrified, poor brute.'

Of course. He'd thought the man seemed vaguely familiar. There was a patch of waste ground on the edge of Roswell Pits where a collection of condemned railway wagons had been parked. He had seen the man once or twice standing in the door of a box-car on the far side.

'He doesn't live in the house, then?'

'Oh no; I don't imagine anyone lives there nowadays. He moved out not long after his daughter died. You can see – look, there – that's where the gate used to be. Look how overgrown it is. I doubt if anyone has set foot in Cuckoo Farm in twenty years.'

'His daughter died?'

Marjorie looked at him sidelong, quite subdued for once, and her voice dropped to a murmur. 'There were some who said it wasn't an accident,' she said darkly. 'They say he was taken in for questioning, but he was never charged with anything. Malicious gossip, if you ask me. The Lillystones were never what you'd call popular; folk were downright scared of them, if you want the truth. I was, too; all of us local children were. My mother was the only person who was ever friendly with them. She was a young woman when old Jack first came here, back in the Twenties, and she befriended his wife, poor woman. He was from up north. Old-fashioned sort – all Chapel, hard graft and strict morals, but his wife was pleasant. Local girl. He'd spent most of his youth at sea, apparently, and lost touch with his roots. I've no idea why he chose to come to Ely, though. Attracted by its Puritan history, I imagine. Cromwell was an Ely man, you know, rot his black heart.'

Drick was confused. 'So it was old Jack's daughter who died?' He pointed vaguely at the blocked-off lane. 'That man's sister?'

'No, his daughter. Young Jack's sister, sensible creature, had more of her mother in her, and went off to live in Huntingdon the first chance she got. I played with her from time to time when we were little, because Mum encouraged me to and she had no other friends, but I only went to the house a couple of times. Her father frightened the life out of me once, and young Jack was touched in the head as far as I could see.'

'How did she die? Jack's daughter, I mean.'

Marjorie frowned. 'I don't know what went on,' she said, and caught his look. 'For once,' she added with a wry smile. 'I didn't live in Ely then. I left in 1964, when I got married. I came back ten years ago, after my dear husband died.'

Drick looked at her, but kindly kept the scepticism out of the look. She was deliberately suppressing what she knew. It wasn't like Marjorie to keep gossip that juicy to herself, and virtually impossible that she shouldn't know the details at all, whether she had been living here at the time or not.

'Well,' she said, putting her brightness back on like a cape, 'We mustn't keep you here talking all day. I'm sure you have important work to be doing. You will be sure to send me a copy of your book, won't you?'

'Of course I will.'

She smiled. 'Frazer! Come here now!'

They retrieved their dogs and reattached their leads. As they were about to go their separate ways, Drick called Marjorie back.

'By the way,' he said. 'What was this daughter called?'

'Kismet. Charming little girl, they say. Took after her mother. Fare thee well, Roderick, and damn the critics!'

Part Three

THE LILLYSTONES

Packet 7

Drick didn't believe in ghosts. Sure, he believed in his capacity to create leprechauns, goblins and double-glazing salesmen by writing in a reporter's notepad, because he had seen the evidence with his own eyes. But he didn't believe in ghosts. Paradoxically, his disbelief sprang from the same rationale: he didn't believe in them because he had once seen one.

He'd been about seventeen at the time, and doing what he spent quite a bit of time doing at that period: lying on his bed in his darkened room, staring alternately at the ceiling, the walls, the crack in the plaster between the wall and the ceiling, and the pattern of fading light leaking round the drawn curtains. The only sound was a faint mumble from the television downstairs. As twilight drew down, the corner beside the window grew darker and darker, until it seemed blacker than any natural darkness, like a rent in the fabric of space. Floating on the edge of trance, he stared into the blackness and saw, with mounting fascination, that it was beginning to assume a form, defined by a dim red glow – a faint aura. The glow grew perceptibly brighter and refined itself into the unmistakeable outline of a person standing in the corner of the room. As he stared, the black began to dissolve into granular light and shade, and the features of a face began to emerge. The face was indefinably familiar, even though at first it was very vague. As the figure became clearer, he became more and more convinced that it was someone he knew, but no more able to say who. Suddenly, his heart thumping, he lurched off the bed and sprang to his feet. The figure was almost fully formed now, but as he lunged towards it, it broke like an image in a shattered mirror and vanished.

He didn't stand there palpitating with fright (well, perhaps a little bit); he stood palpitating because now he knew for certain how ghosts worked. They were a slightly more sophisticated version of the visual effect that lets you see faces in cloud formations. He hadn't believed in ghosts before, but now he felt he had *proved* their non-existence. After all, it is one thing to talk about there being a rational explanation for everything, but to *see* the process of self-induced trance unfold was a revelation.

Therefore, he reasoned now, there had to be a rational explanation for Kismet. The two front-running candidates were that Marjorie was mistaken or that the girl he had met wasn't Kismet Lillystone. He favoured the latter, since it followed on from suspicions he'd had for some time. The girl had taken the name from the street, knew the story, and had assumed the dead Kismet's identity. The question of why she would do this he pushed aside. He also pushed aside the matter of his lost hours with her, his dry jeans, her extraordinary knowledge of him. None of this, he reckoned, would be beyond the skills of the average hypnotist or stage psychic. She wasn't a ghost, and that was that.

Given normal circumstances, Drick would have insisted on asking Marjorie Turnbull a great many more questions about Jack Lillystone and his daughter, but circumstances were anything but normal. He had a lot on his mind; besides, Marjorie seemed to have little to add to what she'd already told him. They'd met again the next day in Springhead Lane, and Drick had brought the subject up again, but either she really didn't know much about it (he found that hard to believe) or she just didn't want to talk about it (which was extremely odd). All he got was a reiteration of the same threadbare account. And so he turned the matter over in his mind, spitted on a slender knowledge and basted in a rich sauce of his own imagination. Oh, if this were a novel, he could have conjured up any number of different accounts to fit what he had seen and been told, but nothing would do but the truth.

It crossed his mind more than once that he should investigate. He thought of searching newspaper archives for information about the death, but he had no clear idea of what period he was dealing with. Some time between 1964 and the early '80s, he supposed; that was an awful lot of newspapers, and he never seemed to have the time to spare.

One of the distractions which took his mind off Kismet was that, after a year of havering and procrastinating, he had finally left Elsa. He didn't have the means to set up home on his own, so in the end he resorted to using the notepad. The notepad was the other thing which occupied his attention.

He had been reluctant to use it for anything significant until he had a better understanding of its powers and the consequences of using them. He had, for instance, been harbouring a deep anxiety about Jonathan Peachment. He had called this poor man into existence simply for the purpose of experiment, and what had become of him since? Drick hoped he was transient; that he had dematerialised as soon as his function had been fulfilled, but Drick couldn't quite convince himself that this was the case; he was out there somewhere, and in what kind of state? An unsuccessful double-glazing salesman working for an unspecified non-company. Had he, after failing to sell his windows to Elsa, gone back to his office to find that it wasn't there; indeed, had never been there? Was he now living on the streets, unemployed and homeless, with nothing but his portfolio and a record of unremitting failure to support him? If so, it was surely Drick's responsibility to do something about it. But what could he do? Annihilate him? He didn't know if it was possible to wipe a human being from existence once created; okay, he had done it to the goblin, but now he wondered if annihilation might not result in the victim being sent to some awful netherworld. (He had started thinking in terms of some bizarre concepts recently in an effort to set this phenomenon in some kind of comprehensible framework.) Perhaps he could kill him in some humane manner. In the end, he used the notepad to send the unfortunate man a couple of thousand pounds (in cash, stuffed into a carrier bag which he would find '*suddenly at his feet as he walked along the pavement*'), and repeated the gift at intervals whenever he remembered.

As for his own life, he was more hesitant. Of course, he imagined all kinds of favours he could do himself, ranging from fame and fortune to an extra inch in height, but didn't do any of them. Leaving Elsa, though, was a more pressing concern, so he set about, with tremendous care, making it happen. The central requirement was accommodation he could afford. He didn't have the nerve to enrich himself just yet, nor create himself a house (the Monkey's Paw still exerting its influence). He heard on the grapevine of a little Georgian cottage in New Barns Road which was being renovated and would be ready to let in mid-October. He made inquiries, and began insinuating himself into it.

The owner was a Mrs Lynn, a middle-aged widow of independent means who lived in Cambridge. When Drick contacted her and told her something about himself, she was only too delighted to let the cottage to him. She had recently developed (just in the past couple of weeks, in fact) a passion for literature, and a fascination with authors – novelists in particular – which would make Marjorie Turnbull look almost indifferent. Such was her enthusiasm for all things literary that, to have an actual novelist as her tenant, she was willing to offer the cottage for the ridiculous peppercorn rent of one pound a month. She could easily afford to do this, since a letter from her accountant the previous week had informed her that she had considerably more assets than had been thought, a turn of events for which the accountant – contrary to his calling – was quite unable to account.

Drick moved in on 21 November 1993. His entire worldly goods barely filled the boot of the taxi which took him to his new home. Elsa succumbed to grief as he packed his things, and begged him to stay. Her show of emotion had more to do with form than feeling, however, and lasted all of ten minutes; she just couldn't keep it up, and in the end she waved him off dry-eyed.

He and Manni inspected their new accommodation appreciatively, admiring the exquisitely tasteful furnishing and establishing which items could be shared and which Manni was forbidden to touch. (Mrs Lynn simply *adored* dogs, even though, strangely enough, she had never owned one herself, and so was happy for Drick to have Manni in the house.)

Another factor which weighed on Drick's mind – or should in all conscience have weighed – was the revision of the manuscript of *The Island*. After a couple more discussions, he had acceded to some of Nick Lovell's less drastic suggestions for improving the text. 'Less drastic' was how Lovell saw them; Drick still thought they were fucking outrageous. He only acquiesced because he had been harbouring a growing feeling lately that something – something profound but indefinable – was wrong with the novel. He was sure it had nothing to do with anything Nick Lovell had identified, but it couldn't harm to be directed (a little) for once in his life. He had promised a revised manuscript by the middle of January, but as November wore on, December came and went, and January leapt out at him like a mugger, as he spent hours gazing at his printed words, he simply couldn't see any way to improve them. He cut, juggled, amended and excised repeatedly, but always seemed to wend his way back to the original. In the end, he set it aside and just worried about it in a vague, abstracted, totally unproductive sort of way, like a tax return (something he knew nothing about at that time). As if that weren't enough, there was the blasted title. 'The Island' wasn't good enough apparently, and could he think up something more, well, *grabbing*? Grabbing bollocks; he had never had much time for titles. Window-dressing; it was the content that mattered. Another worry to nibble away at him in the dark.

In the meantime he devoted himself to the notepad. Studying the phenomenon naturally involved making it perform, and so he spent a great deal of time thinking up ways of doing so harmlessly, and while he thought and planned, he practised the techniques of doing very very small writing.

He found that, by using a Rotring drawing pen with a .1 nib and a magnifying glass, he could produce a continuous script less than two millimetres high which was perfectly legible. Using this technique, he calculated that he could cram over a hundred and fifty thousand words into the notepad; not to mention totally ruin his eyesight and suffer joint-strain and innumerable headaches into the bargain. The ideal solution would be to find some way of printing onto the paper (assuming printing would work). His inkjet printer could produce perfectly legible type at least as small as his Rotring handwriting, but it would only take loose sheets; since he had established that removing leaves from the notepad rendered them inert, this idea was useless . . . Unless, of course, he could create a printer for himself which could print onto the intact pad. He was good with technical things, so he made some sketches of the required mechanics, imagined the machine as vividly as possible, in as much detail as possible, and then wrote it into existence.

It worked perfectly. Instead of a roller-feeder mechanism it had a moving tray below the cartridge into which the notepad would fit. He tested it with an ordinary reporter's notebook, and was delighted by the results. It produced minute lettering with a breathtaking crispness. And when he tried it on the magic notepad (writing himself a silver ring to go with his gold one), it worked exactly as it had with handwriting. Using this, he might be able to get up to four hundred thousand words before the pad was exhausted. That was equivalent to three novels, almost.

Having resolved the mechanical problems, the rather large issue then remained of precisely what fabulous deeds to spend those precious words on. In theory, he should be able to enrich and improve himself and still have enough space left over to make the world a fine, just and equitable place. The first thing to do, though, was to thoroughly explore the possibilities. This might seem an unbelievably dull and pedestrian way to deal with such an exciting toy, but it wasn't. Drick had learned long ago (although he wasn't sure how) that some things in life should be leapt into with abandon, while others should be approached with care; the mistake most people made was having one or other approach hard-wired into their personalities. They missed either the exhilaration of the leap or the infinitely greater profit yielded by careful consideration of the more complex opportunities in life.

To that end, he took out the list of questions he had noted

140

down after his first tentative experiments, and reconsidered them in the light of his experiences.

- ○ *Are the effects of what I create (or change) truly permanent?* There was no way of answering this; only time would tell.
- ○ *Is it always instantaneous and immediate, or can I manipulate things in the past or the future?* He had proved that the event brought about could be displaced in time from the act of writing: into the future (finding the way into Cuckoo Farm) or into the past (Mrs Lynn's love of dogs and literature).
- ○ *Are there limits to what I can do? Could I destroy the universe? Or create a new one?* He had already noted *a priori* that this was immaterial, since he himself (and his notepad) would be destroyed in the first case, and he would be unable to observe the second. However, the question of limits was relevant.
- ○ *Could I, then, bring about the creation or destruction of, say, a human being?* The case of Jonathan Peachment suggested he could, but he didn't know whether he was a permanent or temporary entity. The issue of permanence again, and again only time would tell.
- ○ *Could I change my own life? Make myself rich and successful or better-looking and more charming and intelligent?* (Or at a pinch make the world a finer, juster etc. etc.) He had changed the course of his life in a small way by providing himself with a rented house, but as for *changing himself*, he still didn't know.
- ○ *Can I change other people's personalities?* No. He had changed his landlady's tastes, but that wasn't the same thing. His attempts to make Elsa a better, brighter person had failed utterly.

After some thought, he added a supplementary note at the bottom of the page:

- ○ *I seem to retain a memory of what things were like before I changed them (e.g. Mrs R's previous indifference to me and suspicion of dogs; the railway carriage before I redesigned its occupants etc.). Do other people? Or do the objects and circumstances I create seem to them to have always been so? It seems they must, or I ought to have seen some evidence to the contrary (e.g. stark staring schizophrenic behaviour in the people I've affected).*

There are limits, of course, to how much thought even the most difficult proposition can tolerably be given. He toyed around with his questions for so long that even he began to get annoyed with himself. If he had been having these discussions with another person rather than inside his own head, he would have been slapped across the face weeks ago. Contemplation has its place, but there comes a time when you have to shit or get off the pot. There was a fine line, he realised, between caution and being a dithering little ponce. So you might fuck up your head and make a mess of the world, he told himself – are either in such good condition they'll notice a bit more damage?

To prove himself a man of action, he phoned Jeremy and arranged to meet him in Cambridge for a drink. In preparation, he spent half an hour washing his hair and shaving, then twenty seconds changing his eyes from brown to blue, smoothing out the crooked tip of his nose and turning his newly washed hair a darker, richer shade of brown, adding a raffish curl to complement his improved looks. Jeremy had known him since childhood; if he noticed none of these changes, then the last question on his list would have been definitively answered. He wrote a few more sentences, then left the house.

When he stepped out of his front door, he was delighted to find a gleaming new Toyota Landcruiser waiting for him, in exactly the shade of crimson he had described. (He had considered making it an E-Type, but rejected it as too conspicuous – besides, it wouldn't have room for a dog.) He blipped the locks off with the keys he found in his trouser pocket, opened the hatch and let Manni bound inside. With a sense of immense satisfaction, he slid into the driving seat and switched on the ignition. The deep growl of the engine hinted at something with a little more bite than the manufacturer's specification. And there was a

142

full tank of petrol on board. Nice touch. He eased down the accelerator and smiled as the car kicked the grit of New Barns Road from its heels.

They met at eight in the Old Spring, which was just round the corner from Jeremy's flat and allowed dogs in. Drick parked the Landcruiser discreetly a few streets away to avoid awkward questions about how he had come by it. Jeremy was waiting for him when he arrived, sitting at a table in a gloomy corner of the dimly lit bar. He had a Coke in front of him and a pint of Adnam's for Drick.

'And a merry evening to you too, you old bastard,' said Drick, sitting down and swigging his beer gratefully. 'How's life treating you?'

He watched for a reaction to his altered appearance; even in this low light his curly hair and new nose ought to be obvious.

Jeremy smiled and stroked Manni's head. 'Not so bad,' he said. 'I'm writing up.'

'You're not still at that damned tome, surely? I thought you'd have finished ages ago.'

Jeremy frowned at him. 'I think you've been away less time than you think. If I get written up and submit by May I'll have set a department record; nobody's submitted in under three years in living memory.'

Drick stroked his nose thoughtfully (appreciating its improved shape as he did so). 'Honestly? It seems such a long time ago.'

'It's just over a year. Don't you remember the last Club meeting?'

'Well, of course.' Drick grinned. 'How could I forget? A famous victory, that was. I never got all the drinks I was owed, either.'

'So, how's life as an author?'

'Oh, good, good.' Drick leaned forward, resting his elbows on the table. 'Jeremy, mate. Listen, this might sound like a funny question, but d'you notice anything different about me?'

Jeremy peered at him. 'You've had a nose job,' he said.

'What?' He put a hand up to his nose in alarm, then realised Jeremy was grinning.

'I don't know. What's different about you? You seem a lot more cheerful than last time I saw you. Life without Elsa must suit you.'

'It does. Look, honestly now, can you see anything different about me, physically?'

Jeremy made the peculiar grimace he always put on to show he was considering carefully. 'No,' he said eventually. 'Why? Should I?'

'No.' Drick laughed, overcome by a sudden rush of euphoria. 'No,' he repeated when the laughter had subsided. 'I had a little crisis of identity for a moment there, that's all.'

'Crisis of identity. Yeah, right. Anyway, tell me what it's like to have your talents recognised at last, because bugger a smell of that can I get in my neck of the woods, I can tell you.'

'Oh, fantastic, just as you'd imagine. You walk on air for about two weeks, and then get used to it. Suddenly, just being appreciated doesn't seem enough.'

'You want money as well.'

'Dead right. But there's other stuff as well.'

Telling Jeremy about the trouble he was having with *The Island* brought back just how big his problems were. He wasn't at all happy with the novel. Something really important was missing from it. It wouldn't have been so bad if he'd been able to grasp what it was. Whatever it needed, it was more than some editorial tweezing. He was having profound regrets about having borne the market in mind as he wrote it; it had evidently made him take his eye off the ball.

Having begun the conversation, he now tried to steer it away from his novel, but this was easier desired than done. The only other subjects on his mind – his notepad and Kismet – were no more comfortable; the one would make his friend think he'd marinated his brain in acid once and for all, while the other . . . well, it would do all that and was too personal as well, even to discuss with his oldest friend. Instead, he hedged around the issue, hinting that he had recently come to view life in, shall we say, a different light; been made aware of the importance of

144

creating your own opportunities. In a roundabout way, he gave Jeremy to understand that this new outlook was loosely connected with his career as a writer, and wasn't entirely separate from somebody he'd met.

Jeremy wasn't used to this vague, allusive way of talking; usually when Drick had something to say he said it straight, without regard to feelings – his own or anybody else's.

'You've met another woman,' he said.

'I didn't say it was a woman.'

'You didn't need to. No man's ever had much of an influence on you. Was this before or after you left Elsa?'

'Before. She wasn't the reason I left, though.'

'And are you sleeping with her?'

Drick shook his head.

'She must be something special, then.'

'She was. Is. I've never met anyone remotely like her.'

'What's her name?'

Drick hesitated. 'Look, let's not talk about her, eh?' And he smiled. 'Lady's name in the mess, what? Anyway, what are we thinking of – you haven't given me any good gossip about the old Department. I'm sure I must've missed out on all sorts of bitching and backbiting this past year. Bring me up to date.'

During the week after his evening with Jeremy, Drick began sorting out the nuts, bolts and rivets of his life. In the short term at least, this distracted him from the fact that the superstructure was still breached and torn and flapping in the wind.

Deciding that it was safest not to make himself rich (he still felt a nagging anxiety about the buffer of assets he had bestowed on his landlady – what if she got into trouble with the Inland Revenue or Customs and Excise, or whatever organisation it was that would come round and drag your toenails out with hot pliers if they found out you had more money than you claimed?) he simply sidestepped the need for money. He could just create anything he needed. He discovered by experiment that, without wasting too many pages, he could re-enact events which would, in the real world, normally be repeated; to do this, he simply had to write the thing in the notepad, then overwrite it whenever he wanted it to happen again. This involved some sacrifice of space, since it had to be done by hand in normal-size letters. But by using his Rotring pen and displacing the letters very slightly each time he overwrote them, he found he could get up to a dozen or more repeats before the paper was saturated and began to break up, forcing him onto a fresh patch. He set aside two whole pages for the purpose, and provided himself with food to fill his fridge and cupboards once a week (this didn't take up much notepad space, since he only had to call into existence 'the ingredients for all his favourite meals'); the car was topped up with petrol once a fortnight; and he could get himself clothes as and when he needed them. The only time money was required was to pay his bills, and he covered these by depositing modest, unobtrusive sums in his bank account once a month.

This sort of conservative parsimony didn't come naturally to him. Just like anybody else, he dreamed of colossal mansions, luxury yachts, private jets and guitar-shaped swimming pools. He discovered, though, that it is one thing to dream of fabulous wealth, quite another to enact it. It wasn't want of imagination; rather a surfeit of it. He could imagine all too well the multitude of things that could go wrong. With hindsight, his first notepad adventure had probably shaken him more badly than he had thought.

And so he sorted himself out very satisfactorily without drawing any attention to what was going on. But however securely he tightened up the nuts and bolts and hammered down the rivets, he couldn't ignore the big things. He tried unsuccessfully to improve *The Island* by miraculous means, describing himself waking one morning to find that the manuscript had improved immeasurably. When he read it, though, he found it unchanged; despite a weird feeling of well-being as he pored over words he had only found disquieting the previous day, he knew it wouldn't do. This was perfectly logical when he thought about it, and provided him with another lesson in the workings of the notepad. He could only use it to change things without specifying details of the alterations if they were vivid in his imagination at the time of

146

writing; as in the case of the Russian girl on the train, for example. His Russian adventure bore close examination, in fact; there were some important lessons there on the power to go beyond the written word. Aside from the question of imagining more than was stated, it seemed that, once the situation set in motion had developed its own dynamic force, it could produce details which were far beyond his knowledge and therefore his imagination. Evidence for this included the cyrillic print he had seen and the geography and architecture of Leningrad and its station, none of which he had the slightest previous familiarity with. He had since looked up photographs of the city, and there was no doubting that it was the real, actual Leningrad he had visited (the real, actual Leningrad of nearly half a century ago, moreover), not some figment created out of his imagination.

In summary, then, he could travel spatially and temporally, and create things out of thin air (and send them back to oblivion), but could do none of these if the intended product was not present in either reality or his imagination. And since, as far as *The Island* was concerned, his mind was a blank, the result was: no change at all. Only that odd but totally transparent sensation of satisfaction. Other things being equal, that alone would have been sufficient to banish his anxieties, but he was immune to the amnesiac effect his interventions had on other people, and so he remembered perfectly his feelings as they had been before, and now they returned in force.

An interesting and unexpected by-blow of the attempt, though, was that towards the end of the week Nick Lovell phoned to say that he had re-read the manuscript and decided that every one of his previous criticisms had, on reflection, been unfounded; nothing needed changing, and he was therefore all the more impatient to receive the final draft. Drick said no, absolutely not, he was utterly convinced that Nick had been right the first time, and could he have just a little more time? He was also considering some ideas for alternative titles. Just another week or two, honestly. Nick said very well, but it must be in by the end of January at the very latest.

As he put the phone down, Drick felt despair creep into his

soul. The book's faults were incurable, and he was now firmly convinced that its publication in its present form would be a blow to his self-esteem from which he would never recover. He imagined people pointing him out in the street and hooting with derisive laughter. Of course, he could always use the notepad to make people like the book, but *he* would always know that he had got success through trickery, and he wasn't having that, not after so much effort. He needed a miracle, but not one like that. A natural miracle, he thought, whatever that might be.

Two weeks later, when the deadline was up and he was on the verge of asking Lovell to send the manuscript back and forget about the contract, he got his miracle at last.

Nestled amongst the warren of lanes and alleyways which lay between The Vineyards and Springhead Lane was a cluster of little green-roofed single-storey prefabs which had been erected just after the Second World War to house migrant workers bombed out of the cities. Originally there had been a small estate of them on the hillside above Lisle Lane, with open views of the meadows, woods and river; but now only three remained, hemmed in on all sides by the patchwork of flats and retirement bungalows stitched together at random during the 1960s and '70s.

Drick found the prefabs with some difficulty; they were reached by a narrow muddy track which led inconspicuously off Vineyard Way and wound along between two rows of bungalow gardens. Two of the prefabs were in a sorry state of repair, but the third looked as whole and clean as when it had first been hauled into place. Its concrete slab walls were painted a fresh cream, its steel window frames were crisp white, and the little patch of front lawn was smooth as baize and bordered by immaculate shrubs. This was the house he had been told to look for. He walked up the path and pressed the doorbell.

Earlier that morning, he had bumped into Marjorie Turnbull again.

Perhaps because of his state of mind over the novel (i.e. his willingness to be distracted from it), he had been thinking about

Kismet more and more. He had tried to use the notepad to miraculously learn the truth about her, but had experienced his second complete failure. (It was starting to seem like the demo version of some mega piece of software: he kept expecting a dialogue box to pop up, saying *That function has been disabled. To get the full functionality of Literary Omnipotence, buy the retail version from OmniBook Inc.*)

He was still puzzled by much of what Marjorie had told him the last time they met, and he asked her some more questions about the Lillystone family. Again, all she did was repeat the story she'd told him twice before – vague and full of gaping holes. Also, there were too many contradictions and confusions for his liking: such as the blurred generations of this strange family – Kismet, her mother, old Jack's wife – he had trouble teasing them apart and making three separate women from the singular image he held in his mind; then there was the 'death' of Kismet.

'You're most gluttonously interested in them, young Roderick,' said Marjorie. 'Not thinking of making them the subject of one of your novels, are you?' She accompanied this with a coquettish little giggle which had probably made casting directors burst their fly buttons thirty or forty years ago, but now made her seem rather sadly comical. Oddly, it was this rift between what she had been and what age had wrought of her that stimulated Drick's fondness. In his imaginings, he had created all manner of ways in which she might be pressed into service as a character; there was no way he could have invented her, and she was too good to waste.

'Well, perhaps,' he said. 'Call it native curiosity.'

She couldn't (or wouldn't – he wasn't sure) tell him any more; most of the interesting part of the story had happened while she was living in Surrey. 'There is a person you might talk to, though. Old Finn Bourn.'

'Finborn?'

'Finn. Bourn. Two names, Roderick. He worked for Jack Lillystone for upwards of forty years.'

'Which one?'

'Which Jack Lillystone, you mean? Oh, both of them. The

father first, then the son when he took over the business.'

'What was the business?'

'Well, all sorts, really. Ostensibly they were farmers, but old Jack made his money in other streets than agriculture. A little property here, a bit of scrap dealing there, some building. Young Jack dispensed with most of the allsorts and concentrated on the building side. He was never what you'd call a rich man, but he did well enough.'

'And this . . . what was it? Finn?'

'Finn Bourn. He's a distant relation of mine. My mother's second cousin once removed, I believe. Does that make him my second cousin twice removed? I've never been clear about removals. Are they a generation or a sibling thing?'

'Generation, I think.'

'Twice removed, then . . . Where was I?'

'Finn Bourn.'

'Of course. He's a joiner. Was a joiner, I should say; retired long ago. He's in his eighties.'

'Would he talk to me, do you think?'

Marjorie threw back her head and guffawed. 'I should say so! Until you can't take any more. I can't imagine how he ever got on so well with the Lillystones; they were always a taciturn bunch. Finn could talk the hind legs off a whole herd of donkeys, but he doesn't get much chance nowadays. He doesn't get out as much as he used to. I drop by from time to time to see he's still breathing, when I can get someone to look after Frazer. If there's one thing Finn doesn't like, it's dogs. I could leave Frazer at home if a visit to Finn didn't take so confoundedly long. He gossips so much, I might pop in in the morning for a cup of tea and not be home by dinner time.'

Marjorie must have noticed the look Drick gave Manni. 'Don't worry about him,' she said. 'I'll look after him, if you like.'

'Would you?'

'To be sure. He's adorable, and no trouble I'll be bound. Aren't you, sweetie? See? He and Frazer can play to their hearts' content.'

'When do you think would be a good time to go?'

150

'Well, he goes out on Wednesdays to pick up his pension, and Thursdays he goes to the market. What's today?'

'Friday.' (A sudden sinking in his guts as he said it – Monday was the deadline for *The Island*.)

Marjorie beamed. 'Well, Roderick, there's no time like the present, is there? I could take Manni home with me now. Come and collect him when you've finished.'

She gave him directions to Finn Bourn's house ('a prefab off Vineyard Way, you can't miss it,' she said, not mentioning the maze of bungalows surrounding it on all sides). She took both leads in one hand and left Drick watching a little disconsolately as Manni was led away in tandem with Frazer, tail wagging and without a single backward glance at his master. He was so preoccupied with the dog's display of doubtful loyalty that Marjorie was almost out of earshot when he realised that something else was nagging at him; something obvious.

'Hang on!' he yelled. 'I don't know where you live!'

The face that appeared in the crack above the security chain wasn't quite what he had expected; it certainly didn't look garrulous. He had pictured an old Cheeryble, deeply lined and jowled but still with rosy cheeks and a red nose and merry, twinkling eyes. Instead, the eyes that peered at him past the part-opened door were cloudy and grey, and the face was long and harrowed, with pallid skin the colour and texture of melted wax.

'Hnh?' said the cadaverous apparition.

'Mr Bourn?' said Drick.

'Ar, that's me.' Like his face, his voice was thin and colourless, worn threadbare by age. 'Selling something, are yer?'

Drick chuckled good-naturedly. 'No, Mr Bourn. You wouldn't buy it if I were, would you?'

The eyes narrowed. 'Depends what it is, youngster. What 'ave yer got?'

'Nothing, Mr Bourn. Only this.' He held up the bottle of brandy Marjorie had suggested he bring. The old eyes suddenly lit up; or rather, they cleared slightly and widened under their drooping lids. 'And I'm not selling it,' he added. 'It's a gift. I'm a friend of Marjorie Turnbull. My name's Roderick. She suggested I drop by.'

'Oh, 'er,' the old man muttered. 'Well, yer'd best come in, then.' He released the chain and opened the door wide, letting out an odour of stale pipe smoke and disinfectant. 'Friend of Marjorie's are yer? I 'ope yer don't talk as much as she done. Once she gets 'er fat backside in that chair, it'd take a team o' drays to get 'er shifted afore dinner time.' He chuckled, and the sound was like feet scuffing through dead leaves on a wet day. 'Nivver misses a dinner, that 'un, I'll bet.'

Never taking his eyes off the bottle of brandy, he led Drick into a small, surprisingly bright living room which, despite the fact that it clearly hadn't seen a new stick of furniture since the late 1940s, was in a better state of cleanliness and repair than many a more modern home. It was like a museum reconstruction of post-war mod cons. There were two narrow, high-armed easy chairs facing each other in front of an antique gas fire (which was burning at full gasp and filling the room with a thick, almost unbreathable heat), a neat little utility drop-leaf dining table and an imitation Deco sideboard on which stood a matching monolithic wireless. The old man listened for a few seconds to the cricket commentary oozing out of the cabinet with vacuum-valve warmth, then switched it off and waved Drick to an armchair. He took the brandy bottle, poured out a measure each and lowered himself painfully into the other chair. There was a pipe smouldering in an ashtray on a stand beside the chair, and he picked it up and puffed it back to life before speaking.

'Friend o' young Madge's, then, are yer?'

Drick smiled in what he imagined was a fond manner. 'Yes,' he said. 'She said she would've come herself,' he lied, trying to create a plausibly innocuous reason for his call. 'She's busy, though.'

'Well thank Gawd she din't. Busy 'bout other folks' business, I don' doubt.' He sipped his brandy, puffed his pipe, and fixed Drick with a querulous look. 'So, are you goin'er tell me 'bout 'ow they'm doin' up Market Square an' Mrs Wilson's baby an' all that

152

other business what I either knows 'bout already or don' want ter know 'bout?'

'No, Mr Bourn. In fact, it's you wh—'

'There ain't no need ter "Mr Bourn" me, youngster. I ain't nivver bin Mr Bourn to no man. "Finn" is my given name, and it'll do fine.'

'That's very egalitarian of you,' said Drick with a smile. 'My given name is Roderick, not "youngster".'

The old man grinned. 'Mouthy young snip, ain't yer? So, if you ain't 'ere to bend my lugs on Madge's be'alf, what can I do for yer, young Roderick?'

Drick explained that he was a writer in search of material. He led the old man to understand that, while he wasn't after specific stories, one could never have enough of what he chose to call 'background'. Marjorie had recommended old Finn as a rich source of knowledge about Ely 'in the old days'.

'You know,' he concluded. 'The real stuff, as opposed to what you can read about in books. How people really used to live, and so on.'

'So you wan' *me* ter talk, an' you ter listen? Well, there's a turn-up.' He rubbed a sallow cheek with the stem of his pipe. 'I don' know as there'm be much I could tell yer, though.'

Drick prompted him: 'Marjorie told me you used to work for the Lillystone family.'

'Jack Lillystone, yer mean? Ar, that I done. Forty-sivven year I worked for 'im an' 'is son arter.'

'What work did you do?'

'Well, I started out as a joiner. Least, that were my trade. I was 'prenticed to Thurloe's out in Littleport when I were a nipper, an' I were a good 'un. That was when joinery was joinery – not like now, when common chippies call 'emselves joiners. Back then, if you was a carpenter you was a carpenter, but if you was a joiner, why that was somethin' special.'

'What was the difference?'

'What were the difference? Why, a whole world o' skill, boy. See, when a house got built, the carpenters laid down the joists an' rafters an' wall studs an' the stair strings an' the like, then when they was finished, the joiners come in an' finished off, like. Did all the fine work as you sees on show. Balusters, newel posts, treads an' risers, windows an' doors. The skilled bits, see.'

'And you worked as a joiner for Jack Lillystone?'

The old man grunted. 'Ar, at first.'

'Who was he, exactly?'

'He were what we use' ter call an outcomeling. Come from up north when I were still a 'prentice. That'd be goin' back, oh, 'bout seventy year ago . . .'

Over the next two hours, old Finn proved himself, to Drick's great satisfaction, every bit as much of a talker as Marjorie had promised. He stopped and started a great deal, performing sudden U-turns so that he could fill in some inconsequential detail which he seemed to think essential to his narrative, making huge leaps forward to draw comparisons with how things had declined nowadays, and sometimes forgetting where he was altogether. But with numerous refills of pipe and brandy glass, he eventually gave Drick enough information to piece together an outline of the Lillystones' story.

Jack Lillystone arrived in Ely in 1922. From the start he established a reputation as a dour, uncommunicative, even intimidating
man, and so very little was ever known of his background. It was
believed that he came from an ancient family of Yorkshire
landowners. Rumour had it that he had quarrelled with most of
his relatives as a very young man (over land, money or marriage,
depending on which version of the rumour you listened to; some
of the more fanciful gossips even said he had murdered his own
brother) and had run away to sea to escape the consequences. He
had served as an engineering officer in the Royal Navy during the
First World War, and had seen action at the Battle of Jutland,
where he received the wound which caused his lifelong pro-
nounced limp.

Shortly after the War, he retired from the Navy and lived briefly
in Cambridge before settling in Ely. Using funds saved during his
naval service, he bought a stretch of marshland near the Roswell
claypits and set about draining it. The land, dried out and fertile,
quadrupled in value, and he used the proceeds from the sale of
two dozen acres to build Cuckoo Farm and buy more reclaimable
land. He did business briskly and without ceremony, and
impressed local tradesmen and landowners with his acumen and
his insistence on payment in cash on the nail (even when he was
the buyer). In fact, he did more than impress them; he terrified
the life out of them, and not one of them would have dared
overcharge, bilk or undercut him. There was one story of a
neighbour who tried to regain at an advantageous price some
acres he had sold to Jack for drainage. A dispute developed which

culminated in Jack horsewhipping the man half to death in Ely Market. He dared the magistrates to touch him for it, and of course they didn't. They were all townsmen and maybe thought they'd get a dose of the same treatment.

His business interests expanded rapidly, moving into boatbuilding and scrap dealing as well as land development. Most especially he took up housebuilding, where his talents for land and manufacture could be combined. His workmen were mostly hired by the day, but a small handful were employed on a permanent basis. One of these was the nineteen-year-old Finn Bourn, a newly time-served joiner, who was taken on in 1928 to work on a row of houses Lillystone's were building on Prickwillow Road. He was a good joiner – one of the very best – and a bright boy, too. Jack Lillystone recognised his potential, and promoted him rapidly within the firm. This was most unusual; Jack was by nature suspicious and hostile, and the kindness – fondness you might almost say – he showed the boy was the subject of many uncharitable remarks (though never within Jack's earshot). By the time he was twenty-three Finn was assistant clerk (which was not really a clerical post – more a sort of gaffer-extraordinary) and therefore only third in line of authority after Mr Lillystone himself.

In 1931, Finn's responsibilities increased even more, since at the age of forty-nine, Jack Lillystone finally decided to get married and had to devote a certain amount of time to finding a bride. He settled on Georgina Goodison, the eighteen-year-old daughter of one of that select and ever-diminishing band of neighbours with whom he hadn't quarrelled. Mr Goodison's interview with his prospective son-in-law must have been something to see; rarely can the conventional roles of scowling parent and diffident, eager-to-please suitor have been so firmly reversed. Georgina was willing (she was widely regarded as a bit of a simple creature), and so they were married at Christmas in the Methodist chapel off Lynn Road. (Georgina's father would have preferred the Cathedral or St Mary's Church, but Jack Lillystone's religious convictions prevailed.)

Contrary to what you might expect from a man of such fiery

156

temper, he was an entirely blameless husband. He never beat Georgina, nor even raised his voice to her, even though she tried him sorely with her airy-fairy ways. She loved to paint and read books of poetry and press wild flowers, and showed no sign of any housewifely skills. Far from losing patience with her, Jack employed a housekeeper and let his young wife pursue her idle passions. On that evidence alone, people might have been inclined to think that marriage had softened him, but it hadn't; with everyone other than Georgina he was as much the iron-fist, nose-to-the-grindstone, don't-give-me-any-of-your-nonsense-if-you-don't-want-a-bloody-nose tyrant as ever.

In 1932, Georgina presented him with a son, named Jack after his father, and in 1935 a daughter, Liza. Tragically, Liza's birth killed her mother. According to the story leaked by Mrs Andrews, the midwife, Georgina didn't even survive labour; Dr Cardew had had to cut baby Liza from her mother's dead body.

If Jack grieved at all, he didn't show it. He doted on his daughter, in whom he saw Georgina born again, but he was harsher on the son; cruelly harsh, in many ways. Since young Jack was struck from the same mould as his father, and his father could see it as clearly as he could see Georgina in his daughter, a modern mind might have attributed motives to his stern treatment of the son; but this was the 1930s, and self-loathing hadn't been invented.

As the children grew, so the family withdrew into itself. Jack acquired an office on Fore Hill and a yard on Broad Street, and transferred all his business administration there. Finn – who was now chief clerk and had a family of his own – no longer had an office and quarters in the stable block at Cuckoo Farm, and he and other employees rarely had reason to call there. Social visitors had never been encouraged, and so the Lillystones grew apart from the local community. Liza and young Jack were kept from school; their father held the view that anything he couldn't teach them at home would be of no use to them in life, and he wanted to shield them from the corrupting influence of schoolteachers, whom he regarded as a collection of underemployed busybodies who were simply too idle or too stupid to shift for themselves, and so must be forever trying to foist their worthless book-learned ways on other folks' children.

Georgina, it was believed, would have liked her son and daughter to have playmates other than each other (if only to show Liza that not all boys were bullies like her brother), but none would come to Cuckoo Farm. Alice Turnbull, who had been a lifelong friend of Georgina, tried to encourage her own daughter, Marjorie, to play with the Lillystone children, but her efforts were largely in vain. Little Marjorie got on well with Liza, but was too scared of her father and brother to go near the farm.

Finn Bourn never paid all that much attention to the children, but he was never quite convinced that the local view of them as poor, lonely, unhappy little souls was very accurate. They always seemed contented enough to him. Certainly the boy was forever chasing little Liza, pulling her hair and trying to muddy her dress, but what little boys didn't treat girls that way? And Liza seemed devoted to her brother in a way Georgina had never been to their father. If local people didn't understand the family, that was their problem, not the family's.

Finn only became closely involved with family affairs once. In 1942, Jack commissioned him to build a model ship for his son's tenth birthday. Young Jack, influenced by his father, had developed a passion for all things nautical, and was especially fascinated by the sailing men-of-war of the Napoleonic era. With a childish devotion (which he maintained from infancy through to adulthood), he worshipped Lord Nelson, and took to refighting his battles with paper ships, spending hours crouching on the muddy bank of the Great Ouse, pushing the little folded newspaper vessels around on the sluggish water. His father was pleased by this interest, and young Jack found himself the focus of paternal warmth for the first time in his life.

The model, for which Jack paid Finn fifty pounds, was to be built in wood to a scale of one in forty-eight. The subject was to be Nelson's flagship, the *Victory*. He provided Finn with reference material to work from, and a supply of oak and deal. He also gave his chief clerk as much time off work as would be necessary to complete the model. This was important, since Finn's evenings were no longer his own. On the outbreak of war, he had been rejected by the Services because of his leg (it had been left partially crippled by a childhood bout of polio). Instead he joined the Home Guard, and was placed on the duty rota for manning the pillbox on Ely Common. Each evening, he sat on a stool in the damp brick box, shaping sections of deal with sandpaper and a sharp knife, glancing through the slit from time to time to check that no Germans were making their way down Prickwillow Road.

The model *Victory* was finished in time for young Jack's birthday in October, and it was a sight to behold; the finest piece of woodworking, Finn maintained, that he ever did in his life. It had opening gun hatches, swivelling yard-arms and working pulleys, with rigging made from silk yarn, and linen sails stitched by Mrs Bourn. Finn also made a plinth for it to stand on. Though the model took pride of place on the mantelpiece in the family parlour, it was recognised as the exclusive property of young Jack, and he was allowed to move it to the dining-room table and play with it there whenever he pleased, so long as one of his parents was around to supervise. His reaction when it was first presented to him on his birthday needs no description; sufficient to say that it remained forever his most prized possession, possibly more valuable even than his own life.

Perhaps there was a conscious effort – in gratitude for that one access of paternal affection, maybe – to become like his father as he grew older. Finn wasn't sure about this; he suspected that no deliberate effort was required – young Jack was his father all over again in his blood, and that was that. Whatever, as the two children grew towards adulthood, they became so like their parents in looks, manner, character, and even in the way they regarded each other, that they were for all the world like husband and wife in miniature. Perhaps not surprising, since they had no other example to follow.

In 1953, Liza – seventeen years old now, and pretty as a picture – went away. Or was sent. Neither of the children – even though young Jack was a man of twenty-one now – had ever left Ely in their lives. Finn, who called at the farm to deliver the monthly accounts to Mr Lillystone on the day Liza left, got the very strong impression that something was wrong – like thunder in the air, he thought, but of course he didn't inquire; just got the accounts countersigned and made his exit quickly and quietly. A few days later, Colin Pickett, a part-time labourer for Lillystone's, was found beaten insensible in an alley behind the Three Blackbirds in Broad Street. Finn believed that young Jack Lillystone was responsible: he had noticed Colin hanging about near Cuckoo Farm in the weeks leading up to Liza's leaving, and had once witnessed her brother sending him about his business in an extremely threatening manner. Clearly there was some kind of frustrated courtship going on there, but Finn never found out any of the details. Colin moved to Cambridge and was never seen in Ely again.

About eight months after Liza had left, young Jack went away too; again, Finn had no idea where. Within a week, Liza returned, and Finn imagined that Jack must have been sent to bring her back. But if that was the case, he didn't accompany her; in fact, he didn't show his face at Cuckoo Farm for ten whole years.

When he did return, in 1964, he looked very much older, having aged more than he should have in that time. His hair was greying, and there was a worn, wiry look about him – like dry, age-hardened timber – so that he resembled his father more than ever. He gave no explanation for his absence – at least none that Finn ever heard about – and his father accepted him back with uncharacteristic quiescence, perhaps because he no longer had the verve to do otherwise.

It was as well young Jack came home when he did, because his father was also no longer capable of running the business. He seemed tired and listless, his old aggression only flaring up on rare occasions. His mellowing wasn't really remarkable – he was eighty-two years old now, and could be expected to slow down a bit. He was still physically fit, his fists were still hard, and when the temper took him he was still capable of flooring a man half his age. But his spirit was leaving him; and when it reached its final rapid decline, it took his body with it. Within a year of young Jack's return to Cuckoo Farm, his father was dead.

The new Mr Jack Lillystone (still young Jack to everyone who knew him, so long was the shadow cast by his late father) showed little inclination to take his rightful place as overlord in the Lillystone business empire. Finn was left to run everything as he saw fit, and was no longer even required to present accounts or even verbal reports. In consequence, he never set foot on Cuckoo Farm again. He was vaguely aware of Jack's marriage in 1965 (a private affair which took place away from Ely), but never met his wife; didn't even know her name. He also heard that a child was born, but knew little more than that. He retired in 1975, and watched dismally from a distance as the business he had helped old Jack Lillystone to build and maintain was slowly run into the ground. The last thing to go was the building firm in 1981. He did hear that Jack's child – a daughter – had died, as had Liza. He never knew what happened to Jack's wife. All he heard was that the daughter drowned by Cuckoo Bridge; he thought of the boy Jack, and wondered if she had been playing with toy boats at the time. There was talk (yes, of course there was – there will always be talk about the Lillystones of this world) that Jack killed the girl, but Finn wouldn't credit a word of it. He read in the paper that Jack had been questioned by the police and released; the inquest returned a verdict of accidental death, and that, as far as Finn was concerned, was that. There were no more details, and the little girl, her father, and all the rest of the Lillystones were allowed to slip quietly away into the obscurity of local myth.

VI

truncated sentence, into which a reproduction of the contents of some of the packets had been inserted. Feeling safer, I read on. I can tell you, the words had a bigger impact on me then than they had had three years ago. For one thing, I started to take some of the more fantastic elements in Drick's story a great deal more seriously. Somehow, the mere fact of his total disappearance (how lame that word seems: we're so accustomed to associating it with people who've simply gone temporarily missing) hadn't been sufficient to convince me that the story he told in his funny little packets was anything but a gross elaboration designed to cover up an inexplicable but undoubtedly perfectly earthly ruse. But haven't you ever noticed how much more real and serious things seem when they affect you personally? If he had predicted my actions so perfectly (I was loath to think that his words might have *predetermined* my actions), then what might he not be capable of?

As soon as I turned the last page of the reproduced packet – the story of the Lillystone family – I closed the book, paid for my uneaten lunch, and left the Granary. I didn't trust myself to drive just yet, so I walked about the streets for a couple of hours. Only when it started raining heavily did I go back to my car. Even then I didn't start the engine; I just sat gazing at the rain streaming down the windscreen. The compulsion to smoke is always strongest in me when I have hard thinking to do. I smoked six Gitanes in thirty minutes while the rain drummed on the car roof, which gives you an indication of the thinking going on in my head.

Eventually, it occurred to me – the thought breaking through like sudden sunlight through rain clouds (which, incidentally, is

162

exactly what the sunlight did at that very moment) – that, predetermined or predicted, I was destined at some time in the future to *write down these words*. For the logical circle to close, the story contained in the book (the part concerning me, that is) had ultimately to be written by me. And following logically from that realisation was the conclusion that, at least until this writing had been done, I was, in effect, immortal.

I could therefore drive wherever I liked with impunity, whatever my mental state. I turned the key and started the engine . . . and switched it off again. Immortality isn't necessarily the same as invulnerability; I could be horribly injured without being killed. The force of that thought was so strong that the possibility suddenly seemed like an inevitability: I pictured myself in a hospital bed with half my face missing, hideous burns, and all my limbs broken – all, that is, except my right arm, which was busily writing.

But Drick – assuming he *had* predetermined my life by writing in his infernal notepad (the existence of which I had never seriously believed in until now) . . . he wouldn't have caused anything awful to happen to me, would he?

I took the book out of my pocket and opened it again, fanning through to the place where I had left off reading. Here we were . . . *As soon as I turned the last page . . . compulsion to smoke . . . force of that thought was so strong . . . hospital bed . . . took the book out of my pocket* . . . And here were the closing words of the chapter:

Reassured by the knowledge of my immortality and invulnerability, I started the engine and drove (a bit recklessly, I have to admit, given the condition of the roads after the rain) back to my parents' house, arriving just after six o'clock, safe, sound, and more than a little pleased with myself.

163

'Did you get what you wanted?' Marjorie asked, busying herself with the kettle. 'Tea or coffee, by the way . . . ?'

'Coffee, please. Black, three sugars.'

She stared at him with disgust. 'It'll rot your teeth, you know. My late husband took four, and three spoons of Nescafé – but he was an alcoholic, you know.'

'Actor?'

'Costume designer. He could have had a great career – he was an assistant on *Dr Zhivago* and *Lawrence of Arabia* – but by the time he was forty he couldn't tell the difference between a raglan sleeve and a periwig, dear soul, and died with a hobnailed liver and blood that was ninety per cent proof.'

'Oh well, a little bit of sugar can't do much harm compared with that, can it?'

'Hmm.' She shovelled it in, pulling a face, and stirred. 'You didn't answer my question. Did Finn tell you what you wanted to know?'

Drick settled back on his chair, stroked Manni's head and hummed an uncertain little arpeggio. 'Difficult to say, really. You're right, though; he does like to talk.'

He had left the prefab with his head whirling with the old man's meandering, digressive story, and was only now, an hour later, beginning to sort it into some kind of coherent chronological order. He was certainly better informed about the Lillystones than he had been a few hours ago, but the one thing he had wanted to learn about more than any other had eluded his grasp. Old Finn had seemed to know next to nothing about Jack's daughter

Kismet. Drick had hoped that there would be some explanation – or at least some hint of an explanation – of what he knew to be the case: that Kismet was still alive. (He had abandoned the impostor hypothesis now, and was working on the suspicion that reports of her death had been exaggerated.)

'He does. There you are – black, three sugars. Be sure you brush your teeth when you get home.'

'Marjorie, I've already got one mother. I don't need two.'

'Nonsense. Men your age need all the mothers they can get.' She sat down at the kitchen table with her cup and a bone china pot of camomile tea. 'So,' she said, pouring, 'What *did* you learn?'

'More than I bargained for about the Lillystone family. Next to nothing about Kismet.'

'Not enough to write a book, then?'

'Oh, I could write a book, no problem. My books are made up here' – he tapped his head – 'not out there.'

He had always been vaguely insulted by the almost universal assumption that novels must be built either from personal experience or life-stories overheard. He had noticed, for instance, as soon as he became a published writer, that knowing glances would be turned in his direction whenever family gossip was aired. *Better not say too much in front of Roderick – you might find it in a book before you know it.* Always said as a joke, of course, but he resented it nonetheless. The trouble was, everybody thought their little family dramas – divorces, adulteries, betrayals – were so profoundly unusual and emotive that they must be ripe fruit for fiction; as though he hadn't the wit to make that stuff up a thousand times over. The things he really looked out for, the true jewels of human life, were the little, insignificant things. For example, he had an uncle in Gloucester who had a unique approach to sandwiches. He would lay all the components out on his plate – two slices of bread, a pat of butter, slice of ham and a dollop of mustard – and eat them one by one, in that order, without bothering to assemble them. That, in his view, was how sandwiches *worked*, and nobody could tell him any different. You couldn't invent things like that – or Drick couldn't, not with confidence. He had collected a little store of such idiosyncrasies which he was forever trying to weave into his made-up stories.

'Anyway,' he said, 'I don't want to write a book. I told you that. I'm just curious.' He toyed with the handle of his mug. 'You were about the same age as Liza Lillystone, weren't you?'

'Yes. We were friends, up to a point. About as close a friend as she ever had outside the family, I suppose, for what that's worth.'

'Finn seemed to imply – that is, he seemed to me to be implying . . .' Drick hesitated awkwardly.

She looked sternly at him. 'Out with it.'

'Never mind. Listen, when Liza went away in 1954 she was pregnant, right?'

'I imagine so. That was usually the explanation when unmarried girls were sent away suddenly in those days. She was gone for about the right length of time to have a baby.'

'And Colin Whatsisface was the father.'

'Colin Pickett. Again, I imagine that was the case. I wasn't what you'd call intimate with Liza by then, but it was pretty much established fact that she was sneaking away from the house at night to see him. He had a big mouth, unfortunately, and young Jack took payment out of him for it with his fists.'

'I wonder where they sent her. I mean, they weren't Catholics, so it can't have been a convent.'

'Oh, there were other places you could be sent. And old Jack had relatives in Yorkshire. Maybe he'd made his peace with them.'

'Her brother left shortly after. Do you know where he went? He was away ten years.'

Marjorie shook her head. 'I wish I could enlighten you. He might have gone to sea like his father for all I know.'

'And I don't suppose you know anything about the woman he married? Finn didn't even know her name, let alone who she was or where she came from.'

'Didn't he? I must say that surprises me. But you're getting into a period I know hardly anything about. When my acting career started to take off I spent hardly any time at all in Ely, and then of course when I married Ralph in 1964 I left altogether.'

'You wouldn't know anything about Kismet, then?'

166

'Jack's daughter?' She shook her head. 'I didn't move back here until long after she died.'

Drick paused before asking his next question. So far he had noticed two blatant evasions. The last time they met, she had said about Kismet that she was *a charming little girl, they say. Took after her mother.* Who was *they*? According to Finn, the Lillystones had virtually no contact with the world outside Cuckoo Farm after the mid-1950s. And how could anyone have known that she took after her mother when even Finn, the one person who had any kind of dealings with the family, didn't know so much as the mother's name? Marjorie obviously knew (or had heard, or suspected) far more than she admitted to.

Presumably mistaking his thoughtful expression for something more sinister, she suddenly burst out: 'I know the kind of things people would say about it all nowadays. God knows they said enough vile things back then. No doubt if it was all happening now, there'd be talk of sexual abuse and goodness knows what. People are obsessed with it. A father can't be close to his daughter without some filthy motive being imputed. Well, the Lillystones weren't like that at all, so I hope you're not going to imply that they were.'

Drick stared at her in astonishment. 'It hadn't even crossed my mind,' he said. (It had actually, but he had dismissed it until now.) This was bad; since she was clearly hiding something, he had been hoping to shock her into revealing it, but she was already on the back foot, ready for allegations. But why was she so defensive of the family, when she had no apparent reason to be?

He decided to shock her anyway. 'Credit me with more imagination than that, Marjorie. I'm not talking about child abuse. I think when Jack beat up Colin Pickett, it wasn't because he'd taken liberties with his sister – it was the fury of jealousy.' He paused to assess the shock effect, but there didn't seem to be one. 'A threat, too,' he went on. 'From the description Finn gave me, it seems unlikely that Liza would have been attracted to someone like Colin; he was a pathetic specimen – he hung around because he was infatuated with her. As a result of that, he knew things, and Jack wanted to make sure he never repeated them. The Lillystones

167

might have been aloof, not cared what people in the town thought of them, but even they drew the line somewhere. Because it was Jack's baby Liza took away with her to be delivered in secret and put out for adoption, wasn't it?'

Marjorie gaped at him in horror. 'That's an—'

'And that was why he went away himself, and didn't come back until his father was all set to follow his mother to the grave. Once they were alone together, Jack and Liza resumed the relationship that had been interrupted ten years before. That's why he never told anyone anything about his "wife", isn't it?'

'I don't know. I—'

'Because he never had one; only his sister. And Kismet was the product of the relationship. The only thing I'm not sure about yet is what happened to Liza. Did she die, or what? And *did* Jack kill Kismet?'

Marjorie was gazing dumbly at him now. 'You're right,' she said at last. 'You do have a vivid imagination.'

'Really? What would you say, Marjorie, if I were to tell you that Kismet is still alive? That she didn't drown by Cuckoo Bridge?'

She frowned. 'Why? Do you think you're likely to tell me such a thing?'

Drick hesitated. His torrent of cross-examination had exhausted him, and he couldn't sustain the certainty of his suppositions any longer. 'I don't know,' he said. 'Would you be surprised if I did?'

'Not after what you've just said. I could quite easily imagine you capable of alleging almost anything. If I didn't know you better, I'd throw you out of this house for some of the things you've just flung at me.'

'It wasn't aimed at you personally,' he said gently. No, only at the beliefs she had nurtured for most of her adult life. 'When you first told me about the Lillystones, you didn't sound too fond of them. Why so defensive now?'

She slumped in her chair, suddenly seeming old and drained. 'I wish I'd never sent you to see old Finn.' She looked up, and there were angry tears in her eyes. 'You've got it all wrong. Liza didn't have Jack's baby. I don't know how you can think anything so disgusting. She was in love with Colin Pickett; having sex with him in that horrible little bedsit of his. *She* didn't have Jack's baby. *I* did. He didn't run away for ten years because . . . because . . .' She almost spat with disgust. 'He went because he'd fathered a child on *me* and he didn't want to face the responsibility. There – is that seedy enough for you?'

Drick lay on his sofa with a tall vodka in his hand and *Modern Life Is Rubbish* on the CD player. He gazed vacantly out at the back garden, where Manni was taking apart a plastic flowerpot and scattering the bits across the lawn. It would be dark soon, and an evening frost was already beginning to settle, but Manni was having too much fun to notice.

Drick took another large swig of vodka and turned the music up a notch. Between them, they helped him assimilate what he had learned that day.

Well, he had certainly succeeded in shocking a revelation out of Marjorie. He wondered if she would ever speak to him again. And still she had managed to evade his question about Kismet. Unless . . . No, it was stretching credibility to suspect that Kismet was Marjorie's daughter. Her child had been born in 1955 and adopted. There was no way the Kismet he had met could be more than twenty-five or twenty-six years old.

The tiny, withered nodule in his brain which he liked to think of as his work ethic was trying to tell him he had more important things to think about than the Lillystone family. He ignored it. It was Friday, and he didn't have to speak to Nick Lovell until Monday. He'd work something out, and if he didn't he could always use the notepad to write himself another week's grace.

Now, there was a thought. He could simply have Marjorie phone him this minute and spill the whole story. He could imagine her contrition, her remorse at having been so selfish and evasive, her tearful decision to tell him everything she knew. He tingled with the thought of his power for a few seconds, then put the idea aside. He'd had about enough of Marjorie for one day, and he'd just thought of a more direct way to learn a little more about Kismet. The Kismet who wasn't part of some half-remembered, half-suppressed past; the Kismet who was alive and had walked in and out of his life with so little thought for his sanity.

He went to his desk, switched on the computer, laid the notepad in its tray under the printer, and began to type. It took less than a minute; when he had finished, he pressed Command-P, the tray began to move and the print-head hissed and squawked, squirting out in minute, compressed type:

That Saturday morning, Jack Lillystone woke in his boxcar feeling more ill than he had ever been in his life. His vision was blurred, his stomach churned, and he could barely feel his limbs, let alone move them.

Repulsive as the man might be, Drick didn't want to make him suffer more than was necessary, so he added:

Surprisingly, considering how virulent the sickness was, his strong constitution chased away the bugs with remarkable swiftness; by eight o'clock that evening, he felt completely recovered.

Drick went to bed that night feeling unconscionably pleased with himself. If he hadn't had the foresight to add a little note for himself in the pad, his excitement might have kept him awake all night.

He woke early to find it had snowed in the night, and that made him feel all the better. He loved snow; when he opened his eyes to see the familiar access of glittering light fanning over the top of the curtains, he jumped out of bed and ran to the window, hoping for big drifts. As a child in Wales he had done the same thing many times, peering out of his bedroom window in delight at the deep white swallowing the garden walls and creeping up to the window ledges.

By East Anglian standards, there had been quite a blizzard: on the road, only a few patches of tarmac showed through the snow, and it lay in drifts up to two inches deep against the houses. Still, it was snow, and the world was a better, cleaner, purer place for it.

He dressed quickly and was out of the house by eight, before the thin, fragile covering had been too sullied by passing feet. Manni had been a tiny puppy the previous winter, soft-skinned, delicate and vulnerable to cold, and so had never walked on snow before. He sniffed at it cautiously and scuffed it with his claws, astonished at the way it bit back. He quickly discovered that the best thing to do with it was eat it, and Drick had to haul him along, skidding and scrabbling, stopping every dozen yards or so to sweep great clods of melting slush out of the dog's mouth.

After a long struggle down Kiln Lane, where the snow lay thicker than in the town, they finally arrived at the turn in the road where the hawthorn and bramble hung down, concealing the entrance to the farm lane. Just to be sure, Drick walked on past the bend and a little way down the hardcore track to the waste ground where the railway wagons were parked. The boxcar was shut up tight, and white smoke was pouring from the stove chimney which fed crookedly out of a hole in its end wall. Satisfied that his medicine had worked, and that the beast wouldn't be straying from its cage today, he went back to the farm entrance and burrowed under the prickling, catching curtain. It was even thicker than it had been the last time, and much harder work to get through; the snow made it even more uncomfortable, the fronds flinging icy showers with unerring accuracy down the back of his neck. The broken-down gate looked even more dilapidated now; he hadn't noticed before the wooden plaque that hung by one rusty screw from the top bar, greened and rotten but still partially legible: 'CUC O F RM'. Lying on the ground was part of a broken sign made of white board with lettering painted in red. He picked it up and brushed the snow and debris off. 'TRESPASSE WILL B' it read. Shot? Horsewhipped perhaps, or flung in a pit in a locked outbuilding, never to see the light of day again? From what he had heard and seen of the Lillystone men, he could believe almost anything.

There was something about abandoned farms which had always fascinated and terrified him, and he suspected strongly that the feeling was a universal human phenomenon. Maybe it was their isolation and the smell of death lingering in damp, dark corners; maybe it was something more abstruse than that: farms represented the point at which the domestic conjoined with the wild; a dangerous, unsettling boundary out of place in a world where wild frontiers no longer existed. Every storyteller knows that the perfect setting for a nightmare is a farm. Emily Brontë knew it, and proved its power greater than any gothic castle. Drick's childhood had been haunted by the abandoned farm which stood across the road from his parents' house. For years the crumbling, centuries-old buildings simultaneously drew and repelled him and all his friends. Murders had been committed there, it was said, and he could believe it. Playing in the outbuildings on the edge of the yard was one thing; the house was rarely approached, and he had only summoned up the courage to enter it once. He and Jeremy had loosened one of the boards which blocked off the house-place door and penetrated only a few yards into the darkness before being driven back, terrified by the cracking of a litter of nameless horrors under their feet and the damp, cloying air, like the last exhalations of a hundred mouldering corpses.

Compared with Llanyrafon Farm (odd, he thought, how he should be reminded so vividly of his childhood twice in as many hours), where centuries of malign will billowed from every nook, this place seemed relatively harmless, although now he knew something of the people who had built and occupied it – and still kept vigil against its violation – he approached it with rather more trepidation than he had the last time.

The front door was still ajar, exactly as he had left it. Jack Lillystone must be confident that he had scared off the intruder once and for all, and mustn't have felt the need to bar the entrance. On reflection, he was probably right; if it hadn't been for the miraculous power in his possession, Drick would never have dared to return. He understood now why the house had decayed so little; it would have been a brave vandal indeed who ventured down here (even if he found the way in) to break windows and knock slates from the roof.

173

He didn't leave Manni tied outdoors this time. It was too cold, and besides, if Jack proved after all to have the superhuman strength of will to haul himself out of his sick-bed and patrol the farm, Drick didn't want to leave Manni as a signal of his presence or (worse) potential first target for any buckshot that might fly. After making a cursory inspection of the ground-floor rooms (nothing had altered, as far as he could see), he tested the solidity of the newel-post at the bottom of the stairs and lashed Manni's lead to it. He gave the dog a big rawhide chew he had brought along especially, and made his way up the creaking staircase, crumbled plaster crunching under his heavy walking boots at each slow tread.

The door at the top of the stairs was, as before, closed. He remembered leaving it open, so somebody must have been up here in the meantime. He wiped away the thin accretion of new dust which had settled on the china plaque, and read it again: 'KISMET'S ROOM'. For the second time, he brushed the cobwebs aside and took the brass doorknob in his hand, twisted it, and pushed in the door.

Exactly as before, his first impression as it opened was of blindingly bright light filling the room like a glass bowl. It was a corner room, with two windows; one facing south and the other east, and the climbing sun blazed in despite the grimy panes, breaking into dazzling splinters as it hit the cloud of dust thrown up by the door opening.

So far as he could tell, under the patina which coated everything in the house like a shroud, it was a fairly typical little girl's room, albeit one of a more austere age than the little girls of his generation had grown up in. There were no Sindy dolls or pink plastic cassette players; no white teddy bears, gaudily decorated jewel-caskets or heart-shaped starlet make-up mirrors; none of the weird, incomprehensible things he remembered cluttering the talc-smelling bedrooms of the little girls of his acquaintance.

There were framed pictures on the walls which, under the dust, proved to be of typically girlish subjects: ponies, a blurry watercolour of a cottage scene with people in straw bonnets, anthropomorphised animals messing about in boats. Altogether,

174

there were half a dozen of the blandest prints you could imagine, none giving away the least shred of information about the person whose room this had been. He had the feeling that, like most decoration provided by parents for their children, they impinged on the consciousness only tangentially. Try to recall the pattern on the wallpaper in your room when you were seven, and chances are that you won't be able to; but see that pattern again, and it's like Proust's madeleine, triggering an uncontrollable rush of memories which haven't stirred out of deep storage in twenty or thirty years.

The only apparent hint of the occupant stamping her own personality on the room was above the head of the adult-size iron-framed bed. Four pieces of paper torn from a notebook had been pinned neatly to the wall, right where the morning sunlight through the east window must strike. Drick leaned close and peered at them, but there was nothing to be seen. There had once been writing on them, he could tell that much, but the sunlight had faded it to illegibility. He pulled one sheet gently off its pin; it was dry as a dead leaf, and broke into bits between his fingers.

Apart from the bed, there were four items of furniture in the room. Reading clockwise from the door, there was a tall, plain pine wardrobe, a chest of drawers made of age-darkened oak, a chapel chair with a bible pocket built on its back, and a small bedside table. Aside from the furniture, there wasn't much else in the room: a lamp on the bedside table with a china stand shaped like a tree trunk with a red squirrel climbing up it watched by a badger, and a silver crucifix standing ominously on the chest of drawers.

The only thing in the room that gave him the briefest hint of the creeps was the bed; if it had been neatly made, as though waiting for the dead girl to come back and climb in, that would have been comprehensible; expected, almost. Instead, the covers were thrown back, the sheet was rumpled, and there was a distinct dent in the pillow, as though she had just got up. The impression was heightened by the fact that, alone in the whole house, the bed was entirely free of the skein of dusty webs and fallen plaster.

He shivered, and it wasn't the cold that caused it. In fact, with the sunshine streaming in, it was quite pleasantly warm in the room. He stood between the bed and the window, with the light falling full on him, and wondered what to do next. Beyond seeing the inside of Kismet's room, he hadn't planned his trespass with any particular purpose. Now that he was here, he felt vaguely disappointed. What had he expected? To find evidence that the Kismet he knew was indeed the supposedly lost child of Jack (and Liza?) Lillystone, and that she was living in secret seclusion in her childhood bedroom? Well, actually, now that he came to think of it, that *was* more or less what had been in the back of his mind. He had come here to find her, not to gaze impotently at a collection of morbid relics.

There was the bed, of course; he couldn't believe it had been preserved like that by chance. *Someone* was still using it, in his opinion; someone, presumably, who wasn't fastidious about the state of the room. A squatter, perhaps? No, there'd be more mess. Jack Lillystone, maybe? That thought gave him the creeps for real.

Almost idly, distracted by the impenetrable question of the bed, he opened the door of the wardrobe. A wave of lavender scent fell out through the parting webs and washed over him, sluicing away his thoughts like thistledown. On the floor of the wardrobe, peeping out from beneath the hanging clothes, was a white sun hat with a broad brim and a ribbon printed with bright red strawberries. He bent to pick it up, and something soft brushed against his cheek. Hanging on the back of the wardrobe door, on a scented hanger, was a white dress. He stopped breathing. It made no difference that both hat and dress were made for a child – an eleven- or twelve-year-old, at a guess – he knew without a doubt that they were the very same garments Kismet had worn that day he waded across the river to the garden. It wasn't merely the fact that they were of an identical design (though reduced to child size) that made him sure; it was the pair of large, muddy pawprints on the front of the dress.

The hat fell from his fingers, and he stepped back from the wardrobe. The chapel chair pressed against the back of his knees, and he dropped into it.

He sat there for several minutes, staring blankly and listening to his heart pounding. Then he rose to his feet and quickly, methodically, ransacked the room from top to bottom. The universe couldn't tease him like this, he thought angrily; Kismet herself was one thing, the notepad another, but this was quite beyond the bounds of reasonable weirdness. This was insanity: burbling, gibbering, cross-eyed barking nuts-in-May crazy. Weird shit like this couldn't happen unless *he* was in control of it. There had to be something else here; something that would make sense of it all. He was an optimistic soul at heart; unreasonably so, since all he found was more madness.

He stripped back the bedclothes and found nothing; tore the pictures and papers off the wall and found nothing; looked under the rugs and found nothing; pulled all the clothes out of the wardrobe and found nothing; and, breathing hard by now and sweating, yanked open the drawers and found – a miracle. It took him a little while to realise it was a miracle; in that moment, as he stared open-mouthed into the bottom drawer of the chest, it looked like a thick ream of paper, sitting there innocently with *his name* in carefully hand-drawn capitals on the top sheet.

He stared for a few seconds, then sat down again. There was always more than one possible explanation for any set of observed phenomena; according to Sherlock Holmes (or was it Auguste Dupin?), once you stripped away the impossible, what remained, however unlikely, must be the truth. The possible explanations here were: 1) that Kismet was still alive, she had met him, knew quite a lot about him, and so it was not inconceivable that his name should appear on a piece of paper in a drawer in the room that had been hers (possibly still was hers); 2) that she was dead, but that he had met her anyway in adult form; 3) that his brain had undergone total meltdown. He tended to favour the third hypothesis; it was the only one that fitted all the facts. Holmes (or Dupin) hadn't envisaged a situation in which, when you stripped away the impossible, you were left with nothing. So nothing was the truth, and the truth was nothing. A good Zen principle, but hardly helpful.

He decided to begin again, bearing in mind that the universe where all the impossible things lived was a much smaller and more exclusive place than he had supposed a few months ago. Stripping away the impossible should therefore be easier. First, and being generous to himself, it was impossible that he could have imagined any of the things he had seen. The path his reason took from that point on was too long and tortuous to be reproduced in writing; sufficient to record that his conclusion was simple: to keep his eyes, ears and mind open. It would all make sense eventually. As has been noted, he was optimistic at heart.

Feeling a little better, he took the heavy sheaf of paper out of the drawer and examined it. It was a novel in manuscript (real manuscript, not word-processed – written out laboriously in a rather scruffy, thoroughly familiar hand). Above his name on the top sheet was a title: *The Alchemist's Apprentice*, which meant nothing to him.

He turned it back and began reading the first page. He read it twice, then read on to the second page, then the third. This wasn't *The Alchemist's Apprentice* (whatever that signified); it was *The Island*. With little differences, though. Here and there, unnoticeable to anyone but its creator or the most obsessive analyst, the text had been altered. The changes varied in scale from amendments to the punctuation to the insertion of whole sentences. Elsewhere, single words had been deleted, substituted or added. The overall effect was an immeasurable improvement of the language: it had more bite, better rhythm. Then, in the third chapter, he discovered a much more profound difference between this manuscript and *The Island*. A new character appeared. He was an Algerian fakir-cum-alchemist called Izzat who was befriended and brought into the orbit of the Weiss family by the daughter, Rebecca. This was more than an amendment – it was revolutionary. What was remarkable was that he had once considered including this character, but had rejected the idea; partly because the amount of re-working seemed to outweigh any likely benefits, which he thought would be nugatory, but mainly because it was antihistorical. He had already compromised his principles enough with this book, and hadn't been about to make it worse. He could see now, though, that the result was in fact a huge improvement in the whole structure of the story. *The Island* was a good novel; *The Alchemist's Apprentice* was a superb one. The character Izzat brought a magical dimension which cast the whole story in a new, glittering light. It was, underneath, precisely the same story (so far as he could tell as he speed-read his way through it), but... but so many things. He could see his fortune in it. It was the miracle he had wished for but been unable to bring about.

He looked at his watch. Nearly three hours had passed while he sat reading. He realised that he hadn't heard a peep from Manni for ages. He stood up, pushing the bulky manuscript securely under his coat, and went to leave the room. As he turned, he noticed a small scrap of paper in the bottom of the open drawer, where it had lain hidden by the manuscript. He picked it out. Written on it, again in the handwriting which so resembled his own, were the following words:

<u>Scenario 1</u>: You are a soldier, caught in the midst of a battle which is raging up and down the main street of a small town. Your brain and body are buffeted by explosions; bullets slap and zing off the walls within inches of you. Your life hangs in the corner of your eye, on your trigger finger and on the tip of your bayonet; all around you men are turned on the instant into bursting blood-bags and hunks of chopped meat. Then, in the midst of the smoke and din, you see a man sitting on the kerb playing with a small dog, utterly oblivious to the inferno around him.

<u>Scenario 2</u>: You are a writer, taking a break from work, walking your dog down the main street of a small town. Cars drone slowly up the one-way street, and the pavements are busy with shoppers. You weave your dog in and out, all your concentration bent towards preventing him grabbing at people's shopping bags or jumping up to greet them. Some children are playing with a cat outside the post office on the opposite side of the street, but you are alert and not taken by surprise when your dog lunges suddenly towards the traffic. Deftly, you haul him back to heel, issue a stern command and continue on your way. A few seconds later, thirty yards behind you, the façade of the post office erupts with a deafening noise like rolling thunder, windows

bursting and flinging out a fountain of shattered glass, sweeping away the children, the cat, three shoppers and two parked cars.

    <u>*Conclusion:*</u> *What we call normality or anomaly depends entirely on which end of the telescope we look through. For some, the close-up magnified view is the true normality, while for others it is the tiny, far-away view which is real.*

Drick frowned at the paper, then stuffed it in his coat pocket and walked out onto the landing and down the stairs. To his surprise, Manni was curled up asleep in the bight of wall and stair-foot, the rawhide chew half-turned to sticky pulp lying in the dust by his nose. He jumped up when he heard Drick's tread on the stairs.

'Okay, mate, let's go home,' said Drick, untying the lead and opening the front door. 'Whether it's what we came for or not, we've got something.'

Part Four

THE ALCHEMIST'S APPRENTICE

Packet 10

Drick was glad he had taken the trouble to learn to touch-type properly. He could manage nearly sixty words a minute in an energetic mood, or forty in a more relaxed state. Pushing hard, he'd just have time in what remained of the weekend to transfer *The Alchemist's Apprentice* to disk. He could have done it instantly with the aid of the notepad, but felt that, since the manuscript had fallen miraculously into his hands, he should suffer at least some effort in putting it to print. He didn't waste too much time wondering where the manuscript had come from (nor the slip of paper with it) – it had his name on it, and was in his handwriting. He put aside the fairly obvious suspicion that Kismet had something to do with it; he didn't want to think about that.

And so he typed. He typed all Saturday afternoon and evening; he typed until his fingers tingled, then stung, then ached, then screamed, each keystroke like a hammer-blow on the swelling knuckles. He called a halt at midnight, and walked round the room with his hands stuffed in his armpits, swearing and wincing. The stack of paper, which had lowered gradually by the hour, was still a good couple of inches thick. He had typed forty thousand words; about a third of the novel. He went to the kitchen and put his hands in the fridge icebox; that didn't help, so he tried a bowl of warm water instead. That was better, but his fingers still felt as though they'd been given a going-over with one of those machines they use for battering down tarmac.

He was determined not to give up, so he compromised. He took out the notepad and, holding a pen awkwardly (he couldn't type another word tonight to save his life), wrote a couple of

sentences. The first accelerated the repair to the damaged liga-
ments and muscles in his hands, so that he would be completely
recovered by the morning. The second turned him into the fastest
typist in the world, capable of flinging the keys at up to a hundred
and eighty words a minute. At that speed, he could get the job
done by the end of Sunday with a twenty-minute break every
hour.

When he woke up at seven the next morning, his fingers felt
incredible; they had more than recovered, they felt like new
fingers. A palpable buzz of energy flowed through them, and
their movements were quicker and more precise. He had to take
care in the kitchen as he made his coffee; his hands darted about
so fast he had a hard time keeping track of them. At first, he
tried to control their movements consciously, with unnatural
deliberation, and ended up knocking over the coffee jug and
spilling grounds all over the kitchen floor. He swept them up
with frightening speed, before Manni could lick up more than a
tongueful.

After that, he let his brain get on with the business of
coordinating his hands without interference from his mind. It was
the fastest breakfast he had ever seen in his life: corn flakes, milk,
sugar, coffee, more sugar, more milk, spoons and cup darting
about the worktop in a perfect high-speed dance. Those cocktail
slingers had nothing on him; people would pay to see his breakfast routine.

When he sat down to type, he astonished even himself. His
fingers flitted across the keys in a blur, with a sound like a
sewing-machine. The computer, which had a 40 MHz chip (quite
impressive back then), had difficulty keeping up; he had to pause
for a second at the end of each paragraph to let it catch up.
Incroyable. Roderick Bent and his six-million-dollar fingers. He
wondered what the effect on foreplay would be.

By eight that evening, he had finished and spell-checked his
work. An excitement had grown within him while he typed, the
full force of the improved novel slamming him right between the
eyes. As he fed a block of paper into the printer, he was trembling
slightly. He put the original manuscript in a box-file and laid it

carefully in a drawer under his desk. Three hours later, he had two complete copies in print; one he wrapped up in brown paper ready for posting in the morning, the other he took into the living room, along with a bottle of red wine and a fresh packet of cigarettes, to read at his leisure.

'Nicholas Lovell's office.'

'Hi, Nicholas Lovell's office. Roderick Bent here.'

There was an audible intake of breath. 'Roderick! I was about to call you. I hope you've got a decision for me; if you haven't, I shall be making it on your behalf in about ten minutes. As a token of my greatness of heart, I've decided to bypass the copy-editing process. See how I indulge you? If you can get a revised MS to me by the end of the week or authorise me – ha! authorise! – to use the one I have, I can mark it up myself over the weekend and get it to the typesetter for Monday. It *has* to be Monday, Roderick, or *The Island* dies of financial asphyxiation. Comprendé?'

'Stop it, Nick. Untwist your boxers and listen. I can do better than the end of the week. You'll have the MS on your desk by tomorrow lunchtime, amended, emended, repaired, improved and souped up.'

There was an uncertain pause. 'You've changed it, then?'

'Almost beyond recognition.'

'I see. You haven't spoiled it, have you? It seemed perfectly fine the last time I read it.'

'Nick, who's the writer in this relationship?'

'You are, but I'm the unfortunate publisher. This may be your baby, Roderick, but if you've given it a nose-stud and tattoos I won't have it in my kindergarten.'

'It's better, Nick. Infinitely better. It's going to make us million-aires, I can feel it.'

He heard a long sigh – Nick exhaling his anxieties and hoping to breathe in confidence. 'Very well, Roderick. I'll read it tomor-row evening. Unless it's very much worse, we'll go with it.'

'I appreciate it. By the way, I've got a new title for you. "The Alchemist's Apprentice".'

185

'Aah, yeees. Okay, I can live with that. I don't see how it fits the book, though.'

'You will. Oh, and there's one other thing.'

'Yes?'

'I want to be published under a pseudonym.'

'Okay, plenty do. I presume you've got a name in mind?'

'Madagascar Rhodes. I've enclosed a biographical blurb with the manuscript.'

This was an idea he had been playing with for a long time. He had never liked his own name; at least, not since the mid-1970s. He and Jeremy had both suffered from their names, and it had driven them apart for a while (rather than bringing them closer together, as shared freakishness usually does). When the Jeremy Thorpe case burst over the tabloids and television news like an especially pustulent boil, the name Jeremy became inextricably associated with homosexuality (perhaps helped on its way to infamy by its frivolous syllables; the much duller 'Norman' never suffered in the same way). Children are the world's biggest homophobes, and anything smacking of poufery was there to be laughed at, from insufficiently masculine shoes to Omo washing powder. For a pre-adolescent boy growing up in South Wales, having a gay name was disastrous. Drick, being Bent, had suffered a less catastrophic but more enduring ignominy, and had learned to absorb the teasing by joining in with it and laughing at himself. But his and Jeremy's best-of-friends status threw a whole new slant on the issue and, for several months, they shunned each other (by unspoken mutual consent and without acrimony). Drick was uneasy about his own name for ever after; he never learned to lose the anticipation of gales of laughter whenever he spoke it or heard it announced in public. So, after some deliberation, he had decided to adopt the persona of a character from one of his abandoned novels.

There was another pause while Nick wrote the name down. 'Not sure about Madagascar,' he said. 'Any alternatives?'

'You could shorten it to Maddy, if you like.'

'You'll sound like a woman.'

'And the problem with that is . . . ?'

Another sigh. 'All right, Maddy Rhodes it is. What shall we do about a photo?'

'I've enclosed one of my stand-in.'

'You've got the whole damn thing stitched up, haven't you?'

Drick laughed. 'Goodbye, Nick. I'll speak to you on Wednesday, once you've read and loved the new draft. Cheers.'

Drick had never waited for a verdict on a piece of work with less anxiety. He was so relaxed that, when Wednesday afternoon came and he still hadn't heard from Nick, he jumped immediately to the conclusion that there had been a perfectly routine delay, and that he would hear soon enough. (Any writer will recognise this as a superhuman degree of insouciance.) At last, around midday on Thursday, the phone rang. It was Nick, in ecstatic mood. The new manuscript was *perfectissimo*. Sorry he hadn't phoned yesterday, but he had had to read it a second time because he hadn't been able to believe how good it was the first. He had marked it up for typesetting, and would be dispatching it that afternoon. Drick could expect to receive proofs in a few weeks' time. Incidentally, Obelisk (i.e. Nick himself) had decided to risk their neck and increase the print-run to a thousand copies. Massive.

The sensation of release was phenomenal. At last, the novel was out of his hands and in someone else's; all responsibility could be abdicated, and all that remained was to quibble over jacket designs and wait until it appeared in the shops. It did occur to him that, if he had been in possession of the notepad a year ago, he might be living off a fat advance from a big publisher; but what the hell – he couldn't change the past. (That was a thought that would come back to haunt him.)

Now that *The Alchemist's Apprentice* had been sent out to stand on its own two flyleaves, he could begin trying to make some kind of sense (or at least order) out of all the other stuff. The notepad; Kismet; the Lillystones; Marjorie Turnbull's baby; the miraculous appearance of the new manuscript; and the invisible, magnetic pull that seemed to connect him to this weird island of impossibility. For the first time since it had begun, he traced the chain of events, trying to recall every detail no matter how insignificant. Within that framework, he might be able to construct a sequence of connections. A bit like the diffusionist pottery typologies he had been taught to despise as an undergraduate.

First there had been the dream by the river on that hot afternoon in June last year . . . No, the point of departure was further back; it had to be the writing of *The Island*. It had seemed a perfectly normal thing to do at the time, but it was obviously connected with all that came after. The idea, he recalled, had come to him in pure, germinal form over two years ago. For him, all novels came this way – like his encounter with the derelict outside the Obelisk office – in a single, identifiable moment.

The seed of *The Island* (or *The Alchemist's Apprentice* as he now irrevocably thought of it) had popped into his head one evening in November 1991 as he was walking through St John's College to the Pythagoras School, where the Department of Archaeology held its annual party to welcome (the word is used advisedly) new postgraduates. He was crossing the Bridge of Sighs when a sudden icy blast blew in through the unglazed windows. He was at the peak of the bridge's span, and he stopped walking . . . That was the moment when the idea came to him. He remembered the occasion, because the idea had no apparent connection with what he had been thinking about (cheese sandwiches, if you're interested). Why at that moment? Why there, on the summit of that dark tunnel bridge? He had seen it with the clarity of a slide projection; a sequence of images. A family of Jewish refugees living on Malta. Wartime. The siege. And an Arab alchemist. (And definitely no cheese sandwiches.)

The content of the novel – the idea itself – was irrelevant, he was now sure. Now that he looked back on that evening, he was convinced that it was the bridge that was the important element. Following this hunch, he traced, with growing exhilaration, the origin of all his other novels. There were five of them, not including the abortions. Each and every one, he realised had first entered the anteroom of his imagination while he was standing on, crossing, passing under, or looking from a distance at, a bridge. Moreover, the three abandoned pieces had started while he was, respectively, driving over Hay Bluff, watching *If*, and looking at a tramp in a doorway in Great Newport Street. *The Alchemist's Apprentice* was an anomaly only in that the idea had not even the vaguest association with his surroundings or thoughts at the time it arrived.

The feeling of excitement as these realisations occurred turned to a distinct tingle down the back of his neck when he realised further that his four published stories had begun as ideas which came while he was *immersed in water*.

Why bridges? Why water? Closing his eyes and concentrating, he recreated the sensation he felt whenever he had a good idea. It was easy to do; like getting back the feeling of eating a Flying Saucer just by picturing what they looked like – the dry rice paper meniscus quickly turning to pulp and leaking a fizz of sharp powdery sherbet. Bridges – something about bridges (and water) opened a little spy-hole into an unconscious part of his mind, as though a section had been locked off somehow. A section where all the good ideas were kept. *But why bridges?* And what was the connection with that story Kismet had left on his desk at the college – the story which was *about* him but contained nothing that he remembered, even though – and this was the killer punch – *he had written it*. The handwriting, he now knew, wasn't just similar to his; it *was* his.

Now he could return to that June afternoon, and the dream of the dead girl rising out of the river. Shortly after that, he had first seen Kismet; Kismet who was supposed to be dead – drowned in the vicinity of Cuckoo Bridge . . . His imagination raced ahead – her sketch-pad floating on the water . . . the story of Three Bridges Corner . . . the narratives of Marjorie and old Finn . . . the notepad . . . And he believed he understood at last. The understanding wasn't clear, nor even very coherent, but it was more lucid than the tangle that had been there before. One thing stood out more clearly than any other – he had to speak to Marjorie again.

He would have liked to speak to Jeremy first; running it all past a disinterested third party might have been useful. Jeremy was the only person in the world to whom he wouldn't have to explain every last detail.

He phoned him, but he was busy writing up his thesis and couldn't spare the time for a drink. He should call again next week. Drick couldn't wait that long, so he just went round to Marjorie's house and knocked on the door.

The eyes widened in the round, sharp-nosed face. 'I'm surprised you have the nerve to present yourself here again,' said Marjorie over Frazer's furious barking. 'Be quiet, you hound of hell! It's only Roderick and Mannfred – look.'

The massive Dobermann pushed past her and lunged at Manni; the lead was wrenched from Drick's hand, and the two dogs chased each other manically around the front garden.

'I'm sorry about the other day,' said Drick. 'I overstepped the bounds. Can we talk?'

She looked doubtful. 'If you wish,' she said a little curtly. 'Come in.'

They sat in the kitchen, exactly as before; Drick with a mug of instant coffee in front of him, Marjorie nursing a cup of camomile tea. Drick blandished her with apologies, and she softened surprisingly quickly. It was almost childishly easy to get round Marjorie. The truth was she fancied him rotten, even though she was old enough to be his mother's elder sister. (He learned later that it had been her weakness for young men that had scuppered her chances of a comeback in the early '80s; she'd become infatuated with a young screenwriter who was writing a character vehicle for her – a starring role. She pestered him incessantly, and at that time, though well over forty, she retained enough of her former attractiveness to alarm the screenwriter's wife. Eventually, he was persuaded to drop the project.) Drick had seen the flirtatious look in her eyes from the first, and had been gently amused (even oddly flattered when he watched her film appearances and saw the siren she had once been); now it seemed faintly disgusting. He had seen her private emotions, and the effect was like seeing her aged, fattened naked body. He felt vaguely ashamed of himself now as he played on her weakness, plying her with charm, softening her up to extract more personal secrets.

'What happened to your baby?' he asked gently.

Marjorie sniffed loudly and looked up with a courageous expression, defying the truth to hurt her. 'She was adopted.'

'How old were you?'

'I was nineteen and a Roman Catholic. As far as my parents were concerned, she never existed. I went away to a convent for a little while, and when I came back I was their little girl again. Veronica was never spoken of again.'

'Veronica?'

'I called her Veronica Rita. After Veronica Lake and Rita Hayworth; they were my idols. I don't suppose you've ever heard of them. I've no idea what she was really called, or what happened to her, or whether she was ever told about me. She would have been eighteen in 1974, and I've been waiting ever since for her to get in touch. She never has. She may not even be alive still for all I know.' She gave Drick a querulous, slantendicular look. 'I have no idea why I'm telling you this; you can't possibly imagine what it means to have another human soul conjoined with your own, and to have it torn from you before your eyes.' She shrugged. 'But then you're a writer, so I suppose you must; a writer – a good writer – understands all of human life.'

Had it been anyone other than her, he would have taken it as an ironic sneer; but Marjorie really did have that much faith in writers. Came of being an actress, he supposed; perhaps if you devoted all your time to acting out writers' words, you ended up believing they were the truth.

Oddly, though, he *did* seem to understand what she meant – not in the bland way of common empathy, but as though he had experienced such a thing. Which was absurd, of course.

'You think I'm a good writer?' he asked.

'Of course. I've read all your stories, Roderick, you know that. You don't need my opinion.'

'No. I suppose not.'

She smiled. 'There, you're honest. I like that. Most people would say "Oh, but *everyone*'s opinion is worthwhile", wouldn't they? But everyone's opinion is not worthwhile. Most are worthless, and some are an abomination.'

'Tell me about Kismet, Marjorie.'

She poured herself another cup of camomile tea. (Drick noticed again the resemblance to urine; even the smell wasn't entirely dissimilar.) 'I resented her,' she said flatly.

Drick had expected second-hand facts, not first-hand observation. 'I thought you lived away at that time. Did you know her, then?'

'I came back for several months in 1976. I was estranged from Ralph for a short while, and I came to live with my parents. They were rather elderly by then, and I looked after them more than they me, but still I was reminded of . . . the last time I was with them. I regressed. I hadn't seen Jack for twenty years, but I kept thinking about him, and about Veronica. Eventually, I went to visit him. It was the middle of June, and sweltering. Do you remember the summer of 1976?' Drick nodded. 'The farm was terribly run down. The hedges were overgrown, and the gardens were full of weeds. He and Kismet were all alone there, and he had more or less given up.

'We talked about Veronica – or rather, I talked about Veronica while he stared at his boots and grunted from time to time. As I talked, I found myself despising him and resenting Kismet. She'd had the chance to grow up with her natural relatives, while Veronica . . . Poor child – it wasn't her fault. Veronica . . . by then she would be an adult, perhaps with children of her own. Kismet was still just a child. She didn't deserve . . . I shouldn't have felt that way about her.

'I said – I suppose I must have said something about her, something nasty. That was the only time Jack looked at me, and you've never seen such a look of loathing in a human face; part hatred, part fear.' (Having met Jack Lillystone, Drick could imagine that look, and it made him shudder.) 'He was about to say something back when Kismet came running in from the garden. She was the prettiest little thing, and dressed all in white, like a little angel. She always wore white, apparently, from top to toe; wouldn't stand for more than the merest splash of colour. Jack indulged her remarkably for such a fierce man. Just like his father with Georgina and Liza.

'Anyway, she stopped dead when she clapped eyes on me. I said hello to her, but perhaps she caught a glimpse of what I was feeling in the way I looked at her, because she turned on her heel and fled. I can still hear the sound of her heels tripping frantically down the garden path, and Jack shouting furiously after her to come back. But she wouldn't. That was the only time I ever saw her.'

'What did she look like?'

Marjorie made a rueful face. 'Prettier than anything you've ever seen. She would have grown into a very beautiful woman indeed. Slim and elegant, with long, raven hair. Romany hair, like her mother. I could almost kill myself at how I behaved. It wasn't her fault.

'When I left – That is, I decided to leave right away; Jack and I had nothing more to say to one another. As I was going up the lane towards the road, I bumped into Mrs Parmiter. Did Finn mention her? She kept house for old Jack. He took her on because Georgina had too little room in her mind for housework, even though he detested having outsiders getting close to his family. She retired immediately after old Jack died. Her last role was as nurse to him during his last illness.

'Where was I? Mrs Parmiter. I bumped into her in the lane as I was leaving. She was very old now – nearly eighty – but she still called in from time to time to bring treats for Kismet and to tell Jack all the town gossip – as though he'd have been interested! I think he tolerated her for Kismet's sake. She was a sweet old stick. When she saw me, she looked like she'd seen a ghost, and almost dropped her basket.

' "Why, it's young Marjorie Turnbull!" she exclaimed. "We thought you'd gorn off ter be a film star! Maisie Ryan said she'd seen you, but I said no, you'd be in 'Ollywood." She glanced along the lane and looked knowingly at me. She was a shrewd woman, for all her years. Did you know her grandmother was supposed to have been a witch? She was – over in Wilburton. "Been ter see young Jack, 'ave you? I'll wager you've missed that lad, even with all them mat'nee fellers arter you. There's not many like young Jack, you know."

' "No, Mrs Parmiter," I said. "And Heaven be thanked for it."

'She cackled. "See little Kismet, did you? Queer name, that, for a queer child."

'I asked her what she meant. "Oh, she's a dearie, but she torments a poor old soul something shameful. I'd a'most swear she was possessed."

'I could see she was dying to tell me, so I just nodded, and she told me the strangest tale I've ever heard – or at least, the strangest tale I've ever believed. It seems it was Kismet's custom, whenever Mrs Parmiter called, to greet her at the gate into the yard. She would perform a little curtsy as she passed and say "Good morning, Ma'am". And Mrs Parmiter would greet her in return and walk on towards the house, as though she were the Queen. The rule of the game was that she wasn't to stop and talk; if she did, Kismet would turn her back and walk away. When she crossed the yard and went round to the side of the house, she would find the kitchen door open, and, standing on the step waiting to greet her, would be Kismet again! "Good morning, Ma'am," she would say. "I trust you are well." The first time it happened, the poor old woman almost dropped down dead from shock. Now, you won't be familiar with the geography of Cuckoo Farm, but—'

'I've been there a couple of times,' said Drick, who could guess what was coming next.

'Have you? I don't imagine it's changed much. Then you'll know that the house and yard are enclosed on all sides by hedges and thick woods. There was no earthly way Kismet could get from the lane to the house without Mrs Parmiter seeing her; at least not in the time it would take even an elderly lady to walk the distance from gate to kitchen door. No *earthly* means, as I say. If Mrs Parmiter hadn't been the granddaughter of a witch, and therefore subject to a certain compulsion to take it in her stride, I daresay she'd have never set foot on the place again. As far as she could see, the child had some kind of transmigratory powers.'

Something was bothering Drick; an uneasiness that had

194

nothing to do with transmigration, but he couldn't put his finger on it. 'You believed this?' he asked.

'I believe she saw what she said she saw. Presumably there was some trick involved; but what a trick it must have been, and for a child to do such a thing . . . well, she was a clever girl, and had an impudent sense of humour, just like her mother.'

That was it. 'That's the second time you've said she was like her mother. But you never knew her mother – no-one did.'

Was it Drick's imagination, or did Marjorie colour slightly? 'Did I say that? I mean her grandmother. Georgina. Of course I did.'

Drick studied her face, trying to detect a lie. 'Georgina had . . . what did you call it? Romany hair?'

'Yes. Yes, she did.' Marjorie chuckled, and Drick couldn't help thinking it sounded a little forced. 'How could I mean her mother? I never knew her. Goodness, I didn't even live here then!'

Drick chose his next words carefully. 'Marjorie, I'm not in any way suggesting that what I said last time is actual fact, but . . . but can you swear to me that there isn't the tiniest part of you that has suspicions about Kismet's parentage? Could you swear that?'

'Swear what? Suspicions? Well, I don't really understand what it is you're . . . that is, I . . .' Her voice sank to a meek little whisper. 'Yes, I do.'

'You swear?'

There was a long pause. 'No, I suspect.'

Drick waited a few moments, and then said as gently as he could: 'Liza?'

Marjorie nodded.

'And how strongly do you suspect?'

When her voice came, it was tiny: 'Completely.' Suddenly, she burst out: 'How could I think such a thing, and yet how could I not?' she demanded, and then the words came tumbling out: 'Not a living soul – not me, nor Finn, nor even Mrs Parmiter – ever claimed to know a thing about Kismet's mother; not even her name. There was no wedding that anyone ever heard of. And there were Jack and Liza – alone, so far as anyone could tell – on the farm. And one or two of us who knew them a bit remembered what they'd been like as children. And then the beating Jack

195

gave Colin Pickett. Such violence, even for a Lillystone – they said Colin was crippled for life . . .'

The torrent petered out, and she stared into her empty teacup. 'Such jealousy,' she murmured, almost inaudible now. 'Jealousy like that is more than fraternal.'

Drick got up and, without saying anything, filled the kettle and made her another pot of tea – real tea, which he found in a caddy above the sink. When he sat down again, he lit a cigarette and drew hard on it. 'Okay, so we accept the likelihood that Liza was Kismet's mother, but has it ever occurred to you that Jack might not have been the father?'

Marjorie's face brightened momentarily, then fell again. 'I don't know,' she said. 'Who could the father have been? After Colin, I can't imagine any man daring to lay a finger on her.'

'It's not impossible, though. I don't suppose Mrs Parmiter's still around, is she? She might have some idea.'

'She might have had ideas, but she died seven or eight years ago. Any knowledge she had has gone with her.'

The dogs, who had been sleeping on the floor, began to stir. Manni got up, stretched, yawned cavernously, and scraped a forepaw down Drick's leg.

'That means let me out for a pee. We'd better be going. Thanks for talking.'

Marjorie shrugged. 'Oh, I've got more talk than I know what to do with. You're welcome to come and relieve me of some of it whenever you like.' She stood up. 'Roderick, there was something I meant to ask you.'

'Yes?'

'Last time we spoke, you asked me what I'd say if you told me Kismet was still alive. What did you mean by that? Do you think she might be?'

He sighed. After she had confided so much in him, he ought to tell her about Kismet – or the woman who claimed to be Kismet. If anyone deserved to know, she did, if only in exchange for what she had told him. 'No,' he said. 'I said it to provoke; nothing more than that. I behaved very badly. I'm sorry.'

Out in the street, as he waited for Manni to finish decorating a beech tree on the verge, he realised what else had been bothering him in Marjorie's references to Kismet. How, on the basis of one meeting (especially if it happened the way she described it), did she know that Kismet was clever and charming (he remembered that casual parting reference from months ago) and had an impudent sense of humour? He supposed she might be projecting Liza's personality onto her daughter, or might be repeating an assessment she'd had from the old housekeeper. She hadn't had more contact with Kismet than she claimed, had she?

In the end, he couldn't be bothered to wrestle with the thought, so he shrugged it off.

'Finished?' he said to the dog. 'Come on, then.'

Twins. It was so obvious he wondered why he hadn't thought of it before.

He was in his favourite position: reclining on the sofa with a drink in one hand and a cigarette in the other; his best thinking position, better even than the bath. He had been going over the afternoon's conversation when the realisation opened out like morning glory, spreading its petals brightly and perfectly in his mind; it took him so much by surprise that he sat bolt upright, sending his ashtray bowling onto the floor and nearly tipping red wine into his lap. 'Kismet' was a pair of twins. The two-places-at-once trick she played on the housekeeper. It fitted. And why should anyone outside such a family necessarily know that the one child was two? Even the housekeeper didn't know, because she had retired, and only visited occasionally. Jack wouldn't enlighten anyone; he probably didn't even *speak* to anyone, let alone discuss his private family business, and the girls wouldn't admit to Mrs Parmiter they were two, because it would scupper the fun they had at her expense. Also, and this was the bit that made him jerk upright, it explained how Kismet could die and yet still be alive.

The rush of exhilaration didn't last long. The hypothesis might test well against some of the salient facts, but it didn't satisfy him. Not because it was inherently weak, but because he no longer felt that Kismet was a phenomenon to be explained by hypotheses and facts. He no longer believed that she was any more than a figment; not of his imagination, but of somebody else's – Finn Bourn's, Marjorie's, Jack's, old Mrs Parmiter's. Kismet, the living girl in his mind, was his; Kismet – the little girl drowned – was theirs. This was why he had held her back from Marjorie. His Kismet didn't belong to their story. The more family history he discovered, the further she seemed to recede; the deeper he probed to uncover what lay under the distorting water, the more the river mud blossomed and clouded his view. Surely, somehow, sometime, somewhere, she would return to him. Wouldn't she? If she was his?

He tried to hurry the process along. During the weeks that followed, as February deep-froze the world outside his windows, then March slowly thawed it to dripping damp, he tried many times to conjure her up with the notepad. He described walks where she waited for him as he turned the corner of Kiln Lane, he had her come to his door, he went back to Cuckoo Farm and stood in the wrecked bedroom, waiting for her to appear as he had ordained. He wrote dozens of scenarios, where dozens of combinations of circumstances brought her back to him, but it was no good. *That function has been disabled.* He wasted four whole pages of his notepad before accepting that, so far as Kismet was concerned, it was utterly powerless. She was beyond its reach, subject to her own laws. If Kismet wanted to be found, she would come to him, as she had come to him before, in her own good time.

In the meantime, while he waited for her to reveal herself, he corralled what he had of her in his mind, and began to deal with her the only way he knew how. He put the notepad away, took out some normal, ordinary paper, and wrote about her. If he couldn't have her for real, he would fictionalise her into submission.

He didn't write about her directly, because it wouldn't serve the purpose he had in mind; instead, he divided her story into pieces and assimilated it into others. This is how he went about it.

Since discovering the source of his inspiration, he took to crossing bridges at every opportunity. He re-routed his daily walks with Manni to include as many bridges as possible. There was Ely High Bridge, the walkway over the river between Waterside and Babylon, and any number of little ditch-crossings in the fields around Roswell and Springhead Lane. Taking advantage of the

Landcruiser and its perpetually full fuel tank, dog and master travelled further afield for their walks, crossing every bridge in Cambridge and the villages for miles around.

The spy-hole opened, and ideas for novels came at him like catseyes on a night-time drive. Ninety-nine times out of a hundred they were useless, rejected as fast as they came. But a few stuck. He noted them down carefully and put the notes in manilla folders, neatly labelled, in the bottom drawer of his desk. When he had collected the seeds of three books, he stopped his bridge-twitching and set to work.

In order of occurrence, he entitled them (with typical utilitarianism) *The Tenant*, *The Musician*, and *The Model*. Disregarding order, though, he worked on them all simultaneously, turning away from one when inspiration dried and concentrating on another.

He worked away at Kismet's story like an overgrown and tangled tree, hewing it down, splitting the trunk, sawing, sanding, planing and polishing; woodsman, carpenter and joiner by turns. He cut and shaped, dowelled, glued and jointed the pieces into his new fabric until nobody but him would recognise in its grain the tree from which they had come.

At first, he was pleased with the image of himself as a craftsman, but couldn't really sustain it. Now he came to think of it, he had always found the common claim that writing was a *craft* a precious piece of false humility. Nauseating, really. For one thing, if it was a craft, it would be a damn sight easier to teach. It wasn't a craft, it was a . . . something different. Casting about for another image, he found himself recalling a passage from *The Alchemist's Apprentice*. Setting aside his work, he got the manuscript out and leafed through it. Yes, here it was.

> . . . *Izzat went to his lectern and opened the great leather-bound volume which lay upon it. He ran his long, creased forefinger down the page and stopped at an illuminated entry.*
>
> *'Here, child,' he said. 'Let my grandfather's words speak for me. If you will understand alchemy, you can do no better than hear him.'*
>
> *Rebecca stepped up beside him and peered at the page. She thought it a beautiful thing, with its bright red and gold illumination, and the*

deep brown, florid script covering the waxy vellum like wheat in a field. But she could make no sense of it; the writing swam before her eyes as she attempted to unravel words from it.

Izzat saw, and he smiled. 'You cannot read it? Then I shall demonstrate.'

He handed her down from the lectern and escorted her across the laboratory to the great oak table where the implements of his art were arrayed. Jeroboams, retorts, flacons, tubes and pipes; dishes of porcelain and glass, bottles stoppered with wax seals; all arranged about the centrepiece – a great alembic of copper and glass, as tall as a man, and mounted upon a tripod over a polished brass spirit stove.

'Medusa,' he murmured. 'I call her that for her snakes.' He laughed his harsh, breathy laugh as he fingered the pipes of glass and polished copper which fed from the alembic's upper and middle chambers. 'Come, my little apprentice, fill this for me.' He removed the copper bowl which formed the belly of the apparatus and handed it to her. She took it to the lead trough in the corner of the laboratory and filled it from the pump. When she brought it back, she found he had lit the stove. He took the bowl from her and reattached it.

'Now,' he said, as the violet flames began to lick the planished, blackened copper, 'while this warms, we take our remaining elements: Earth –' and he took a chunk of some dark substance from a shallow dish and placed it on a platter connected by a coiled pipe to the pot-belly of the alembic '– and Air.' He attached a pair of leather bellows to another pipe. 'And now for our agents and reagents. Both Allah and Shaitan are necessary to the purpose of creating gold, you see.'

Rebecca watched, hypnotised, while he began to open bottles and flacons. Using a silver spoon, he measured a quantity of iridiscent purple crystals into a porcelain dish, then let fall some drops of a clear fluid from a flacon onto them. A great balloon of purple smoke burst from the dish, and he set it aside. He performed many tricks like this, producing yellow fumes, red flames, and even a loud bang which made Rebecca's ears judder. Then he took the residues from each reaction and mixed them all together in a mortar of green stone, grinding them to a paste with a delicate-looking silver pestle.

'This is our filter,' he said when he had finished mixing and had begun spooning the paste into the belly of the alembic. 'What is base

201

and would be gold must pass through this. It is in the transmigration between here and the head that the transformation occurs. From head to hand is purification.'

He closed and sealed the belly. From a high shelf he took a small lacquered box; inside it were three balls, each about the size of a gull's egg. 'The three base elements,' he said. 'My grandfather had the knowledge of them from his grandfather, and he off his grandfather, and so back to the time of Mohammed. No other alchemist has ever discovered their secret. There is lead, which even the lowest infidel knows about; but here is also amber – the fools in their northern forests where it is plentiful, prize it for itself – is it not ironic? And thirdly, there is salt purified from the shores of the Dead Sea. Simple, you say? Their combination has eluded the greatest minds since before the time of prophets.'

One by one, he took the spheres from the box and placed them with infinite care, each within its own capsule of muslin and beeswax, in the lowest chamber of the alembic.

'The temperature is right,' he said, touching the copper vessel of water. 'The process begins. Now, quick, apprentice! Attach this to the pump.' He handed Rebecca the end of a long, flexible leather hose. She placed it over the mouth of the water pump and fixed it tight by means of an ingenious arrangement of small levers and springs. 'Now work the pump, apprentice! As fast as you can!'

She worked the handle up and down, and the leather pipe swelled and stiffened with the force of water. The pipe fed into a copper tube which spiralled over the alembic, twisting round and round the 'Medusa snakes' and then returned via a sluice to the trough. When the water began to gush out, Izzat commanded her to stop pumping.

'The temperature is regulated thus,' he explained. 'Now stand beside me, and watch alchemy at work!'

The towering apparatus vibrated, bubbled and hissed; from time to time, the noise intensified, and little jets of steam and coloured vapour were ejected from valves which protruded from the copper flasks like warts on a toad. Every so often, Izzat would lean forward and place his cheek close to some part of the alembic – now the belly, now the head, now the filigree of pipes – and declare that the temperature was growing. Then he would order Rebecca to operate the pump: 'Gently, child . . . a little more . . . now stop!' Then he would lapse into an attitude of intense contemplation, resting his beard on his knotted knuckles and gazing at his machine.

At last, there was a deep gurgling sound from the head, and a thin yellow fluid began to run down one of the three glass pipes, draining into a porcelain vessel. 'The first distillate,' said Izzat. 'And now the second,' he added, as a clear fluid dripped from the tip of another tube into another vessel. 'The third distillate, which a perfumer would call the essence absolue, *is collected via the silver pipe.' He indicated a slender strand feeding out of the very top of the alembic. Instead of draining away like the first and second substances, the contents of this pipe were carried off to an elaborately engraved chamber standing upon its own tripod to one side of the table. After what seemed a painfully long time, she began to notice a gentle hissing emanating from this chamber.*

Izzat noticed the expression on her face, and grinned. 'It occurs,' he said. 'The process reaches its conclusion.'

When the sound ceased, he disconnected the silver pipe and lifted the chamber off its tripod with reverent care. 'This must be left to cool,' he said. 'It is of absolute importance that impure air does not touch it before it has consolidated.' He placed the chamber in a bowl half-filled with white sand. 'This ensures that it does not cool too fast,' he explained, and turned over a large hourglass. 'The cooling will take one hour and thirty-three minutes precisely.'

While they waited, Izzat sat his apprentice alongside him before the fire and lectured her on the process of distillation. He described how his grandfather's grandfather's grandfather had perfected the particular application of it in this alembic. ('His original, which was constructed in the famous workshop of the smith Gamal at Khokand, was far superior to this,' he said, 'but it is no longer possible to obtain the materials nor the workmanship. This equipment functions well enough, but is a poor substitute. Alas, all things decline in time.')

At last, the sand in the glass ran out, and Izzat rose to his feet. He lifted the chased copper chamber out of the sand and set it on the table next to a candlebranch. 'Behold, apprentice,' he said, 'the fruit of our work.'

Rebecca held her breath as he raised the circular lid of the chamber

203

and lifted out a small, perfectly spherical pearl of bright, gleaming metal. He held it between the tips of finger and thumb, and for a second the candlelight seemed to shine right through it, suffusing it with a deep, immeasurably rich glow.

'Gold!' she exclaimed.

That was more like it. He could see himself more as an alchemist than a woodworker: conjuring fictional gold out of the base materials of life. *Fictional* gold, indeed. He read on.

. . . Izzat grinned; a great wolfish grin that made his forked beard stick out like elephant tusks. 'Gold indeed,' he said. 'Now watch.'

He rolled the sphere round and round his palm, then tossed it high into the air; it glittered briefly at the top of its arc, then fell. Izzat's arms swept out, and he clapped the falling sphere between his palms. When he drew them apart and held them out to the light, there was nothing to be seen but a dusting of whitish powder clinging to the folds of skin.

Rebecca cried out in alarm. 'What happened to it? Where did the gold go?'

He brushed the dust off his hands. 'Scattered to the winds,' he said. 'An illusion.'

'I don't understand.'

He looked sternly at her; his dark, slanted eyes never looked more terrifying, and she shrank back. 'You think gold can be created so easily? Pah! You know how long it takes to create that quantity of pure gold?' Rebecca shook her head dumbly. 'Five years! Five years of sweat and toil, five years of careful separation, distillation and rectification. One tiny little error and poof! all is gone, and you must begin again. This is your first lesson, apprentice; that the beginning and end of alchemy is patience.'

Yes, closer. Perversely, it occurred to him that a writer was more like a reverse alchemist, changing the gold of life into the base metal of words, but that wasn't the truth. Words were the base metal, life was the reagent, and writing was the gold. Illusory gold perhaps, gold that would collapse into dust under pressure, but while it lasted it would glister brighter than oily yellow life.

As the spring months passed into summer, he worked away at his three novels. Not all of that time was spent writing; much of the work went on in his head. Slowly, he charged the chambers of his imagination with the raw elements and distilled them gradually to an essence which drip-drip-dripped into flacons, ready to be poured out onto paper. By the beginning of June, he had discharged about seven or eight chapters of each book, and had sketches of two dozen more. With each one, he had passed the critical point where he knew that he would finish the book and finish it well. From that moment on, he wrote obsessively (and quickly – he still had his remarkable fingerpower, and could write or type as fast as he could think the words): he ate breakfast and wrote; he walked Manni and played out dialogues and descriptions in his head; he ate lunch and wrote; he wrote all afternoon and evening and sometimes long into the night. Eventually there came a midsummer afternoon when he looked inside himself and found that Kismet was gone. Her *essence absolue* had been mixed among the pages of the three new manuscripts, and there was none left.

The novels were complete: three thick stacks of printed paper sitting on his desk. He laid them in the bottom drawer side by side, closed it and left them to settle. About six months should be sufficient. Sometime around Christmas, he would get them out and see how they were doing. The heavy sediments would have settled, and he could comb through them, filtering out impurities, adding new elements, and they would then be perfect. Not gold, of course, but a fairly good substitute.

To celebrate, he took out the notepad and created himself a feast. He gorged himself on exotic fruits and roast meats and fowls that would never be found in a supermarket; he drank wines from vintages long consigned to history. Peeled, honey-glazed Tuscan grapes were slipped between his lips by gorgeous serving girls clad in a variety of serving-girl-type outfits, ranging from Roman slave to Geisha, by way of Restoration wench and Parisienne *demi-monde* waitress. (Actually, they were fantastically sophisticated synthetic replicants; he didn't want to be hampered by scruples when it came to consigning them to oblivion afterwards; but they looked, acted – and felt – exactly like the real thing.) There was music from every period of history, and an atmosphere of unparalleled, unrestrained, and eventually unclothed debauchery reigned all night, until he eventually collapsed from exhaustion shortly after dawn, lying on a litter of cushions amongst a tangle of naked and half-naked female limbs.

(Manni, by the way, slept through the whole thing on his beanbag upstairs, but was very happy the next day when he discovered his bowl filled with the leftovers from the feast. No dog in history ever ate so well.)

Packet 12

It was nearly midday when Drick was woken by the sound of hammering on the front door. He swung out of bed feeling refreshed and revived, as though he had enjoyed a true sleep of the soul; his body had been combed through, and every twist and niggle of weariness removed. Even the persistent dull ache in his left shoulder – the product of prolonged bad typing posture – had vanished. He sprang like a faun across to the window and threw it open, letting in a wash of warm, clean summer air. Jeremy was standing on the pavement below, looking up at him. 'Down in a minute,' he said.

Before opening the door, he checked the downstairs rooms for tell-tale signs of the previous night's orgy, but there were none that he could see. His serving girls, true to the letter of their contract, had cleared away every trace, gathering up the silver platters, goblets, wine pitchers and leftover food, and taking the whole lot with them to oblivion. Drick had seen to this very smartly, he thought. There was a pantry (or scullery or laundry room – he wasn't sure which, only that it contained a large Belfast sink and was a little too damp for storing food in) which opened off the kitchen. He had ordained that the serving girls, at the first light of dawn, would open the pantry door, walk through, and instantly vanish; not be teleported elsewhere, but simply wink out of existence.

There was no evidence in the living room to suggest that anything had happened here; the girls had not only taken all their paraphernalia with them, they had also tidied up. A yucca Drick had kicked over while dancing with his Restoration wench had been righted and all its scattered soil swept up. A red wine stain on the sofa had been miraculously removed, and a broken pane in the French window had been replaced (he examined it, and found the putty still soft). Since he had forgotten to order cleaning and tidying, he was impressed by the girls' dedication to duty and thought perhaps he should reward them somehow. Perhaps he could call them back into existence and bestow permanent, independent life on them. On the other hand, maybe that wasn't such a great reward. He'd think about it.

He was even more impressed when he found that they had filled Manni's bowl with leftover scraps: to anyone else, it would look like any old mash of slops; only Drick knew there was ptarmigan in there, and roast guinea-fowl with wine gravy, honeyed sweetmeats from Crete and *kefir* from beyond the Aral Sea. The vet would have had a fit.

Satisfied that the coast was clear, he let Jeremy in at last. 'Wotcher, cock,' he said. 'Are you a doctor yet?'

Jeremy rolled his eyes. 'God, don't talk about it. I've got my viva on Monday.'

'No kidding. Who with?'

Jeremy named the two eminent archaeologists – one from Cambridge, the other from Reading University – who had been booked to examine his thesis. 'I've got to wear a gown,' he said miserably. 'Can you believe it? I've hired one for 50p from the Graduate Union.'

Drick sniggered. 'You'll walk it,' he said. 'I feel it in my water.'

Jeremy looked about the room. 'Where's poochy-chops? Don't tell me you've taken my advice and hired him out as a cart-horse.'

At that moment, Manni, scarcely able to believe his luck, was devouring the contents of his bowl; for once in his life, his breakfast was more exciting than visitors. When he had finished, he came trotting into the living room, licking his lips and trying unsuccessfully to reach a speck of Tashkent melon which was stuck on the tip of his nose. He greeted Jeremy with his usual whirl of limbs and claws and great huffs of gravy breath, then ran back to the kitchen and returned with a sandal in his mouth. He dropped it at Jeremy's feet and sat waiting for praise. Jeremy picked it up by a broken thong and held it out like a killed rat.

'Might this belong to your mystery woman, young Drick?' he grinned.

Drick recognised it as belonging to Flavia, his Roman replicant. She had been his favourite, with an irresistible combination of demure, virginal appearance and unspeakably licentious tastes, and he had cavorted with her more than with any of the others. Evidently, those flimsy little sandals weren't built to withstand that degree of exertion, and this one must have slipped off as she crossed the threshold of the pantry on her way to outer darkness.

'Undoubtedly,' he said. 'It looks like one of hers.'

'So, are you going to spill the broth this time? Who is she, and do I get to meet her?'

'Oh, I doubt it. She's not around any more. Her name's Flavia, and she was born around AD 75. Gorgeous girl, but I had to send her back where she came from. I couldn't stand the pace.'

'Okay, I'll mind my own business.' Jeremy tossed the sandal aside. Manni seized it and began pulling it to pieces. 'So, what *did* you want to talk about?'

'What did *I* want to talk about?'

'Last time we spoke, you seemed desperate to talk about something. Sorry I couldn't oblige, by the way; you can imagine the amount of work I had on.'

Drick smiled. 'I've written three novels since then, you know.'

'Sure you have.'

'No, seriously. Three of them.' He took out a cigarette and threw the packet to Jeremy. 'Try these, they're Turkish. What I wanted to talk about . . .' He hesitated. It was on the tip of his tongue to tell the whole story: Kismet, the notepad, the drowned daughter of Jack Lillystone, but the desire wasn't really there any more. 'I don't want to talk about it any more.'

Jeremy lit his cigarette. 'We used to tell each other everything, Drick,' he said. 'At least,' he added, inhaling deeply, 'I did.'

There was such a tone of suppressed hurt in his voice that Drick gave in. Even so, he didn't tell the story as it had happened; instead, he presented it as the basis for a novel. The story of the Lillystones he told as fact, exactly as he had heard it from Finn and Marjorie; the rest, he made out, was merely a fiction he had a notion to build on top of it. (Having distilled and poured the whole thing so methodically into the three novels, this didn't feel like much of a lie; none of it seemed very real now.)

'Twins,' said Jeremy as soon as he heard the account of the trick played on the housekeeper.

'That's what I thought!' Drick exclaimed, leaning forward; then, remembering himself, he slumped back in an attitude of dejection. 'Is it that obvious?' he asked. 'I hoped it might be a surprise.'

Jeremy was looking at him oddly, with an expression that might have been faint distaste. 'Depends how you work it. Twins is a pretty obvious device, though.'

'It is, isn't it? I'll come up with something better.' Drick's dejection suddenly became real; he'd thought twins was a pretty neat idea, and had used that aspect of Kismet's story as the pivot for *The Tenant*. 'What do you think about the girl?' he asked casually.

'Kismet? I think she sounds . . .' Jeremy grinned. 'D'you remember Ellen Rees? That peculiar cadaverous girl you were in love with at junior school?'

'She wasn't cadaverous; she was ethereal.'

'She always looked underfed and had that not-all-there look in her eyes.'

'You were just jealous because she held my hand all through breaktime while you couldn't get Sandra Bryant even to look at you.'

Jeremy gaped in outrage. 'You're fantasising, man. Didn't you see her dance with me at Duxy's birthday party? Right through "Telegram Sam" *and* "Tiger Feet".'

'Only because you promised her your dinner money for a week. It was shameful; prostitution at nine years old, I ask you.'

'You're blathering, boy; I wouldn't rely on your memory for yesterday's date.' Jeremy stubbed his cigarette out. 'Except for Ellen Rees. I didn't think she'd have left that big an impression.'

'You're saying Kismet's based on her? She isn't, you know. Not by a mile.'

'Sounds just like her to me. Do you remember what happened to her?'

Drick shrugged. 'No idea. She vanished just before we went to Croesy Comp. I remember her being in Mrs Darke's class, but then . . . nothing. Must've moved away. Anyway,' he added, 'Kismet is not based on Ellen Rees, whatever you think.'

And he stuck by his assertion; Jeremy noticed, though, that mention of his infatuation with the strange little girl brought a peculiar faraway look into Drick's eyes, and that it didn't leave for the rest of the afternoon. He was wrong, though; the look had nothing to do with Ellen Rees. What had occurred to Drick was how much Flavia had looked like Sandra Bryant – or rather, like his image of Sandra Bryant as a nineteen-year-old. He had last seen Sandra aged ten, just before she and her parents emigrated to Canada, and he had forgotten all about her until Jeremy mentioned her. He was astonished at the way she had lain unnoticed in his memory for nearly twenty years – not even dormant, but slowly growing to adulthood. That was why he looked so preoccupied. That, and something else. One of the small number of things Jeremy didn't know about Drick was that Sandra Bryant had stopped him and snogged his face off as they walked home through Paddock Woods after that very same birthday party. He hadn't needed to part with any dinner money at all, and the incident had warmed him for weeks after. He'd imagined himself glowing visibly like a Ready Brek kid. Remembering it now, he was amazed at how guilty he still felt about the betrayal.

The feeling was profoundly uncomfortable. After Jeremy had gone home, Drick, feeling the need for distraction, got his notepad out and, with reckless fatalism and two short sentences, took himself off to the Upper Palaeolithic for a holiday.

He had never cared overmuch for the period – sure, they had some very attractive cave paintings, but he had always thought their material culture unendurably dull: all those flint flakes and bits of antler, with only the occasional fat-titted figurine to break the monotony. Its one redeeming feature, though, was the sparseness of its population. He had once calculated, for the purposes

211

of a second-year essay, using Binford's studies of hunter-gatherer land-use patterns as a model, that the population of Europe *ca* 14,000 years ago would have been somewhat less than two hundred people. Yes, he could do with some of that solitude right now. Unfortunately, being an archaeologist, his perception of the past, however remote, was inextricably associated with humans, and he materialised slap in the middle of the biggest bison hunt the Périgord region had seen in over half a century.

He only managed to escape being trampled to death by hurling himself over the edge of a small precipice, thus avoiding both the thundering hooves of hundreds of terrified, steaming bison and a fall over the much steeper drop towards which they were being driven by a dozen screaming men who brandished sharpened poles from behind hurdle fences. He lay in the dust, battered and bruised, his hands clamped over his ears to keep out the deafening screams of men and beasts as the herd bore down on the edge, reared up momentarily like a swelling wave, and then broke, cascading down the bluff in a nightmare of flailing limbs and hell-bound bellowing. They landed, broken and twisted, in a sort of corral, also built of hurdles, behind which more men with pointed poles waited for the torrent to cease. When the last animal had hurled itself off and landed with a loud, scrabbling thud, they leapt over the fence and began spearing the dozens of bison which had been left unkilled by the fall and still wriggled and bellowed pitiably amidst the heap. Meanwhile, the drivers scrambled down the bluff and joined in the slaughter.

Drick didn't wait around to watch the butchering; while the men were engrossed in slicing up the carcasses with their flint blades, he stole away and made for a wood half a mile away across the plain. He was appalled by the waste he had just seen. There were around twenty or thirty men in the hunting party; even if each man represented a large extended family, they couldn't use all the meat lying in that corral. Even if they'd had the technology to preserve the unused portion, they couldn't eat their way through it in a hundred years. It was ironic that it was these people's descendants, a thousand generations down the line, who would garner a reputation for rapaciousness; a few thousand more of

212

these guys, and Europe would be a barren wasteland before the Neolithic got under way. But then, he reflected, how else could you kill thundering great beasts with nothing more than pointed sticks and bits of flint? Europe's fauna was paying the price for humankind's pathetic technology. Now, *there* was food for thought.

Understandably, he liked the Upper Palaeolithic even less after that. His notepad had survived the fall (fortunately, he had put a cord through its spiral binding and hung it round his neck, in anticipation of unforeseen circumstances), so he sat under the forest eaves and created himself a civilised meal. A vegetarian meal. He also acquired some warm clothes. The Arctic began only a couple of hundred miles north of here (Britain lay buried under ice sheets), and it was terribly cold. After he had eaten, he got up and walked. He travelled for several weeks, and soon found the solitude he had come looking for. He stood on the coast of the Mediterranean (a good few miles further out and lower down than it was in his own time), and savoured the air of the Côte d'Azur: it was cold, clean and pure, and the nearest holidaymaker was fourteen millennia away.

He created himself a boat, and sailed out to a small island where, at last, he had his holiday. He stayed for three weeks, living a life of sublime isolation in a small house he wrote for himself on a knoll overlooking the sea. (As the island would be covered by water when the ice sheets melted in another four thousand years or so, he figured it didn't matter if he left behind a few anomalous artefacts.) Eventually, when solitude began to feel like loneliness, he said goodbye to his house, his island and the early stone age, and wrote himself back into his living room, arriving about forty minutes after he had left. Manni, who had been asleep on the sofa for the last hour, looked up in surprise when he materialised, then stretched, yawned, and fell asleep again.

Drick went on to have many more adventures. The travel bug hadn't merely bitten him, it had sunk its teeth to the bone and wouldn't let go. After his Palaeolithic outing, he was more cautious about how he sent himself, picking his locations with more regard to safety, and ensuring that he went appropriately attired for the period and place.

At first, he designed each trip carefully and wrote it in the notepad. But with the precautions needed for safe travel, he soon found that its pages were being consumed at a frightful rate. He hit upon an ingenious solution which suggested itself one evening when he was thinking fondly about his serving girls and wondering whether he should call them back for another party. The idea was very simple: he turned the pantry door into a magic portal. Whenever he wished to travel, he merely had to clear his mind, concentrate on where he wanted to go, and step through the pantry door. He had created his very own Mr Benn changing room. Another, equally neat idea obviated the need to take the notepad with him. He simply endowed himself with the ability to create anything he needed by an unwritten act of will (a trick, incidentally, which only worked within his adventures; the notepad couldn't give him omnipotence independent of itself in his own 'real' time and place). And to return to his kitchen safe and sound, all he had to do was click his heels at any time and say, 'There's no place like home'. (Well, what other method could any self-respecting dimension-jumper use?)

He walked the streets of Victorian London, staring openmouthed at depths of poverty and heights of opulence whose surface Dickens, apparently, had barely scratched; he sat in the newly built hall of Trinity College amongst a press of undergraduates who stank of sweat and damp, eating fatty pork and drinking rancid wine while the icy fenland wind howled in through the unglazed windows; he watched Neolithic farmers building a long barrow in the Wiltshire hills, and was massively delighted at how catastrophically wrong his former fellows were about almost every aspect of construction, organisation, function and ritual; he stood on a hill above Botany Bay and watched the *Endeavour* sail by; he bought a meat pie from the cookshop in Great Newport Street whose upstairs rooms would one day be the offices of Obelisk Press, and stood eating it in Charing Cross, watching them tearing down the old Golden Cross Inn to extend the great new square, the needle of Nelson's Column rising

214

gradually into the smoky, smut-strewn air; he was chased through the back-streets of Paris by an angry mob who had taken him for an English aristocratic spy (just for the sake of getting the full Revolutionary experience, he let himself get taken as far as the tumbril before clicking his heels and getting the hell out).

He went through a brief spate of meeting famous people from history, but gave it up when he discovered that they weren't nearly as interesting as he'd imagined. Napoleon, for instance, turned out to be little more than a morose, balding little man with a foul temper. Certainly he had charisma, but beneath the layers of myth, he was no different from the politicians of any other age, full of piss and banal messianism. One politician Drick did take to was Abraham Lincoln, who was actually more interesting than his image, with a fund of good anecdotes and an acid sense of humour. Also, his views on slavery were more complex than Drick had been led to believe.

The more he adventured, the more adventurous he became. He had read his science fiction, and he knew the possible consequences of time travel: the risk of changing things in the past. There were two basic schools of thought. One argued that making the slightest alteration to any period in history (say, stopping someone in the street of, say, sixteenth-century Heidelberg to ask the time) would cause a chain of ballooning consequences which would make the present unrecognisable when you returned to it (America a Third World state while the rest of the globe suffocated under the heel of the Lithuanian Empire). The other school contended that changing things would simply be impossible; your presence would be imperceptible to the people in the past, and, since you did not technically exist in that time, interfering in it would be a logical impossibility. The truth, as some people had suspected, lay somewhere in between. Drick found that he could act in the past, doing things, making things different from how he found them – but he couldn't alter the course of history. History *had happened*, and the consequences of any act he might commit were simply what history had determined. Had he, for instance, put himself aboard the *Titanic* and tried to prevent disaster, then it would have turned out that it was

215

his preventive actions that drove the ship onto the iceberg. (He never tried this, by the way; he learned from smaller, accidental incidents how time worked, and so avoided big gestures.)

This stricture on changing things didn't seem to apply to the present; there he could alter to his heart's content, so long as he wasn't in the past when he did it. The 'present', he discovered, was not confined to the passing moment, but consisted of an indeterminate period of time culminating in the right-now. The depth of the present varied according to what aspect of reality he tinkered with. The determining factor seemed to be how directly the phenomenon in question was being played out in the present. If it was a person, then the alterable depth went back to their birth; if it was an idea or invention (the Internet, say), the cut-off point was the inception of the idea. There were limitations: deeply entrenched ideas (like communism or democracy) couldn't be changed; only recent conceptions which retained a certain ephemeral quality could be messed with.

These discoveries brought him back to considering the questions which had so exercised him when he first acquired the notepad: 1) Could he kill a person with it? 2) Could he bring them back to life? and 3) Could he wipe a person out of existence altogether? Replicant serving girls were one thing; a real, living, breathing human was something else. He decided to settle all three questions once and for all.

He thought long and hard about who to kill. It had to be someone who wouldn't be greatly missed; whose death would make the world a better place. However, they shouldn't be so bad that their resurrection would be completely disastrous. After considering and rejecting several candidates, he finally settled on Anne Widdecombe, a woman he objected to on aesthetic as well as political grounds; a woman as ugly physically as her views were morally, snarl-mouthed and distended with spite. But not an utterly monstrous blot on humanity to rank with, say, Nikolai Ceaucescu or the inventor of mustard gas.

He killed her in a particularly violent road accident. She was driving from her constituency office to her home when a prison van pulled out of a side road, causing her to swerve into the path of a Golf GTi containing a gang of joyriders. She was the only fatal casualty. The car thieves escaped from the scene, as did the occupants of the prison van (all of whom had been wrongly convicted under recent get-tough initiatives). Drick watched the news reports to check that she was definitely dead, his emotions a strange brew of glee and horror as he looked at the footage of the scene. Then he brought her back to life. Or, rather, he erased her death (resurrection, he decided would be going it a bit strong). The prison van arrived at the junction a split second earlier, and she was merely forced to brake sharply. For good measure, he also improved her a little, recreating her as the much pleasanter person she is today, and backdated the upgrade to her birth so that there would be no noticeable hiatus. (I can picture your expression – believe it, she was worse before.)

For his next trick, he wiped out Ewan Brereton. You've never heard of him, of course, because by the time Drick had finished with him he had never existed.

A little history lesson. Until August 1994, Ewan Brereton was the most powerful, most unpleasant, most detested member of the Conservative Party after la Thatch herself. He was loathed even within the Party for the unscrupulous, corrupt, power-mad bastard he was. Only Thatcher liked him; he was her Rottweiler (said the press imaginatively), guarding her back against plots by members of her cabinet, helping to preserve her premiership when it was challenged in late 1988 by Douglas Hurd. Brereton was also the man who, as Trade and Industry Secretary, promoted the sale of nuclear weapons technology to Iraq; in two separate terms as Home Secretary, he became known to the press as Blood And Guts Brereton after sending in troops to break up miners' picket lines in 1984. He did the same against the Poll Tax demonstrations, an action which led to sixteen gunshot casualties among the demonstrators – three of them fatal. As Defence Secretary during Desert Storm he was responsible for initiating secret orders (actually not so secret, once they were leaked by an appalled civil servant) for testing chemical agents on Iraqi prisoners of war. It was this last piece of outrage which led to the great outpouring of scandal which precipitated the 1991 general election (the items listed here were just the most salient of Brereton's great achievements; he was more corrupt than a month-old carcass). Ironically, amidst the electoral slaughter, Brereton was one of the few Conservatives to keep his seat.

Drick annihilated him without the least compunction. But when he went to the library afterwards and mugged up the revised history of the past two decades, he was startled at how little the world was changed by the excision. It was better in some ways, certainly, but some of the events he had thought Brereton largely responsible for (such as the Falklands War) had happened without him. A definite downside was that Labour lost the election (which had moved to '92); a shame, because Neil Kinnock had actually made a surprisingly good prime minister, and some classic performances in the Commons were lost forever when Drick unwittingly pushed him back into opposition. The Prime Minister was now some shop dummy called Major, and the Labour Party was under a man called Blair. Where the hell had *they* come from? Who were they? They looked like a pair of estate agents. He was even more bewildered, talking to people, to find that nobody else had a very clear idea how the two leaders had got where they were; they had just risen suddenly in the dark, like fungus.

Disappointed by the effects of his intervention, Drick didn't take up the moral improvement of the world as a full-time occupation. So far as he could see, it was so irremediably fucked that trying to unfuck it was beyond the powers of even the near-omnipotent. If you pulled at one piece of the tangle and straightened it out, the effort only caused an even worse snarl elsewhere. Miracles couldn't save mankind. Even God had been forced to admit defeat; he had resorted to flooding the bastards out, guilty and innocent together; his only mistake had been letting Noah's gang escape and start the whole rotten process over again.

Drick gave up trying to make the world better; as a kind of penance for his failure, he decided to go and study just how bad it could be. He took up travelling again.

In the world outside his house, people's lives moved on. Jeremy took his viva, passed and received his doctorate. Elsa sold up her business and moved back to Norfolk. Marjorie Turnbull received a second stab at reviving her acting career. She was contacted by an associate of her former agent and offered a starring role in a series of ads for a brand of wholemeal bread. This led to a part in a West End revival of *Entertaining Mr Sloane* and a succession of small film offers. She continued to live in Ely, however, and was to be seen regularly walking with Frazer round the fields and lanes. Finn Bourn suffered a mild stroke and was moved out of his prefab into sheltered housing. And *The Alchemist's Apprentice* was published amidst a raging torrent of apathy and indifference. Obelisk hoped for reviews in local papers, the *Literary Review* and other semi-invisible places, but nothing had come to light as yet.

All of which mattered to Drick rather less than the colour of the dustman's underpants. He had his mind on other things.

For his second round of great journeys, he decided to go and see what war was like. Like many overgrown boys, he had always harboured a slightly morbid, slightly childlike fascination with battles and weapons. The fact that it conflicted with his generally peaceable nature only made the fascination more piquant. Now he was going to bring that conflict to a head; he would select the very worst of warfare and force himself to view it from close quarters.

He was more circumspect in his preparations for these trips: period clothing and an unobtrusive manner wouldn't protect him from bullets and bayonets, so he had his pantry portal render him invisible and invulnerable. He was only going to observe, so there was no sense in putting himself in physical danger. Besides, his purpose was to expose himself to *other people's* fear and suffering, not his own: he was out to shock and horrify himself, not garner some kind of assuagement of his guilt by sharing the danger of war.

He began his tour systematically, starting with recent wars and working his way back. From the Basra Road to Thermopylae, he stood on the sidelines and saw what damage humans could do to each other. He watched the waves of landing craft lumber in to Omaha Beach, launching their cargoes of men into drowning water and curtains of machine-gun bullets; he stood in the German lines on Thiepval Ridge on the first day of the Somme and watched the gunners reaping down the advancing lines of British infantry; he floated above the field at Gettysburg and watched the Union cavalry charge the Confederate lines; he looked down from the Causeway Heights as the Light Brigade tore through clouds of smoke towards the Russian batteries, shot cutting great lanes through their dressed ranks; he saw the 27th Inniskillings at Waterloo, standing their ground hour by hour while the French artillery broke them down, blood and bone; the English archers at Agincourt, arrows spent, tearing into the overcrowded flanks of the French men-at-arms with their heavy mallets, smashing heads and crushing limbs; Trajan's legionaries forming a jostling, rippling wall of shields against the screaming suicide charges of Dacian warriors ... The images ran together, forming in his brain a single continuous, unrelenting reel of violence.

And he was shocked – but not in the way he had anticipated. Startled, perhaps, rather than shocked, at how little he felt. It was like seeing the action on a cinema screen – true, if it was cinema it was fifty-foot high Cinemax with 3-D surround sound, dynamic seating and piped-in smells, but somehow it wasn't really like *being* there. No, that wasn't the problem; he felt present physically, but he didn't engage with the horrors around him at any real emotional level. Surely the fact that he was seeing real men, not film extras, killing, wounding, screaming in rage and agony; that the blood bursting from their bodies was real, not cosmetic, should have jarred his brain and shocked him to the depths of his soul. It didn't, and it wasn't merely because he wasn't in mortal danger himself. A battle, he decided, was too much to encompass in its entirety; where he expected gut-level shock and disgust, he only got a blurred sensation of unease and ... yes, he had to admit it – excitement too.

It might have been significant that the only sights which really jarred him were ones he hadn't expected. The German machine-gunners on the Somme, for example. Like everyone else, he'd had an image of the soldier crouched behind his gun, gripping its handles and directing its fire across the ranks of the advancing enemy. The guns he saw didn't have hand-grips; they were secured on their traverse-plates with friction screws, and the gunners moved them by knocking the side of the breech with a block of wood at regular intervals of a second or so: *bladabladablada*–knock-*bladabladablada*–knock-*bladabladablada*–knock – without even looking at their targets – from one end of the traverse to the other, then back again, concentrating on feeding in the ammunition and keeping the supply of barrel coolant flowing. *That* gave him a jolt. So did the sheer impossibility of making *any* sense of what was going on at any point during the day at Waterloo through the constant drifting, dragging curtains of powder smoke. He'd expected white plumes spurting out and dissipating in the breeze, not a permanent, impenetrable fog. There were other things that registered (the incredible din of a battle at close quarters between armoured men with hand-weapons, for instance – more brain-curdling than anything from the age of explosives), but none that provoked the war-sadness or rage he had believed he should feel.

He didn't make all these trips and see all these sights in one long tour, of course, but over a period of weeks and months; in the gaps between, he wrote down his impressions. It was only then, forming the sights (he didn't feel justified in calling them experiences) into writing, that he came close to producing an emotional reaction, and he wondered whether he was only capable of understanding when the *out there* was brought inside through the medium of written words.

While he wrote, he drank. He had always found that alcohol eased the transition of thoughts from head to paper, but now the process seemed to require extra lubrication. And the more he wrote, the more he drank. He worked his way up to two bottles of red wine in an evening, then added a third to get him through the afternoon.

He wasn't aware of it at the time – or if he was, it was only in the vaguest, most distant, intangible way – but he was trying to find something. Even had he been aware that he was looking, though, he would still have been no wiser about *what* he was looking for. His efforts to change the world; when that failed, his journeys after horror its most hideous corners; when they failed, his attempt to retrieve something from writing about them; when that was only partially successful, his pouring-on of blinding wine – through all of it, he was seeking something. Some*one*.

For as long as he could remember, he had felt as if a part of him had been torn out, but that the rupture had been so skilfully sutured he couldn't find the place; there was no scar, not even any *pain* as such, just an indefinable sense of loss. The feeling had been with him for so long, he no longer thought about it. *Something* had reminded him, though; something recent.

It all caved in on him on New Year's Eve, when he had been living alone in his cottage in New Barns Road for just over a year. He had spent the afternoon describing his walk through the woods and cornfields round Sharpsburg in the aftermath of the Battle of Antietam, trying to breathe the stench of fresh corpses onto the paper – it was an indescribable smell of sweat and serge and leather and blood mixed with the linger of spent powder and burning – like an abattoir in a farmyard next to a steel works.

There was one picture that had stuck in his mind; out of all he had seen on his travels, it was the only one he couldn't assimilate. Lying on the edge of a wood near the Dunker church was a dead horse; its rider, a Union cavalryman, was sprawled beside it, his face laid open by a sabre cut from eye to mouth. He was alive, but only just, and a comrade was trying to give him a drink from his canteen. Most of the water sloshed out, pink with blood, through the hole in his cheek. Drick moved closer, and heard the dying man speak. *Josh*, he said, and spluttered with the effort. *Is Josh dead? I thought I saw him dead.* The soldier kneeling beside him said no, he'd seen Josh riding off the field with Hooker's staff. *Are you sure?* Yes, Henry, I'm sure. The wounded cavalryman seemed satisfied by the news and, with a faint smile, turned over and died.

That was it, a simple and probably commonplace enough

scene, but it bothered Drick for some reason. Who was Josh? Was he cousin, brother or friend to the dying Henry, or something closer? And why did his survival mean that Henry could die contented, as though his death was of little importance compared with Josh's life? If they were so close, surely Josh would be devastated to hear of Henry's death; he shouldn't be succumbing happily, he should be raging against fate for dictating that only one of them should survive. How could he be so selfish? He was shuffling off his mortal coil there under the beech boughs, and was happy to accept Josh's grief – perhaps lifelong grief – as the price of being spared a few moments' bereavement himself. Drick found himself enraged by the irrationality of it; he felt like going back there just so he could kick Henry's corpse.

He tried to get some sense out of the incident by writing an account of it, but finally accepted defeat. The sun was going down over the Cathedral, and the room was getting too dark to write. Rather than switch on the lights, he put aside his pen and paper, and reached for the wine bottle.

As the evening grew, he found himself thinking for the first time in months – for the first time since dissecting her and sealing her up in the three manuscript sarcophagi locked in the drawer under his desk – about Kismet. He wanted, needed, desperately and pitifully yearned for her. Not . . . no, not in the way you – or even he – might have expected: there was nothing sexual in his longing. He couldn't have told you *why* he wanted her, just that he did.

He got the notepad out and tried, as he had tried before, to conjure her up; and, as before, he was unable to do it. His last memory of that night was of stumbling out into the street, with Manni leaping round his legs, and finding his way into the park. There, he sank down on his knees in the middle of the football pitch and rolled over onto his back, staring up at the stars, listening to the distant sounds of revelry and ringing church bells, while the ice-cold dew soaked through his shirt and he called her name over and over and over. She existed for him then as she had never existed before. The more he had learned about her, the less real she had seemed – his meetings with her had seemed almost like fugue episodes, and perhaps had been – but he believed in her existence now as surely as he believed in his own. Not because she had grown more real, but because he felt less so. He was sliding into a twilit corner of semi-existence from which he could see no escape.

Somehow he must have made it back indoors and up to bed, but he couldn't think how; the last thing he remembered was hot dog-breath on his face and neck as Manni fussed round him, nuzzling and nudging. For the first few seconds, he thought he was still on his back in the park, but this was dry and warm; he was in his bed, and Manni was nuzzling him again, pushing his cold nose into the crook of his neck. He pushed the dog away and rolled over.

'Go 'way,' he mumbled, pulling the duvet up to his chin, but Manni was insistent. He turned back and found the dog had his forepaws on the bed, staring down at him in the dark, a grey, ghostly shape with mournful ears like a cowl. 'Settle down, for Chrissake,' Drick growled, pushing the dog down. 'You're *not* going out in the middle of the night. Cross your bloody legs.' The dog hesitated, and pawed at him. '*In your bed!*' he roared.

There were padding steps across the room, then the rustle of the bean bag. A pause, then more rustling, and the padding came back towards the bed. Now, as he pawed, he whined pitiably, then hurried over to the door and began scratching at the panels, his cries turning to yipping, jabbering barks, a noise he hadn't made since he was a small puppy. That was what made Drick sit up and take notice. When Manni needed a pee in the night (and it was rare), he just nuzzled and poked and wouldn't take no for an answer. He never whined, especially not in that infantile, fearful way.

His head still heavy with the evening's wine, Drick heaved himself out of bed and went over to the door. Manni ran round him excitedly, then resumed scraping and sniffing. Drick sniffed too, and smelled smoke. He clapped his hand over the dog's snout and listened: there was a distinct hissing, rushing sound coming through the door. Without thinking, he flung it open, and was

224

almost knocked backwards by the rush of heat. The hall was thick with fire, and the flames were creeping up the stairs towards him under a breaker of smoke.

'Manni! Stop!'

The dog flew across the landing and stood on the lip of the stairs, hackles up, barking furiously at the advancing flames. Drick, choking on the smoke, rushed forward and grabbed him by the scruff.

'This way! Come on, there's a good boy – follow me!'

By a combination of cajoling, commanding and physically dragging, he managed to hustle the dog into the spare bedroom. It was at the back of the house, and its window overlooked the kitchen extension. He slammed the door, flung up the sash and, with an access of unexpected strength, heaved the big dog bodily over the sill onto the flat roof. He was about to follow when he realised he had no way of getting the dog to the ground. He lowered the sash again and ran back to his own bedroom, tore the duvet off the bed and made it back to the spare bedroom just as the fire reached the top of the stairs and spilled over onto the landing. He could hardly see now through the smoke and tears; he stumbled blindly across the room, opened the window again, and climbed out, pushing the bundled duvet ahead of him.

He found Manni padding cautiously round the edges of the roof, looking for a way down. Drick grabbed him, threw the duvet over him like a cloak and tucked it under his body. Then, without pausing for reflection, he pushed him over the edge and jumped after him.

Packet 13

'Nice flat.'

Jeremy looked up in surprise. 'You think so?'

'Well, it's . . .' He struggled for a word.

'Small? Pokey? Overcrowded?'

'All those things and more. At least it's not a burnt-out shell.' He touched Manni's head. There was a tiny scab forming above the eye, pushing back the fur. He'd been lucky; another inch down and the holly branch could have taken the eye out. Still, it was better than landing on the stone flags.

'I suppose it's not bad for rented accommodation. Most places in Cambridge I wouldn't lodge a dog in. Sorry, Manni, no offence.' He looked at Drick's clothes again – or the lack of them. 'Are you sure you don't you want to change?'

Drick peered down at his smoke-blackened T-shirt, bare, scratched legs, and the torn duvet still bunched around his body. 'Into what?' he asked.

'I'll get you something of mine. You'll need some trousers at least.'

He got up and went through to the bedroom. Drick stroked Manni's head and listened to the sounds of drawers opening and closing.

The fire engines had arrived within a couple of minutes of his and Manni's daredevil leap off the extension. They disentangled themselves from the holly bush to the sound of sirens and made their way round the side of the house to find a straggle of neighbours standing in the street looking up at the burning cottage, swirling blue lights illuminating their rag-bag nightwear.

Only one or two of them noticed him; the rest seemed hypnotised by the flames and smoke.

The ambulance arrived while the firemen were unreeling their hoses. Drick was tracked down by a paramedic and a fireman in a white helmet. Was there anybody else inside? Drick shook his head. Nobody, he said. He described how Manni had alerted him to the fire and how they had escaped over the extension; he didn't know why he told them this story – what use could it be to them? – other than a feeling that something was expected from him, and that was all he had to offer. They gave him an oxygen mask and a blanket and tried to get him to sit in the ambulance; he wouldn't get in without Manni, so in the end he sat on their wheelie stretcher with Manni at his feet and the mask over his face. They wrapped some more blankets round him, he wrapped the duvet round Manni, and together they watched the waterspouts play over the cottage walls, teasing the flames that danced in the windows.

Dawn was breaking when the firemen began reeling in their hoses. They had managed to prevent the fire from spreading to the roof, but most of the rooms were pretty well gutted. Drick sploshed along the flooded pavement to the front door and peered in (the ambulance had left an hour ago; the paramedics, having satisfied themselves that he wasn't suffering from smoke inhalation, had left him in the notional care of the next-door neighbour, a middle-aged woman Drick had never seen before in his life). He was forced to back off as two firemen in breathing gear – they looked like deep-sea fishermen applying to become spacemen – came out, crunching over a litter of unidentifiable, charcoaled rubble.

'This 'ere's what's caused it,' said one, peeling off his mask. He held up a buckled, blackened object which Drick eventually recognised as the electric heater he kept in the understairs cupboard to ward off the persistent damp. He remembered leaving it on yesterday afternoon. 'Left it switched on, din't you?' said the fireman.

Drick stared at him, biting back the observation that there'd not have been a fire if he hadn't, would there? Stating the bleeding obvious seemed to be the first thing they taught you in emergency service school. *Out late, aren't we, sir? That's a nasty cut, sonny. That petrol wouldn't have caught fire if you hadn't slung a lighted match in it.* Instead, he just nodded.

He wandered through the blackened, dripping rooms like a stranger, thinking that the stench of wet charcoal was probably the most dismal smell in the world. He picked up defamiliarised objects and examined them; some he kept, most he dropped again. There was a large puddle in his office, and he stood in it in his borrowed wellingtons, freezing his toes off and surveying the wreckage. His computer looked as though it had been painted by Dali; it was intact on one side, while the other sagged dismally and had begun spreading across the burnt desktop. There were flakes of burnt paper everywhere – books mostly, from the collapsed shelves. Lying on the floor next to the skeleton of his swivel chair was a small object which at first he took for a spring. He picked it up and realised, with a sickening jolt, that it was the spiral binding from the notepad, its plastic coating all melted off, its pages part of the sludge of sodden ash under his boots. Oddly, his first thought was, *Oh well, Jonathan Peachment won't get his money any more . . .*

'Here you are,' said Jeremy, coming back from the bedroom with a pair of jeans he'd spent the past five minutes ironing. 'I'll get you a jumper as well.'

Drick shrugged off the duvet and started pulling on the jeans. Jeremy was a couple of inches narrower round the waist, and they were a bit tight, but the length was right. 'Thanks,' he said when Jeremy came in again and handed him a thick woollen jumper. 'I never said thank you for collecting me. It must've been quite a shock. Especially on New Year's Day.'

'Not as much of a shock as it was for you,' Jeremy said. 'It must've been one hell of a party.'

'It was a heater under the stairs.' Drick pulled the jumper down over his head, and felt surprisingly comforted by its dry, scratchy warmth. 'There wasn't a party.'

Years later, Jeremy would remember this conversation and reflect on how having a dramatic New Year's Eve non-party seemed to be a Bent trademark. Now, he just asked, 'Did you lose much? In the fire, I mean.'

Drick sighed. 'Everything, pretty much. Except my manuscripts. They were in a steel drawer – a chest of drawers under the desk. They survived, just about.'

It had been a marvellous discovery, opening the drawer and finding them there; they had begun to yellow at the edges in the heat, but hadn't caught fire. They were all there: seven of them including *The Alchemist's Apprentice*. Also in there were most of his notes – travel and otherwise.

'Oh well,' said Jeremy. 'They're your bread and butter, aren't they.'

Drick looked at him sharply, but he didn't seem to be being ironic. 'Yes,' he said. 'I suppose so.'

'How's the book doing, by the way? I saw it in Waterstone's the other day.'

'I don't know. I spoke to my publisher the other week, and he was a bit vague. Talked about subbing, whatever that is, and said there'd been no returns.'

'Returns?'

'Don't ask me. Could be tax returns for all I know.'

'Do you get royalties?'

Drick laughed. 'Yes, I got a cheque just before Christmas for six hundred and thirty-six pounds.'

'That's not bad. How often do you get that?'

'Twice a year.'

'Oh. Bad after all, then.'

Drick shrugged. 'Not really. By the time the book's in the shops, the work's so far behind you the royalties seem like free money.'

'Were you insured?' Drick shook his head. 'Will you be able to manage?'

'Yes. You know me – always fall on my feet. I'll sort something out.'

Though God knew what. While he was waiting for Jeremy to collect him, and then during the drive down to Cambridge, he had gone over his situation in his mind. His notebook was gone. That was the tolling undertow of all his thoughts. Gone forever, and he didn't know how to cope without it. It wasn't just the adventures; he'd lived so long now with the absolute liberty it gave him – liberty from money, from worry, from the mundane here and now – that he couldn't imagine how you lived without the ability to create whatever you needed out of thin air. Food, for God's sake – did you really have to go out and carry it home? You had to hand over cash for *bog rolls*? Bills came, and you couldn't simply *put* the money there to pay them? Christ's trousers, what the hell was he going to do?

He could sell a few things, he supposed. The Landcruiser would fetch a good few thousand pounds, but he couldn't tell Jeremy that, because he didn't know it existed; Drick had never been able to think up a rational explanation of how he had come by it, so it had remained secret. Even more secretly, it now contained in its boot, hidden under a soiled hospital blanket, a cardboard box full of items which, taken together, would make an antique dealer's eyes leap out on stalks. They were items he had collected on his travels – souvenirs of time and space. Only a few pieces had survived the flames, but they were impressive enough. There was a Roman legionary's helmet cloven across the crown, a silver locket containing a miniature in oils pickpocketed from the Duke of Wellington's discarded coat during the crisis at Waterloo, some small pieces of silverware filched from Trinity College in 1663, a Woolwich-pattern Hussar's pistol picked up from the valley of death after Balaclava, some pieces of Delft china with Napoleon II's crest on them. There were some other small odds and ends, but these were the prime pieces. The sale of the Landcruiser should keep him for a while; if he needed more money after that, he would fall back on his mementos.

He smiled, rather thinly and unconvincingly, he suspected. 'I'll be fine. In the meantime, can I stay here while I get myself sorted out?'

They lasted a week and a half. The sofa was too small to sleep on, so they had to share Jeremy's double bed. It was just like the sleepovers they'd had when they were kids, even down to the dog snoring on a blanket in the corner (back then it had been Gina, Jeremy's black labrador, belching on the ice cream and sweets they fed her), and they lasted longer on the nostalgia than they would have without it. Ten days was the limit, though.

Drick sold the Landcruiser (he told Jeremy he was raiding his savings account), which provided enough money to rent a little thatched cottage in Arrington, a no-horse village about eight miles from Cambridge. A flat in the city was of no use to him with Manni, and the rents charged for Cambridge houses gave a whole new slant to the dictum that property is theft. There was enough money left over to live on for a few months, and enough after that to buy a rusty little Nissan for the run to the super-market (the only retail facility in Arrington was a post office which the postmistress ran from the front room of her house – if you wanted anything more complicated than a newspaper or a pint of milk you were stuffed without a car).

He could have gone back to live in Ely – a bit more expensive, but he wouldn't have had to buy a car – but he didn't want to. Besides, he'd always fancied living in a thatched cottage. Like most fancies, this one turned out to be a turd in a rusty tin can.

To say Crow Lodge was a step down from his cottage in Ely was like saying it was a step down from the kitchen roof to the holly bush. The patchy carpet smelled vaguely of joss-sticks and strongly of cats, while the furniture looked like all that stuff you took to the tip when your grandmother died. Bulky was one way of describing it; ugly was another; and brown – God it was brown; it was like the aftermath of a vomiting contest between the Bisto kids and the Oxo family.

The January wind that came howling over the hills blew straight into the house; it found routes through gaps between the timbers and the crumbling daub, crept under the thatch, and hummed audibly through the quarter-inch gaps that yawned round every door frame. The only heating was from an open fire in the sitting room and an ancient panel-heater which hissed and crackled alarmingly when Drick plugged it in. Understandably, he only used it when he was desperate, and then watched it like a hawk. (Sometimes the buzzing and fizzing noises took on the form of words in his numb head. *Was that dumb or what?* they said. *Oh, I won't waste my notepad curing a damp problem – I'll use this crappy old heater instead.*) Typically, the bathroom was the furthest room from the fire; he took to storing his milk on the window-sill above the cistern, where it kept a good couple of degrees colder than in the antique fridge.

On the first night in their new home, he and Manni sat huddled close to the miserable fire and shivered, listening to the wind droning over the thatch. There was a shed full of logs out the back, but nothing to chop or cut them with; Drick used up all the sections of a Saturday *Guardian* kindling a flame out of the driest log he could find, which burned fitfully for half an hour then went out. Half a can of lighter fluid got it going again, but not for long. By ten o'clock he was exhausted (shivering constantly took up a lot more energy than he would have imagined) and went to bed. He was so cold he broke his *numero-uno* golden rule of master-dog relationships – he let Manni sleep on the bed with him. He'd always thought a thatched cottage would be warm and cosy – the perfect insulation, he'd imagined. Precisely why the idea of a house built of worm-eaten sticks and crumbling mud topped off with two feet of damp hay should appear cosy was beyond him now.

He settled in eventually, after a fashion. He got used to having to shop for food and cook it, got used to the rattle and whine of the old Nissan in place of the smooth power of the Landcruiser, even grew acclimatised to the cold (wine helped); what he never learned to cope with was the loneliness. He blamed this on the remoteness of the cottage and his poverty, even though he had felt the same before the fire (it was this same sense of despair which had caused the drinking which in turn had led to the fire); the only difference was that now he had no distractions.

Around the beginning of February, he began work on a new novel, called, with typical utilitarian bluntness, *The Fuckup*. Contrary to what that might imply, it wasn't autobiographical in any way. The title referred to the dropping of a small tin of baked beans on a busy street in Manchester, out of which small incident he had imagined a chain of events, ballooning in magnitude, leading ultimately to nuclear confrontation and the annihilation of half of western Europe. It was a good premise, and he had in mind a fantastically clever sequence of connections which would bring down the climax with terrifying inevitability, but he couldn't summon up any enthusiasm for the story; the trouble was, he no longer believed that small events had much, if any, influence on big ones. Even big events seemed to have only limited influence on each other. History had its own logic, its own momentum, its own leaden inevitability. It didn't grow fractally from, say, treading on an ant in the Iron Age. History followed an unstoppable course, like an oil tanker; it wouldn't be halted – or even diverted – by a speck of plankton, nor even a dolphin or a whale. A massive iceberg planted directly in its path might cause it to change tack temporarily, then it would resume its pre-programmed course, leaving behind it just a minor deviation in the froth of its wake.

It wouldn't be true to say he abandoned the book; he simply set it aside with the intention of coming back to it, but never did.

Perhaps as a means of regaining some grip on his own history, he began to develop a growing obsession with dates and ages. He calculated that, notwithstanding having – entirely on a whim – frozen himself at twenty-eight years old, he had been born exactly twenty-nine years, four months and two days ago, whereas Manni was one year, seven months and sixteen days old. Crow Lodge had been built about 1590, extended *circa* 1930 and last re-thatched nine years ago. His Nissan was exactly the same age as the thatch, and in similar condition. The main road that ran past his front door had been laid down in the first century AD, the route between London and the Humber for legions of marching Romans. The milk on his bathroom window-sill would expire in two days, the cheese in his fridge considerably sooner. The sheep in the field beyond the back lane were ten months old, and probably ripe for slaughter.

He went around the house and surrounding countryside enumerating ages and life expectancies like some sort of temporal auditor. Calculating on the basis of an average of all his known ancestors, he estimated that his own remaining span, barring accidents, was about forty-two years and six months. Longer than the milk, but less than the Roman route north.

Far from making him think of the relative imminence of his own mortality, the calculation brought an overwhelming impression of the long emptiness of his remaining years. From ages and spans, he started to brood on the moment of death. He took his box of loot from the cubby-hole under the stairs and itemised the deaths associated with each piece.

The legionary who had worn this helmet on the first Dacian campaign died when it was punched through by the heavy, hooked point of a native sword. The Duke of Wellington died peacefully in his bed, an old man; still bewildered, Drick liked to imagine, by the mysterious disappearance of the locket he had carried with him on the Waterloo campaign nearly forty years before. Another violent death had attended the owner of the cavalry pistol, but Drick didn't know the precise nature of it; he might have been one of the riders plucked from his saddle like a rag doll by roundshot, or possibly the one or two who had simply vanished in a shower of mud and blood.

One by one, he worked his way through the items. The last was a small tortoiseshell snuff-box; anonymous and valueless itself, it merely served as a container for a two-inch length of faded, stringy gold braid cut from an epaulette.

All the world knew how, where and when the owner of this little fragment of regalia had died; they even knew – or thought they knew – the words he had uttered as he lay dying. This was a souvenir of the only bit of battle-tourism that had left a deep, lingering impression on Drick. Not for what he'd seen, but for something he'd *thought* he saw, and for something he had done.

It hadn't been at all like the painting he had once seen, but then he hadn't expected it to be, really. The artist, of course, hadn't been there. The first thing you didn't get in the painting was the noise: the rolling thunder of cannon and crackle of musketry on the decks above; the pitiful, soul-scouring wails and screams of agony as the surgeon worked away with his knives and saws, the buckets about his feet filling with discarded limbs; the thwap and bang of

234

shot against the hull; all against the deep creakings and groanings of a thousand overstressed timber joints. The second thing was a powerful cocktail of a hundred foul stenches: sweat, powder smoke and blood; vinegar, tar, wood, paint and hot iron, along with damp rope and clothes, and the burning coals in the surgeon's brazier and seared flesh as wounds and amputations were cauterised.

But even if sound and smell had been switched off, the scene didn't even *look* as the myth would have you believe. True, an assortment of ratings and officers were gathered in a circle illuminated by the glow of a lantern (which stank of tallow), looking down with expressions varying from pity and grief to downright horror at their dying commander. Thereafter the resemblance became shaky. Nelson was indeed lying on a make-shift bed of sailcloth and uniform jackets, with his own fantastically ornate dress coat, frosted like a Christmas tree with decorations and orders, draped over his legs as a blanket. But he wasn't gazing soulfully into the middle distance, nobly handsome with one limp hand outstretched like the Virgin Mary. His pig-tailed peruke was gone, and sweat was pouring down his grey, shaven skull; his eyes were screwed up, and little gasps and grunts of barely contained agony slipped between his clenched teeth (which were brown and rotten) as a surgeon, red to the elbows, tried uselessly to dig the musketball out of his body. In the end, he was ordered to give up the attempt, but who gave the order wasn't clear. A portly man with tousled black hair crouched down at the Admiral's side and gripped his hand. This, Drick realised, must be Hardy, Nelson's Flag Captain and commander of the *Victory*.

Drick, invisible and imperceptible, eased himself forward and knelt close by; if Nelson was going to speak his famous valedic-tion, he wanted to hear it. Was he going to make a comment on fate or ask for a token of affection?

Right now, he didn't seem about to say anything; he was in too much pain; bordering on delirium, in fact. He was slipping away fast. Drick edged closer and closer, until he could smell the decay and hear the rattles in the dying man's breath.

And at that moment, he suddenly became aware that he wasn't the only one watching and listening. No, not the officers and men who were gathered round – apart from them. There was somebody else there, lurking unseen, holding their breath, straining every nerve to hear what words would pass this man's lips. Invisible like him; he could sense the presence, and the force of will – echoing his own – urging the Admiral to speak. He thought he perceived a faint shimmering in the air beside Hardy, but wasn't sure in the dim light, and when he looked directly at the spot, the movement – it had been like a heat-shiver in the air – disappeared. He looked back at Nelson.

His lips were moving helplessly, inarticulately, and his eyes rolled towards Hardy, who leant closer.

Go on, said Drick silently. *Say it; two words or three . . . K— K— Come on, man . . . Ki— . . . Ki— . . .* He was so close now he could see the circle of men and the glare of the lantern reflected in the man's glazed, dulling eyes. Ki– . . . Nelson's mouth moved, the tongue stroking the upper lip, and there was a faint croak in his throat.

Hardy waved the other men to silence. 'His lordship wishes to speak,' he said.

Ki— . . . Ki— . . . Kis—

'Yes, my lord?'

'*Kis . . .*' The voice was hoarse, barely audible. '*Kismet, Hardy.*'

Drick sat back on his heels, his heart pounding. He heard the sailors behind him murmuring among themselves, trying, presumably, to decipher the half-heard words. He looked round at them: some looked stern and noble; they clearly thought they knew what they had heard. When he looked back, Hardy, with age and weariness suddenly piling up behind his eyes, leant down and kissed his Admiral on the grey, sweat-greased forehead.

Nelson was dead. At last, Drick knew for certain what his last words were. Nothing. An inarticulate death-rattle, with the words *Kismet, Hardy* laid over it in a desperate, urgent whisper. Not one of the eye-witnesses, of course, had the slightest suspicion of the imperceptible presence crouched close in the centre of the scene; they merely heard – or misheard – the words and were completely unaware that they had come not from Nelson, but from Roderick Bent, the invisible visitor in their midst.

Kismet indeed.

He twisted the piece of braid between his fingers for a few moments, rolling it like a cigarette, holding it up to his nose and sniffing – it smelled of sea-spray and cologne – then put it back in the snuff-box, which he placed, with a delicacy that was almost like reverence, on a shelf.

'I'm probably the only person in the world – the only person in history – who knows that Nelson's actual last words were most likely "Ah, I'm hit!" I say *probably* – I *am* the only person who knows. Apart from yourself, of course.'

A million microscopic needles pricked a wave up Drick's spine. He stood motionless for two heartbeats, then, very, very slowly and with careful deliberation, turned round.

'I was there too, you see,' said Kismet. 'I think you sensed me at one point – you looked right at me, but then decided you were imagining things and looked away.'

She was sitting on the sofa; Manni's chin was resting on her lap, and she was toying with his ears. She smiled at the look on Drick's face and, realising he probably wouldn't be regaining the power of speech for a good few moments yet, went on: 'Oh, you were perfectly visible to me. I'd never seen you in' – she giggled – 'in "real" life then, so I wasn't totally sure who you were.' She assumed a serious expression, but couldn't quite hold onto it. 'This is going to be difficult to get a grip on, but although you only went there a few months ago in your own time scale, *I* was there years ago. When we met in my garden, I knew for certain who you were.'

Drick's eyes were practically out on stalks; his jaw was going up and down now, but nothing intelligible was coming out. 'W-w-w-w- . . . h-h-h- . . . I-I-I-I- . . .'

Kismet giggled again. 'So, the dying words that *you* put into Nelson's mouth were suggested to you by *me*, knowing what you were going to do with them. I got them, as I told you, from my father, who got them from some historical source or other.' She put on a deep, husky tone: '*Kismet, Hardy*. Don't you just love it when history comes full circle like that? Quite the most satisfying part of time-travelling, I think; probably the only good reason for doing it, dropping these little paper boats into the stream and seeing where they wash up.'

Drick got the use of his tongue back at last. 'How did you get in here?' he asked.

'Did I magic myself in, you mean? Am I a phantom?' She smiled. 'You left the back door open. You really should be more careful, you know.' She looked about her. 'Not that you've got much to steal. I was so sorry when I found out about the fire.' She looked it; her eyes glistened momentarily. 'You lost your book, didn't you? I know you; you wouldn't be living like this if you still had it.'

The phone started ringing. Drick stared at her, a great juddering conflict of emotions jarring and squirming inside him from his chest down to his toes: exhilaration, joy, fear, relief, anxiety.

'Hadn't you better answer that?' she asked.

'Answer what?'

'The phone. It's ringing.'

'Is it?' He had to look away from her to listen; the sight of her swamped all other sensations. 'Yes, I'd better, but I'm not going to.'

'Why?'

'Because you might go away again.'

'I won't. Not yet, anyway. I really think you should answer.'

He crossed the room and picked up the phone. 'Bent,' he said, keeping Kismet in view by staring at her white plimsolls, nestled against Manni's hip – he still couldn't look directly at her without feeling deaf mutism coming on.

'Roderick. How are you?'

'Fine,' he said, wondering who the vaguely familiar voice on the other end of the line was.

'I've got some news for you.'

Nick Lovell. The man *never* introduced himself when he called; damn him, did he think he was the only person Drick ever got phone calls from?

'Oh yes?'

He listened to Lovell's news without any appearance of interest, as if he were hearing a repeat of last Monday's shipping forecast. Occasionally he made a deep grunt of acknowledgement, but that was his only contribution to the conversation apart from saying goodbye at the end.

'Well?' said Kismet.

Drick went on staring into space, his hand still resting on the cradled receiver. She prompted him again, and his head turned towards her, his gaze following a couple of moments behind.

'It was my publisher,' he said. 'Some news about my book.'

'Book?'

'*The Alchemist's Apprentice.*' It occurred to him that she knew perfectly well what book, but he didn't point it out. 'It's been doing better than expected, apparently.'

'How well?'

'Hnh? Oh, quite well.' He looked down at his hand with a bewildered expression, and lifted it off the phone – carefully, finger by finger, as though it was glued. 'The first print run has sold out. He's ordered a further run of a thousand – he hasn't got the capital available to pay for more than that. He's in a state because he's got orders in from bookshops amounting to fifteen thousand copies.'

'That's good, isn't it?'

Drick nodded abstractedly, a gesture which managed to convey neither agreement nor even acknowledgement that she had spoken. 'He doesn't know what to do. The orders keep coming in, and Obelisk can't meet more than a fraction of them.' He looked at Kismet, seeming to focus on her at last. 'There was a big review in *The Times* last month, which nobody saw fit to tell me about. Nor did they tell me about the features that appeared in most of the papers shortly after. It seems a lot of people like *The Alchemist's Apprentice*. Like it a lot.'

Drick repeated the rest of what Lovell had said, with all the enthusiasm of a secretary reading back the minutes of a particularly dull committee meeting. Obelisk was out of its depth; they had never had a successful book on their lists before, and simply didn't have the commercial resources to follow through. Lovell was considering selling out the publishing rights to a bigger company. Several of them had been spotted hovering on the sidelines, waiting for an opportunity to rush in with buckets of cash. He reeled off a list of names: Drick couldn't think of a single big (or even medium-size) publishing house that wasn't on it. Lovell would keep them at arm's length while Drick made up his mind, but wouldn't be able to fend them off forever once the frenzy began, as it surely would once people in the trade discovered just how snowed under the company was. He recommended that Drick talk to one of the literary agents who had already been probing for information. He had a friend who was in the agenting line, and he knew a fair bit about which agencies would best suit a young and potentially bestselling author like Drick; or even a middle-aged mystery-man like Maddy Rhodes. None of the agents, by the way, had figured out yet that he was pseudonymous.

One word struck Drick like a gong. *Bestselling.* (Some part of his brain edited out the 'potentially'.) Did fifteen thousand orders constitute a bestseller? He had no idea. He remembered the air-punching cowboy-whoops he had done when he heard that Obelisk wanted to publish the book, and wondered why he felt so flat now.

Kismet, of course. He looked at her. 'Are you responsible for this?'

'What?'

'I don't understand . . . I think, I feel like you've made this happen. Somehow, for some reason.'

She shrugged. 'It's got nothing to do with me.' Then she smiled. 'Why? Do you think I could make something like that happen?'

'I could . . .' He paused. He'd been about to say, *I could've made it happen, before.* 'How did you know about the notepad?'

She seemed about to speak, then changed her mind. She drew a finger under one of Manni's ears, held it out for a moment, then let it fall. 'He's looking healthy, isn't he? Country air must agree with him.'

240

'Bugger the country air. How did you know about the note-pad?' Even as he said it he was conscious that this was possibly the least bewildering thing about her, but in a way it seemed to stand for everything else, all the questions he wanted to ask. 'How did you know?' he repeated.

Kismet smiled at him and went on stroking the dog's head. 'Oh dear, Manni, he's going to get cross in a minute.'

'Yes, I am as a matter of fact.'

'You're a writer; you know the conventions of dialogue, or you should. When the lady, confronted by a direct question, begins stroking the dog and talking about the country air, it means she's not going to answer.'

Drick smiled in spite of himself. 'And I suppose, if the questioner is a gentleman, he doesn't press the lady any further?'

'Right.' She stood up and walked towards him. It was only a couple of steps across the room, but it seemed to him that she was walking from much further away, as though he was seeing her through the wrong end of a telescope. He was startled when she touched his cheek, and he flinched. 'I'd like to ask *you* a question,' she said. 'If you're a gentleman, you'll answer – gentlemen don't have the prerogative of being evasive.'

'Go on.'

'If you think I made that happen' – she indicated the phone – 'it must mean that *you didn't*. Otherwise, why would you accuse me?'

'*Accuse* you?'

'You said it in a tone of accusation. Why would it be such a terrible thing? Why *didn't* you use the power you had at your fingertips to make yourself famous? You'd already made yourself rich. Effectively rich.'

'You know an awful lot about me, don't you,' he said with heavy irony, then caught her look; it told him he was going for the ungentlemanly evasion. 'I'd never have known if . . . whether it would've worked out that way anyway.'

He couldn't have put it much less eloquently, but she nodded serenely, as though she understood him perfectly. 'You're not ready for this, are you? Close your eyes.'

He obeyed, expecting her to tell him to hold out his hand. Instead, he felt her lips brush against his. 'September,' she said. 'The fourteenth. This year. *Then* you'll be ready.'

He waited for her to say more, eyes still closed. And waited. When at last he opened his eyes, she was gone. The back door was open, swinging gently in the breeze.

The spell broke, and he ran out of the house, up the garden path, and slithered to a halt in the muddy lane. There was no sign of her. If she hadn't magicked her way in, she had certainly magicked herself away. *September?* He wasn't sure he could live that long feeling as desolate as he felt now.

'Come back!' he yelled. 'Come back *now*!'

Packet 14

Drick began keeping a diary. No, not a diary exactly – more a sort of *aide-memoire*. There was no need to record his feelings, since, at some instinctive level, he knew he would remember them perfectly without assistance. What he wouldn't remember would be the chain of events. His obsession with dates, spinning on like a flywheel, simply compelled him to record everything that happened, and in what order. Later, he would be able to hang his memories on the dates.

What made him so sure he would remember the feelings was how simple, thin and threadbare they were. He *should* have felt elated, exultant, rich; he should have felt that his future was waiting to greet him with a warm grin and a hearty handshake, not lurking in the shadows wearing a sallow, sarcastic sneer. He wanted to be able to sift that period; analyse the feelings and find out why he didn't react to success the way he thought he should.

Perhaps it was also a sort of insurance: with only the dates and events recorded, and the feeling largely glossed over, he might look back from some better futurity and convince himself that he *had* felt good about it all.

These were some of the things he put in the diary.

Sat. 28 January 1995.
Received cutting from The Times *via Obelisk (at last). Book highly praised – '[The] kind of novel your friends will know by heart without reading it, because you'll talk of nothing else . . .'*

  Filed this away along with other cuttings from Mail on Sunday, Mirror, Independent, Guardian, Scotsman *et al.*

Mon. 30 January.
First approach by agent. Small independent. Greasy-sounding voice on phone. Much talk of large money. Had to put on vaguely S. African accent. Told him he could suck my cock and get five per cent. Asked NL not to give out my phone no. to callers – agents can contact me through Obelisk only.

Why had he been so hostile to Kismet? Not hostile exactly, but . . . no, given how much he had wanted her, he *had* been downright hostile.

Wed. 1 February.
Wine and nibbles at Waterstone's in Charing Cross Road with agents, publishers and booksellers, organised with great expenditure of energy by NL. (Don't know why – had assumed it would be a matter for Obelisk alone – I mean, they own the publishing rights, don't they?) Took Manni, just to measure tolerance afforded to rising star. Good level of tolerance, even when nibbles table knocked over and corn chips trampled into winey paste all over carpet. Passed self off as illegitimate son of M. Rhodes, who never leaves his home on Malta. Had no patience with business and deals, so would do pretty much exactly as I recommended. Heard much effusive praise, and no complaints even when two esteemed literary agents had skin scrapings taken from shins by M.

Wed. 8 February.
Agents had no apparent distinguishing characteristics to choose between, so went with NL's recommendation (not his pal, as it happens). Am (or rather MR is) now represented by one Noel Crixus (God help us all), mercurial hub of large, well-established agency and owner of largest collection of gaudy ties and fashionable spectacle frames in London. Believes in Maddy Rhodes (whether as genuine personage or literary supernova is unclear).

Thu. 9 February.
10 a.m. Meeting with Crixus in his office in WC1 (large, glass walls, pot plants, coffee). Revealed myself as the unprepossessing reality behind Maddy Rhodes – had to in order to sign form

244

committing me to this agency and get things under way. Sat in wicker chair and watched this man handling his phone like a six-gun, firing shots at the feet of every publisher in London. Had them dancing like can-can girls by lunchtime. Knocked half a dozen (who weren't 'players' apparently) out of the auction while shovelling takeaway couscous into his face. Bidding levelled off at £250,000 around 2 p.m. Left him issuing charmingly phrased threats at ten past and went to catch train.

Appears that what's happened here is completely out of the ordinary. Crixus told me during a lull in the auction that normally *(is there really a 'normal' in this business?) Obelisk would have sold the paperback rights direct to a big house. Rather foolishly, they overlooked these rights in my contract – they've never published in paperback, so didn't think to put the relevant clause in. So, completely uniquely in his experience, Crixus is, in effect, acting for both me* and *Obelisk, selling both* my *pb rights and* their *hb – and other – rights (of which I get a 40 per cent cut).*

Fri. 10 February.
Phone call from Crixus. Auction has resulted in four serious bids, which I am offered like a dish of canapes. This one looks delicious but comes with a rather unpleasant sauce; another, also very inviting (I'm told), is likely to crumble down my shirt-front the moment I bite into it; and so on. This is his metaphor, which tells me two things: a. he is more food-fixated than can be good for his health (he's thirty-five and already shaped like one of yesterday's doughnuts); and b. he probably tried to be an author before becoming an agent.

Told Crixus I would go with whichever publisher he thought was best. Headline, apparently. Cut short his explanation of why they were best, telling him to just do the deal and send me the contract.

Thu. 8 June.
The Alchemist's Apprentice *re-published simultaneously in hard-back and paperback. (With – presumably for time-saving reasons, for there can be no other – Obelisk's piss-yellow maze on the front cover.)*

No launch, no signings, no interviews. Maddy Rhodes remains a man of mystery.

Sat. 17 June.
Offers received this week (at current exchange rates):
    £77,600 for German translation rights
    £101,240 for US rights
    £21,550 for Italian translation rights
    £17,300 for Dutch translation rights
    Earnings this week: £227,690 for no work at all.

Mon. 19 June.
Final royalty payment from Obelisk: £3,756.49.

Sat. 24 June.
List of countries who have bought rights in book now includes France, Japan, S. Korea, Brazil, Spain and Turkey. Haven't actually received any money yet, so still living in Cold Lodge, which is now only tolerably warm despite hot weather (only insulation value of thatch appears to be in keeping warmth out*).*

Fri. 7 July.
Eye-slicing headache from reading and signing contracts. Crixus tells me they are all fine, but read them anyway from sheer bloody-mindedness. Should get some money soon.

Sat. 8 July.
No. 1 in Times *and* Guardian *Top 10's for fourth week running. Selling approx. 14,000 copies per week. Surely there aren't that many book-buyers in the country? People must be using them as briquettes.*

Sat. 15 July.
Weekly sales 21,000. Checked style supplement for articles on building garden tubs from unwanted paperback novels.
    Checked bank balance. £821,884.23. Represents proceeds of about two-thirds of the deals I've signed so far.

Sun. 16 July.
Flying Legends air show at Duxford with Jeremy. I paid for both of us.

Sat. 22 July.
Requests turned down this week: Interviews with Radio 1, Radio 4,
The Late Show; *features in the* Independent, Guardian *and*
Elle.

    Have concocted fake interview with Crixus, which he will sell to
whoever wants it (virtually everybody). Having given this account of
himself, Maddy has left Malta and resumed his randomly itinerant life.
This, hopefully, will throw the growing hack-pack off his scent. Only
risk is that someone in Wales will recognise Lionel Bent in jacket
photo; blurriness and false moustache makes this unlikely, however.

It appears from his diary that all Drick did that summer (apart
from going to an air show) was obsess about his book and how
rich he was getting. Since recording its process was the purpose of
the diary, that impression is hardly surprising. However, in reality,
he hardly thought about it at all. He did a lot of stuff that
summer, and thinking about his growing fame and fortune was
only a small fraction of it.

He bought a house, for instance. That was, admittedly, *connected*
with fame and fortune, but he didn't think of it that way. All he
thought of was avoiding another winter in that cottage. It was
like living in an upturned colander. He spent three weeks of July
looking for (and £180,000 buying) a suitable place. He scoured
the country, from Wales to Yorkshire, and from Cornwall to
Cambridge (he had bought a new car – a Landcruiser, you may
be mildly amused to learn – for the purpose), before settling,
with a heavy interior sigh, on Ely. No 70 Waterside was a large
Georgian house with a view over the river and marina. It had got
sadly run-down under the ownership of a Mr Thornley, a
certifiably insane ex-naval officer and furtive homosexual, and
Drick had to plough a further fifty thousand into the place to
make it habitable. He moved in near the end of August, while
work was still going on. Even in that state it was more comfortable than Cold Lodge. Not that he spent a great deal of time
there. In the meantime, he had bought (with the assistance of a
sixty per cent mortgage this time) a flat in a converted warehouse
in Wapping, near St George in the East. Ignoring his agent's

advice, he didn't get an accountant; he collected and spent his money with a sort of dismal recklessness – he couldn't bring himself to care about it enough to pay someone to manage it for him.

He also completed a novel. *The Fuckup* he abandoned in favour of a bleaker, darker story called *The Traitor*. (Success hadn't given him any greater facility with titles.) It was shorter and more austere than his other works, and quite brutal. In retrospect, it was easy to see the sublimation of his emotions in that manuscript. He sent it to his agent and his editor, expecting them to express reservations. After all, it was hardly in the life-affirming vein of *The Alchemist's Apprentice*. Reservations he didn't get. They couldn't have been more unreserved if they'd tried. They loved it. He wondered if they'd have loved it quite as much if it hadn't been preceded by a knockout bestseller that stacked up in bookshops like bricks in a builders' merchant. As a test, he told them he'd had second thoughts about *The Traitor*, and sent them a synopsis describing what, if he had written it, would have been the most awful novel in the history of the world, filled with every senti-mental cliché and creaky plot device he had ever heard of, together with the most long-winded, tedious philosophical premise (to which no fewer than three opening chapters would be devoted) he could think up without actually giving himself a brain haemorrhage. They hated it, and said so. Reassured, he let them go ahead with *The Traitor*, and a notional publication date of July 1996 was set.

Apart from the air show in July, he didn't see much of Jeremy. They had little in common in their lives now (an interest in vintage aeroplanes being one of the few remaining things), and besides, Drick was beginning to find his friend's deepening poverty difficult to reconcile with his own wealth. With his doctorate a year behind him and his research being published, he was still living on a thin gruel of Income Support and Housing Benefit. There were few vacancies in universities, and always hundreds of applicants for every one. The two of them were too alike for Drick to offer help. Just as he hadn't been able to use the notepad to help *The Alchemist's Apprentice* on its way, he knew

Jeremy would stand or fall by his own merits alone.

Riches, houses, writing and friends in need took up their share of time (or not, as the case may be). The big thing, occupying his thoughts more than all of them put together, was Kismet. September the fourteenth, she had said. The day before his thirtieth birthday. Or the day before what would have been his birthday if he still had them. She hadn't told him where or at what time she would meet him, and he didn't wonder about it; she would just be wherever he was at whatever time she chose.

As the appointed day approached, he decided to force the issue anyway. Or try. For a start, he decided to be in London that day. He hadn't spent enough time there to feel that London was his own turf, but it certainly wasn't hers. Moreover, he would spend the *entire day* in a comfortable little bar he knew in Soho (the evening too, if necessary). He didn't know for sure why he felt so antagonistic towards her; probably because of the wilful way she kept popping in and out of his life without a by-your-leave, mercilessly messing with his head. *This* time, *he* would at least choose the place where they met.

On the afternoon of the thirteenth, he was packed and ready to leave for Wapping. As he was carrying his bag out to the car, he heard his name called.

'Roderick Bent?'

He looked up and saw a uniformed man in a peaked cap standing astride a red bicycle. 'Mr Roderick Bent?' he repeated. Drick nodded, and the man thrust a small envelope at him. 'Telegram.'

Drick watched the man cycle off. He looked down at the grey envelope, then at the receding uniform. 'Oi!' he shouted. 'Come back here! Telegrams don't exist any more!'

But the man had gone. He looked at the envelope again, and tore it open. Inside was a slip of paper with his name typed and a short white stripe across the middle with one word printed on it: 'STOP'.

He screwed it up angrily and threw it into the gutter, then picked up his bag again and tossed it onto the back seat of the car.

★ ★ ★

Three hours later, when he should have been making his way through rush-hour traffic on the Mile End Road, he was sitting at his desk, fuming impotently as he watched Ely rain coursing down the French window.

No impenetrable barriers had been put in his way, just that one-word telegram. Then, as he sat behind the wheel and started the engine, it began to rain, and he was suddenly overcome by a wave of unspecified dread. Mile End and Whitechapel in the rain; white Transits and streams of car headlights; the dockland skyline under louring evening clouds; a landscape of lurking grey malice. He could no more go there than eat his own stools. He turned off the engine, got out of the car and went back indoors.

He knew he was being manipulated, and he resented it. At least he thought he resented it, told himself he wasn't going to stand for it, having someone unseen taking liberties with his destiny. Underneath, though, there was a small, soft-spoken part of him that quite liked it. So quietly did it speak to him that he took a while to detect its presence, and when he did, it made him all the more angry. It was all part of the puppetry: manipulate and at the same time convince the puppet it doesn't mind having its strings jerked about.

He hadn't drunk much since the fire (God, how long ago it seemed – more like nine years than nine months), but he broke the abstinence habit that evening. He got a bottle of Bulgarian out of the kitchen cupboard and ripped the cork to shreds in his haste to get it open. He downed the whole bottle in less than an hour; disgusting stuff, but with a good solid kick to it. He opened another bottle – Burgundy this time – and made an evening of it.

When he was woken by a pounding door-knocker and hammering temples and looked at the clock, he thought instantly that the previous night's wine had been put in his path. Christ, he couldn't even get pissed of his own volition! Normally, he got up at seven-thirty sharp and took Manni for a walk – rain or howling gale, rested or tired, fresh or hung-over; it was the one lynch-pin of discipline in his haywire life, and he stuck to it with an almost religious, flagellatory dedication. Last night, though, he had got so steamed he must have forgotten to set the alarm. Quarter past nine had crept up silently on him, and he was right where the puppet-master wanted him. The last nail in the coffin of free will.

Swearing loudly, he dragged on yesterday's clothes and stumped down the stairs. 'All right, all right!' he yelled as the knocker thundered again. 'You've kept me waiting eight months – you can wait another two minutes!' He let Manni out into the back garden first, then went and opened the front door.

He had so conditioned himself to expect Kismet's slight, bright figure on the threshold that it took several seconds' blinking against the sunlight for him to realise that he was looking not at a woman in white but at a man in several shades of dismal grey and brown, wearing a savage, uneven number-one cut and an expression of timid determination. This was a man obviously used to having doors slammed in his face, and he spewed out his prepared speech in one stammering breath, before Drick had time to react. As he spoke, in a voice that sounded like a thousand nights of smoke, cheap spirits and damp sheets, he held up an identity card which was so creased and crumpled that the print was virtually illegible (his name began with Jo – that was all Drick could make out), while the postage-stamp photograph could have been anyone from John the Baptist to John F. Kennedy.

'Hello sir I w-w-w-won't take up much of your time and I'm not asking for money but c-c-c-could I tell you a bit about my story it's a [*unintelligible*] and as I say it w-w-won't take up much of your time I represent [*unintelligible*] and I've lived on the streets and you might w-w-want to hear about how I've pulled myself up and sorted out my life c-could you spare a c-c-couple of minutes of your time?'

He was beginning to go blue in the face as he blurted out the last few words, and gasped for breath, wheezing and looking as if he was about to keel over. Drick looked narrowly at him. Chronologically, he couldn't have been more than thirty, but his vital organs, to judge from the noises he was making, would be

251

rejected by an organ scrapyard. If this was him *after* he'd sorted his life out, what was he like before? He stank like a fishmonger's dustbin, too.

'You're not selling God, are you?'

The man, who was wiping flecks of yellow spittle from the corners of his mouth, tried to speak, but couldn't gather the breath; instead, he shook his head. His eyes stared with mute, forlorn hopefulness at Drick.

'If you're not one of God's donkeys, you must be after money. Why should I be interested in your life story?'

'Cos . . .' He clearly hadn't bargained for this; it wasn't in his script. (He'd probably never got beyond the end of his opening speech before.) He fell back on his prepared lines. 'Cos I got my life sorted out, and—'

'So you said. Good for you. You want money, don't you?'

'No, I—'

'If your life's so sorted, why haven't you got a job?'

'It's not that easy.'

'Why not? If you can sort out your life, you can sort out a job. Have you worked before?'

'Yes, I—'

'Then do it again.' Drick could sense a rant coming on, but couldn't stop himself. 'Think yourself lucky you've got control over your destiny, man! Pull yourself together, get off your arse, go out there and take life by the throat. Some of us don't have that luxury, you know. Have you got any idea what it's like having someone else control your life? Not being able to make a decision without having it fucked about with?'

The poor man quailed under the onslaught, and started to back off.

'What did you do before?' Drick demanded.

'I w-w-w-was a s-s-salesman.'

'Then go and be a suh-suh-salesman again! Get a grip on yourself.'

With that, he finally slammed the door in the man's face. He stormed through the house, feeling worse rather than better for having given vent to his spleen. He was half-way up the stairs, on his way to the bathroom, when he froze in mid-step. *I w-w-w-was a s-s-salesman . . .*

He flung the front door open and ran out onto the pavement, looking frantically up and down the street. He ran to the corner, and saw the dishevelled shape further up the hill, walking disconsolately away from a house near the corner of Lisle Lane. Drick ran full tilt, and caught up with him before he turned down Broad Street. The man heard the footsteps behind him, and turned, cowering back against the wall, his arms raised ineffectually to shield him from the attack he thought was coming.

'Show me that ID again,' Drick demanded. 'And calm down – I'm not going to hurt you.'

The man's bloodshot eyes were wide with alarm, like billiard balls wrapped in streaky bacon. He reached inside his grease-stained anorak and took the card out, flinching back as Drick snatched it from him.

It was no easier to read up close than it had been at arm's length. He could make out that it had been issued by some sort of christian organisation, the name of which had been eroded away. The signature at the bottom wouldn't have been legible when it was fresh, and all that was left of the name above it was 'Jona . . .'

'What's this say?' he asked, pointing to the name.

'Eh?'

'What's your name?'

'J-J-J- . . . J-J-J-J-'

'Come on, I haven't got all day!'

'J-J-J-Jonathan.'

'Jonathan what?'

'P-P-P-Peachment.'

Drick's skin kept flushing hot and cold, and his head was spinning. He listened to the rush of the hot water tank and the churning of the washing machine. After a few minutes the hot water stopped flowing, and squeaky-bath splashing sounds came from upstairs.

He got up from the sofa and went through to the dining room.

253

There, he unlocked the filing cabinet and took out two hundred pounds in cash. It was all he had in the house; he would go to the bank later and get some more out, he decided, riffling through the wad of brown notes and putting them in his trouser pocket. He'd buy some clothes while he was at it; the man's own rags probably wouldn't survive the boil wash he was giving them, and Drick's cast-offs wouldn't fit him.

In the end, he did better than that. By mid-afternoon, Jonathan Peachment, former double-glazing salesman and derelict, had three new changes of clothes, a bank account in his name with a thousand pounds in it, a comfortable attic room at 70 Waterside, and a job as Drick's secretary-cum-gofer. Washed and shaved, he looked quite respectable.

He was a little suspicious of his good fortune, plainly worried about what might be expected of him in return, but equally plainly terrified of going back on the streets. Drick could hardly explain to him why he felt so obliged to help him, so, by unspoken agreement, they left the subject unbroached, pretending that the situation had simply, and with a sort of ineffable inevitability, happened (which, after a fashion, was true).

In the midst of all this, Drick quite forgot about Kismet. He remembered at four o'clock, while he and Jonathan were having afternoon tea and cakes in the kitchen. (Jonathan already had a big lunch inside him, but he stuffed the large, sticky Danish pastries in as though they were vol-au-vents.) Drick happened to look at the clock, and realised that something that was meant to be happening today had still not occurred.

'I've got to go out,' he said.

Jonathan looked up, cheeks bulging with masticated pastry.

'You know where all the food is. Just help yourself if you're still hungry. Watch TV, listen to some music, do what you like.' He stood up. 'I'll find you some work to do tomorrow.'

He put Manni's lead on and, aware that both of them (the dog too, possibly) were thinking what a major act of trust it was, left Jonathan alone in the house.

VII

Even though I've got more money nowadays, I still live in the same little flat in Cambridge I moved to in 1994 after finishing my PhD. The only noticeable difference is that the phone doesn't get cut off any more, and I have my own computer. If you look very carefully, you will spot one more slight difference.

In the hall bookcase, beside my old hardback copy of *The Alchemist's Apprentice*, three other novels are lined up, all with my name on. They differ from *The Alchemist's Apprentice* in two important respects: firstly, they have an objective existence outside my flat and my head; secondly, I actually like these novels. Well, it would be a bit strange if I didn't, wouldn't it? I was never able to figure out how Drick could write a book like *The Alchemist's Apprentice*. Not that it wasn't well written; in fact, it was quite beautifully written. More than that, the story was good up to a point, and so were the characters. There's the trouble: *up to a point*. That point being where it departs from truth. Not truth as in what actually happened (although it was historically unauthentic), but truth in a profounder sense. One of the many things Drick and I shared was a devotion to the truth. (Probably the reason why both of us were attracted to – but ultimately couldn't make it in – the academic world). I'm aware that proclaiming a devotion to the truth sounds, at best, naïve; at worst, self-righteous and pompous, but there you are: that's what we believed in, and we tried to live and work by it as best we could. We were also deeply sceptical by nature; which is ironic, given the things that have happened to us. If I weren't so anti-superstitious, I'd imagine we had been picked out by the gods for our scepticism and been punished with a sort of twisted Cassandra syndrome. I mean, who would ever believe either of us?

In a sense, then, it seems appropriate that, with *The Alchemist's Apprentice* gone into oblivion, here, masquerading under its covers, is Drick's true story.

On the day after my trip to Hay, which was a Sunday, I read the rest of the book. I learned a few things from it. At one level, I found myself seeing the contents of Drick's packets in a whole new light, believing at last what I read in them three years ago. That, of course, might be the reason why Drick left it for me, knowing the difficulties I would have with the story the packets told. What else I learned from them is obvious: I learned the course of my immediate future.

The first item on my future's agenda was to begin writing the account you've been reading. That's what I'm doing right now. I decided to do it without reference to the book I found in Hay: when I've finished, I'll check the two versions against each other. If they match, I'll know conclusively that destiny (or Drick, whichever you want to call it) really has had me firmly in its grasp. I know what you're thinking, but you're wrong: I'm not merely parroting his version verbatim; my memory may be good, but it's not that good. And I'm not copying, either: *The Alchemist's Apprentice* (new) sits unconsulted in my bookcase, next to my three books and *The Alchemist's Apprentice* (old). Three fictitious but otherwise true novels sandwiched by a fictional lie and a true story; I like that.

Anyway, I think it's time now (and this *is* memory serving in addition to instinct) for me to pause. I feel some more of Drick's packets coming on. If I remember right, this is the one where he gets to hear the truth about Kismet.

Shortly after that, he gets to hear the truth about himself.

Part Five

KISMET

Drick wasn't fooled for a moment. She wouldn't turn up at his house, not if he waited a million years; she had no intention of coming to him. He was going to her.

He paused on the pavement outside his front door. If there was a pre-ordained inevitability going on here, he could test it, introduce a random element. He unclipped Manni's lead.

'Off you go,' he urged.

Manni looked momentarily puzzled at the unexpected liber-ation, then, not a dog to look a gift horse in the mouth, took advantage. He took off across the road – setting up a blast of car horns – and cantered along the quayside towards the park. Drick waited for the cars to pass, then crossed the road and set off after him. Wherever Manni went, he would follow.

It was a long and meandering route, with many cut-offs and doublings-back as Manni investigated the scents of the river and park, checking that all was as it should be, following up unusual smells with the fussy thoroughness of a filing clerk finding 'Squirrel' under 'J' and 'Beer, Spilt' under 'Q'. Whenever he turned back and trotted towards his master or looked at him for guidance, Drick would stop and wait; entirely random, no direc-tions to come from him.

Gradually their zigzag course took them east along the river, through the park and fields beyond, then the woods and Kiln Lane. To Drick's slight surprise, they passed by the entrance to Cuckoo Farm without pause. The bushes and brambles had, if anything, grown even thicker since he had last come by here; if he hadn't known about the concealed gap where the road turned, he would never find the entrance now. Which was irrelevant, because Manni was leading him enthusiastically on past, down towards the water works and Cuckoo Bridge. They crossed the mouth of Roswell Pits and the river, and took a break near the pumping station, where Manni demanded a drink of water.

Drick was very surprised when, instead of heading back west, Manni started off along the Queen Adelaide road. Suddenly, about a hundred yards along, he leapt down the bank, across the narrow strip of ground, and skidded to a halt at the edge of the river. He stood there, ears waving in the breeze, barking frantically at something on the surface of the water below. When Drick caught up with him and looked down, he saw a small paper boat stuck under the lip of the overhanging bank. A bent reed stem had pinned it there, and it spun round and round as the breeze tried ineffectually to send it on its way downstream.

'You want the boat?'

Manni broke off barking, swiped his paws down Drick's legs, then went back to staring down at the boat, head cocked on one side.

Gripping a tuft of coarse grass, Drick leaned over the edge of the bank and reached down. At the full stretch of his arm, he managed to grasp the boat's conical crown and free it from the reed; he brought it up, shaking off drips of water.

'Sit.' Manni sat, gazing up with open-mouthed longing at the soggy boat. 'Good boy. Here you are.'

Drick fully expected him to seize it and pull it to tatters, which was what he invariably did with paper; instead, he took it between his incisors with the utmost delicacy, like a maiden aunt nibbling the edge of a crustless cucumber sandwich, and trotted off with it. He headed back the way they had come; at the pumping station, he set off across the field, the boat still dangling from his mouth and swaying gently from side to side.

As they approached the spot opposite Kismet's garden, Drick watched the far bank, expecting to see her waiting there. He wasn't disappointed. She stood above the derelict landing stage, her hat tilted back on its ribbon, a silhouette in white against the dark background of woods and hedges. She raised a hand in greeting and, as before, Drick could see her face even though it was out of range of his eyesight. She was smiling patiently, and he sensed that he was later than she expected, a realisation which gave him huge satisfaction.

As before, Manni leapt into the water and swam across while Drick waded behind. And, as before, when they scrambled up the bank and found themselves in the garden, they were dry.

'You've brought me a present again,' said Kismet to Manni as he sat before her. She took the boat from his mouth and held it up to the light. 'Is it another note? No, no writing here.' She smiled warmly at Drick as he approached. 'He's learned some social graces since the last time he came here,' she said, glancing at the politely sitting dog and touching the front of her dress.

'Has he? Well, I suppose he's grown up a bit. He was just a big puppy then. In dog years he's as old as me now.' Drick gazed steadily at her. 'So, are you going to tell me what you want?'

'What *I* want?'

'You brought me here.'

'You're the one with the questions to ask. You've prepared a whole list of them, haven't you?'

Drick opened his mouth to speak, then closed it again. It was true, he *had* prepared questions: a whole list of them, as she said. His dumbfounded goggling days were over, he had decided. This time, once and for all, he would go away with it all explained.

'Well,' she said, 'ask away.'

He reached into his back pocket.

'You haven't written them down, have you?'

'No,' he said, taking out a rather crushed packet of cigarettes and lighting one. 'Force of habit,' he added, waving the cigarette. 'I always smoke when I think. Aids comprehension.'

'I see. I thought for a moment you were going to produce a questionnaire.'

'Right.' Drick took a long, deep draw of smoke. 'Okay.' He blasted the smoke out through his teeth. 'Now, are you a twin?'

She paused. 'Hold on.' She stepped into the alcove in the privet hedge and brought out a wrought iron chair. She set it in the centre of the lawn and sat on it, taking off her hat and laying it

261

across her lap. 'There. The interrogated should always be seated; it emphasises the dominance of the interrogator. When you say "Now, are you a twin", do you mean, am I a twin now?'

'No, I mean—'

'So you're using the interrogative Now – the Now that means "Okay, pay attention". You *don't* want to know whether I am, at this moment, a twin.'

'No. I mean . . . well, *of course*. How could you be a twin then and not—'

'When?'

'What?'

'A twin then? When?'

'When . . .' He'd been about to say, *when you died*, but she evidently hadn't died. 'When . . . when Kismet Lillystone – I mean Jack Lillystone's daughter – died. Drowned, whatever.' He grimaced inside; he could feel the conversation slipping out of his grasp like a slithering fish. He had to grip tighter.

'Which one? Kismet or Jack's daughter?'

He hesitated. 'They're not the same person?'

'I don't know. You're the one who separated them. *Are* they the same?'

Drick sighed. '*I* don't know. Listen. One: are you or are you not Kismet Lillystone?'

'Yes.'

Good God, a straight answer! It was, oddly, more disorientating than her evasions, and his brain reeled for a moment. 'And that has been your name since you were bor— . . .' *Wrong* – that was just inviting a smartarse answer. 'I mean, has that been your name since you were a baby?'

'To the best of my knowledge, yes.'

'And is Jack Lillystone – the younger Jack Lillystone – your father?'

'As good as.'

'As good as? What's that supposed to mean? Ah, you mean he's your adoptive father? Then is – was Liza Lillystone your mother?'

'As good as.' She caught his look, and relented. 'Yes,' she said. Encouraged by the tone of admission, he grew excited, and only just stopped himself pointing his cigarette at her accusingly as he followed up: 'And do you – did you – *have you ever* had a twin sister?'

She smiled, and he felt the moment of advantage slip away in the upturned lips. 'From time to time,' she said.

He carried on doggedly, choosing to ignore the disingenuous answer. 'Was it your twin who drowned by Cuckoo Bridge?'

'No.'

'Then the drowning story is false?'

'No.'

'So who drowned?'

She looked down at her lap. 'I did,' she said quietly.

He snorted contemptuously. 'Sorry, I don't believe in ghosts. You're as solid as I am. Look.' He reached down and took her hand. In the fraction of a second before they touched, he had a sudden, almost overwhelming sense that his fingers would pass through hers like water, and experienced a rush of irrational reassurance when they didn't. He wrapped her hand in both of his, even more reassured by its warmth.

'Nor should you,' she said, looking at their enfolded hands. 'It's possible, of course; anything is possible, but you shouldn't believe in something if it doesn't fit in your universe. If ghosts aren't right for you, you shouldn't believe in them.'

Extricating her hand from his, she walked a full circle round him, looking appraisingly at him, the accustomed serene smile on her lips. 'Watch and learn,' she said softly. She tapped his sleeve and fetched the paper boat from the table. 'Here, Manni,' she said brightly, and tossed the boat high in the air.

It fluttered briefly at the top of its arc, then turned back on the breeze. Manni launched himself like a rocket, limbs stretched fore and aft, head thrown back, jaws flung wide to grab the boat, and . . . Nothing. The boat hung in the air, bracketed above and below by the great curved canines. The dog described a great arc of forelegs, neck, chest, wasp waist and rear legs, frozen in mid-leap. Drick was struck by the way the expression of delight, caught in a single millisecond, looked indistinguishable from ravening savagery, teeth suddenly like fangs in the gaping jaw, eyes staring wide. He reached out a finger and nudged the boat, but the soggy paper was as solid as steel.

He heard Kismet giggle, and turned to look at her.

'You think you're the only one with miraculous powers?' she said. 'Watch.'

She snapped her fingers – quickly, left and right – and it was as though half a dozen frames of film slipped through the projector: Manni's ears jerked forward, his jaws snapped on the boat, and then the scene froze again. She did it again – *click-ick* – and his back legs began to catch up with his body, curling under his belly.

'That's beautiful,' she said. 'We'll leave him like that a moment.'

Drick became aware that a profound silence had settled over the garden. Time – the world's time, that is, outside the envelope surrounding the two of them – had stopped.

'I don't have miraculous powers,' he said. 'Not any more.'

'Well, no. You gave up too easily.'

'Gave up?'

'Didn't it ever occur to you to wonder *why* you were given such miraculous powers? You tried to make the world a better place, but you gave up before you'd really got started. You're probably not the only one; it's quite dispiriting when you find how little you can really do. I think – and this is only surmise, by the way – they don't like it. Of course, they tolerate a certain amount of self-indulgence' – here she paused and looked at Drick, and he felt she could see everything, *every*thing, he had conjured up for himself with the notepad – 'but they have their limits.'

'Who's *they*?'

She gazed steadily at him. 'The source. As I said, this is only surmise.'

'And there are others? Other people who can do these things?'

She shrugged. 'I think so. Very few, I think, and not at the same time. I've sensed their . . . *presence*, shall we say, in the past. Traces of those who've gone before, like very faint footprints.' She looked at him, and, for once, there was a slightly puzzled look in her eyes. 'I get – that is I always *got* the impression that we only appeared on Earth once in an era, and certainly that only one of us could exist at any one time.'

'And you get your power taken away if you don't change the world?'

'That was my theory. I watched you, and it seemed to be confirmed. It nearly happened to me. I began to lose hope of making things better, and stopped trying. Luckily, though, unlike you, I didn't lose it all in a puff of smoke. I felt it slipping away from me gradually, and I had a pretty shrewd idea of what was happening.'

'So you succeeded? In improving the world? When I tried it, I just seemed to make things . . . well, if not worse, then equally bad.'

She reached up and stroked Manni's side. 'You were on the wrong track,' she said. 'You were too . . . idealistic. You thought the world's history could be repaired like a broken engine. Do you want to know what I did?'

'What d'you mean?'

'How I made the world better.'

He nodded. 'Go on.'

'I caused a war.'

'A *war*?'

'Yes, a war. A very big war, actually.'

'And that made the world a better place?'

She nodded. 'Mm-hmm. Do you want to see?'

'See?'

'I can show you what I did. Come on.'

She led him out of the garden by a short-cut, a narrow, winding track leading through the woods. It opened onto Kiln Lane, a little way beyond the bend in the road. When Drick looked back, he couldn't for the life of him see the gap they had come through; just a solid wall of brambles.

'This way,' she said.

They walked together the quarter-mile or so up Kiln Lane to the junction with Prickwillow Road. Just before they reached it, Kismet ducked through a gap in the fence, and Drick followed her. They walked through a small copse and came out on the common. It was a long, narrow strip of rough grassland bordered down one side by the road to Prickwillow and on the other by trees. Drick knew it well – it had been a staple part of dog-walks while he lived in the cottage on New Barns Road – but for some reason it looked different now. It took a full minute before he realised that the housing estate on the other side of Prickwillow Road wasn't there any more. Just open fields, which he could see clearly because the hedges along the edge of the road weren't there either.

About half-way along, on the left-hand side, was a Second World War pillbox, nestling into the hedge. Drick had always thought it looked as though it was trying to sleep, gun-slits narrow and drowsy, pulling the undergrowth over itself like a blanket. Fat chance. It was used by local kids as a drug den. He had once fought his way through the nettles and had a look inside: painted on the blast-wall inside the entrance was a cannabis leaf and a palimpsest of druggy slogans. This, he had since worked out, would be where Finn Bourn had spent his wartime evenings, watching for enemy invaders and carving the pieces of young Jack Lillystone's model ship.

Like the view over the road, though, the pillbox looked very different from how he remembered it. It stood out more from the hedge, for one thing, and it seemed to have . . . well, tilted a little, if such a thing were possible. Also, someone appeared to have lit a fire inside; there were wisps of smoke curling up from the gun slits. As they came closer, he saw that the grass around the building was scorched black, as was the building itself. The brickwork was scarred and, just to the left of the east-facing slit, pierced right through by an almost perfectly circular hole, around which the bricks were dished in as though a giant fist had punched the wall. Drick took a few more steps towards it, then stopped. The objects he had taken for burnt logs, stacked beside the pillbox, were incinerated corpses. Two of them; or maybe three, he wasn't sure. Looking back the way they had come, he realised also that the gouges in the turf which he had assumed were made by a tractor were in fact the ruts of tank tracks.

Kismet, realising he was no longer following her, stopped and looked back at him. 'Come on,' she said. 'We've got to be quick.'

'What is this? Is it the war you caused?'

'Of course not. This is what really happened.' She shrugged. 'What really happened *before*,' she corrected herself. 'Now hurry up. This isn't easy to sustain.'

'What isn't?'

'*This*.' She swept her arms about her, taking in the scene. 'Going back is one thing – easy enough. Going back and then *sideways* is very different. It takes concentration, and I can't keep it up forever.'

She turned away, but he called her back. 'Hold on,' he said. 'One question. When is this?'

'September nineteen-forty-one,' she replied, and walked on. 'The seventeenth,' she called back over her shoulder. 'Eighth day of the battle.'

'*What* battle?' he demanded, but she wasn't listening. He jogged to catch up with her, then walked along at her elbow as she led the way off the common and along Prickwillow Road towards the centre of the town.

He recognised most of the houses they passed – the ones that still stood, at least – although they all looked slightly different. Different window frames (most panes shattered), different colour front doors, wistaria where there had been bare brick, pebble-dash where there had been thick ivy. And, lying in the dust of the road, the occasional dead body. Old men, mostly, Drick noted. In fact, he realised, old men exclusively. No young men, no women, no children. And all in army uniform. Here and there armoured vehicles were pulled up at the kerb, and soldiers with rifles and submachine-guns at the port loitered near doorways.

In Brays Lane, a tank was parked outside a factory building where Waitrose should have been. As they passed, it fired a round into the doorway and sprayed the resulting cloudburst of dust with machine-gun bullets. Kismet hurried past, and he followed.

The hub of activity seemed to be the marketplace. Here, buildings were burning, and a handful of the defending troops (old men again) had been herded together and lined up against the Almonry wall – precisely, Drick realised, where, in his interior map, the war memorial stood (*had* stood? would stand? should stand?). There were more vehicles and soldiers scattered about. The battle seemed to be over (although sporadic gunfire and the occasional distant explosion echoed down the streets), and many of the soldiers were engaged in looting. Not that there was much to take. A group of half a dozen or so were dragging furniture out of a shop and depositing it in the street. One came out carrying a bulky, old-fashioned cash register; he dumped it on the pavement and set about the locked drawer with his bayonet. The register jangled at the repeated blows, as if ringing up sales on a busy day.

Slowly, Drick became aware that Kismet had stopped walking and was speaking to him. 'Sorry?' he said. 'What did you say?'

'This isn't a major battle,' she repeated. 'The main front line is about twenty miles south-west of here, beyond Cambridge.' She smiled grimly. 'I shouldn't think there's much left of your old cottage; some of the fiercest fighting is going on in that area. That's why the defenders here' – she pointed at the group of prisoners, who were being jabbed and prodded with bayonets – 'are so old. When the invasion came, every man under fifty who could stand up was thrown into the army. Men over fifty and cripples were formed into resistance pockets in less important places. Like here. Their only purpose is to slow down the enemy advance.'

They watched the scene for a while in silence. Drick was trying to figure out what it was about the invading troops that didn't look right: they were familiar from any number of old film clips, yet somehow strange. Eventually, he gave in and asked Kismet to explain.

'It didn't happen quite how people think it . . . *would have*,' she said, and grinned. 'I was going to say "did" – it's difficult to manage your tenses in this situation. You've probably read those crypto-history novels, where the Nazis win the war – German tanks in British streets, German sentries standing guard while Nazi officers get out of Mercedes staff cars in front of London hotels. The Swastika flying over Buckingham Palace. That sort of thing. That isn't quite how it happened. When the invaders came, they were—'

268

'French,' said Drick, who had finally figured it out for himself. The vehicles had German markings, and the soldiers wore German-style coal-scuttle helmets and carried German weapons, but their uniforms were French.

'Yes,' said Kismet. 'Oh, there were Germans too, but most of the troops were French. I'm afraid to say they behaved rather worse than the Germans did. You know, atrocities.'

'But . . . the *French*? How come?'

'Better to ask how *not* come. I'll tell you quickly—'

'For once,' he interrupted.

'—because I can't keep this up much longer.' She took a deep breath. 'Have you ever noticed how most of the big things in history have a sort of malignant – or sometimes benign – inevitability about them? The American Civil War, the Union forces winning it, the fall of communism, the abolition of slavery, the decline of empires. It's virtually impossible to imagine history happening any other way. What's more, people who were there at the time – intelligent, knowledgeable people – could see these things coming. But there are other events and outcomes which, even with hindsight, not only couldn't have been predicted, but even confound all expectation and beggar analysis. In the 1930s, war in Europe was one of the former type of event, but the eventual course – as you know it – was one of the latter. That's why it's such a favourite with crypto-historians.

'I grew up with what really happened. It was horrible, and so I set out to change it. I read every book about the war I could find, in order to identify the key moments, and, basically, I changed three things. First, I made Winston Churchill Prime Minister in place of Lord Halifax. Then I had Hermann Göring persuade Hitler to stop the German army short of Dunkirk. Then, later in 1940, I had him – Göring again – switch the Luftwaffe offensive away from airfields and onto cities. The results of those three changes were that the core of the British army wasn't wiped out on the beach waiting for an evacuation that came too late, the British–German armistice of October 1940 was never signed, and nor was the non-aggression pact that followed. German forces didn't have the breathing space to consolidate themselves and absorb waves of French soldiers, and nor did they have a free run at Britain in 1941, nor did they manage to close the door against American involvement. And . . . and so on. You know the rest.'

'Yes, I know,' he said. 'And you think you made things *better*?'

'I did. I prevented the invasion you see going on here, I hampered the invasion that still took place in Russia, I enabled the Allies, ultimately, to win a war which, in real history – the inevitable kind – was lost before it even started. I've estimated that I saved – or rather I *enabled* the saving – of over seven million lives.' She gave him a sardonic look. 'I don't know about you, but I'd call that making things better.'

Drick was about to reply when he was distracted by a commotion in Market Street. A boy burst out of a shop near the market building carrying a bundle in his arms, pursued by two soldiers. There was a cry of alarm, and a woman who had been standing on the other side of the street started running towards him. *Billy!* she yelled. *Billy! Stop!* One of the soldiers chasing the boy halted, cocked his submachine-gun and fired a long burst. The woman (the boy's mother? or sister?) was caught in the wild spread of bullets, and the side of her dress, from armpit to waist, was torn open in a splatter of red, like gravel thrown on water. The boy fell sprawling with one bullet in his midriff and another in the back of his head. His rag bundle rolled across the road, unwrapping itself; inside was a chicken, which squawked and fluttered indignantly for a moment, then calmed down and started pecking at the ground between the two corpses.

'Maybe you're right,' said Drick. He felt nauseous; it was odd, but the scene affected him much more than any of the far worse scenes of slaughter and suffering he had witnessed in his travels. Even though, now, or *then*, or however you expressed it – in his own timeline – this had *never happened*, and was, in its way, a sort of fiction.

His surroundings – the people, the buildings and the square – began to shimmer slightly, focus becoming uncertain, and he thought he was fainting.

'It's going,' said Kismet, strain beginning to show in her eyes, and he realised the shimmering wasn't in his own vision.

270

She clicked her fingers, he experienced a moment of profound giddiness, as though his head was being sucked down through his own body, then he found himself back in the silent garden. The light was still the deepening gold of a late September afternoon, and Manni was still half-way through his leap, with the paper boat clasped between his teeth.

'Lemonade, I think,' said Kismet, and two tumblers of cloudy effervescence appeared in her hands. 'That sort of thing always leaves me thirsty.'

Drick downed his in one long, glugging swallow, and felt immediately better. Kismet sipped hers daintily, walking round the leaping dog, tilting her head from one side to the other, admiring him from every angle.

'More?' she said, noticing Drick's empty glass. He nodded, and it was full again.

He sipped it thoughtfully. 'This theory of history,' he said. 'Inevitability and so on . . .'

'It's not a theory,' she said. 'I've seen it happen. The only hypothetical part is what causes it.'

He furrowed his brow. 'I think I can guess. The parts you think "what if" about – the uncertain bits – are the result of . . . interference.'

'Yes. And not only those. Historical events which defy analysis, like . . . like . . .' She searched for an example.

'Kennedy,' he suggested.

'Exactly. Events that seem, on the face of it, inexplicable. Those too, I think.'

He smiled. 'So, anything that's grist to crypto-historians and conspiracy theorists has probably been caused by people like you.'

'People like me? You make it sound like there are dozens of us.'

He mused, half to himself: 'I wonder what disaster was averted by Kennedy's assassination.'

She shook her head. 'I don't know. Nuclear war, for all we know.'

'It's possible. He came close to it once, even in the new improved version. I've often wondered why people think he was

271

so fantastic; if he hadn't had good advisers, those Cuban missiles would have gone zinging over the Gulf of Florida in nothing flat.' He laughed. 'So it wasn't the CIA after all, or the Mafia – it was someone up in the future with a magic notepad.' He looked at her. 'Or magic fingers.'

She nodded. 'It can be awkward. I've found that changing things has another effect: it leaves behind imperfections.'

'Imperfections?'

'Flaws. Like historical flotsam.'

She looked at him, expecting to have to explain further, but he was nodding his head.

'Makes sense,' he said. 'I've seen some. I met someone once who'd spotted a whole raft of *your* imperfections.' He looked at her and chuckled. 'Conspiracy theorist. If only he'd known.'

He gazed at the lowering sun, halted in its descent beyond the Cathedral octagon, and took a long draught of lemonade. It made so much sense; the first time in ... the first time *ever* he'd had something explained to him which did that, where everything seemed to fit. Which was ironic, considering that—

'You haven't got what you came for, have you?' she said gently.

'What?' He stared at her, blinking, and seemed to see her clearly at last: a slight, pretty, disconcertingly childlike woman in white. Not Death, the destroyer of worlds, gripping history between her thighs and riding it full-tilt over impossible hurdles, which was how he had begun to perceive her during the past couple of hours.

'Tell me,' he said.

'Tell you what?'

He shrugged. 'Everything. Everything I don't know.'

'I don't know about that. Everything you don't know could take rather a long time.' She gave him an ironic look. 'Have you got a century or two to spare? Why don't you tell me what you do know – or think you know – and I'll fill in the blanks.'

'Will you?'

'I promise. First, tell me the story of Kismet Lillystone.'

It took a long time. At least it seemed a long time by his own

272

interior clock – in the world outside, Manni still hung at the top of his leap and the sun stood motionless above the Cathedral. (He noticed, incidentally, that the hands on his watch remained stationary at three minutes to six even though, bizarrely, the mechanism went on ticking.)

Ever the storyteller, he went right back to the beginning – the elder Jack Lillystone's arrival in Ely – and brought the narrative right up to the present moment. He included Finn Bourn's version, and Marjorie's, as well as the second-hand account of Mrs Parmiter, synthesising them into a continuous plot by the addition of his own surmises and inferences. Ever the academic (though he would never have admitted it), he was careful to indicate his sources, and where evidence ended and conjecture began. He did everything short of hand her a printed bibliography. He was pleased with how coherent it all seemed (it helped that he had written it all down some time ago, in three or four different versions, shortly before converting it into a suite of novels), and Kismet seemed to think so too. She maintained an expression of genuine interest throughout, and didn't interrupt once. That gave him confidence, and he rode his story to the end, sure that all his conjectures were correct.

The climax of his story was the death of Kismet – or rather, Kismet's twin sister – by drowning in the river near Cuckoo Bridge. (He glanced apprehensively at her when he broached this, but her expression didn't alter. If there had been pain – and surely there must have been – it didn't show now.) There were, he said, three possible explanations. One, Jack killed her. Two, Kismet killed her. Three, her death was accidental. The third was the version accepted officially, but the police had suspected the first. No charges were brought against Jack Lillystone, presumably because of lack of evidence. The second possibility, that Kismet – or the woman he knew as Kismet – had killed her twin, he discounted. She wasn't capable, he judged. No, he inclined to the view that the death was accidental, and that the guilt detectable in Jack was due not to culpability but to having deprived the surviving twin of companionship with other children which might have compensated for the loss of her sister. Oh, and by the way, the mysterious father of Liza's twin daughters was none other than Finn Bourn, old though he had been. This wild surmise was based on the fact that this was the only part of the story on which the loquacious old man had been reticent.

Kismet was silent for a long while after he finished talking, and he had to prompt her for a verdict.

'Well?' he said. 'Am I right?'

'You seem very set on this idea of twins,' she said.

He shrugged. 'It's the only explanation. Both for the trick you played on the housekeeper, and for the fact that you're here.'

'Perhaps I am a ghost after all.'

He shook his head, and couldn't keep a superior cast out of his expression. 'I told you, I don't believe in ghosts,' he said flatly.

'Oh, well that's my goose cooked, then.' And she vanished.

The supercilious expression dropped off his face like a fried egg off a spatula, and he stared about him, aghast.

'Only joking,' she said, rematerialising beside him. 'Just a reminder that it's not a good idea to bandy assertions about what your *beliefs* will permit to exist in the world when you're talking to someone who can do this . . .' Her fingers clicked, and she vanished again, reappearing instantaneously ten yards away, hovering six feet off the ground. 'Or this,' she added as a floating maroon sofa appeared behind her. She sat on it and smiled down at him. 'Is it?'

'I still don't believe in ghosts,' he said, conscious that it was a faintly absurd thing to say to a dead girl sitting on a levitating maroon sofa (whilst frozen in time).

'But you believe in twins.'

'Of course.'

'What about triplets?'

Two identical Kismets appeared, one on each side of her, on the sofa.

'Or more?'

She waved her hand, as though she were casting seed, and an eye-paralysing infinity of Kismets surrounded him, filling the garden and the fields beyond the river.

'You see?' they all said in unison, and vanished as suddenly as they had come, with a noise like a cork from a bottle.

The sofa, bearing the one solitary original Kismet, drifted down through the air and settled on the grass. She patted the cushion beside her, and Drick sat tentatively on it, prodding the fabric uncertainly, slightly surprised to find it solid and, it has to be said, quite extraordinarily comfortable.

'Point taken. That's how you pulled the trick on Mrs Parmiter, isn't it?'

She smiled coquettishly at him. 'At last, a conclusion that fits the observable facts. Assuming,' she added, 'that you *believe* her story.'

'I do now.'

'And the twins?'

'I don't know.' He shifted in his seat and tried to look sternly at her. 'Why don't you just *tell* me about it, instead of dazzling me with illusions?'

'They aren't illusions.'

'Well, tricks, then. I feel like Alice; I keep expecting a white rabbit to come running out with a big watch.' He caught a glint in her eye. 'Don't even think about it,' he warned. 'There's a fine line between putting me in my place and simple showing off, you know.'

'All right,' she laughed. 'No more "tricks", as you call them.' She spread her hands. 'See, all normal.'

'Normal?' He looked around, taking in Manni, the garden and the sofa. 'You call this normal?'

'Very well, if it'll make you feel more comfortable . . .'

The sofa was replaced by a garden swing with a red-and-white striped canopy. She snapped her fingers, and time switched itself back on: Manni completed his leap, landing on his forepaws with a grunt, and trotted up to Drick, offering the paper boat; the gentle sounds of fields and river resumed; and the second hand on Drick's watch started moving again.

'No more tricks?' he said.

'Nope.'

'Okay.' He dug his heels into the turf and set the swing moving gently, while Kismet, sitting at the other end, drew her legs up under her and made herself comfortable. 'Now tell me the true story of Kismet Lillystone,' he said.

She met his gaze briefly, then looked down at her hands, picking alternately at the ruffle on her right wrist and the watch strap (white, like everything else she wore) round her left. Suddenly, she seemed small and vulnerable – an illusion if ever there was one – and hesitant. No more diversions, just the unvarnished truth; he wasn't sure *she* was going to be able to cope, never mind him.

'I'm surprised,' she began, 'your friend Marjorie didn't tell you the truth. She guessed, I know she did.'

'Guessed what? When?'

'When she came to the house all those years ago. It was such a hot summer.'

'1976. I remember it. We went to Bournemouth on holiday. There were swarms of ladybirds washed up on the beach.'

She looked at him bleakly, and he realised with a jolt that the visit Marjorie had described to him – she had never mentioned this fact, and it had slipped by him – could have been only weeks, perhaps even days or hours before little Kismet's death. Alleged death. Miraculously faked death?

'What did she guess?'

'That she knew me. She looked at me in such a way . . . I ran away. I had to get out of the house. She was the only person who could have known who I was. It was more than a resemblance, you see.'

Drick frowned, bewildered. 'I don't think she guessed anything. She thought you ran away because you could see how much she hated you.'

'For having the life that Veronica didn't?' She smiled thinly. 'Father told me about Veronica, and I found out more myself. I visited her, although she didn't know it. She owns half of Hertfordshire now – or at least her husband does. Three children, spends most of her time riding. Very keen on amateur dramatics, too.'

'Marjorie hasn't the slightest idea what happened to her.'

'That's probably for the best. Veronica hasn't the slightest idea

276

that her parents aren't her natural parents.'

Drick stroked his chin. 'When you said she guessed, I thought for a moment you were going to tell me you were Veronica.'

She chuckled. 'Hardly. I was ten years old. Veronica was already married and expecting her first child. I doubt if even the strongest wishful thinking could collapse ages that dramatically.'

'So, what did she guess? Who did she think you were?'

Kismet entwined her fingers and stretched out her arms like a cat. 'Liza.'

'Liza? Your mother?'

'We were ... Madge and Liza were childhood friends. Madge was the only person outside the family who knew her at all.'

'And she thought you were your mother?'

'More than that. She *knew* I was.'

He had seen and done at least half a dozen impossible things that day, but it still took him a little while to chew this over and swallow it.

'And you're telling me she guessed right?' he asked.

'Yes.'

'You're *Liza?*'

'Yes.'

He managed to keep a straight face. 'You're looking good for fifty-eight.'

'Would you say so? I thought I looked not too bad for twenty-nine. Better still for eighty, I suppose you'd say.'

Drick still kept his face straight, though other positions suggested themselves. 'Look,' he said, 'would it save you the effort of telling me more if I just started gibbering and squawking right now?'

'Not really.'

'You're going to tell me anyway, aren't you?' He sighed. 'You're Liza *and* Kismet?'

'In a manner of speaking. Liza died giving birth to me, just as Georgina died giving birth to her. We – Georgina, Liza, Kismet – are one soul.' She saw his expression, and dropped the portentous tone that had taken over her voice. 'Don't look at me like that. And don't ask me to explain – I don't understand it myself. All I know is that I feel – have always felt – much older than my age. I *remember* things that predate me. I remember Liza's life, and Georgina's. I remember a world before *I* was born, and I remember it through their eyes.

'One of the things I remember is a dreadful scene, between . . . *me* – that's how I see it – and my first husband, Jack. It was the only time he ever raised his voice to me, and it was terrifying. For the first time in our marriage I saw the side of him that he showed to the whole world. He was convinced I had cuckolded him, though who he imagined it could have been with was a mystery. How could I possibly be expecting a child, when we hadn't shared a bed in nearly a year? I . . . *She* didn't understand it either. There had been no man.

'Jack must have believed her, because there were no more rows, and when I – I mean, when Liza was born, he loved her as his own. More, if anything; certainly more than the son who was without doubt flesh of his flesh. And the son loved her too. Perhaps each saw his dead wife or mother in her.

'When she died giving birth to me, my uncle became my father – took the role upon himself without complaint – and named me Kismet. What other name could he choose? The momentum of fate must have seemed irresistible. But he never recovered from the death of his sister and his father. He did what he could for me; did everything a father could – and I wasn't an easy child, I can tell you. What child would be, with the lives of two previous generations piled up inside her head?'

She fell silent then, lost in her memories. After a while, she shook her head, clearing away the tangle of thoughts. 'I always felt, from the moment I was born' – she touched her chest – 'born as myself, I mean. I always felt that there was a part missing; that, in passing from Liza to Kismet, I'd had something removed.'

A sense of excitement bubbled deep inside Drick as she said this. At first he was only vaguely conscious of it. When she went on, though, it burst suddenly, and his hands began to tremble.

'When we talked,' she said, 'I made sure you didn't remember what we talked about. From the first moment I saw you, I knew *you* were it – the piece that was missing. I'd lost track of you, you see, but I knew when I saw you. This thing about twins; I know why it held your imagination so tightly. I thought I'd healed it, but interference so often leaves these little errors.'

Normally, he would have got impatient with the evasive, allusive way she was talking. Not now, though; he had an overwhelming sense of seeing – vaguely, like an approaching figure on a heat-shimmered horizon – where she was heading.

She ordered her memories and went back and, without any further digression, told him the story of a week in a hot summer, nineteen years ago. When she came to the end, Drick was limp and breathless, feeling as though he himself had been dragged half-drowned from the depths of the river. Now he knew everything. Understood . . . well, no, but at least he knew.

The little girl stood on the hearth-rug, looking up at the marvellous, magnificent sailing ship, cradled on its stand on the mantelpiece. She remembered it being made for her father, being presented to him on his tenth birthday. Her own tenth birthday was several weeks away, but it was unlikely she would be given a gift as wonderful as this. She could create one, of course, but that wouldn't be the same; it wouldn't have the hours of intricate care carved into every line, joint and stitch.

He was obsessively jealous of this ship, her father; nobody but he was allowed to so much as touch it. Breathe on it, even. The one time he had struck her had been when she was seven, and he caught her climbing up on a chair to stroke its silken rigging.

He wouldn't see if she touched it now, though. He was out in the old stable, trying to mend his father's old mantel clock. Her double was with him, so he wouldn't suspect that she was in here, plotting an unforgivable transgression. (He had no more idea of her powers than Mrs Parmiter; just like the housekeeper, all he knew was that she was 'special', an uneasy perception which left him slightly, inexplicably in awe of her.) She climbed up on a dining chair and ran a finger along the gunwales and rails, touching the tiny protruding cannon. It was amazingly detailed, right down to the spoked wheel and the tiny copper plates lining the hull. She wondered if it would float.

Glancing over her shoulder (completely unnecessarily, since she could see her father hard at work through her double's eyes, but even the most gifted child can't resist these furtive impulses), she decided to find out. To do so, she would use a trick she had learned long ago but had only recently perfected.

Shutting her eyes and crossing her fingers, she entered the silent world of stopped time.

She wasn't strong enough to lift the model off its cradle, so she stepped down off the chair, laid her thumbs over her crossed fingers, and raised the ship by willing it. There was a tiny creak as the cradle relinquished its burden, then the ship sailed down through the air and floated before her.

It was exacting work, and she had to concentrate hard to keep time, the ship and her double from slipping out of her grip. She guided the ship out of the room, across the hall and out through the kitchen door. Had anyone been able to observe it, it would have made a strangely beautiful sight as she guided it down the garden path, through the gap in the hedge and across the lawn to the landing stage. She lowered it into the water and uncrossed her fingers, ready to grab hold of time again if the ship should start to sink.

It floated. She jumped up and down on the bank, clapping her hands with glee. The sails bellied slightly in the breeze and, with stately grace, the ship turned and began to warp ropeless away from the shore. Then, without warning, the breeze strengthened, and the ship heeled to starboard, turning more sharply and heading out into the sluggish current.

She panicked. She crossed her fingers again and, tired and overstrained by the combined effort of halting time and maintaining her double, her powers drained from her body like yolk from a blown egg and deserted her.

In the stable, Jack started back in horror as his daughter vanished like a ghost before his eyes, while on the Great Ouse, his precious *Victory*, sails set full, rode on downstream, heeling sharply now and taking on water through her open gun-ports.

She turned and ran – back across the lawn, through the hedge, across the garden and under the trees, crashing through the undergrowth, weeping and swearing at the brambles and nettles that tore and stung her bare legs. She burst out of the woods onto Kiln Lane, and ran down past the water works to the riverbank. The *Victory* was heeling badly now, and starting to sink; the mainsail was trailing in the water, and the quarter deck was partly submerged. The ship had entered a terminal curve, veering left now, towards the entrance to Roswell Pits.

She ran onto Cuckoo Bridge and clung to the rail, watching in despair as the crippled ship drifted towards her. If she were to climb out over the rail and stretch down, she might be able to grab the top of the main mast. She would only have this one chance before the ship sailed on through and finally sank in the deep water of the Pits. She tried briefly to lift it up by force of will, but there was no strength left in her. So, eyes filling with tears of fright for herself and anxiety for the ship, she clambered over and stood on the outside of the bridge. Lowering herself into a crouch and clinging on with one white-knuckled hand, one eye open and peering downwards, she reached down and grabbed. The truck of the foremast brushed against her fingers; she grabbed again, and managed to get a grip on the main mast and hold it against the ship's momentum. Now, if she could make her way back to the bank along the outside of the rail, keeping hold of the mast as she went . . .

Holding her breath, she moved her fingers along the rail, like a paraplegic spider – a few inches to the left . . . a few more inches . . . one more . . . Then, as she tried to shuffle her feet along to catch up, her left shoe struck a nail, the right one slipped, and she dropped like a stone. Her chin collided violently with the bridge as she fell, and she hit the water unconscious.

That, at least, was the verdict of the inquest. Her body was found by an angler some hours later, half-submerged in some reeds in the mouth of the Pits. There was no sign of the *Victory*, which had floated on for twenty yards and sunk without trace.

The body's broken jaw provided some confusing circumstantial detail to a case which otherwise would have looked like a simple accident. By a freak coincidence, the injury resembled exactly the result of a punch to the jaw. This aroused the suspicions of the authorities, and Jack Lillystone spent two long, soul-wracking days in a cell in Ely police station. He was profoundly confused, and unable to give a coherent account of himself. As far as he was concerned, the last time he had seen his daughter had been in the stable, when she vanished before his eyes. Naturally, he didn't tell them *that*. It helped him slightly that the officers interviewing him (one of whom had a father who had known old Jack Lillystone) found him decidedly frightening, and went easy on him.

Due to lack of any other evidence, he was released without charge. The pathologist who examined the body was extremely thorough; perhaps more than was necessary. As well as the normal post-mortem opening of the chest and abdomen, he removed the body's hands and bagged them separately, in case this should prove to be a murder case. However, he found no evidence of assault (sexual or otherwise) and concluded that death had been caused solely by drowning. The injury to the jaw, he conceded at the inquest, would be entirely consistent with violent contact with the bridge railing during a fall. The coroner recorded a verdict of death by misadventure, and the body was released.

Jack, to the disgust of the townsfolk (many of whom were sure he was guilty) insisted on taking his daughter home. There, he would conduct a private vigil whose solemnity would compensate for the indignities her remains had suffered at the hands of the law. She was handed over, hastily and rather crudely stitched back together by the pathologist's assistant, in a cheap plywood box. Jack had an undertaker provide a burial gown and a proper coffin, which was laid, unlidded, on the dining-room table at Cuckoo Farm. While he was about his business, the undertaker did his best to conceal the dreadful incisions made by the pathologist's knives, and to persuade Jack that, without proper ... er, storage facilities, the seven days until the funeral would be, er ... Jack told him to stop mincing and speak plain; if he meant that the body would rot, then he, Jack, didn't care. He would carry out his vigil no matter what the cost.

And so he did, and the body did not rot. For seven days and

282

seven nights Jack sat beside the coffin, leaving it only occasionally to eat a few dry crusts or drink a cup of water, or sometimes to sleep on the floor in front of the fire. Mostly, he slept fitfully in his chair; whenever he woke, he would jerk upright with a little gasp, and go immediately to the coffin to gaze down at the body. Then, with a deep sigh, he would go back to his chair, settle down and slip eventually back into a doze, in which he would dream once more that his daughter still lived.

At the eleventh hour on the seventh night, he looked into the coffin for the last time. On the table beside it he had laid out the eight brass screws and a screwdriver, ready to secure the lid. She looked unchanged. Unchanged, that is, since the undertaker brought her home. Nobody ever looked so peaceful and yet so utterly dead. Her skin, which in life had been milky, with a bloom of pale pink, had been bleached translucent white by the liberal quantities of formalin in which the pathologist had bathed and infused the body (and which had presumably kept it in such a remarkable state of preservation). With another deep sigh of regret, he took the lid and laid it on the coffin.

When the undertaker arrived with his assistants the following morning, he was surprised to find the coffin lid screwed down. Strictly speaking, that should have been his job. However, one look at Jack and he lost all inclination to make an issue of it. He had never seen a face so harrowed by grief, nor so close to unspeakable fury. The coffin was carried out to the hearse in silence, taken the short drive to the cemetery in Beech Lane and buried in a plot in the north corner, under the boughs of a great horse chestnut. The only people present at the graveside were Jack, the undertaker and his men, and the Methodist minister. It had been made clear that other mourners would not be welcome. Not that any would sincerely mourn; the only thing that might have brought people from the town to the funeral would have been morbid curiosity.

Afterwards, Jack went home, gathered together a few essentials from the house, and left without even locking the door. He never again, as long as he lived, set foot inside. The house, the farmyard and the garden were left to fall into decay.

283

While Kismet told her story, the sun sank and set. By the time she had finished, it was pitch-dark over the river. She conjured up a ring of lanterns, and they sat together on the swing in their yellow glow, sharing a reflective silence.

'Sad story,' said Drick, when several minutes had passed. It hadn't, after all, been quite what he expected. 'Who really got buried in the cemetery? It wasn't you, obviously.'

Her expression was difficult to read in the soft glow of the lanterns, but she seemed to be smiling. 'No, it wasn't me.' Then she laughed, a clear peal of delight. 'What took place on 30 August 1976 in Beech Lane cemetery was the solemn burial of approximately fifty-one pounds of bricks.'

With an unmistakeable grin, she watched the expressions chase each other across Drick's face: astonishment, realisation, disbelief, comprehension, astonishment again, and back to disbelief. 'You really were expecting a twin to turn up, weren't you?' she said.

Suddenly, she got up onto her knees, making the swing jerk violently. 'Look,' she said, and began unbuttoning the bodice of her dress. 'Bring that lantern closer.'

Bewildered, he took one of the lanterns off its pole and held it up as she finished unbuttoning and held the front of her dress open. He gasped. Running the length of her torso was the longest scar he had ever seen. Starting below the base of her throat, it passed down between her breasts, over her belly, kinked around her navel and disappeared among the shadows in her groin. It wasn't merely the length of it, though, that was shocking, but the ugly crudeness of it, ridged and puckered like a railway track.

'Pretty, isn't it?' said Kismet. 'That hamfisted incompetent stitched me like a pig carcass. Here too.' She undid her wristwatch and took off the white ruffle. Both her wrists bore bracelet scars as unsightly as the one on her body.

She looked at his face, and saw in it exactly the same expression Jack had worn when he saw her eyes open just as he was about to slide the coffin lid into place.

'You doubt me,' she said, but gently, without rancour. 'Touch, if that will help you believe.'

He glanced at her eyes, hesitated, then stretched out a finger and touched the ridge below her throat, tracing it slowly down to her abdomen. It was hard and gnarled, as though a long ash twig had been inserted under the skin.

He withdrew his finger and said: 'I don't disbelieve you.'

'It doesn't cross your mind that this could be another so-called trick?'

'Not for a moment.'

'Good. Because it isn't.' She buttoned up her dress and replaced her watch and ruffle. When the scars were all covered up again, she sat for a moment in silence. 'I lost all my powers,' she said eventually, talking as though to herself, gazing into the distance. 'And I died. The moment I hit the water, it was as if my mind was jolted right out of my body, and I could see myself, unconscious, sinking under the surface. Then everything – the water, the bridge, the banks – faded away to grey, and I think I fell into a sort of oblivion as my body died. When I woke, I was in utter darkness. There was no sensation other than the sight of darkness and the sound of absolute silence. No sensation at all, you might say, except that I was aware that the dark and silence were ... *absences*, not nothingness. As though something was waiting to speak and be seen. Also, I felt that I was being watched. Eventually, whatever it was that was watching me made itself visible and spoke. I've no memory of what it looked like or what it said, just a memory of ... terrible, absolute awe. That I was being regarded with a disapproval that was superhumanly profound. I felt ashamed and naked. I don't know why I was being so disapproved of, except for a vague notion that I'd left something behind, or left something uncompleted.

'After a while – I've no idea how long, and I suspect time was an irrelevance in whatever place it was I'd found myself – I felt I was drifting, moving along an immensely long tunnel. At the same time I knew I wasn't proceeding onwards, but going back. I was being *sent* back. That must have been what – or part of what the *something* had said to me. Go back and complete whatever it was I was meant to complete.

'As I travelled along the tunnel, I began to perceive a bright light in the distance. It got brighter and more intense as I moved closer, until I wanted to close my eyes, but I couldn't. It was so bright, they hurt – as bright as the sun. Just when I thought my eyes would burn out, the light disappeared, and I found myself lying on my back, in a coffin, looking up at my father. He was standing with the coffin-lid poised ready to put in place, wearing the most startled face I'd ever seen.'

She looked at Drick and grinned. 'Until I met you, of course. Owner of the largest repertoire of startled faces in the world.'

'Well, I think I've seen quite a bit of startling stuff these past couple of years,' Drick replied. 'Not to mention alarming, bewildering, confusing and downright bloody frightening. It takes quite an extensive repertoire to cope, you know.' He thought for a moment. 'Why did your . . .' He stumbled through the appellations – son, brother, uncle – before settling on the one she seemed to prefer, even though it was the only one that was untrue. 'Why did your father act the way he did? Abandoning the farm, I mean, acting as though you really were dead.'

'Superstition, I think. Maintaining an appropriately bereaved appearance? I don't know. He went to live in his railway carriage, and that was that. I *think* – and I know him pretty well, as you can imagine – that after I came back like that, he became quite afraid of me. In his entire life, he'd never known what it was to fear another human being. Even his father didn't scare him. He left me to live as I wished in the house; he seemed to feel that his only role in my life – or his – from then on was to guard the place, as a sort of sanctuary.'

'You live in that place?' said Drick, thinking of the dust and decay and spider webs.

'Not as you see it, no. I live in a . . . a version of it. It's difficult to maintain, but I manage. In the version I inhabit, the garden always blooms, the sun shines perpetually, except when I feel like letting night or rain fall. This part' – with a sweep of her arm she indicated the riverside lawn – 'is the only bit of my version that intersects with everybody else's. From time to time, I come here and step out into the real world.'

'And that's when we've met?'

'Yes. You see, that's the reason I was sent back – I figured it out quite quickly, of course. I was sent back to keep an eye on you.'

'On me?'

'Yes.'

'Why?'

She paused. 'Well, I was responsible for you, in a manner of speaking. Having created you.'

She waited, watching the effect.

'Hmm,' she said, 'I haven't seen *that* one before. Your repertoire's even more extensive than I thought.'

If he looked startled, it was probably just habit; inside, he just felt numb. He also thought of Jonathan Peachment and didn't feel he had the right to be sceptical. 'You *created* me?' he repeated, in the same tone as he might say, You speak *Chinese*?

'Yes, I created you. Quite inadvertently, of course.'

'Oh, well that makes it all right, then. How can you create someone inadvertently?'

'By expressing an insufficiently specified wish. You remember I told you that I'd always felt that something was missing? That something had been removed?'

He nodded, but didn't tell her that he had felt exactly the same thing for as long as he could remember: as though something had been cut out of him and the wound so perfectly sealed that you couldn't find the join, that was how he had expressed it.

He didn't need to tell her – she could tell from his expression that he understood her perfectly. 'Well,' she went on, 'I wished so hard for that empty space to be filled that . . . it was. But of course, I couldn't imagine what or who was meant to fill the space, and so it was decided for me. I willed it indirectly, you see.'

'When did this happen?' he asked. 'It's important when it happened.'

'I know. Don't worry, it wasn't retrospective, like that poor man you brought into the world. I willed you straight into your mother's womb, and simultaneously Kismet appeared in mine.'

He nodded, ignoring the barb. 'So I was definitely born normally? I wasn't backdated?'

'Abnormally conceived, but absolutely normally born, yes.' She

287

hesitated, then appeared to force a decision. 'You and your brother,' she added.

He shook his head. 'I haven't got a brother.'

She gazed at him silently for a moment. 'This is going to be difficult,' she said apprehensively. 'You weren't created alone. You were one of a pair. Twins.'

To her surprise (he would have been pleased that he had managed to surprise her, but he wasn't conscious of it at the time), he laughed out loud. 'No, I'm not having that,' he said. 'A twin I didn't know about? That stuff's for novels, not real life.'

'You forgot him. I *made* you forget him. I wouldn't have interfered if it hadn't been necessary; you'd have gone out of your mind if I hadn't. I don't think I did the job perfectly, though. I think I left traces. Haven't you wondered why you found my story so fascinating? Why you couldn't let it alone?' She waited for a reply, and when it didn't come, she went on: 'I thought about giving you the memory back, but there was too much trauma still. I probed you about it when we met, and saw it was no good.'

'When we met?'

'Here in the garden, that afternoon, and the other time. That's why you can't remember much of what we talked about. I cleared your memory of our conversations, in case I'd said anything clumsy that might nag at you afterwards.'

'So why tell me now?' He frowned at her. 'You're not going to erase my memory again, are you? I don't want to lose all the other stuff.'

'I won't erase your memory. I'm telling you now because I think, for better or worse, it's time you learned the truth. Or regained the truth.' She leant towards him and pressed two fingertips against his forehead. 'You may feel some discomfort,' she said.

The spy-hole in his head opened up, but now *it* seemed to be peering through *him*. He was lying on the floor of the locked cell, and the aperture burned with searing light. The hole enlarged, as though a thermal lance was boring through the reinforced steel;

288

white-hot molten metal dripped down the surface of the door and fizzed on the cold floor.

He shut his eyes against the glare. If this was discomfort, he'd hate to know her idea of pain.

Shutting out the light only made the noise more intense – an excoriating hiss that was partly like steam from a ruptured boiler, partly like sandpaper burnishing his eardrums, partly like a barrage of shells passing overhead.

He opened his eyes, and saw the brutal steel structure of a vast bridge soaring above him. He shut them again, and felt grateful for the noise.

When the noise stopped – leaving a long, raucous ringing in his ears – he opened his eyes timorously. The cell door had gone. He crept up to the open doorway, stepping over the puddle of cooling metallic lava, which now glowed a dull cherry-red. He peered through and saw . . . well, what he *didn't* see was a fantastic landscape of rolling hills, purple mountains and fairy castles climbing through threads of silver cloud, which was what he expected to see. What he saw was a cell identical to his own. It had dripping stone walls like his, a flat stone bed like his, and lying on the bed was a figure which . . . The figure looked up. The figure smiled.

So *that* was pain. He came reeling out of the trance, gasping and sobbing like a child, clutching at Kismet as she wrapped her arms around him and gently rocked the swing with her foot.

As he came out of the bathroom, Drick noticed that Jonathan's office door was half-open. (As well as a bedroom on the attic floor, he had this room to himself; dignified – and, in a sense, authorised – by the title 'office', it was really more of a private living room-cum-kitchen, which allowed the two of them to share the house without too much housematiness, preserving an atmosphere of boss-employee.) He knocked on the frame, and Jonathan appeared. He looked a lot better now than he had a couple of months ago: he shaved regularly (more regularly than Drick did, anyway) and his hollowed cheeks had filled out a little. He still had that look, though – even at funerals people would probably nudge each other and say *Who's that miserable-looking bloke?* At least, the ones who didn't notice his hat might say that. *Who's that weirdo in the silver bobble-hat?* would be a more likely inquiry.

Drick had got used to it, and barely glanced at it now. 'Coffee, Jonathan?' *Go on, crack a smile; it won't kill you.*

'I'd love one.'

Drick clapped him on both shoulders. 'Good man. Make a big pot while you're at it.'

The oldest tricks were the best, he thought, as he tripped happily down the stairs. Besides, Jonathan ought to earn his living somehow. He had very little secretarying to do, and he hardly earned his keep on the strength of his laugh-a-minute personality. Drick had decided to metamorphose him gradually into a sort of quasi-butler and then take it from there. The two strengths he had uncovered so far – making coffee and being tidy – had pointed the way.

He found Jeremy in the dining room. (Another misnomer, since this was in fact an office, where Drick kept all his reference books, his files and his computer, and even, from time to time, did a little work.) He was admiring Drick's new Macintosh.

'Quadra 950,' he said. 'Nice.'

'Certainly is.'

'It's got the Power PC chip, hasn't it?'

'Yup.' He watched Jeremy's face for a moment. Jeremy didn't have his own computer; on his income, he couldn't have afforded a pocket calculator. 'Look, I wish you'd let me buy you one.'

Jeremy looked sharply at him. 'I've told you, I'm not becoming your kept boy for anything.'

'Come on, don't be a wet fart all your life. Call it a loan.'

'N-O spells no, Drick. Anyway, there are some British Academy fellowships coming up next year. I'm sure to get one of them.' He stood back and took a long view of the Mac. 'It's a lovely piece of gear,' he said. 'But do you really need *quite* such a big desk to display it on? I mean, ten people could eat their dinner off there.'

'It's not normally like this. Jonathan's tidied it again. He does it twice a week – Mondays and Fridays.'

'I never thought I'd see the day when you'd get a domestic.'

Drick shrugged. 'That's being filthy rich for you. Anyway, he's not exactly a domestic. Tidying the desk is his hobby. I call him my *aide d'escritoire*.'

Jeremy smiled. 'You've been waiting a long time for a chance to deliver that line, haven't you?'

'About three weeks. What d'you think?'

'Don't put it in one of your novels. Not unless you've got a character who specialises in really crap aphorisms.' Jeremy dropped his voice to a confidential whisper. 'I don't mean to pry—'

'God forbid.'

'—but why has he got tin foil on his hat?'

Drick grinned. 'You noticed. It's to keep the government out.'

'What?'

'The foil deflects the mind-reading rays from government

291

satellites. They've been seeing into our brains for years, apparently, looking for subversive thoughts. Jonathan read about it in a magazine.'

Jeremy frowned. 'Doesn't it concern you?'

'What? Satellites seeing into my brain? No, I can't say I worry overmuch about it.'

'I mean sharing your house with a high-juice fruit-loop.'

Drick mimed making a note. 'That's good. D'you mind if I use it?' He put the imaginary note in his pocket and looked serious. 'He's not mad. He just has this slightly eccentric notion that there's this invisible outside agency messing with him, which manifests itself in this belief. He's completely rational apart from that one thing. Give him a break – he's had a difficult life.'

Jeremy shrugged. 'I suppose we've heard weirder, you and I.'

'You don't know the half of it.'

'It's a pity he didn't show up when the Club was still active.'

Drick's mouth tightened. 'Those jerks? One exposure to Jonathan and they'd have been wandering the streets of Cambridge in reflective headgear chanting *Follow me.*'

He dismissed the thought with a shake of his head. 'Anyway,' he said, 'enough of Jonathan. I've got something to show you.' He opened his filing cabinet and took out a thin manilla folder. 'I'd like to know what you think,' he said, handing it over.

'Really?'

'Really.'

Jeremy took it over to the sofa, and opened it gravely. He'd never been asked for his opinion of Drick's writing before (fortunately, perhaps, in the case of *The Alchemist's Apprentice*, which he hadn't liked much), and he thought he should take it seriously. Inside the folder were about a dozen closely printed pages.

'It's a short story,' said Drick.

Jeremy lit a cigarette and began to read. While he was looking at the first page, Jonathan came in quietly with a tray, on which stood a pot of coffee, two cups, a bowl of sugar lumps and a small jug of cream. He placed it on the desk and left as quietly as he had come, retreating to his office with his own small pot of coffee and two Kit Kats, of which he was inordinately fond.

'Duxy!' Jeremy shouted suddenly. 'I don't believe it! Is it him? Yes it is – to the life! Who else ever called you Bender? And *Spam*!'

Drick grinned. 'You remember him. I sometimes wonder what happened to them all. My fantasy is that Spam is immensely handsome and successful, smelling like a whirlwind in a perfume factory and with a gorgeous wife who calls him Simon.'

'Off beam, I'm afraid. I saw him last time I was in Wales. I think he still wears the same jumpers. He's got three kids; the eldest is about to start comprehensive school. His wife looks older than his mother, and about half as good-looking.'

'I remember his mother. All the beauty and elegance of a bus pile-up. What about Duxy?'

'I met him a couple of years ago. Grey as a ghost, with a beer gut like a sack of soil. Made you wonder why you'd ever looked up to him.' He paused reflectively. 'Jimmy Hughes still looks good, mind. Doing very well in sales, I heard.'

'Hmm. Anyway, read on.'

'What is this? Autobiography?'

Drick smiled enigmatically. 'Sort of.'

While Jeremy read on, Drick poured out the coffee. When he put Jeremy's cup on the arm of the sofa, he received a quizzical glance, and when he sat down at his desk, he saw that Jeremy was wearing an ever-deepening frown.

'Not good?' he asked.

Jeremy looked up, seemed about to speak, then carried on reading. When he finished, he laid the story on the sofa beside him and, obviously playing for time, sipped his coffee, lit a cigarette and gazed out of the window.

'Well, what d'you think?'

Jeremy, his little stock of evasive gestures exhausted, had no choice but to speak. 'Cribbo's surname was Taylor, not Evans,' he said. 'And you didn't come up with the word Rampike. I did.'

'Bollocks. *A*, it was Evans. My dad worked with his at Panteg. *B*, Rampike was mine. I got it from *The Red Pony*. And *C*, you know perfectly well what I'm talking about.' He strode over to the sofa, seized the sheaf of paper and brandished it like a manifesto. 'Why the bleeding, creeping, suffering *Christ* did nobody ever talk to me about this?'

'We tried!'

'Who?'

'I don't know – everybody. Me, your mum and dad. You wouldn't let them. Then you went weird. Where is it?' He grabbed the story from Drick and leafed through it. 'Here it is. You say it yourself.' He read the paragraph out loud:

'Remembering the looks on their faces as they gathered round him, it seemed clear that they had been more frightened by the incident than he had. Jeremy especially; he seemed reluctant even to talk about it. Rod discovered he had a strange, unexpected power: whenever he talked about it, his friends clammed up and looked nervous. They became easier to persuade, and would often do his bidding.'

'Fucking hell!' Jeremy shouted. 'You can say that again. You gave everyone the creeping heebie-jeebies. I was the only one who could stand to be around you. They – we all thought you were . . . I don't know. And this was the version you were carrying around in your fucked-up head?'

'Yes. I forgot even that after a while.' Drick sank down on the sofa. 'Why didn't anyone ever tell me about him?'

'Who? Raymond?' Jeremy looked at Drick with a slightly alarmed expression, as though he'd caught himself saying 'cunt' in front of his grandmother, but there was no visible reaction. 'You know, that's the first time I've said his name in nearly twenty years? You don't realise how powerful names can be, do you?' He frowned deeply. 'Like I said, we tried. You wouldn't let us. You either went catatonic or blew up into a frenzy.' His voice became gentler. 'And now you've remembered? After all this time?'

'No, I was . . .' Drick hesitated. 'Yes, I remembered.' He got up and opened the filing cabinet again. 'I've written another version. I want to know if this is the way you remember it.' He smiled.

294

'Apart from the Rampike. I'm still claiming that, whatever you say.' He handed Jeremy another folder. 'This is what I've been— . . . what I remember.'

This time he watched with a distinct air of anxiety as Jeremy read. Jeremy's expression grew graver as the pages turned, as it had when he read the previous version. But when he finished and laid the pages aside, he looked at Drick with the profoundest sympathy in his eyes.

'Did you ever feel a weight fall off your shoulders?' he said.

'Not exactly.' Drick tapped the paper. 'Is that how *you* remember it?'

'Pretty much. Maybe not as clearly. Memories must keep better in cold storage.' He paused. 'How d'you feel about it?'

Drick shrugged. 'Okay, I think. Not traumatised all over again, if that's what you mean.'

Jeremy picked up the pages again and flipped through them. 'I still say *I* christened the Rampike,' he said.

They looked at each other: for a moment the near-telepathy that had once bound them together flickered between them again, and they laughed until they cried.

Duxy was the leader. It wasn't up for discussion: he led, and that was all there was to it. If there had been a vote, Duxy would still have been leader, so where was the point of democracy? Nowhere, that's where; a waste of time that would be better spent on other things. The only one who might have been a serious challenger was Raymond, but he didn't put himself forward. He preferred to stay close to Rod. Twins they might be, but their relationship had evolved at an early age into that of big brother-little brother. They didn't look alike, and their personalities were as different as brothers' personalities could be: Rod looked up to Raymond, and Raymond led and protected Rod. Jeremy was friends with both of them, and tried not to show preference, but he was naturally drawn to the more forceful character of the two.

Although Duxy led, it was Raymond (at Rod's prompting) who chose the place wherein he should lead them. Three Bridges Corner was a ready-made adventure playground, and was a favourite with all of them, but Rod was especially – perhaps a little abnormally – fascinated by it.

As the whole area was hemmed in by dense woodland, it was obvious to any boy with half a brain that Three Bridges Corner made the best, most challenging follow-my-leader course in the world.

And, as always, Duxy went first. That gave him the prerogative of dictating the order of followers. Jimmy Hughes, who was actually the best climber and should on those grounds alone have been leader, went second. After him came little Christopher Evans (Cribbo), who was more than a year younger than the rest

296

of them and a weakling with it. Technically, he should have gone last, but he happened to be Duxy's poodle, and he wouldn't let the snivelling little bugger out of his sight. Then there was Spam Williams (who stank like a dead fishmonger's socks), then Jeremy, then Raymond (who turned down Duxy's offer of second place) then, in last place, came Rod. He didn't mind being last (not as much as he minded being called Rod, anyway), since it meant long pauses while the boys ahead of him negotiated the obstacles, leaving him free to study the structure of the bridges, which was what interested him about the place.

'Oi, pay fuckin' attention, Roddyprick.'

Rod looked at Duxy. 'Eh?'

'Orders, spaz.'

Duxy had a way of being abusive without rancour: he did it with a sudden grin (scaled up to a giggle if he called you something really foul) which managed to convey that, even if he meant it, it didn't matter that he meant it, because he was such an irresistibly great mate. It fooled Rod every time, even when Duxy called him Roddyprick, or Bender.

'Listening, Dux.'

Duxy surveyed his troops, a charismatic half-smile on his thin lips. He always adopted this expression, implying that he was about to deliver a long talk, when he was going to do something unexpe—

'*Rampike!*' he yelled, turning and crashing off through the woods, whooping like a Red Indian.

They took up the cry as they followed, dodging between the trees, ducking under branches, leaping clumps of undergrowth like so many Chingachgooks, oblivious to the brambles that scraped at their shins. All order vanished in the race to be first to the Rampike.

Duxy was first out of the wood, hitting the tussocky grass of the pasture at a headlong run, with Jimmy and Spam close behind. Then came Raymond, Rod and Jeremy, with Cribbo trailing behind, flapping his arms like a gull. (Cribbo could never be shaken in his belief that this eccentric habit helped him run faster.)

When they had all slapped the dead trunk and paused to get their breath back, they fell into line and began the course. First they took turns to climb the Rampike, shinning up the unscorched side, hand-over-handing out along its horizontal branch and dropping to the turf. That was easy enough, except for Spam, who landed feet-first slap in the middle of a fresh cowpat. Some of it went up his legs and lapped over the tops of his shoes (he didn't care; it added to the festering bouquet he always carried with him), but most shot in a great green spout up Cribbo's side.

'*Yes!*' Spam cried. Amidst the laughter, he tried to persuade Rod to drop on the remains of the cowpat. If Duxy had joined in, he might have done it, but Duxy was torn between laughing and making sure (with a stern glance) that the tears welling up in Cribbo's eyes didn't spill over. When Raymond and Rod had made the drop, Duxy set off back across the pasture at a trot.

'Follow on!' he called, and stamped a foot on the fringe of another fresh green dollop, taking care to hit it at an angle, so that the spray shot away from him. Jimmy did the same, Cribbo pretended to stamp on it, and Spam ran right through the middle of it. That amused him so much he doubled back for another go, kicking up a big slobbery clod that splattered up Cribbo's back. (Duxy wasn't looking, fortunately.) By the time Jeremy reached the pat, all that was left was a patch of slippery grass, which he could stamp on with complete impunity.

Duxy led them a tortuous route through the woods, then down to the riverbank, where they had to leap like mountain goats from rock to rock (the most convincing impression being by Spam, who smelled like one) as far as the foot of the road bridge, where they climbed up onto the concrete pier and ran through to the far side. While he waited his turn to get up from the last rock, Rod looked up at the underside of the bridge. There were birds nesting up there, he noticed. He tapped Raymond on the shoulder and pointed. Raymond grinned.

'Shoulda brought the air-gun,' he said. Then his turn came, and he levered himself up and ran on, leaving Rod staring after him, aghast. That wasn't what he'd meant at all.

On the other side, the bridge was revetted by a steep grass bank. Scrambling up it got harder and harder as the leaders destroyed the few handhold tufts in their haste to pull themselves up. By the time Rod made it up to the roadside, the front-runners had crossed over and were disappearing down the entrance to the footbridge. When he got there, Duxy was climbing over the wire fence at the far end and heading off back into the woods, with Jimmy vaulting like a gymnast after him. Rod pumped his legs faster, shoving Raymond in the back to urge him on. Raymond passed the shove on to Jeremy, who was being held up by Spam. Spam was sweating like a pig (his fund of near-perfect animal impressions seemed limitless – sweated like a pig, smelled like a goat, scratched like a dog, belched like a cow – he was a one-boy menagerie) and beginning to tire badly. Jeremy studied the back of Spam's jumper, looking for a clean place to shove. (Clean being a relative term with Spam, who owned a selection of filthy jumpers which he wore in all weathers, even today's sweltering heat, temperature being more or less regulated by the number of vests underneath. The jumpers came in a variety of jazzy patterns, but all had the same grey, greasy pall and spotty collection of stains.) He found an area near the left shoulder where the cowshit splatter hadn't touched, and pushed. Spam grunted and almost fell, but pressed on harder.

Luckily, Duxy was tiring too, and he paused a little way into the woods, on the pretext of letting the poufs and ponces catch up. When they were all gathered, Rod noticed that he had that expression on his face again, and he braced himself for an extra special challenge, thinking he could guess what it might be. There were a few obstacles they hadn't tackled yet, but only one which engendered that degree of sly anticipation. The pipe bridge. Rod and Raymond glanced at each other. If there was one characteristic they shared, it was a horror of heights.

They guessed right. When he judged that even the weakest of them were recovered (i.e. when he had got his own breath back), Duxy led them to the tall iron gates. The padlock had been broken off years ago, and the thick steel chain which had once secured the gates against intruders lay caked in rust amongst the litter. The gate squealed on its hinges, and Duxy started to climb the narrow steps to the left of the pipe. They were as steep as a ladder, and Rod used his hands to help himself up. When he reached the top, he had to make a deliberate effort to stand upright and step out onto the metal walkway. On either side, and between the slats of the walkway itself, he could see the river thirty feet below, swirling with yellow froth as it licked the edges of the jagged rocks. Concentrating on the slats and letting the view between and around them go out of focus, he took two steps forward and joined the queue. At the head, Duxy was crouching and peering down through the gap between walkway and sidewall.

'Here,' he said.

Raymond looked back over his shoulder, and Rod saw apprehension in every line of his face. He had seen what Duxy was planning to do, and Rod could guess. Merely crossing the precarious walkway wasn't daring enough, apparently. About a third of the way along its span, the pipe bridge passed over the footbridge, and Duxy was going to try dropping from one to the other. Rod put a hand on the sidewall to brace himself, and looked down through the gap. From ground level, the two bridges appeared to pass very close, but from up here the concrete footway and its steel girder rails looked almost as distant as the river beneath.

Leaning out like this, he could watch Duxy make his attempt. He sat down on the walkway and grasped the lip at the bottom of the sidewall. His face tense, he rocked his hips back and forth, and Rod could see his lips moving silently: *one, two, three . . .* Then, with an audible grunt, he took his weight on his hands and swung forward, dropping down through the gap. He probably intended to swing by his hands before dropping, but the momentum of his fall whipped his fingers off the slippery steel, and he went straight down. After what seemed like a horribly long fall, his baseball boots hit the concrete with a loud thump, he rolled over and over, and came up yelling in triumph, shaking his fists in the air.

'C'mon!' he shouted. ''Seasy!'

Jimmy went next. Inspired by Duxy, he deliberately took the drop in one go, and landed like a paratrooper. Cribbo took a lot longer, lying out flat on the walkway before swinging his legs out over the drop and twisting his body in search of a handhold. While Duxy called encouragement and Cribbo tried to get a firm grip on the lip of the sidewall, Rod dragged his eyes away and concentrated on the bridge, looking for some feature to study. At the centre, a stub stuck out from the pipe, and he fixed on that; it led into a big metal box with a ladder up the side and a large black handwheel on top. He tried to work out what it was for, shutting out the grunts, gasps and cries from the boys ahead of him, and the instructions – *Left a bit – nuh, right – back the other way, spastic!* – being called from below. He concentrated hard on the peculiar device and heard nothing.

He didn't see Jeremy or Raymond go. When he brought his mind back to the game, he found himself alone on the bridge, and they were all yelling at him to hurry up. He edged along the walkway until he judged he was exactly above the footbridge. Not having watched the last few jumpers, he found it difficult to tell which precise spot they had dropped from. He gazed down, and suddenly his attention was caught by something in the river below the edge of the footbridge. For a moment, he thought he saw himself reflected in the water, peering back up at him, but it didn't seem like a reflection; it seemed as though the face was *under* the water. It only lasted a split second; he blinked, the reflection was lost in a froth of turbulence, and then he was looking down into the faces of Cribbo and Spam, both wearing expressions of abject terror. They must have seen that he was setting himself up to drop from the wrong place, so he shuffled a little to the right. There was no sign of the others; they must have lost patience with him and run on. He thought Jeremy and Raymond might have waited.

He laid his hands on the lip, rested his weight on them, and with a single heave of his hips, launched himself down through the gap.

The drop made no visual impression on him whatsoever, not even a blur. He felt a brief sensation of falling, then a sharp clout on the chin, and thought for an instant he had hit the lip of the pipe bridge. Something scraped violently up his side from knee to

301

armpit, and when his vision returned, he found himself clinging like a monkey to the outside of the footbridge rail. His left arm was hooked over the top girder, and the rest of him hung in space. He stayed there for a few moments, feeling surprisingly calm; then he glanced down at the river swirling by far below his swinging feet.

Jeremy, soaked to the skin, was being hauled onto a rock by Duxy and Jimmy. He was coughing up water, choking and yelling above the roar of the river. They backed off in the face of his fury, letting go of him; immediately, he turned and dived back into the river. Then Rod saw what the commotion was about: lodged up against the concrete footing of the road bridge, on the far side of the river, a body was floating. It was face down, but Rod would have recognised that blue-striped T-shirt anywhere. There was blood on his head; a thick ooze turning the froth pink.

He had no memory of getting back over the rail. The next thing he knew, he was lying on his back on the concrete, with Cribbo and Spam looking down at him. Whether he'd hauled himself over, or they'd helped, he had no recollection. Other faces joined theirs: Jimmy and Duxy and, a minute or two later, Jeremy. There was water dripping from his hair, and his left cheek was red, as though he had been punched. That reminded Rod of his own injured jaw, and he realised where the horrendous pain in his head came from, and why his vision was blurring. The faces faded, sounds deadened, he felt as though he was dropping from a great height again, and everything vanished.

He didn't go to Raymond's funeral. He didn't speak to anyone – nor give any sign of hearing anyone who spoke to him – for a whole week. It took him that long to work out in his mind what had happened.

Cribbo and Spam had been left to warn Rod not to jump, while Duxy and Jimmy followed Jeremy down to the riverbank. Jeremy dived in twice to try and rescue Raymond, who was swirling unconscious in the water, but it was useless. The looks of terror Rod had seen on Cribbo and Spam's speechless faces as

302

he looked down from the pipe bridge had been caused by the realisation that he was about to drop from the same spot Raymond had chosen.

Everyone but Rod had seen Raymond's misjudged jump. He had dropped too far to the right, and hit the parapet of the footbridge full-on. His heels went out from under him as he struck, he fell backwards, striking the back of his head on the girder rail, and tipped over the edge. Jeremy himself nearly drowned in his first attempt to rescue him. A wasted effort, since the adults said Raymond was probably dead or nearly dead before he even hit the water. At most, the river merely finished the job three-quarters done by the steel girder.

As soon as Rod got a picture of what happened clear in his head, he promptly forgot it. Or rather, he remembered a version of it, from which Raymond had been excised. He didn't *try* to forget his brother, but he lost him from his memory as utterly as he had lost him from his life.

He didn't play at Three Bridges Corner from that day onwards, although he did go back occasionally to look at the great stone-and-steel N. What puzzled him, having no idea now that anything other than his own mildly calamitous fall had ever taken place there, was that the others stayed away from it too. Even more surprisingly, they didn't take the piss as he'd expected; they never even mentioned his fall. As he got older, it seemed to make sense. Remembering the looks on their faces as they gathered round him, it seemed clear that they had been more frightened by the incident than he had. Jeremy especially; he seemed reluctant even to talk about it. He discovered he had a strange, unexpected power: whenever he talked about it, his friends clammed up and looked nervous. They became easier to persuade, and would often do his bidding. He grew in confidence, and the diffident little boy he had been went away, replaced by a new, more robust model.

Within a couple of years, he had forgotten the incident entirely, although he did sustain a deeper attachment, stemming from that day, to Jeremy. He didn't know it, but he saw in his friend a

303

substitute for his lost twin brother. A substitute that didn't quite work, because although he had no memory of Raymond, he always retained an uneasiness, a feeling that something had been taken away from him, the point of detachment so thoroughly smoothed over that he couldn't detect it.

After Jeremy had gone home, Drick harnessed Manni up and took him for a walk. It had been a bitterly cold day, even for November, and the ground retained a hard frost in places where the bright sunshine hadn't reached. The sun was fading down the sky now, but there was still a good hour of daylight left.

They took a detour up the hill to the High Street, pausing to look up at the windows of Elsa's old flat. They had been double-glazed, he noted, which tickled his sense of irony. Presumably at the expense of the person who now owned the gift shop, which still stocked the same old lines, judging by the window display of ecclesiastical teddies, wooden fruit and doilies.

From the shop, Drick and Manni followed their old route: across the High Street, through Steeplegate, and across the Cathedral green. Down Back Hill, past the station and out along the Stuntney Causeway to the Queen Adelaide Road. There they crossed marsh and field, following the riverbank east. When they reached the point opposite Cuckoo Farm, Drick indulged in another reflective pause. So far as he could tell, there wasn't a trace of frost on the riverside lawn, even though the hedges must have kept most of it in shade all day. Frost didn't settle here, and if it did, it was only at the proprietor's behest.

He closed his eyes, made a small, silent thought, and when he opened them again, a bridge spanned the river, opening invitingly before his feet and crossing to the garden. It was a Chinese bridge, with red rails carved in geometric patterns, tiny pagoda roofs capping the upright posts, and silver bells hanging from the rails, tinkling softly in the breeze.

He smiled. This was better than last time, when, leaving the garden after that eternal evening, a bridge had materialised which was an exact replica of the footway at Three Bridges Corner. His own fault for being careless in imagining a crossing when the newly rediscovered memory was so fresh in his mind. Still, not at all pleasant. Almost freaked him right out, in fact.

He stepped onto the pagoda bridge and walked across, delighted by the way the rhythm of his footsteps was taken up by the jingling bells. When he reached the far side and stepped down onto the grass, he found himself in a different day. It was still four o'clock by his watch, but the sun was riding high and hot in the sky. The hedgerows were thick with dog-rose, and sitting on the velvet grass with a glass of lemonade in her hand, was Kismet.

Packet 17

There isn't much left to tell. As we're so close to parting, I'll address you directly one last time.

I suppose I could have ended there, on that last page. It has that end-of-story quality, don't you think? Maybe it doesn't for you; you still have some unopened packets in the box, or – depending on whom I'm addressing – a thickish chunk of book in your right hand, so you're probably not in an end-of-story mood yet. I am. Besides, those thoughtful end-moments are harder to come by than you might think, and I was very tempted for a while there just to stop myself on that bridge, with Kismet waiting for me, and draw a line. But that would chuck a rather large spanner in the mechanism, wouldn't it? Okay, go on, I'll give you the real ending, which, for me, is only now about to happen.

Everything is prepared. It's New Year's Eve, and I've just made the phone call which will set it all in motion. A New Year party seemed the most plausible excuse. So, I've got a few hours left to get things finalised. Virtually everything I've ever written (barring shopping lists and these last few pages) has been carefully pack-aged, labelled and boxed up. There's a lot more of it than I'd thought; I've had to discard the little box I originally intended to use, and get a much bigger one. In addition to these special packets whose contents you've been reading, there are parcels containing the manuscripts of:

9 novels, finished
4 novels, unfinished
17 short stories, completed

5 short stories, in note form
12 outline sketches for novels
8 essays

I hadn't realised quite how much there was until seeing it all gathered together. For someone who's always taken a perverse pride in his laziness, I've been a bit industrious, haven't I? Oh, and while I'm listing, let's not forget,

1 novel, published, shortly to be obliterated

But of course you don't want to know this. You, Jeremy, already know what the box contains, while you, whose name I don't know (sorry, but there are limits even to the kind of powers at my disposal), probably don't care. What you *will* want to know is where I am going, how I got there, and why I chose to leave. Well, I assume you will. Since you've come this far with me, the least I can do is take you the last few yards.

I'm afraid length of exposure hasn't made public nakedness any easier to endure, so you'll excuse me if I slip back into character for the last act.

He took to visiting the garden more and more frequently as the winter months passed. By the time the new year was more than a few weeks old, he was going there every morning and spending the whole day with Kismet in the garden's perpetual summer. (They tried out spring and autumn, and once or twice allowed a heavy snow to settle, but nine days out of ten it was high summer in the garden.) One warm July evening in late January, they had a conversation which changed both their lives for good. It went something like this.

They were lying out on the grass, watching Manni grinding down a big marrowbone, when Drick decided to broach a subject that had interested him for a very long time, but which he had refrained from asking about before because it seemed a little . . . well, personal.

'It's funny,' he began cautiously. 'When I first met you, I was struck by the way you seemed . . . older than you looked.'

'Does it show?' she smiled.

'Not exactly. It's a sense of age. What's strange is that you appear to be the same age as me—'

'I am – I'm precisely the same age as you.'

'Well, yes, in a manner of speaking. But you're also . . . I don't know – seventies, eighties? Or maybe older. Were you anybody before you were Georgina?'

She plucked a blade of grass and rolled it into a ball. 'Not that I remember. If you don't remember something, it didn't happen, did it?'

'You might have had your memory tampered with,' he said pointedly.

'I don't think so. I have . . . not a memory exactly, more an awareness that there was nothing – a kind of pleasant blankness – before.'

He looked at her. 'Really? What was it like?'

'Nice.' She giggled. 'Not very informative, is it? But for once *nice* is a perfect description. It was simple and pleasant, like a sort of unconsciousness without dreams.'

He grunted, not knowing what to make of this. 'Do you feel old?' he asked. 'I mean, having lived three lives. Do you feel as though you're . . . however old you are?'

She grinned. 'It really bugs you, doesn't it? That on the surface I'm as young as you are, that underneath this mature-yet-still-young-and-beautiful skin, a wrinkly old lady is lurking. To answer your question, no I don't feel as old as I am. I'll be eighty-three this year, but I don't have the body *or* the mind of my age. I *know* I've been Georgina and Liza, that I've been married once and given birth to four children and seen war come and go and new inventions and all the rest of it. But I don't *feel* I have. I have those memories, but they don't have the immediacy of real memories. Being Kismet is a memory, but being Liza and Georgina is like something I read in a book. The longest, most detailed first-person novel in the world.' She looked at Drick and smiled, a tiny hint of mockery in her eyes. 'So consider me young. I do. Don't be disgusted by your desires.'

He looked sharply at her. She seemed to have an ability to look right into his mind, and he wasn't sure if some of the thoughts she might find in there were entirely appropriate. Should he regard her as a friend, or as some kind of sister or even a mother? Rather than ask her outright, he approached the subject in a roundabout way.

'When I was growing up – I mean, when Raymond and I were growing up – when Raymond and I and *you* were growing up . . . were you aware of me? I mean us.'

'Did I watch over you, you mean?'

'Well, yes.'

'Not exactly. I don't have a crystal ball. I couldn't see you.' She chewed her underlip and frowned, trying to disinter a deep memory. 'I did sense you, though. I felt a kind of presence, a . . .' She looked at him. 'What are you grinning about?'

'Sorry,' he said. 'It's all getting a bit . . .' He affected a deep frown and breathed heavily. '*I sense a disturbance in the Force. A presence I've not felt since . . .*'

She looked blankly at him. 'Pardon?'

He looked surprised. 'A disturbance in the Force,' he repeated.

'I haven't the faintest idea what you're talking about,' she said.

'You've never seen *Star Wars*?'

It was obvious from her face that she'd never even heard of it. He rolled on his back and crowed with delight. This had happened a couple of times, and it never failed to thrill him: however feeble it might seem, it gave him indescribable pleasure to find these odd gaps in her knowledge. Huge and – in his opinion at least – profoundly important gaps. (Had he thought about it, he could have read off his feelings of inferiority in her presence in direct proportion to his delight in her occasional ignorances.)

'Sorry,' he said when he had got his breath back. 'You were saying?'

She thought for a moment, retrieving her thread. 'It was like standing in the centre of a perfectly flat, perfectly still lake, surrounded by an impenetrable fog. There may be somebody else out there somewhere, standing in the water, but you can't see them. Every so often, though, they move, and the ripples they cause radiate out and lap against your legs. It was a bit like that. I suppose, if we were to compare notes, we'd find that the times when I felt your ripples were times when something important was happening to you. For instance, the time when I felt the most obtrusive ripples was . . . well, you can probably guess.'

'The bridge?'

'Exactly. I think it may even . . .' She shook her head. 'No, I won't say.'

311

This time, though, he saw her thoughts suddenly as clearly as she routinely saw his. 'It was what made you fall, wasn't it?'

She nodded mutely.

He examined his own feelings, alarmed by a rush of what looked at first glance like satisfaction, or even pleasure. But when he scrutinised it, he found it was a peculiar sense of consolation: having had some profound influence on *her* life – her death, indeed – made him feel less like a helpless puppet, less like an aimless walk-on character in somebody else's novel, an incidental by-blow, created inadvertently during a moment of stress.

Following right on the heels of this thought came its obvious sequent: how, in any meaningful sense, was his creation any different from anybody else's? 'Created inadvertently during a moment of stress' could apply to a whole hell of a lot of people. No, bugger objectivity; this *was* different.

They sat in silence for a long while, the only sounds bees bumbling in the hedgerow and Manni's teeth grinding with single-minded determination at his bone. There are moments in anybody's life – whatever their circumstances, and however they came into the world – which can only be addressed by posing one particular question. It may be the end of an era or the end of a game of ping-pong; the only thing to do is take stock and ask.

'What are we going to do now?'

Kismet looked at him. 'I've been wondering when you were going to ask that,' she said.

'Really? How long?'

'Oh, ever since I've known you.'

He laughed. 'Okay, so I'm asking at last. Have you got an answer?'

'No, but I suspect you have. Let me help by asking you a question of my own. Are you happy, Roderick?'

She had never called him by his name before, and it gave him two simultaneous jolts: first, the realisation that she had never called him by his name before, and second, that she chose the version which only his mother and Marjorie Turnbull ever used. If anything was guaranteed to add yet another layer to his complex about how he should view his relationship with Kismet, that was it.

'I'd rather you called me Drick,' he said.

'Of course. Whatever you want. Are you happy, Drick?'

There had been a time, not very long ago, when he would have laughed out loud at her question. In his view, happiness was a transitory state: happy one moment, down the next, excited the day after that. In the sense that she meant it – *are you having a happy life* – it was absurd. How should he know? Notions like that – happiness, fulfilment, passion, disappointment – as unitary states were half-baked psychotherapeutic no-brainers. But now . . . Now what? Could he really take the question *Are you happy?* seriously? Not if the half-sneer on his face was anything to go by.

He wiped the look away and, instead of laughing in her face, told her a story.

'There was a king once,' he began. 'An ancient Greek king, if I remember rightly, whose name escapes me. He was immensely successful – he increased the bounds of his kingdom, won all his wars, achieved immense popularity and colossal personal wealth, and had many beautiful children. It must have seemed that, of all men in creation, he was especially favoured by the gods.

'However, there was one thing missing. An objective, dispassionate judgement – without this, how could he ever know whether he had won all he possessed through merit or through luck? Of course, none of his courtiers could be relied on to judge him impartially, so he went to see an oracle. He had one simple question he wanted answered.

' "Do you think I've had a lucky life?" the King asked.

' "How on earth should I know?" the oracle replied. "You aren't dead yet."

'The King went away far from satisfied. For the rest of his life, the oracle's words must have haunted him, as his children died, his wealth dwindled, his enemies encroached on his kingdom, he toppled from his throne. And more than haunt him; they must have tormented him as he lay dying in poverty and obscurity, reflecting that, of all men in creation, the gods must have picked him out for especial punishment.'

Kismet smiled. 'And the moral is?'

'Don't ask for premature judgements.'

'Okay.' She paused. 'Are you happy, Drick?'

'You're not going to give in, are you?'

'No.'

He laughed. 'Right. Since you insist, yes, I've never been happier. When I'm here with you, that is.'

'And when you're not?'

He shrugged. 'Dunno. That's real life.'

'You don't like being a bestselling author?'

He opened his mouth to speak, then closed it abruptly. He had been about to say, of course he did – who wouldn't? He was a writer; getting rich from a pursuit he loved was a dream come true. But he remembered his diary: the week-by-week itemisation of deals done and money piling up; and he remembered his lack of feeling about the whole thing. He just wasn't sure the book he'd written merited so much profit. If it had been one of the others – the sincere ones that had been written without the market in mind – then he might, just might, have felt different.

'I'm not one,' he said. 'Madagascar Rhodes is.'

He glanced at her. She was nodding, as though she knew what he meant. And so she should – he had told her at length how he felt about *The Alchemist's Apprentice*; at such length that even he had begun to find the long-winded writerly maundering about integrity and truth tedious. But he was right to feel uneasy, even ashamed. He decided to tell her about the Trays.

The Trays (he had begun capitalising them in his mind as they grew to assume a dark, menacing significance out of all proportion to their appearance) had been instituted by Jonathan. Since his creator/employer had taken to disappearing each morning and not returning until after dark, Jonathan had been forced to develop secretarial skills he hadn't previously dreamed of. Mostly these were to do with the specialised art of secretarial evasion. Deflecting calls from Drick's agent and editor, replying vaguely to

314

letters asking when the revisions to the manuscript of *The Traitor* could be expected. Or not replying, as the case may be, to letters from various translators working on *The Alchemist's Apprentice* asking what this or that English, Yiddish or Moorish colloquialism might mean. The letters to which Jonathan couldn't reply on Drick's behalf, along with little notes detailing phone calls received, piled up weekly in a red plastic tray on Drick's desk. Each morning after breakfast, before disappearing for the day with Manni, Drick would go into his dining room/office, look at the red Tray (look *at* it, not through it) with a despondent expression, and leave it untouched. It never seemed to be the right time to deal with it; he had to be in the right mood for that sort of shit. And so, each day the pile grew perceptibly higher, more alarming, and more disheartening. (There was also a yellow Tray, which didn't even bear glancing at in passing. It was piled with brown envelopes – some as thick as novels – marked Inland Revenue, HM Customs & Excise or National Insurance Contributions Agency. The yellow Tray, unlike the red, couldn't really be described as a worrying presence; it was so frightening, Drick didn't even acknowledge its existence.)

Then, as if that weren't enough, last Monday morning he had gone into the office and found yet another Tray – a green one – sitting next to the red one. At first he thought it was there to catch the overflow, but apparently not. Jonathan came in while Drick was looking under the sofa for a rubber ring Manni had lost the previous evening; he deposited a large manilla envelope on top of the precarious pile in the red Tray, then – with a strange, hunted glance at Drick – put a small blue envelope in the green one.

Puzzled, Drick watched him go out, then went over to the desk and looked in the green Tray. There were three letters in there, all with handwritten addresses (Mr Maddy Rhodes), over which his publisher had stuck labels printed with his home address. Fan letters. There had been a time when his editor vetted them himself before passing them on, but the sheer volume had quickly overwhelmed him. So Jonathan had begun a special fan-letter tray, had he? All the envelopes had been opened – it was Jonathan's job to read all Drick's mail and sort it into categories, so that Drick could ignore it systematically.

The first letter was from an elderly lady in Cirencester, who had been given *The Alchemist's Apprentice* by her daughter for Christmas and thought it was the best book she had read in years. The second was from a man in South Africa who had been so inspired by it, he had immediately gone out and booked a holiday in Malta. Well, that wasn't so bad, now, was it? He thought he even felt a warm little glow.

His good humour didn't last long. He opened the letter Jonathan had just added to the tray and scanned the first few lines. *A beautifully written novel . . . read on the recommendation of . . . undoubted achievement . . . utterly ashamed of yourself.*

He actually performed a double-take at that last phrase, and read it again. *To make use of the sufferings of millions of people to make a profit may in your view be an undoubted achievement, and indeed you have carried it off with undeniable style, but in my view (the view of somebody who, unlike you, was actually there) it is disgraceful. You should be utterly ashamed of yourself.*

Drick read the rest of the letter with a feeling of indignation. It was the grossest misrepresentation of facts and motives he had ever come across. To make a profit? Well, he *had* made a profit, of course, but that hadn't been his motivation. Had it? Did Thomas Keneally get letters like this? Probably, so that didn't help much. Did Primo Levi make a profit, and if so, had he donated it all to charity? The letter also accused him of making light of suffering, of taking liberties with historical realities. But he had never intended it as a Holocaust novel; all that had been kept in reserve, hovering there as a dark background against which to set an ultimately optimistic story. Was that making light of suffering? Of course not.

Had the letter been a one-off, he could quickly (though not necessarily easily) have dismissed it. But a few days later, he got another. Again he was accused of making light of suffering, though this time by a correspondent who supported his argument with a series of instances quoted from the novel. All torn brutally out of their context, of course, which infuriated Drick, especially as the letter was from a professor of Holocaust Studies who had no more first-hand knowledge than Drick had himself. But . . .

Oh, but but but. *But* the man's argument carried unavoidable force. *But* the novel *did* make light (in places) of a very serious subject. *But* Drick himself had never felt entirely easy about the novel. Or rather, he had felt a little *too* easy. While he was writing it, he had operated an internal gauge which told him what to include and what to play down. He had never done this before or since, and had only done it then because he was convinced it was necessary for popular success. Whereas normally he practised no bars on what could be portrayed, with this novel, if something disturbed him slightly, he put it in, because it heightened the drama; if something disturbed him quite a lot, he still put it in (toned down, he now realised with a prickle of cold sweat), because it hinted at tragedy; but if something actually *distressed* him, the barrier came down, and it was excluded.

Result: enough darkness to make it a good novel – even, from a storytelling point of view, a superb one – but not enough for truth.

If it hadn't been so profitable, he would have wished he'd never written it – an insight which would have given his first correspondent immense satisfaction, no doubt.

'I'm just glad I wrote under a pseudonym,' he said.

Kismet smiled sardonically. 'If only they knew the alternative. What happened in what I still can't help thinking of as "real" history.'

'Why? What happened?'

'Well, put it this way – you wouldn't get those letters. Not a single European Jew survived, apart from a handful who escaped to America before the war, and a lot of those were deported later in the name of maintaining German-American relations. The German lobby in America was far stronger than the Jewish one in that version of history. What made it even worse was that the world didn't care. There was no Israel, no Holocaust memorials, no histories.'

Drick sighed. 'That doesn't make any difference. To what I've been saying, I mean. What happened happened, I wrote what I wrote, and I did it insincerely.' He laughed, but there was no trace of humour in it. 'My one successful rewriting of history. Inside a million people's heads, I've created a past – a better, more palatable flavour of history than the world could produce by itself. Pathetic, isn't it? Do a million minds make it real?'

As he looked at her, he realised the simple truth which lay beneath what he was saying: the truth he had known before he even got those letters, that he had been pushing to the back of his mind whilst unconsciously acting on it by ignoring the papers building up in the Tray.

'I don't want to be a writer any more,' he said.

She shook her head. 'I seriously doubt that.'

'Well, I don't want to be the writer of *The Alchemist's Apprentice* any more.' He stood up suddenly. 'Shit!' he yelled. 'What the fuck have I done?'

'I don't know. What have you done?'

He stared desolately at her. 'I've sold my fucking soul, that's what!'

'Sit down,' she said gently, patting the turf. 'Calm down and sit down.'

He obeyed the second command, but not the first. 'What am I going to do?' he moaned.

She looked at him with a half-smile. 'You've gone from "What are we going to do" to "What am *I* going to do" in under an hour,' she said. 'That's an impressive shift of perspective. But what you're really asking is what *I'm* going to do to help you. Aren't you?'

That was exactly what he'd meant, and he felt reassured by her tone: it implied that she *could* do something, and would. He nodded.

'What would you like me to do?'

'Wipe out *The Alchemist's Apprentice*,' he said without hesitation. 'Don't look like that – if you can change World War Two, you can erase a lousy novel, surely.'

His voice rose again, and Manni, distressed by the sound, came and nuzzled at his neck. He stroked the dog's head absently, gazing at Kismet. 'Can't you?' he asked.

318

'What about the money? Your house? Could you live without those?'

'Of course I could.'

'And Elsa?'

He frowned. 'Elsa? What about her? She's long gone.'

'She isn't, you know. You are your past; you carry it with you wherever – and whenever – you go. The book is entwined with it. Any change we make has to act retrospectively. There are a number of ways we could go about it. For instance, I could reach deep into your past and remove your ability to write.'

He flinched visibly. 'No,' he said firmly. 'Just the one book. I want it erased.'

'Well, the least extreme form of interference would be to stop you making the alterations which you're so sure made the book so popular.'

'I don't know. Couldn't you make it so that I never wrote the wretched thing in the first place?'

'I could. When exactly did you write it?'

'Three years ago, more or less.'

'When *exactly*?'

'November ninety-two to February ninety-three. I *should* remember,' he added, with a touch of bitterness. 'It was when I was first . . .' His voice trailed away.

'Living with Elsa? There now, you see what I mean. Remember the irrational way repercussions work themselves out when you go messing about with the past. Who knows – you might never leave her.'

'Well, what do you suggest?'

She smiled wanly. 'What do *I* suggest? I suggest you think carefully before you ask for your life to be changed.'

He followed her advice. He went home that evening and, with snow settling thinly outside the window, began to think. When the snow melted, he was still thinking; winter took its sharp teeth away and skulked off, and he was still thinking; spring warmed through, curled up and gave way to summer, and still he thought.

319

He went back over his entire life, remembering it with a clarity he had never known before, and scrutinised each disinterred moment, dusting them off and laying them out like potsherds: this moment going with that one, some more pieces set alongside parts of another, until all the past twenty-eight years (actually it was nearer thirty, but he had stopped having birthdays) lay before him, ordered and susceptible to study. He divided them into categories – Triumphs, Disappointments, Mistakes, Accidents, Achievements – and found that the largest group by far was Accidents. If he had been a more old-fashioned archaeologist than he was, devoted to typologies and culture-history, he would have isolated Accidents (strongly associated with Mistakes) as the type characteristic of the Bent Culture. Bent artefacts would be found to be fashioned almost entirely in the form of Accidents, and Bent funerary sites would be a mixture of Disappointment Barrows and the rather less imposing Achievement Cemeteries.

In amongst the cultural typology were three anomalous artefacts. One was a great, monumental Stonehenge of an anomaly which embodied all five characteristics of the culture: *The Alchemist's Apprentice* was a commercial triumph, but a literary disappointment. The idea had come to him by accident, and writing it, while an achievement of sorts, had been a mistake. He had altered history twice: once by writing Ewan Brereton out of it, and again by writing a false, syrupy, good-natured optimism into it. If he really had done it purely for profit, it mightn't have seemed so bad – at least there would have been a cold rationalism about it. What made the whole thing so ugly and tawdry was that the novel had come out the way it did because the sugar-frosted story had seemed so *likeable*. If he had messed with history in a truly offensive *Springtime For Hitler* kind of way, it wouldn't have been so bad – at least that would have shown some spirit, however tasteless. Instead, he had turned the story of the Holocaust – or one family's part of it – into an episode of *The Waltons*.

The second anomaly fitted none of the categories, although there was accident and disappointment associated with it. The accident was a sudden plunge from the walkway at Three Bridges Corner; the disappointment – a profound, heart-rending disappointment – was Kismet's inability to bring Raymond back. The first time he visited her after regaining his memory, as he crossed the imaginary bridge to her imaginary garden, Drick imagined that Raymond would be there, waiting beside her. But it was impossible, she claimed, to erase his death. He argued with her, pointing out all the examples where exactly that had been done, from Anne Widdecombe to World War Two, but they were different, she said; Raymond wasn't a normal human being. Nor is Anne Widdecombe, he said. She explained that when people like Drick and Raymond – and herself – who weren't of natural birth, died, they died irremediably. They could be sent back, but that decision was out of their hands. He stared at her for a long time when she said that. This was something she did from time to time, letting little nuggets of knowledge about people 'like us' fall out like coins from a leaky purse. He demanded to know what she meant by it – angels, space aliens or what? – but she said there wasn't really a cosmological category into which they fitted. Nobody knows about us, she said. I wasn't given a job description and a contract, you know. So we're like some sort of astral special agents? He tried to say it jeeringly, sounding peeved, but didn't quite carry it off because of the sudden thrill he felt at the idea. She'd had three lifetimes to think about it, she told him, and had tentatively made her way towards the conclusion that 'we' represented the closest you could get to divine intervention in a universe dominated by the exercise of free will. If you *knew* that your ... she hesitated and settled grudgingly for 'mission' – If you knew your mission was to improve the world, then didn't that mess fatally with free will? You had to *choose* to do good. Or not, as the case may be.

The third anomaly was Kismet herself. Or rather, his feelings about her. He kept remembering that look she had given him, and her admonition: *Don't be disgusted by your desires.* She had seen right into him. It was true, he did desire her, in spite of her ambiguous relation to him, and – yes, it had to be said – in spite of the hideous scars on her body. And if neither of them were natural

321

human beings, then why should he not? And, while he was on the subject, was his unnaturalness – or supernaturalness – the explanation at last for his lifelong feeling of never having fitted in? Never being understood properly by anyone? He asked her about it once: No, she said, that's just perfectly normal self-obsession. Everyone has that. Which, in an odd sort of way, was simultaneously disappointing and reassuring.

Eventually, as the summer of 1996 was drawing to a close, he surfaced from his long reverie with a decision, freshly dug from the deepest layers of earth, shining in his hands. He was standing at his bedroom window, gazing down at the boats chugging past on the river, when his mind, tired and muddied from its digging and sorting, crawled back up to the front of his brain and peered out through his eyes. He blinked in startlement at his surroundings, like a hermit emerging from a cave. He turned to look in his bedroom mirror, half-expecting to see a long, matted beard hanging from his face, but he was clean-shaven. He felt as though he'd been away a long time, and his bedroom had that familiar yet strange look about it, the way home looks when you return from a long journey.

He went out onto the landing, and ran right into Jonathan, who was coming up the stairs with a steaming mug in his hand.

'You've got a visitor,' Jonathan said, with a weird, uncharacteristic brightness in his voice which reminded Drick of the way nurses in old folks' homes talk to the residents. Which was rich, if you like, coming from a man wearing *that* on his head.

'Who is it?' Drick asked.

Jonathan started, as though he'd encountered a talking horse. 'Oh,' he said. 'You're back, are you?'

'Who is it?' Drick repeated.

'Dunno. Dining room.' Giving him one last puzzled look, Jonathan went into his office.

Drick called him back. 'Why the, er . . . ?' He nodded at Jonathan's new headgear: a bright red motorcycle helmet. 'What happened to the bobble-hat?'

Jonathan's eyes rolled upwards. 'This? Oh, the foil wasn't strong enough to deflect the rays.'

'And that is?'

Jonathan nodded awkwardly, as though the gesture cost him some effort. 'It's lead-lined,' he said. With that, he went back into his office and shut the door behind him.

Drick rubbed his eyes. 'What time is it?' he called, but there was no reply. 'What *year* is it?' he added, to himself.

He went downstairs. As he reached the hall, the letter-box clattered and spat two envelopes onto the mat. It must be morning, then. He picked them up and, acting on his mood of decisiveness, opened them. One was from his bank manager: its tone, which stopped just short of hectoring, implied that this was not the first but the latest of several attempts to interest him in investments. Since the combined balance of his two accounts now stood at . . . He stared at the figure: £1,854,122.56, wondering whether he had made the right decision. That was a fuck of a lot of cash. He opened the second envelope, and found a three-page screed from a rabbi in Boston condemning him in terms of almost biblical wrath, calling him a whore and a crypto-anti-Zionist. The writer's accusations hinged on a chapter near the end of *The Alchemist's Apprentice* in which the Weiss family not only decide not to settle in Israel, but also use their re-established fortune to support the Muslim Izzat and his estranged family. Drick had never intended to give the impression that these two acts were connected, but he could imagine, on reflection, how the laziness of that chapter's sentimental writing could be ambiguous. And now he came to think of it, the glib way Mr Weiss regained his wealth amidst the ruins of post-war Germany was not only antihistorical, but monumentally absurd.

He looked at the bank manager's letter again. No, he had made the right decision. He opened the dining-room door and walked in.

Kismet was sitting at his desk, feeding cookies to Manni. 'Hello,' she said. 'Your, er . . .' She searched for a word. 'Lodger? Butler? Nice helmet, by the way. He explained all about it while he made us coffee. I don't think he realised I can't drink it.'

'Eh?'

'I can't drink coffee.'

'Oh, right. You being from another world, you mean?'

She looked blank. 'No, I'm allergic to caffeine. I can't have tea either.'

He began to laugh, then stopped abruptly when he saw the state of his desk. How long had he been away? There were now three red Trays containing 'official' correspondence, and *four* green ones brimming with personal letters. Most would probably be fan mail, but he didn't doubt there'd be a few in there as poisonous as the one from the Boston rabbi. He added the latest mail to the relevant heaps and turned to Kismet.

'I've made a decision,' he said.

She gave Manni the last cookie and stroked his ears as he chomped. 'I know.'

'I suppose that's why you're here? You sensed it in the ether?'

'No, I came round to find out why you hadn't been to visit me for so long. I can see you've made a decision from the look on your face.' She gave him a slantendicular smile. 'I don't *always* use the powers available to me. Sometimes I like to pretend I'm a normal person.' She paused. 'I also wanted to tell you, my father died a couple of weeks ago. He had a stroke.'

'Sorry,' he said automatically. 'Are you? Sorry, I mean.'

She nodded. 'I know what you mean. Yes, I'm sorry, and yes, it did occur to me to stop him dying, but no, I didn't do it.'

'Why?'

'He was ready to go. I visited him, and it was written in every line of him. He wasn't old, but he wanted to die. There was nothing left in the world for him but me, and I . . . I couldn't change that.'

They sat in silence for a while. 'What will happen to the house and garden?' Drick asked.

'As far as I'm concerned, nothing. As for the real world, I don't know. I'm the last of the Lillystones, and I'm dead, officially. I suppose Marjorie's daughter may have a claim. I don't know.'

'I could buy it,' Drick suggested. 'Then it could remain undisturbed.'

'For whom? It's very kind of you, but you needn't rescue it on

324

my account. I don't need it.' She smiled brightly. 'Anyway, you haven't told me your decision. You've taken long enough arriving at it, so it must be worth hearing.'

He sat down on the sofa and beckoned her to join him. 'I want to ask you a question,' he said when she had settled beside him. 'Have you ever obliterated anyone? I've done it; erased a man from history.' She watched his face silently, and didn't answer. 'What happens to them?' he went on. 'A person who gets wiped out like that? Do they simply pass into oblivion, or do they go somewhere?'

'It depends,' she said quietly. 'There *is* a place, but . . .' She hesitated.

'But what?'

'It's . . . I've never been there, but I got close. I told you once what happened when I died. The darkness and the silence – that . . . I think that was on the way there.'

'Are you talking about Heaven?'

The disgust and disappointment in his voice made her grin. 'No, not Heaven.'

He sat forward suddenly. 'Does Heaven *exist?*'

'I don't know.'

'Oh. Just thought I'd ask, on the off-chance, you know.' He sat back again. 'Tell me about this other place.'

'Well, it's where all the people who don't exist . . .' She shrugged. '. . . *exist*, I suppose.'

'The people who don't exist?'

'They have to be somewhere.'

'And this is a *place?*'

'If you like. Although it isn't really that, since like the people who live there, it doesn't, strictly speaking, exist. Call it a dimension or an alternative plane or something if it makes you feel more comfortable.'

'I see.' He wasn't sure if he should take her seriously. 'So, to take an example . . .' He tried to think of an example. 'Ulysses lives there?'

'Probably. I mean, I don't have the electoral roll or anything, but I'd imagine he'd be there. All fictional people are.'

'And King Arthur?'

'Yes.'

'What about Sherlock Holmes? And Watson? Harry Flashman? Robinson Crusoe?'

'Yes, yes. All of them.'

It was almost too much for him to take. '*Darth Vader* lives there?' he asked, his mind boggling. 'And Gandalf?' He stared at the carpet. 'Jesus,' he murmured.

'Very probably.'

He looked at her. 'No, I— . . . Oh.' He let out a long, slow breath. 'Wow.'

She waited a while for him to go on, but he was just gazing at her in silence. 'Your decision?' she prompted.

'Yes. My decision.' He stood up abruptly and paced up and down on the Persian rug between the desk and the French window.

'Don't tell me you've come over all uncertain again?'

He stopped pacing. 'No. No, I haven't.'

'Then just ask me. I know you're dying to ask me a big question.'

He sat down again and stared deep into her eyes, wishing he could see into her the way she seemed able to see into him. There were two things he wanted to ask, and he decided to put them both into one question: 'Can you take me there? To this place?'

She didn't answer right away: she reached out and stroked the side of his face. He was startled by how chill her fingers felt.

'Can you?'

'Drick, you do realise you'd never be able to come back?'

He nodded, and spoke without knowing where the words came from: 'I came from there, and I want to go back.' He coughed, as though something had got stuck in his throat. 'Shit,' he said, 'I did come from there, didn't I? *You* called me into existence.'

'Yes, but inadv—'

'Inadvertently. I know.'

'I couldn't bring you back again.'

'I won't ever want to come back. You still haven't answered. Can you take me there?'

'I . . . I can send you there.'

His face froze. 'I want you to—'

'I know. I can't come with you. I was put here, and I have to stay here until I'm permitted to leave.'

'But you were put here to look after me! Once I'm gone, you can go too.'

'I don't know that; it's only surmise. There may be others who need me.'

His expression hardened. 'Not as much as I do.'

He hadn't anticipated this. He hadn't exactly expected that they would go off anywhere together, but then he hadn't imagined that there was anywhere to go; he'd pictured an absolute state of non-existence. But if the thought of going without her was desolate, the alternative gave him a profound nausea: to go back to his life with Elsa, perhaps never to leave; to return to a time before he had known Kismet, and perhaps never find her this time. Either way he would lose her. The more he looked at the choices open to him, the more attractive the third choice seemed: to stay here with her and carry on living his earthbound life. But that was out of the question. One glance at the piles of paper-work in the Trays on his desk told him he couldn't cope with the consequences of this thing he'd created. More importantly, there was Kismet herself. Once or twice during his last few visits to her, she had hinted – without being conscious of it, he was sure – that she was now older than she had ever been before; that is, she had reached an age as Kismet which she had never reached as either Georgina or Liza. And as Kismet she had suffered more than in either of her previous incarnations. He had noticed – he saw it now in her eyes – that she was weary; the spark that animated her was fading, and he suspected that he was in some measure responsible for wearing her out. If he stayed, how long would she last before having to return to the chrysalis and start all over again? A plan flowered briefly in his mind. He could buy Cuckoo Farm and live there with her: when her time came and she shucked off the shell of Kismet, he would bring up the child as his own, just as young Jack Lillystone had done. With a wash of sentimental fondness, he pictured himself cradling the baby in his arms. He even had a name in mind: Christany, after the two characters in his books who most fully embodied (or enliterated?) Kismet. The warmth evoked by the image lasted a couple of seconds before turning to sickness. He would still have *The Alchemist's Albatross* slung round his neck; worse, far, far worse, he would have to watch Kismet die. He could bear all that – just – but what would crush him utterly would be raising the little girl knowing that, somewhere inside her, inaccessible to him, Kismet lived on; she would look at him with her child's eyes and *know* what he had once felt about her – how he would always feel about Kismet. *Don't be ashamed of your desires.* Maybe not, but there were limits.

He looked her in the eye, and tried to keep his voice steady. 'I'll still need your help,' he said.

'No, what you need is this,' she replied.

'What?' He realised she was holding something out to him. With a yelp of astonishment, he recognised his notepad. He took it from her and flung back the cover. It was the very one! It was all there: the Moscow–Leningrad express, Jonathan Peachment, the silver ring, his orgy, the Landcruiser; everything. 'Where did you get this?' he demanded.

'I . . . Well, let's say I had it reconstituted. It isn't perfect. It's more powerful than it was before, but you can only use it once, so use it wisely.'

'More powerful?' He tweaked its spiral. 'You know, I always felt its limitations more than its potency? Strange, isn't it – it was like a demo version of a piece of software.'

She smiled in a way that told him she hadn't the faintest idea what 'software' was, but she got the point. 'We have to have limits imposed,' she said. 'Otherwise we might get ideas above our station. Mine is that I can only do things from my garden.'

'Ideas above our station?'

'Well, if we were omnipotent . . . Remember, we seem to be put here – I mean, I was put here – you're really a by-blow – for a specific purpose: to help put right the hideousness humans have made in their world.'

'If we choose to,' said Drick. 'But if you can only do stuff in your garden, what about when you visited me at Cold Cottage?'

'And I vanished? That's easily enough explained. I wasn't really there.'

He remembered her twin trick, and nodded. 'I see. Are you really here now?'

'Of course. This is an important occasion. I couldn't entrust it to a double.'

'So you're . . .' He grinned. 'You're powerless?'

She met his grin with an inscrutable smile. 'Only in that one sense.'

He closed the pad and stroked the cover. 'The full retail version,' he murmured. 'It can do *anything*?'

'Within the constraints of its own version of logic, yes. But only once, remember.'

'I can use it to . . . to . . . ?'

'To go wherever you want. Literally anywhere.'

Before she left him that morning, he did something he had wanted to do since the first moment he saw her. He touched her. Not merely an idle, glancing touch, but a slow, deliberate caress. He probably wouldn't have done it if she hadn't prompted him.

As they stood in the middle of the room, she at a loss for once what to say, she decided, with typical contrariness, to tease him.

'Isn't there something you'd like to do before we part?' she asked, with a sly smile.

He leant towards her and kissed her on the cheek.

Her smile deepened. 'Not that,' she said.

'I know. You mean something more like this.'

He touched her hair and stroked lightly down to the crook of her neck, then traced a line which ran over her collarbone, followed the shallow swell of her breast and feathered out across her belly. It had worked for him before, and to his indescribable satisfaction, it worked now: she closed her eyes and shivered, and when she opened them again her own desire was there, unveiled at last. She was more earthly than he had thought. At that moment – as at every previous moment, had he only shown the courage to push at the barrier – she was his for the taking. Now

329

the barrier was down. Not to take her used up every ounce of self-restraint he possessed.

'No,' he said. 'Not here. Not now. It would ruin everything.'

He didn't specify *what* precisely it would ruin, or how, but she nodded dumbly and, without saying goodbye, they parted. She was close to him, but, in a strange reversal of the first time he saw her, she seemed immeasurably distant – a white speck on the horizon – as she turned away; the last sight he had of her on earth.

There was plenty of space in the notepad. He hadn't realised how parsimonious he had been with its pages, and was surprised at how many were still unused. He sat down at his desk, and after a moment's thought, set aside the notepad, took out a block of ordinary 80 gsm and a black biro, and began to write.

There was no hesitation: he had planned exactly what he would do given this opportunity; the only surprise was actually being given it. He wrote continuously all that day, and all the next, and the day after that, at lightning speed, sometimes with a pen, sometimes directly into the computer, stopping only occasionally to take a brisk turn around the room – loosening up the flow, he called it – to eat a little food or attend to Manni's needs. As he wrote, happinesses (little discrete packets, not an overwhelming contentment) bobbed to the surface of his mood like bubbles from a sinking ship. If he couldn't out-think her, he wasn't the man he thought he was. Of course, the fact that he had been proved once already not to be exactly the man he'd thought he was gave him periodic pause, but he answered the fact with fatalism: by the time he found out, it would be too late, and that would be that.

When he had written it all and was satisfied that it was perfect, he got the notepad out and began transferring the body of text to its magic pages. After some preparatory sentences (which were of a technical miracle-working nature and need not concern us here), he began copying:

Let me tell you about Madagascar Rhodes; I can't describe how he has been on my mind recently. Old Madagascar;

Maddy to his post-colonial cronies and his readers. The former were entirely fictitious, of course, but the latter were very real and positively legion, and they all knew him as Maddy . . .

On the evening of the seventh day of writing, he put down the last sentence: '*All there was to do now was wait.*'

Then he closed the pad, laid down his pen, and rested.

The next day, he began typing up sections from his work, which he printed out and sealed in separate packets. He put them in a cardboard box he found under the stairs (it just happened to have the logo 'RHODES' stamped on the side, which appealed to his sense of humour), along with all the manuscripts of his novels and stories. He had decided long ago that if anything of him was worth preserving, it was his fiction, and that if anyone was to take possession of it, it should be Jeremy, the closest thing he had to a brother.

Everything was prepared. The change would come about shortly before the turn of the year. All there was to do now was wait.

Postscript

VIII

The last packet ends there. So, incidentally, does the book I found in the dump-bin in Hay back in January. Therefore, what I'm writing here is of my own creation, not guided or predetermined by anybody.

At least, I think it is. For all I know, there may be other pieces of paper lurking out there which have dictated the course of my entire life. It's summer now; six months have passed since my trip to Hay, and nothing has shown up yet, but then neither has the notepad, so I suppose I'll never be sure he didn't ordain more than he put in the book. I guess it must have disappeared from the world along with its owner, but I've learned never to trust obvious certainties.

Drick, it seems, got what he wanted, and I hope he's happy wherever he is. And I hope he's happy with who he's with. I forgot to mention that I never took custody of Manni; contrary to the covering note (which he must have written and sealed up in the box some time before he left), Manni wasn't at the stated address. There was just a plump and dishevelled old woman and a Dobermann called Frazer. Neither, apparently, had ever heard of Drick, Manni, or me.

He must have found that he could (or couldn't not) take the dog with him. I have a very vivid mental image of them going off together, walking away across a long bridge over still, glassy water. The far end of the bridge is lost in haze, and as they walk, they too are swallowed up and vanish. Whether that's my own imagination, or a picture put in my head by Drick, I'll never know, but it's the story I tell myself. I was quite sorry about it, really; I was very fond of Manni. I only hope my story is right; that when Drick went away and time-space shook out the loose threads, the poor dog didn't get caught up in some irrational fold, winking out of existence perhaps, or worse, ending up in some kind of nether limbo.

Whether Drick found what he was looking for is something else I'll never know, so I can't tell you about it. What I can tell you about is an encounter I had a couple of weeks ago, which may (or then again may not) shed some light. It has certainly made me wonder about the unpredictable consequences of interfering with history that Drick writes about in some of the packets.

I had just finished writing out my version of my part of the story. (Incidentally, it did match the version in the book, word for word, although it took me far longer to write than Drick claims it took him.) I felt an urge you've probably felt yourself from time to time: to go and look at the places I had read about. It's a common enough thing, and I often experience it when I've read a book. Something to do with the inadequacy of our own imaginations, I daresay: we want to go and *see* the scene for ourselves; or perhaps it gives us a sense of involvement in the narrative, of somehow standing inside it. Although why I should need to look at the scenery in order to feel involved in *this* story, I don't know.

I've been to Ely plenty of times, but I've never really explored it. I've done the Cathedral, the museums and the shops, and that's about it. I had to consult a street map to find my way to Prickwillow Road and the top of Kiln Lane. I parked the car and walked down the narrow road which runs between tangles of scrubby woodland, winding around the lakes which fill the old claypits. It's an eerie place, Roswell; it feels haunted, pervaded by an atmosphere which I'm sure has nothing to do with the name or the stories which, for me, are associated with it. Even though the weather was sunny and dry, the woods seemed dank and drippy, and there was something unpalatable about the blackberries that clustered thickly in the hedgerows.

It was a longer walk to the bottom of the lane than I'd expected. When I found myself in what appeared to be a group

336

of warehouses, I realised I had come too far. I would have liked to go further, and look at Cuckoo Bridge, but my way was barred by high metal gates. There was a notice on the gates saying that the bridge was closed due to its dangerously unstable condition.

I turned back and retraced my steps. After a hundred yards or so, I came to a place where there was a sharp bend in the road, and I realised this must be where Drick eventually found the way into Cuckoo Farm. I found the entrance much quicker than he had. It was difficult to imagine the problems he'd had; difficult, even, to know how I had managed to miss it on the way down the road. There was a gap between the hedgerow and the woods with a gate in it. The gate was painted bright sunflower yellow, with a sign on it saying 'CUCKOO FARM'.

I stared at it in a stupor for several minutes, then approached warily. It was chained and padlocked. Remembering Drick's encounter with the owner, I almost backed off, but there was some other impulse driving me. Not the will of Drick, I think; just simple curiosity. I climbed the gate.

There was a time, when I was a kid, when I was very good at climbing things, especially gates and fences. Every five-bar gate has its own distinctive wobble, to which you have to attune yourself if you are to time your leap from the top. (You can circumvent this by clambering over, but that was never my style; I always went for the ascent-and-vault.) Unfortunately, the years had rusted my sense of timing; the gate's wobble (a sort of syncopated wa-*wob*ble-da-doof) caught me off balance, my foot slipped, and I went crashing into the lane on the other side, knocking all the breath out of my body and twisting my ankle quite badly.

As I heaved myself up, staggering and brushing mud and grit off my clothes, a voice spoke behind me.

'Hello, a customer. Bit eager, aren't we? We're shut, you know.'

I looked at him. He was about fortyish, with curly, prematurely grey hair, and a soft voice which I would have taken for a woman's if I hadn't seen him.

'Customer?' I said, but he didn't seem to hear me.

'Mondays to Thursdays,' he said. 'We close on Fridays. We only

337

have so much produce to sell, you see. Now, let's have a look at that ankle.'

He knelt down and took my ankle in his large, knotty hands. He had a remarkably gentle touch. He kneaded softly, and I yelped.

'Painful, eh? I imagine it would be. Nothing broken, though. You must have bones like old tree roots.'

'I've never broken one yet,' I said, and smiled. I don't usually take well to strangers, but I felt curiously comfortable with this soft-spoken man. Technically, he had just caught me trespassing, but seemed intent on regarding me as a perfectly legitimate visitor. Even at the time I was sure that this wasn't the reason I felt disposed to be pleasant, but it helped.

'Come up to the house. Milly will dress it for you.'

I followed him up the lane. At the end was a broad yard, half of which was gravelled, while the other half was given over to a kitchen garden. There was a red Espace parked on the gravel in front of the farmhouse. I gazed at the house in wonder. It was exactly as Drick had described it, except for its condition: the windows were clean and gleaming in the sunlight, and behind them I could see bright curtains. I looked around for some sign of the dilapidation I had expected, and eventually saw the tumbled-down stable building on the left-hand side of the yard.

My good Samaritan saw me looking. 'Haven't got round to that yet,' he said. 'It'll make a terrific little shop building one day. Still, one thing at a time, eh?'

He walked towards the house, calling out *Milly! We have a guest!* A woman came out of a door at the side of the house (the kitchen door, I guessed). She saw me and smiled. I had expected her to look like . . . Well, you can probably guess how I expected her to look, but she didn't. She was short and plump, with bobbed blonde hair. I'll tell you who she did remind me of, though: a smaller, more compacted version of Elsa.

Her warm smile wavered with concern as I hobbled towards her. She took my arm, and with the man (who I took for her husband) on my other side, I was helped around the side of the house to the back garden, where there was a small terrace on which chairs and a table were arranged.

While Milly went back to the house for bandages and hot water, I looked at the garden furniture. The table seemed hauntingly familiar. It was wrought-iron and painted white, and didn't go with the wooden chairs.

This man seemed to have an ability (which would have been unsettling in anybody else, but oddly wasn't in him) to read my thoughts.

'The chairs are ours,' he said. 'I know the table doesn't go with them, but we rather like it. The previous owner left it. It used to be down there.' He pointed down the garden, across the vegetable patches, to where there was a tall privet hedge. 'We moved it up to the terrace a few weeks ago, when the weather got warm. We like to sit out here in the afternoon and drink lemonade.'

I stared at him. 'Lemonade?' I said.

I realised too late that I'd reacted as though he'd said *We like to sit out here and drink bat's vomit*, but he just nodded serenely and took a deep breath, savouring the air before letting it out in a long, slow sigh of contentment.

'Have you lived here long?' I asked.

'Not long. Three and a half years, give or take.'

While I was thinking that one over, Milly came round the corner of the house, carrying a steaming enamel pitcher, with a polished copper bowl clasped under one arm and a towel draped over the other.

'Here we are,' she said. 'We'll soon have you up and about. Take your shoe and sock off.'

She set the bowl on the flags in front of my chair and took some long, emerald-green leaves from the pocket of her apron, rolled them between her palms, and dropped the crumbled pieces into the bowl. When she poured in hot water from the pitcher, a ball of sweet, slightly antiseptic-scented vapour rolled up and engulfed me.

'Bathe your ankle in there,' she said, 'while I get the bandages ready.'

The pain, which had been throbbing more and more insistently, sending exploratory shoots up my calf (no doubt to see if my

339

knee was worth colonising), began to ebb away rapidly the moment I sank my foot into the hot, fragrant water.

'That's amazing,' I said. 'What are those leaves?'

Milly didn't answer; she just smiled and directed me to take my foot out of the water and dry it on the towel. 'Here,' she said, and started bandaging my ankle. I looked at it and saw that even the swelling had begun to go down. 'It's only a slight sprain,' she said as I put my sock and shoe back on. 'Shouldn't give you too much trouble.'

I stood up and put my weight tentatively on the injured ankle; it hardly hurt at all. 'You've worked wonders,' I said, but Milly had cleared up her pitcher and bowl and gone back inside the house.

The man smiled benevolently at me. 'You've never seen a miracle worked before?'

'You've done wonders with the house as well,' I said, with an effusiveness which, for me, was quite abnormal. He gave me a quizzical look, and I realised what I'd said. 'I mean, I heard it was quite run down.'

'Really?' He looked up at the house. 'No, I wouldn't say that. Not considering her age.'

'Sorry? Whose age?'

'The previous owner. Charming widow lady; quite delightful. Some sort of artist, I believe.'

'A writer, dear,' Milly corrected him.

I looked at her, startled – partly by what she said, partly by the fact that I hadn't seen her come back and sit at the table. She seemed to have materialised there, like a ghost. 'A writer?' I asked. 'What was her name?'

'Mrs Lillystone. Her son died a few years ago, and she had no other living relatives, so . . .' Milly shrugged. 'She said she was getting too old to keep the place up by herself, so she sold it to us. We got it for an absolute song, didn't we, dear?'

'A song?' he said. 'More like the introduction to a song. We offered more, but she wouldn't take it.'

I was only half-listening. 'Her son died?' I repeated, trying to work it out in my head. 'Did she say what her name was?'

He glanced at Milly. 'Mrs Lillystone,' he repeated.

'No, I meant her first name.'

He frowned. 'I don't believe she ever said. Did she?' He turned to Milly. 'I imagine it would be on the deeds.'

'Georgina,' Milly said. 'She told me her name was Georgina. I remember it well, because . . .' She smiled in what I took to be self-mockery. 'Well, it was a bit embarrassing, you see. She told me as though . . . well, all I could think was that she thought I'd recognise the name. I didn't, of course. I've looked for her books since, but I can't find any.'

'They'd be out of print, I imagine,' the man said.

Milly smiled sadly. 'Poor old dear. I wish I could trace her, because she left something behind when she left.'

I looked at the table. Milly saw the look and shook her head.

'No, not that. A book. One of her manuscripts, I imagine. It's a lovely object; leather bound, like a proper book, but all written by hand. I found it when we were clearing out the attic. I started reading it once, but I never got beyond the first few pages.' She smiled at me. 'I can get it for you if you're interested.'

I nodded. 'I'd be very interested.'

Interested, but destined to be disappointed. She went back into the house, and was gone quite a while. When she came back, she was empty-handed. She hadn't been able to find it, she said. She furrowed her brow, and held a little inquisition, asking herself where she might have seen it last. Eventually, she gave up.

'Come again tomorrow,' she said. 'I'll find it. Do you live locally?'

'Yes. Cambridge,' I said, and she smiled delightedly, as though I'd said *Yes. The Garden of Eden.*

'Good. I'll find it.' She folded her hands together. 'Now, you'll have a glass of lemonade before you go, won't you?'

I never got to see Georgina Lillystone's book – if that's really who the old lady was – *if* the old lady ever really existed. I went back to Kiln Lane the next day, and . . . you're not going to believe this. I couldn't for the life of me find the entrance to Cuckoo Farm. Not anywhere. I scoured the hedgerows for a hundred yards either side of the bend in the road; or rather, where I remembered the

341

bend being. The road seemed, in the interval, to have shaken itself down, and where the sharp left-hander had been, there was now just a vague waver. No bend, no yellow gate and, so far as I could determine, no Cuckoo Farm.

I've been back from time to time since, and I'll probably go back again. One day, I'm sure, I'll find the bend, the gate and the house beyond, and I'll get to see the book. The more I think of it, though, the less sure I am I actually want to see it.

I have this strong mental image, you see, of myself sweeping the dust off this great leather-bound volume, raising the cover, and gazing at ancient, expensive vellum pages covered with fine antique script. I turn to the first page of the first chapter and read the first lines. They say, *Let me tell you about Madagascar Rhodes; I can't describe how he has been on my mind recently . . .*

I don't think I could handle it. Perhaps it's better if I imagine it never existed.